THE
DECEPTION

Copyright © 2022 by Brian Marotto.

Name: Brian Marotto, author/editor/illustrator

Title: The Deception

Description: First Edition

Series: The Creature Within; Book Two

Identifiers: ISBN 979-8-9855207-5-0 (ebook) | ISBN 979-8-9855207-4-3 (paperback) | ISBN 979-8-9855207-3-6 (hardback)

Printed in the United States of America

First Printing Edition - 2023

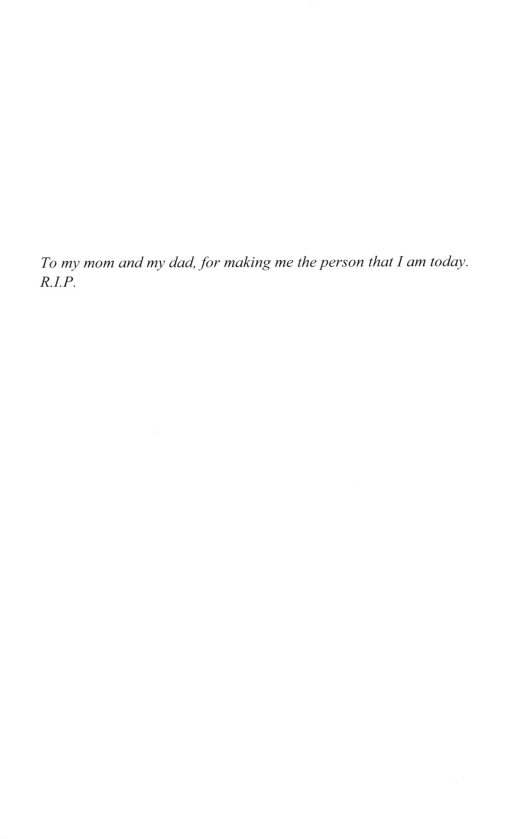

To my mom and my dad, for making me the person that I am today.
R.I.P.

THE CREATURE WITHIN
BOOK TWO

THE
DECEPTION

BRIAN MAROTTO

CHAPTER 1

Claw marks were etched across the scorched mountainous walls as the remains of animal carcasses were scattered throughout the floor. These were the sights that Owen witnessed as he woke up. While he wiped the loose gravel and dirt from his body as he stood up, Owen noticed he was only wearing his specially-made shorts for transitioning.

The lighting was dim due to the sparse, battery-operated lights attached to the walls which were the sole light source that kept the darkness away. Owen's eyes narrowed as he surveyed the room and that is when he noticed that one of the walls was not made of rock, but steel. This steel wall appeared to have a higher concentration of scorch and claw marks. Owen then turned his head to look in the opposite direction and realized it wasn't a room, but a large corridor. As his mind became less hazy, he realized where he was. He was standing in the corridor where the large trucks would enter the mountain to assist in digging for the gem. The steel wall appeared to be a barricade that was used to seal the chimera inside.

From the appearance of the barricade, the chimera caused heavy damage. Owen wondered how much longer it would have lasted if he didn't transition back. He pounded his fist against the steel a few times and it appeared to be sturdy. Realizing that there was no way out from this end, Owen followed the path back down into the mountain to find another way out. As he walked, all he could hear was the sound of his feet crunching on the dirt and gravel. It was quiet…too quiet. The more Owen descended into the mountain, the more he was preparing himself for the air to become colder, but oddly enough it didn't happen. As he pondered why this was the case, he entered the large digging site and scanned the empty room. All the equipment and vehicles that he was expecting to see were already removed. Apart from the uneven ground where the digging took place, one would not know that this was ever an excavation site. Owen observed one area that had a hole deep enough to hold a pool of water, along with a few more animal carcasses scattered throughout the dimly lighted digging area. With everything else removed, Owen was surprised they left the dim lighting behind.

"Hello!" Owen yelled out but the only response he heard back was the echo of his own voice.

As he peered at the large stone bridge above, memories returned of his battle with the manticore. A quick realization, followed by a crinkled brow, erased his current thoughts as he was baffled by the fact that he could see the bridge. He remembered before that even with more lighting, all he could see was a black void and nothing else. How could he see it now, Owen wondered? He took a moment to take a few deep breaths in case he was in transition. Once he was done, nothing changed. He could still see the bridge and he wasn't in transition. He figured either his eyes had adjusted to the darkness, or maybe it was a side effect of coming out of a full transition. In time, he presumed he would be back to normal. For now, he had to concentrate on finding a way out of the mountain.

From what Owen could see, there was no way back from where he was standing. It appeared that the only way to exit the mountain now was through the small door that his friends and himself went through as they pursued Klayden. Immediately after that thought, Owen's mind drifted from exiting the mountain to his friends. So many questions ran through his mind about them. Did Avery, Bailey, and Michael recover from their injuries? Were Cassandra and Ethan able to locate Kyra and did she survive her fall? How did Hailey feel about him after he bit her and then poured his heart out to her? Owen lingered on that last thought since he kept wondering if she had forgiven him, or now hated him. That thought began to concern him enough to briefly contemplate staying in the mountain a little while longer. Owen shook it off. If he was going to see his friends again, he needed to find a way out. Only one solution presented itself and that was to scale the wall of the pit back to the bridge.

Owen transitioned in order to gain access to his claws, but once again, something peculiar happened. He was able to transition, but it was too easy. Typically, it took a lot more effort and concentration to get to that level of transition. This time, it took minimal effort to access his claws. Minus the slight increase in aggression within him, he felt normal. It must be another side effect of the full transition, Owen concluded. That, or maybe what Klayden said about having more control after a full transition was true. He figured it was a question he could ask Isaac or Marcus later once he escaped the mountain. For now, he would simply accept the unexpected gift that was bestowed upon him.

Owen leaped onto the wall and climbed his way to the top with ease. He pulled himself onto the bridge and just as easily as he transitioned, he was able to transition back to normal as well. Owen smiled, for he was happy that he reached the top, but it didn't last long. The eerie silence, accompanied by the emptiness that surrounded him, made Owen feel uncomfortable. This place once housed his friends, as well as a battle between the chimera and a manticore. Now, nothing remained but an odd pile of rubble on the bridge. Owen figured it must have been loose rocks, from above, that fell at some point.

"Hello!" Owen yelled again but received only another echo in return.

After a few moments, he proceeded up the stairs and down the small corridor. Flashbacks from the battle with the minotaur and pushing past all the guards in the rooms within the hallway entered his mind. Once again, nothing but relentless silence surrounded Owen as he followed the dim path to the exit. He was now eager to leave the mountain for none of the memories he had from here were pleasant ones.

Owen smiled and let out a sigh of relief as the wooden door was not barricaded. He proceeded out the door and welcomed the fresh air that rushed against his face as he exited the mountain. As he strolled out into the sunlight, he shielded his eyes as they adjusted to the sudden change in brightness. He then simply stood in the sun and let its warmth embrace him. Owen closed his eyes and slightly tilted his head back as he took in a deep breath through his nose, and then gently smiled as he slowly exhaled.

As he opened his eyes, he noticed the area was different from the last time he saw it. The assortment of leaf colors was all green now. With that, past the mountain's base was a variety of flowers that have bloomed. The area around the base of the trees that were once partially covered with fallen leaves was now covered with a range of colors, with purple, yellow, and white being the dominant colors. Of course, Owen noticed no evidence of the battle between him and his friends against the mercenaries and the oni.

"How long was I the chimera?" Owen muttered.

"You were inside the mountain for about seven months," said a familiar voice from behind him. Owen turned around and saw Marcus and Anders approaching him from around the mountainside. It was Marcus's voice he heard.

Owen smiled as he approached the two and he leaned in and gave Marcus a quick hug, while the two also exchanged a few strong pats on their backs. Owen then turned and gave Anders a hardy handshake. "It's so good to see you guys! Wow, seven months. That would make it…early spring?" Owen asked.

"April to be exact," Marcus responded.

"I can't believe it has been that long, but I guess it is better than coming out here in the dead of winter," Owen remarked, followed by a quick glance toward Marcus. "Even in springtime you still got a suit on. Really?"

"Well to be fair, my jacket is off and my sleeves are rolled," Marcus playfully rebutted with a slight smirk. Anders, who was wearing just a black t-shirt and gray cargo pants, simply grinned and shook his head at Marcus.

Owen's brow arched while he glanced himself over. "I feel like I should be filthy after all those months but I don't seem to be that dirty. I only see some dirt from me walking around and climbing out of that pit."

"As you know, the body resets itself during a full transition for both the creature and the human. It's common in the beginning for someone to think that relates only to injuries and illnesses. It also applies to hygiene, which is most fortunate for the individual, as well as the ones around that person," Marcus replied.

"I can imagine," Owen said as he chuckled. "That's a good perk to have. It's what is allowing you guys to stand as close to me as you are now." The three of them laughed at his comment.

Owen then turned his attention to Anders, "What brings you out here? Don't get me wrong. I am happy to see you, but I figured you would be back out in the field. You know…the whole loner thing and all."

"I do prefer working out in the field alone, but Isaac wanted me to come here and help protect the mountain," Anders responded.

"Protect it from what?" Owen's brow crinkled as he asked.

"You," Anders quickly replied. Owen responded with only a puzzled look. "Well, not so much you, but more the chimera. We could not risk anyone going into the mountain with a chimera inside. Also, if the chimera ever did escape, we needed a creature that could stand up to it. Isaac figured my Amarok would be such a creature."

5

Owen nodded, "Makes sense. I imagine that the barricade you constructed to keep the chimera inside was a big help," Owen added as he glanced over to the steel door that blocked the large entrance.

"Indeed it was, but if you only knew how many times we had to reinforce that steel door. It was to the point that Isaac was starting to worry if we were going to run out of materials or not." Marcus commented. Owen understood his comment from observing not only the two steel beams and multiple wooden beams bracing the steel door, but also the many broken wood beams that littered the surrounding area near the steel door.

"Say what you will, but I believe the bigger concern was how to change the batteries if any of the lights went out," Anders added, followed by a smirk.

"I am quite thankful that the batteries in those units had a long-lasting life," Marcus replied and then glanced back at the mountain.

"I can imagine," Owen said after a quick raise of his brow. "By the way, where is Isaac?"

"About to be on his way," Marcus responded while he raised the walkie-talkie to his mouth. "Isaac this is Marcus. I need you at the front entrance of the mountain. There is something you need to see."

Marcus held the walkie-talkie to his ear for a moment, then everyone heard Isaac speak. "Mysterious way of phrasing that but I am on my way."

"Where is everyone else?" Owen asked.

"I presume you are referring to your friends," Marcus replied.

"Of course, but I wouldn't mind also seeing everyone else too. Cassandra, Ethan, Duncan, Livia, and hopefully even Kyra. I felt like it has been forever and I would really like to see everyone." The urge for Owen to see his friends again was beginning to make him feel restless as he began to fidget in his spot.

"That's an interesting statement you just made," Marcus said as his eyes narrowed.

"How so?" Owen asked while he slightly shrugged.

Before Marcus could respond, his eyes drifted over Owen's shoulder. He turned around to see what diverted Marcus's attention. That is when he could see Isaac flying from over the tree line behind him. He slowly descended not too far from Owen. As the yellow from his eyes and the red feathers on his skin vanished, Isaac smiled while he approached. Owen returned the smile as he gave Isaac a quick hug.

"It's so good to see you again," Owen remarked. He didn't realize how genuinely happy he felt to see Isaac until that moment.

"I'm delighted to see you again as well," Isaac said as he glanced Owen over. "You look so…normal."

"Um…thanks," Owen replied. His brow was knitted since he was confused by Isaac's comment.

Isaac looked over to Marcus, "Have you observed any differences?" Owen's brow furrowed even more as he tried to figure out what was going on.

"Initially, my answer would have been no, but now I am not sure," Marcus responded.

"What are you guys talking about?" Owen asked.

"Why is that?" Isaac asked Marcus, ignoring Owen's question. Owen looked back and forth between Marcus and Isaac with his jaw slightly lowered now, frustrated that they were leaving him out of the conversation.

"It appears that the time did not pass for Owen in the blink of an eye like a typical full transition. Instead, he felt the full weight of the two months that passed." Marcus's response was directed at Isaac but he kept his eyes on Owen the entire time.

"Wait. You said I was in full transition for about seven months," Owen said as he took a few steps toward Marcus.

"No, I said you were inside the mountain for about seven months. There's a difference," Marcus calmly responded.

"Then someone needs to explain the difference!" Owen snarled while his lip curled.

"We will but you need to calm down first," Isaac softly spoke.

"No, I will not calm down!" Owen snapped at Isaac as he quickly turned around to face him. He could feel the anger bubbling inside of him as he began to breathe heavier.

"First, my friends and I go through one painful battle after the next to reach Klayden. Not just physical pain, but emotional pain as well. I witnessed them get injured and wondered if I would ever see them again. Frightened if any one of them would be here one moment and then dead the next. Then, after all that fun, in order to save everyone and stop the manticore, I had to transition into the chimera. Something I wasn't planning on doing for quite a long time. Battling a manticore is not easy. Now, I will admit it was satisfying to kill the beast, but it wasn't easy and painful at times. On top of all that, I can't remember if I killed Cassandra or not. I recall Cassandra staring at me, which made me feel both aggression and fear, so I attacked her. What is confusing to me right now is that I remember feeling justified in my reaction to Cassandra, which is weird to me now because I also remember Cassandra being my friend. Anyway, I was about to make the kill but I blacked out for whatever reason."

By that time, Marcus and Anders made their way to Isaac, standing side by side with him. Everyone's eyes were wide open as they looked back and forth at each other. "Owen…"

"I'm not done!" Owen expressed in a deep, animal-like voice as he cut Isaac off in his response. "When I came to, there was nothing around. I spent my time searching the entire inside of the mountain, trying to find a way out. Nothing but the dim lighting all day every day, to the point that I couldn't tell what time of the day it was, or even how long I was trapped in there. The only interaction I had were with the deer, mountain goats, and brown bears that I'm guessing somebody let into the mountain. At first, I would make the kill right away because I was hungry. After a while, I would wait before I made the kill. Why…because it was something else alive in there besides me! Of course, that didn't work too well because they were all scared of me. I even resorted to pathetically staring at that pool of water just to see my reflection. At least that didn't run away in terror." Owen gritted his teeth and balled his fists in anger. His eyes then began to well up as his anger became slightly diluted by the upsetting memories he remembered from being trapped in the mountain.

"You remembered everything while you were the chimera?" Marcus asked in amazement as his eyes widened.

"Everything and to clarify the misconception that your kind has against me, we are more than just raging beasts. We have all the same feelings as you. For example, when I was trapped in that mountain, I felt fear, loneliness, and anxiety. Before that, when I was with my family, I felt love, comfort, and security. When your kind killed my family and trapped me in that gem, that is when I felt anger and rage." Owen responded as he slowly approached the group. His eyes were narrow and his fangs were showing, as he was filled with hate after his last sentence.

Isaac raised his hands in submission, "You are confused Owen and a lot has happened. Come with us and we can explain everything."

Marcus began to walk toward Owen, "Please come with us so we can help you." Marcus put his hand on Owen's shoulder. Within that same instant, Owen quickly grabbed Marcus's throat. Marcus tried to break the hold but Owen's grip was too strong.

"Don't touch me," Owen sternly, yet slowly, said through his teeth. Marcus's eyes became dark as he transitioned but he still struggled to breathe. He tried again to remove Owen's hand but to no avail.

"You are not even in transition. How are you so strong?" Marcus asked. The words barely made it past his lips as he strained to talk as Owen's grip around his throat increased. Owen did not respond. Instead, he tossed Marcus aside with one arm and watched him tumble across the dirt.

9

Anders immediately went into transition, and then charged at Owen. He slashed at Owen, but he was able to catch Anders's wrist before his claws could lacerate his chest. Anders followed up with another slash to Owen's midsection, but he was able to catch the other wrist as well. Anders tried to break free but Owen's grip was too strong. Anders briefly had a dumbfounded look on his face but his expression became more intense as Anders transitioned deeper, with fur now encumbering most of his body. His claws and fangs grew longer as the pale-yellow eyes of the Amarok stared back at Owen. Anders was now beginning to push Owen back.

"Strong, but not stronger than me." Anders snarled.

A low growl came from Owen as his chimera eyes appeared, along with his claws and fangs as he stopped himself from being pushed back by Anders. The amber eyes of the chimera glared back at Anders as Owen began to drive him back.

"I'm just as rare as you and I'm more transitioned than you. How is this possible?" His remark was strained as he tried to overcome Owen's raw power.

Owen responded with a sinister grin right before his hands were engulfed with flames. Owen released his grip as Anders yelled and reared back while he held his burnt arms in pain. Before Anders could react, Owen followed up with a swift punch to his chest. The impact caused Anders to fall backward and onto the ground. Owen glanced at Marcus, who was almost back to his feet. His eyes then drifted to Isaac. As Owen began to walk toward Isaac, he could see his eyes become yellow while red feathers layered around his eyes. As Isaac lifted into the air Owen pounced and his claws dug into Isaac's legs as he pulled him back to the ground. Isaac and Owen quickly rose to their feet.

Immediately after Isaac stood up and grimaced from the pain in his legs, he looked over Owen's shoulder and quickly raised his hand to direct someone to stop. Owen turned his head and saw Marcus and Anders coming to a halt about ten feet behind him. He then turned his attention back to Isaac who was lowering his hand.

"Owen, a lot has happened, which is causing your thoughts to be in disarray. I want to help you but I can't do that if I'm dead," Isaac cautiously spoke.

"That's unfortunate," Owen coldly responded.

Isaac transitioned back to normal. "You need to believe me. I am not lying to you. You need to trust me like how I trust you won't do anything rash." Isaac remained calm as he spoke. Owen transitioned back to normal and slowly approached Isaac, stopping just a couple of feet from him. Isaac didn't budge and kept on acting normal. For a moment, nobody spoke. They simply just stared at each other. Finally, Owen broke the silence.

"You say that you trust me," Owen said with a hint of a smile.

"Yes, of course," Isaac responded as he smiled.

Owen scoffed. "Then why could I hear your heartbeat grow faster the closer I got to you?" Owen asked as his face became absent of expression. Isaac's smile disappeared and his eyes widened in fear. Before Isaac could respond Owen quickly, with both hands, reached up and snapped Isaac's neck. His body fell lifelessly to the ground while Owen stood over it.

"No!" Marcus bellowed. Both he and Anders stood there in shock. They could not take their eyes off Isaac. "Do you know what you have just done? He wasn't in transition! You killed him!" Marcus added as the sorrow he felt began to leak from his eyes. His jaw dropped and his eyes remained widened as Marcus could not take his eyes off Isaac. Owen turned and responded with a sinister smirk. Both Marcus and Anders, who were both breathing heavily and trembling with rage, went further into transition and let out mighty roars before charging toward Owen.

In response, Owen transitioned and projected flames toward the two, roaring as he did. Anders dove off to the side to avoid the flames while Marcus took advantage of his gargoyle's limited flight ability and glided over the flames. As he landed, Owen moved his

11

hand toward Marcus, but Marcus was too close and the stone skin of the gargoyle gave him enough protection from the flames to engage Owen. He rammed his shoulder into Owen's chest, driving him onto the ground. With the flames extinguished, Anders continued his charge.

While on top of Owen, Marcus raised up into a mount position and swung wildly at Owen. His first two punches pounded on both sides of Owen's face before he was able to shield his head with his arms to block the remaining few punches. Marcus ceased his barrage of punches and raised his hand high in the air and extended his claws. As he was about to slash down at Owen, he was able to quickly grab Marcus's shoulders. Owen's grip tightened, causing his claws to dig into Marcus's shoulders. This made Marcus stop his attack and grab Owen's wrists, wincing in pain as he did. Owen held his grip and then threw Marcus aside and rolled away before standing up.

At that time Anders took a swipe at Owen's head, which Owen was able to duck and follow up with a slash of his own toward Anders's chest, ripping through the flesh as he did. Anders grunted but quickly shook it off as he used his arm to deflect another slash from Owen. Then, Owen stuck his hand out toward Anders and unleashed more fire. Luckily, Anders was able to grab Owen's arm and hold it up, causing the flames to shoot into the sky.

While Owen was caught off guard, Anders slashed at Owen's thigh, tearing through the meat. Owen yelled and followed up with a backhand to Anders's chin, causing him to fall hard to the ground a few feet back. Owen stopped the fire to grab his leg while he watched Marcus and Anders both stand up in front of him. The two extended their claws and showed their fangs as their aggression could be heard through their growling. Owen began to breathe heavier as his rage brewed within him. He then let out a mighty roar and as he did, fur appeared all over his body. His muscles bulged while he too extended his claws, snarling as he showed his fangs.

"Be careful. He's going to turn." Anders commented to Marcus.

12

"Funny, I don't feel anywhere close to a full transition," Owen said in a grizzly voice as he charged them. Before Marcus and Anders could react, Owen had already closed in on them and thrust his fists forward. Each fist slammed into the chest of Anders and Marcus, causing them to fall back to the ground. They both got to one knee while holding their chests.

"What's the matter? Not used to the so-called monster having a chance to fight back. This is for all the fallen chimera who did not deserve the fate you dealt them." The hatred could be heard in his voice through his razor-sharp teeth as his hands ignited.

"Owen, stop!" A female's voice called out from behind him. Owen peered over his shoulder and saw Livia standing only ten feet away from him, slightly trembling. The fire vanished, along with all his fur. As he slowly approached Livia, his fangs and claws disappeared as well, leaving the chimera's presence only in his amber eyes. As he neared Livia, Owen looked over his shoulder back at Marcus and Anders. The two did not move from their position and were slowly coming out of transition. Owen turned his attention back to Livia.

"Before you say anything else…answer me this. Why should I trust anything that comes out of your mouth?" Owen asked without emotion.

"You have no reason to trust me. I'm hoping that between your instinct and my gesture of standing here talking to you, knowing that you could easily kill me at any point, will help mitigate any doubts you have about me."

Owen scoffed, "You won't die with that ring on your finger."

"True, but how many more times will it save me before the magic runs out? If I could take it off I would, but its magic won't allow me to do so. In any case, I'd rather not have to experience you killing me over and over until the ring gives out. Trust me when I say, each time I die, that experience stays with me." Livia's eyes began to water.

Owen could hear her heartbeat racing but she already admitted her fear. Her gesture and words caused a conflict within Owen as he transitioned back to normal after her comment. "I can't keep all my thoughts straight. Part of me says to trust you yet the other part of me is saying the opposite. It's like there are two minds in me at the same time, but at times they are one. I can't explain it." Owen shook his head as he held his forehead, his eyes straining in pain as he did.

"I just want to help you. Everything will be explained later, but we need to get you stable first." Livia said as she slowly raised her hand toward Owen's head. Without warning, Owen grabbed her wrist as his eyes transitioned back to the chimera's eyes.

"I seem to remember how you looked at me in horror when you found out I was a chimera, so I ask again, why would you want to help me?" Owen asked in disgust.

"It was wrong of me to act the way I did. Discovering you were a chimera brought up some painful memories for me but not all chimera, or humans, are evil," Livia replied as her eyes became glassy.

"Painful memories...if you had the memories I possessed then you would truly know what painful memories are." Owen snarled as his fangs and claws returned. He then tilted his head with a curious look. That look quickly switched to anger as he let go of Livia and turned around, sending a wild slash with his claws as he did. His attack just missed Marcus and Anders, causing them to pause in their advance.

"Restrain him," Livia called out.

"You mean, kill him. He killed Isaac," Marcus responded. His brow furrowed from being both agitated and confused by her request.

"He's not in control of himself. Think of what Isaac would want in this situation!" Livia exclaimed. Her sympathetic eyes stared back at Marcus.

Marcus paused; the pain evident on his face. "Fine," Marcus grumbled. Anders and himself lunged at Owen and they each grabbed an arm. With the same momentum, they were able to twist his arms behind his back, being careful to stay away from his hands in case Owen used his fire attack again. Anders grabbed Owen's chest with his free arm while Marcus used his free arm to lodge the crook of his arm under Owen's chin. Owen began to struggle and growl as he tried to break free.

Livia approached Owen and once again, raised her hand to his forehead.

"I'm sorry," Livia said softly.

Owen responded with a loud roar just inches from Livia's face before her fingers gently touched his forehead. As her fingers made contact, the chaos within his mind began to ease. Owen started to feel tired as he transitioned back to normal. At that moment, the world around him began to fade away as he fell unconscious.

CHAPTER 2

Owen's eyes opened to a view of a wooden ceiling. He was laying down on a couch that had a tan sheet covering it and as he sat up, his brow creased since he was confused about where he was. As he glanced around the room, his brow eased when he realized he was back at Duncan's cabin. He swung his feet over to the floor, but as he did, he winced in pain. Owen forgot about the injuries he sustained from his battle earlier. As he looked down at his wounds, he noticed he was wearing a robe. Not only that, it seemed someone applied some basic bandages to his wounds. He could see smears around the bandages, along with his hands and other random places on his body, from where someone attempted to wipe the dirt and blood away. At that time, he heard someone come into the room from the kitchen. Owen turned and noticed it was Livia.

"I'm glad to see that you are awake. How do you feel?" Livia asked. She smiled as she handed him a cup with a reddish liquid inside before she sat down in the chair in front of Owen.

"Fabulous," Owen replied sarcastically. "Is this what I think it is?"

"Vampire blood. It should do the trick," Livia responded.

Owen slurped down the cold drink and was thankful the blood was mixed with other fruity liquids to help mask the taste. "Thank you."

"Not a problem. Now how do you really feel?" Livia asked while she gently smiled as she took the glass away from Owen.

"I can focus more and I feel a lot calmer than before. Yet, I'm so confused," Owen replied.

"Well before we continue, let me explain everything. That should help clear up a lot of your confusion and get you caught up to speed." Livia responded while leaning forward in her chair.

"I killed Isaac. It's all coming back to me now. I killed him. Why are you helping me or why am I even alive?" Owen was distraught as he began to breathe erratically.

"Owen…" Livia began to speak but was interrupted by Owen.

"Isaac was like family to me…like a grandfather in a way. He is one of the reasons why I even made it out of the facility," Owen added. He could feel his eyes begin to swell up. Owen felt horrible…so horrible that the weight of his shame kept his head down.

"He's alive," Livia commented.

Owen's head jerked up to see Livia with a slight smile on her face.

"How is that possible? I looked into his eyes before I snapped his neck and they were normal," Owen inquired as he wiped his eyes.

"Apparently, he was able to transition just enough right before his neck broke to survive. As gruesome as it sounds, his head was twisted away from you so you would not have been able to see his eyes," Livia replied.

Owen let out a huge sigh of relief as a smile appeared but it quickly vanished. "Wait! How are Marcus and Anders doing?"

"Physically they are fine after they had the same drink as you. Emotionally…those wounds may take longer to heal. If it helps, Isaac is world-renowned for his forgiveness and I'm sure he will ask the other two to extend that same sentiment to you," Livia gently responded as her head tilted slightly and she had a hint of a smile.

17

Another sigh of relief left Owen. "Still, my question remains. Why am I still alive?"

"I will answer your question with a question of my own. Why did you become so hostile and violent?" Livia asked.

"Because at the time, I wanted them to die or at least feel the same pain that I…well the chimera felt when the chimera's loved ones were killed. It was like I could feel the chimera's pain and rage all at once. Its memories seemed so real to me that they felt like they were my own. So real, that it was like the chimera took control of my body in a way. Other times it was just pure chaos. It was like I was bouncing between minds or even sharing the same mind with the chimera." Owen slowly shook his head while staring off into the distance, trying to make sense of it all.

Livia tapped his knee to regain his attention. As Owen refocused, she smiled. Her smile caused Owen to relax as he leaned back into the couch.

"Let me finally fill in the blanks and explain what is going on," Livia said as she leaned back in her chair. "I will tell you everything I know from what I observed to what Isaac, Marcus, and Anders explained to me. Let me start by saying Marcus didn't lie to you when he said you were in the mountain for seven months. You were, but not as the chimera per se."

"Typical Marcus with the wordplay," Owen commented as he shook his head.

Livia smiled, "Quite true. As I was saying, you were in the mountain for seven months, but for the last two months, you were a living, breathing chimera. The previous five months you were a statue of a chimera." Livia paused as Owen's mouth slowly opened and his eyes widened.

"How is that possible? Cassandra shouldn't have been able to turn the chimera into stone unless…she became a gorgon." Owen's eyes grew wider with both shock and concern. "Is that what happened? It would explain why I remember killing the manticore and trying to reach Cassandra, but then in a blink of an eye, I was standing there on the bridge all alone in silence. She fully turned, didn't she? Is everyone else okay? Please don't tell me she turned everyone else to stone before Ethan could stop her." Owen was becoming frantic with concern.

"Calm down. I can imagine all your worries and questions going through your mind but they are causing you to not think straight. Just breathe and let me continue," Livia calmly responded. Owen took a deep breath and nodded in agreement.

"Thank you. Just as a side note your friends are safe and Cassandra didn't turn into the gorgon until after she turned you to stone. The thing is, you're right. Only the gorgon itself could turn you into stone, and in a way she did. Everything happened to line up just right for you to be encased in that stone cocoon for five months. To this day we don't know how that happened. Too many factors in play between you and the chimera's biology, the magic from the gem inside of you, and the right amount of time and intensity from the gorgon's gaze from Cassandra. To Isaac's knowledge, this is the first time that this has happened. In any case, we could not break you out of there because it would have either killed you or best case...your mind would have been broken beyond repair."

"How so?" Owen couldn't help but ask.

"From what I could sense from when you...the chimera was temporarily turned to stone, you were undergoing some metamorphosis. We had no idea what you would look like or how your personality would be once it was complete. All we knew was we had to let it run its course." Owen was captivated by the words flowing from Livia's mouth. The more she talked, the more things began to make sense. Seeing Owen's full attention, Livia continued.

"During that time, we had two groups in the mountain. One group searched for the gem while the other group kept an eye on you. Their job was to notify everyone as soon as they saw any ounce of change in the statue. That group consisted of only Isaac and Anders, while Marcus led the dig down in the pit. I must say Klayden wasn't joking when he said they were close to finding the gem. About a week after you turned to stone, we found it. The thing was, the gem was closed inside a small wooden chest that was magically sealed to the point that it could not even be moved from where we found it. It took about a month for Isaac and me to find a way to unlock the magical seals. Probably could have done it sooner if we had a witch close by, but with all our years of experience, we were able to handle it."

Owen raised his hand as if he was in school. Questions were now starting to form in his mind based on what Livia was telling him.

"Save your questions until the end of class," Livia said. She then gave him a quick wink while smiling. Owen grinned and nodded his head. He had to do his best to make a mental note of the questions that were popping up.

"As I was saying, once we were able to move the gem out of the mountain, we cleared everyone in and out of the mountain away. Only Marcus, Anders, Isaac, and I remained to keep an eye on you. Months went by and finally, your statue began to crack. It didn't take too long at all before you broke free. From then forward all we could do is observe from a great distance and keep you secure and alive inside the mountain. Each day we wondered if the chimera was your new form or just you in full transition. Heck, even at one point we wondered if maybe it was your mind in the chimera's body. We had Isaac test that theory since he was the immortal one in the group that can also fly."

"I remember that. He was slowly walking into the bottom area of the pit and as soon as I realized he wasn't one of the usual animals to eat, I decided he must be a new item on the menu. Almost got him too. Isaac doesn't look like it but he can be quite fast when motivated." Owen said while Livia and he chuckled over Isaac's misfortune. "Still, at that time it didn't register that it was Isaac. It was just another human that was no more than just food. A threat that had to be dealt with. My mind was everywhere," Owen replied.

"And that is why you were able to remember what the chimera saw during the full transition when normally nobody remembers. The chimera's memories became yours and vice versa. Today, you were experiencing that same confusion when you were battling the others earlier. Your mind was chaotic. Seriously, there was no order or control over your memories and personality. Everything inside your mind was randomly switching between Owen and the chimera, and even both at the same time. Honestly, I'm surprised how you were able to keep a coherent thought in your head for as long as you did. Once I was able to temporarily shut your mind off, it allowed me time to truly find out what was going on," Livia responded.

"Which is?" Owen nervously asked.

"What would be the best way to explain it?" Livia replied as her eyes drifted up for a moment to ponder how to word it. "Remember when this first started and it was explained to you that you and the chimera were in two small separate rooms with a door that separated the two of you? That door symbolized the magic of the gem. Your job was to keep that door closed and only open it just enough to get what you needed while in transition. Any more and you risked the chimera breaking through, which meant you would fully transition."

"I remember. How can I forget when I spent each day meditating to make sure that didn't happen, as well as keep my emotions in check from the chimera," Owen responded while he slowly shook his head in defeat.

"With the change that you went through while in the mountain, that is now all gone and replaced by one large room. A room that both you and the chimera inhabit, with no door separating you," Livia calmly said. She then raised her hand to stop Owen who was about to speak. "I can see the fear all over your face but before you worry yourself more, let me explain what that now means." Owen took another deep breath and nodded again, trying his best to contain all the emotions he was feeling as his leg began to bounce. He felt nauseous from the thought of trying to keep the chimera in check with no door dividing them.

"Before, the gem's magic was a focal point inside of you. Now, that is gone. It seems like it has fully infused into your body. To the point that it is as much a part of you as your own blood. As for the room analogy, before I stepped in, there was chaos inside the newly remodeled large room. Both your mind and essence had just as an equal right and say as the chimera. That is why your emotions and actions were so unpredictable and confusing. This is compounded when the thoughts are combined. The two of you now share the same memories and at that time, it was hard to distinguish whose memory belong to whom. That is why you went after everyone earlier today. The memory from the chimera, accompanied by the emotion behind it, drove you to act like it was one of your own experiences." Livia remained calm in her explanation.

"It seemed so real. I felt every ounce of pain and anger that the chimera felt when it happened. Is that my life now? I'm now a walking mess that could explode at any moment on anybody. Might as well lock me back inside that mountain," Owen frustratingly said as he shook his head with worry and disappointment.

"That may have been the case but I have remedied that," Livia responded as she smiled. Owen's head tilted to one side while his brow crinkled in both curiosity and anticipation of how this was done.

"Everyone is still in the large open room. All I did was draw a line down the middle of the room and set up a rule that no one crosses the line. It is a partnership now. However, that line may have been drawn to give you slightly more room, making you have the final say in your actions and emotions." Livia replied, followed by a wink.

"Before I get too excited, explain to me what all that entails," Owen responded with a nervous smile as he leaned forward.

22

Livia giggled, "That means that the chaos inside of you is gone. Not only that, you have full access to the chimera without the encumbrances that you once had to deal with before. With the magic now infused inside of you and the two of you sharing a room that you have control over, the best way to put it is you are a hybrid. Not the technical hybrid you once were but a true hybrid. Just in your normal state alone, your strength, speed, agility, healing, instincts, and even your senses have increased significantly. With that, you have full control over your transition. You can even transition to phase three and make it back without any issues. You know you can…everything I just said you experienced during your battle a little while ago. Keep in mind that I don't think you will be able to bounce back quickly from a full transition since regardless of what I did in your mind, the chimera would be in control. You will still remember everything it sees and does but it's important enough for me to repeat again that your mind won't be in control if you fully transition."

"I believe you and I will take what I am now over what I was before any day of the week!" Owen exclaimed with glee as his face lit up and he smiled from ear to ear.

Livia's smile grew with Owen's reaction. "I'm glad you approve of your revamped mental state, but it is more than just your mind and powers that have changed. Take a look at yourself. Even your body has become more toned and your muscle mass has increased some."

Owen quickly glanced himself over and sure enough, he could see a difference. It caught him off guard but before he could comment, Livia continued. "Also, if you haven't noticed, you are not having to keep your emotions in check. It's not just during transition, but in everyday life as well. There may be even more advantages that we haven't even scratched the surface of yet. This is new to us all."

Owen shot up from the couch and leaned down and gave Livia a huge hug. "Thank you. You have no idea how much this means. I don't know how I can repay you but if you ever need anything, you can come to me," Owen said before releasing his hug.

"I'll keep that in mind," Livia commented while she grinned.

Owen then felt a knot in his stomach. "I am afraid to ask but what is the catch?"

Livia paused as her eyes wandered briefly before she responded. "I can't think of any but if I had to guess the first one would be the unknown. As I said, this is new to all of us. To our knowledge, you are one of a kind. There may be unforeseen disadvantages are issues down the line or there may not be. As things come up just let me know and we can try to work it out. Also, the chimera is still part of you. Even with you in charge, its personality is a part of you now and could alter how you react to certain situations…even with you in charge. How much remains to be seen, but you must keep in mind that you are not the same Owen anymore. You are the hybrid of Owen and the chimera. The last thing I can think of right now is that you will share its memories since you and the chimera are now one. Just like with your memories floating into your mind for whatever reason, so will the chimera's memories as well."

"The unknown does sound scary and the fear of finding out the hard way will stay with me for some time, but I will deal with it. Anything is better than what I was going through before and at least I don't have that daily internal struggle anymore," Owen replied after a large exhale.

"Good. Now that I have caught you up to speed, what questions did you have for me?" Livia inquired.

"Why could you not do this for me or even all the recruits that survived the third day after receiving their gem? It would have made life so much easier without having that terrible internal struggle," Owen inquired.

"A fair question with an easy answer," Livia responded quickly with a gentle smile. "The magic from the gem, in the state that it is in when it infuses with a person, prevents me from making any form of mental adjustments. Trust me, I wish I could and I have tried, but without success. Your case is different after your metamorphosis."

"I hate that for everyone else but I understand. I was asking more for my friends. I was hoping they could enjoy the benefits that I now have after you helped me but it doesn't seem that way. At least you have tried," Owen added.

"I've been trying various ways to help with that for hundreds of years, but without success. I wish I could find a way. I still try from time to time in hopes that I do succeed in my endeavor," Livia replied.

"Speaking of my friends...where are they?" Owen asked, fearful of the response he was going to receive.

Livia stood up. "Before I answer, just so you know, Isaac instructed that we tell none of your friends about you until we knew how this would turn out. As far as they know, you died when they saw you turn to stone. I'm sorry." Livia briefly put her hand on his shoulder. He could hear how genuine her apology was in her voice.

Owen scoffed. He didn't know what to say at first. He could only imagine how they must have felt seeing him being turned to stone. With so much time that has passed, he wondered if they have all moved on with their lives. At best, maybe just a thought of him might enter their minds occasionally. He wouldn't be mad if that was the case. He would prefer them happy rather than in mourning. Finally, after those thoughts quickly sped through his head, Owen finally replied, "It's okay. I understand and it makes sense to not give them false hopes. Are they okay?"

"I haven't been keeping track of them, but from what I hear from Isaac, they seem fine. Hailey and Avery are back in the states on an assignment but you can ask Bailey and Michael themselves when they get back from gathering supplies for the barn and cabin," Livia responded.

"They're here? They still don't know I am alive?" Owen asked. He was excited that he could see them but also anxious about how they will react once they saw him.

Livia smiled. "Yes, they are here, and no they are not aware of

25

your resurrection. Bailey and Michael were originally guarding the mountain while the search for the gem was ongoing. That allowed them to help but not be around your statue. Hailey and Avery stayed at the cabin spending an immense amount of time meditating and talking with Isaac and even Duncan. They seemed fine before they left but after they witnessed you turn to stone, they were quite upset and lost. To the point, we thought we may wake up to a thunderbird or a cyclops or both. Anyway, once the gem was found and extracted, we gave it to Bailey and Michael to return it to the cabin."

"I feel horrible they had to go through all of that to get over me but I am relieved they were able to pull through it. I appreciate everyone that helped my friends grieve and move past my death, which just sounds weird saying that out loud," Owen chuckled to himself as Livia smiled. "So, the gem is here now?"

"No, it's with Hailey and Avery. Not too soon after the gem made it back here, we had multiple attempts from people, some with creatures within them, trying to steal the gem. We had Bailey, Michael, Hailey, and Avery head out in two separate directions. Each posing like they had the gem. The ruse worked for a while before whoever is looking for this gem figured out Hailey and Avery had it. By then, they had already made it back to the United States and were en route back to the facility," Livia replied.

"If the gem made it back to the facility, then why are they still on assignment?" Owen asked.

"Because they couldn't make it to the facility. There were too many people scouting the mountain area to make it through unseen. Also, it made Isaac nervous that these people have an idea of where the facility is located, as well as their constant pursuit of the gem. Now they are radio silent and hiding out. Moving from place to place, fighting every step of the way, until we can figure out what to do next. Isaac contacts them occasionally to just check in and to get an update," Livia responded.

"Wow! That gem must be important. Were you able to find out

what creature is inside of it?" Owen asked. He wondered what powerful creature was so important to warrant such a fuss over one gem.

"I couldn't find out. I can only tell what creature is inside of a human, not the gem itself," Livia responded. She appeared glum for a moment as her head drooped. Livia then regained her focus back on Owen. "We had some other people in mind that may be able to tell us but they are being stalked as well. Right now, we are just buying time and keeping it away from whomever this person is that wants it so badly until we can figure out a way to get it to the facility to secure it."

"Maybe I can do something to help now that I am back on the playing board. Curious, what about the others? Cassandra and Ethan and even Kyra. I know she fell into the pit but I was hoping she somehow made it out alive," Owen inquired. He was hopeful until he saw Livia's eyes drift down as she slowly shook her head.

"Wait…you said earlier that Cassandra turned into the gorgon after she turned me to stone. If so that means Ethan had to turn into the golem. Did the golem kill the gorgon?" Owen asked. His eyes widened and his jaw slightly dropped as his nerves increased with the anticipation of the response.

"The golem and the gorgon fought and long story short, the golem walked off the bridge while it held the gorgon. Isaac said that everyone that fell into the pit had died," Livia responded, solemnly.

Owen's eyes transitioned as he growled. He then turned around and kicked the couch. The force of the hit made the couch slide across the room, tumbling everything over in its path.

"Owen, it's okay," Livia quickly said while touching him on his shoulder. Owen turned to face her. Even though he was still agitated and in transition, Livia didn't back away.

"It's not okay. They are dead because of me and I don't want to hear 'it wasn't me it was the chimera' because that doesn't mean much. I transitioned into it out of my own free will and now I will have to live with that. They were good people and they didn't deserve any of it!" A couple of tears rolled down his anguished face as he spoke. Owen's words were full of anger, yet laced with pain.

"That's right. You did and you want to know why? It's because Klayden purposely transitioned into the manticore. He left you no choice. If you didn't turn, the manticore would have killed everyone and the gem would be in the wrong hands. Cassandra still would have used the gorgon's gaze and with that creature, she either would have died or ended up transitioning anyway." Livia voiced with a stern face. Her face then lightened up as a small, compassionate smile broke through. She then put her hand gently on Owen's chest. "Stop beating yourself up. You did what you did to save your friends and loved ones."

Owen's eyes transitioned back to normal and wiped his eyes. "I guess you are right. Still, I would have rather seen them survive," Owen softly replied. Even though he felt sorrow for the friends that didn't make it, he began to feel more at peace with his decision. Then, his brow crinkled and his head tilted while his lips tightened. "Wait a second. You said friends and loved ones. Why did you say loved ones?" Owen asked.

"I'm a psychic who got a little curious when I was in your head fixing everything. Sue me." Livia winked and smiled slightly as she walked off. Her response made Owen chuckle as he shook his head and grinned.

As Livia approached the door, Owen called out to her, "How long will the stuff that you did to my mind last?"

"It's permanent unless you happen to make another psychic angry," Livia responded with a quick raise of her brow as she opened the door. She signaled with her head for Owen to follow her. As Owen walked onto the porch, he could feel the brisk air as he gazed at the orange sky with purple streaks throughout it.

"Nighttime will be here sooner than we think. I will go talk to Isaac and the rest and update them. Then, we can eat some food and get some much-needed rest. Walk with me," Livia kindly requested. Owen followed her across the field to the corral where a few horses were walking about. The horses appeared to be well kept by their non-matted, long-flowing manes and clean bodies. The horses ranged in an assortment of brown and black colors, while some were a combination of the two. He even noticed a few horses with white spots.

"Stay here. I will let you know when you can come into the barn," Livia said while she opened the gate to the corral.

"Why can't I come with you?" Owen questioned.

"Because honestly not only am I updating them on our conversation, I am reassuring and smoothing things over as well. That battle really stuck with them." Livia replied. Owen slowly nodded while looking down.

"I wouldn't worry about it. As strong as men claim to be you guys are sensitive." Livia smiled as she playfully slapped Owen in his arm before walking off. Owen smiled at her comment and was thankful he had at least her on his side for now. She entered the barn and after a few minutes, Duncan exited the barn. As he approached Owen he smiled and gave him a handshake over the corral fence.

"It's been a long time. How are you doing?" Duncan asked.

"Still adjusting but a lot better than I was before. Oh, and sorry about your cabin. I may have…rearranged your furniture. I can fix it though," Owen responded as his face squinched from feeling embarrassed for his previous actions.

Duncan chuckled, "No worries. Besides, I am sure Isaac has money set aside for things like this. I'm just glad you didn't burn the entire cabin down."

Owen's eyes widen, "You know what I am?"

Duncan rested his arms on the corral fence, "Not at first, but being one of Isaac's recruits I knew you weren't human. Then, when Isaac said he and everyone else will need to stay at my place a lot longer than expected, that made me uneasy since he has never asked that of me before. He was kind enough to fill me in on what happened and the need for the extended visit."

"Well, at least he was able to ease your mind under these unusual circumstances," Owen commented. Then, a curious look appeared on Owen's face. "You know the first time I was here I wondered not only if you knew what we were but also if you were like us. It's strange. Now it's like I can sense that you too have a creature. You don't have to tell me what it is, but am I at least right?"

Duncan's brow arched while he smiled. "Centaur. I guess your senses are heightened."

Owen let out a slight chuckle, "I guess so. I appreciate you telling me what you are. You didn't have to."

"It's only fair since I know what you are," Duncan replied.

"So, is that why you enjoy tending to the horses and living all the way out here?" Owen inquired.

"What…because a centaur is half-horse? It's also half human as well," Duncan countered.

"Good point. I didn't mean any offense by it," Owen responded. He hoped he didn't upset Duncan.

"None taken. I was just teasing you. Besides, I can see how one would think that. I live out here and do what I do by choice, but it wasn't always by choice," Duncan said. He could see the inquisitive look on Owen's face so he continued.

"I used to live in the city but it wasn't working out. The centaur's love for women and wine was something I was still struggling with. I could not keep it under control and when I felt I was not getting enough, the centaur's violent nature would shine through. I can't tell you how many bar fights I have been in over the years. Eventually, Isaac sent me here and gave me the new assignment of tending to this safe house. At first, I felt like it was a prison. He even sent some people to ensure I didn't leave the property. Over time and with increased meditation, it began to feel more like home. I felt at peace here. Even when the people watching over me left, I didn't have the urge to run off and relive my old ways. Even when I had to make supply runs into town, the urge was there but only faintly. I just love living out here. Being around nature and tending to the horses is just very peaceful to me. That and horses are easier to deal with than humans."

Owen laughed at Duncan's jest, "Understandable. So why aren't you in there with them now?"

"I got the highlights from Livia. That is all that I needed. The rest of the business they were going to discuss I didn't need to be in there. I rather just know what directly involves me," Duncan responded.

Before Owen could respond he noticed the barn door open as Livia's head popped out. Owen nodded his head toward her. "I guess it's safe for us to return."

"It appears that way. I guess there is only one way to find out," Duncan said as he opened the gate. The two made their way to the barn. As they walked, Owen made sure to watch where he stepped. It was getting darker and he didn't want to walk in anything that a horse left behind. As the two entered the barn Owen noticed Isaac, Marcus, and Anders standing in the middle of the barn, huddled together. All their heads turned toward Owen as he entered. Their faces were absent of expression, which caused Owen to gulp with uneasiness.

"It's okay. Just talk to them. I have explained everything and all is well," Livia whispered as she closed the barn door behind them. Duncan strolled off to the side and began to straighten up some of his supplies.

Owen approached the group. "I know Livia talked to everyone already but still, I am sorry for my actions. I don't know how to make it up to everyone but I am willing to try." Even though his words were sincere, inside he was terrified. Enough to make him fidget as he firmly pressed his lips together in anticipation of their response.

"The idea of cleaning all the horse manure for a few years came to mind but we may have better use for you elsewhere," Marcus replied as he smirked.

"I was overdue for a good sparring match so if anything, you did me a favor," Anders added with a hint of a smile.

"I'm alive and you were not yourself. All is forgiven. Just try not to maim or kill any of us in the future. It would be much appreciated," Isaac mentioned as he smiled and took a few steps toward Owen.

"I'll do my best," Owen jested. "Seriously though…thank you everybody for your understanding. I really appreciate it," Owen added as he and the rest of the group exchanged pats on the shoulders and handshakes.

"Now that this is all past us, and we have some time before we have to prep dinner, let us discuss what lies ahead," Isaac suggested to the group. With everyone slightly nodding, Isaac continued. "As of now, Hailey and Avery have been bouncing from state to state within the northeast trying to shake their pursuers. The gem is safe but our main objective still holds. It is imperative that the gem reaches the facility. Once it is inside the facility, we can toss it through the door that leads inside the cavern with all the other gems. The magic within that door will find a spot for the gem. Then, the only way someone can find it is if they are chosen for that creature. While we work on this objective, if we can also find out what is inside this gem or why it is so important, then that would be ideal. Both for our knowledge and so that we can confront and neutralize the threat."

"Do we have any leads on the gem or even who is behind all of the attacks and pursuits?" Owen asked.

"Besides it being a ruby about a fourth of the size of your palm, then nothing more than what you haven't heard already. As for the person in charge of this group, that is still a mystery. From what we can gather, they are quite organized and not short on numbers. A vast majority of the attacks have been from either humans or people with common and uncommon creatures. Some purposely fully transitioned as soon as they got in range. The past few months have been taxing, to say the least, but that is not what concerns me the most." Isaac responded as he rubbed his worried face.

"I'm afraid to ask but what is the more concerning thing that is bothering you?" Owen inquired as he too became worried.

"What concerns me is the large amount of effort being put into the acquisition of this gem. The same gem that was magically sealed away and buried inside a mountain. What creature warrants such an effort to conceal it from the outside world? I'm also concerned that they are aware of the locations of the safe houses and facilities. There are even people scouting the facility that you were in back in Pennsylvania. Now I presume Klayden gave up the locations but the bigger concern is, how do they know of some of the older locations? Ones that Klayden would not be aware of unless he really dug through the archives, which I can't imagine him doing for such obscure locations. At the same time, he was quite thorough. He made it his business about knowing all the details about anything he put his mind to." Isaac's eyes drifted to the side as he appeared to be deep in thought.

"With all the rare creatures in this room, even while I was a statue, why couldn't you push through while Hailey, another rare creature, and Avery followed behind you? I'm sure you could have powered your way into the facility," Owen commented.

"The idea did cross our minds but it is not that simple. The problem is that whoever has the gem gets constantly bombarded with attempts at stealing it away. It's hard to power through if you can't even get the star players into the game. Now that you are here, I have a new game plan," Isaac said with a mysterious grin on his face.

"I'm not going to like this, am I?" Owen asked as he cringed.

"You might. If anything, I think you may even really enjoy it. Owen, right now everyone thinks you are dead. That means no one is looking or expecting you. If Hailey and Avery can secretly hand off the gem to you, then you will be able to transport it back to the facility unchallenged."

"The plan is sound," Marcus commented while slowly rubbing his chin.

"It may be sound but there is a big flaw in it…me," Owen countered as he began to pace back and forth in front of the group. "There still may be some unknown aspects about me that may jeopardize your plan. Do you really want that? Maybe it would be better if I just stay out of Hailey and Avery's way. That way, I can help clear the path for them, and then you guys can assist in getting them into the facility."

"Are you more worried about the unknown aspects of yourself or the unknown reactions from Hailey and Avery?" Livia added from the other side of the barn.

"Honestly both," Owen replied as he turned his head to address Livia. His attention then went back to the other three. "I am not sure how everyone will feel about seeing me again or how I will be around them. I just don't want to mess anything up with anybody or be the reason why the mission fails. Don't get me wrong. I want to help and I will. I'm just not sure if I am fully on board with your plan," Owen said as he stopped pacing and faced the group. His eyes bounced between the three as he waited for any of them to respond. He felt a little clammy due to being nervous about what they would say and hoped they would accept his counteroffer.

At that time Owen heard the barn door open. As he turned to see what was going on, his eyes widen as he took in a deep breath. It was Bailey and Michael.

CHAPTER 3

The two stopped dead in their tracks as they gasped. Silence filled the room as everyone awaited Bailey and Michael's reaction but they were speechless. They simply stood there with crinkled brows and their mouths slightly opened, dumbfounded.

"How...how is this possible?" Michael finally broke the silence.

"I saw you turn to stone. How are you alive? Is this some trick?" Bailey asked as she looked over to Isaac for any form of explanation.

"No trick. Just a long story," Owen replied as he smiled and walked toward them, but Bailey and Michael didn't move. Bailey once again looked back over at Isaac, to which he grinned and slowly nodded his head.

"You must have had some extra lives we didn't know about. It's good to have you back," Michael said as he smiled immensely. He then grabbed Owen's hand and pulled him in for a hearty hug.

"It's more like someone restarted the game," Owen commented as Michael gave him a confused look. "I'll explain later, and yes, it's good to be back," Owen added.

As Michael moved away Bailey immediately went in for a big hug herself. As Bailey let go of their embrace, she punched Owen in the shoulder.

"What was that for?" Owen asked with a furrowed brow.

Normally, the blow would have hurt him but this time he barely felt it. Not only that, he hardly moved. Bailey shook her hand from the impact.

"I don't know. There are so many to choose from. For starters, you made me hug you and you know I am not a hugger!" Bailey sternly responded.

"Well…technically I didn't force you to hug…" Owen stopped talking and raised his hands in surrender as Bailey's eyes narrowed as she raised her fist at him. Even though Owen ceased talking with Bailey's obvious frustration, he could not help but smile.

Bailey lowered her fist before she continued. "Next, we can go with how you sacrificed yourself for us when there had to be some other way to deal with the situation. Do you have any idea what it is like to have a friend die, right in front of you, in order to save you? Do you have any idea how that messes with your head? How can I have your back if you just go off making crazy decisions?" Bailey asked as she quickly wiped a tear from her eye, yet her knitted brow from her angry face did not change.

"I didn't realize you were friends with the chimera," Owen whimsically replied. Bailey immediately raised her fist again.

Owen put his hand on her shoulder and softly said, "Sorry. I hate that you had to witness what you did. It was the only thing I can think of at that moment to keep everyone alive and safe. Regardless, my death would never be your failure."

Bailey scoffed and lowered her fist. "Of course, when you word it like that it makes me sound like a selfish idiot." A crooked smile then formed on her face. "You're forgiven, just try using all of your brain next time you make a big decision." She then shook the hand that she hit Owen with earlier. "Geez Owen. Does the chimera have some kind of armor that I don't know about or are your shoulders where the goat's horns lie?" Bailey rhetorically asked as she rubbed her hand and wrist.

Owen chuckled. "Your guess is as good as mine when it comes

to the horns," Owen responded while he shrugged his shoulders.

"You seem different although I can't quite place it. Something other than how you took that punch. It's your demeanor or something," Bailey commented as her eyes scanned over Owen. His robe masked the obvious physical changes he went through.

"I'm definitely different, and it should make for an interesting dinner conversation. Why don't we all head back to the cabin to discuss while we eat?" Owen suggested as he glanced around at everybody.

"It's getting late so I think that is a good idea," Isaac replied as he gestured for everyone to follow him.

As the group was about to leave, Marcus walked beside Owen. "I hope you do realize that my forgiveness of the events that occurred earlier today in no way erases my memory of it," Marcus said in a calm, low tone of voice so that only Owen could hear him. Owen remained calm as he turned to face Marcus who also turned to face him. "If such an event were to happen again, I will not care if you are yourself or not. I promise you that I will kill you without any hesitation or remorse." Marcus's demeanor was still calm as he stared into Owen's eyes.

"If I lost control of myself like before, then I sincerely hope you follow through with your promise," Owen calmly responded. The two gave each other a quick head nod before parting ways.

The entire group left the barn and made their way back under the night sky to the cabin, with the moonlight illuminating their path. Once they made it inside, everyone pitched in to make dinner. Before Owen assisted everyone else, he quickly washed his hands and face to remove any remaining dirt and dried blood from himself.

The meal consisted of fresh trout and pike that were grilled, along with an assortment of vegetables. The group sat scattered throughout the main room of the cabin eating their delicious meal. As everyone ate, Isaac and Owen took turns catching Bailey and Michael up to speed with what happened with Owen. The two were so astonished by everything they were hearing that they forgot they were eating. At one point the two began to scarf down their food before it became any colder. The rest of the group had their own side conversations for they already knew Owen's story. Once the meals and discussions were finished, everyone again used teamwork to clean the table and dishes from dinner.

"Well, I enjoyed everything but I think I am going to retire for the night. We will continue our discussions about our next steps tomorrow. Have a good night, everyone," Isaac said as he walked to the back of the cabin and out of sight. Everyone else seemed to go their separate ways after he left. Duncan and Anders went back to the barn while Livia and Marcus went in the same direction as Isaac. Bailey and Michael began to unfold the couches out into beds.

"I only see two couch beds. Where should I sleep?" Owen asked.

"The floor is always an option," Bailey sarcastically replied.

"The bed is big enough we could share," Michael suggested.

"The floor is looking better and better now," Owen jokingly countered. The three chuckled at Owen's comment.

"Thank you," Owen mentioned to Michael as he helped him make the rest of the bed. Afterward, Owen sat on the edge of the bed, deep in thought.

"What's on your mind?" Bailey asked as she sat on the edge of her bed while Michael sat next to Owen.

"Part of Isaac's plan has me thinking." Owen paused as he saw Bailey and Michael give him a curious look. "The part where he wants me to get the gem from Hailey and Avery and bring it back to the facility."

"I think you will be fine. No one will know who you are and if you happened to get attacked, you will have people there that will have your back. Heck, you probably could take them on yourself from what I heard," Michael commented.

"I know. That's not the part I am nervous about," Owen countered.

"You are nervous about seeing Hailey and Avery…well more Hailey. Isn't it?" Bailey inquired. Owen slowly shook his head in agreement. "What about seeing her is making you nervous?" Bailey asked.

"Well, the last time I saw her, things didn't go so smoothly. In the camp, she pretty much rejected me and deemed me as some monster. Then, since making things worse is a special talent of mine, I bit her in the mountain to subdue her. To top it all off I did the one thing she asked me not to do…convey my feelings to her. So yeah…I'm nervous about seeing my ex-girlfriend. To the point that I rather clear an entire valley of creatures than face her," Owen replied as his eyes bounced back and forth between Bailey and Michael.

"I understand your fear but you obviously didn't see her after that day in the mountain," Bailey added as she looked Owen in the eyes. "She was a mess. Both she and Avery but for Hailey…she felt terrible for how things were left between the two of you. It took the two of them months to be able to function due to their emotions. Not even that…the depression they felt overwhelmed them. They were so hurt that at times, Isaac didn't let them help defend this cabin from the attacks. He feared they would either get themselves killed because their heads weren't in the game or they would easily fully transition. Once the two of them were able to mourn and move on, that is when Isaac gave them the gem and asked them to get it to the facility. He made it seem like it was the best move to keep the gem safe but I feel it was also to leave their heartbroken memories behind."

"Yeah, Bailey is right. They both took it hard but if you are worried about Hailey lashing out at you, or even hating you, I doubt that will be the case. I'm sure the two of them will be just as happy and relieved to see you as Bailey and I was," Michael added.

"Even if that was true, do I want to reopen old wounds? It would be better to just let them live their lives without me adding a bunch of drama. There may be some unknown, terrible things that I may be capable of now that I am this true form of a hybrid. I can feel that I am different. What if they don't like the new Owen?"

"Do you want some cheese with that wine or do you think you can fix your skirt and see them again?" Bailey said without emotion as she looked at Owen.

"Well, I can see you are still the sweet and compassionate one of the group," Owen responded as he rolled his eyes while Michael quietly giggled.

Bailey smirked. "All I am saying is that it is a small world and eventually you will run into them, so you need to be ready for that. Besides, are you doing what is best for them…or you?"

"Both," Owen replied while slowly shaking his head in defeat. "I guess you can add smart to your list of qualities," Owen said as he smiled and looked at Bailey.

"And you better not forget it," Bailey quickly replied as she slapped Owen's knee while she stood up. She then walked over to the side of her bed and lied down, but propped up so she could play her handheld video game. At that time, Michael got up and followed Bailey's lead. Owen simply just stared at them.

"What? I need to unwind before I get ready for bed," Michael commented.

"It's good to see you two have embraced nature," Owen joked. Bailey and Michael both smiled while their eyes were fixated on their games.

Owen decided to get cleaned up before going to bed. The hot shower felt relaxing after everything he had been through today. Once he was finally cleaned, Owen went to look at himself in the mirror. He hesitated because he was nervous if he would recognize the person staring back at him. He took a quick deep breath and wiped the condensation from the mirror. Minus the more toned body and the slightly increased muscle mass, he looked like himself, which was weird of him to think, Owen thought. He even stared at his face as if the chimera would show itself without invitation. He knew it was silly to think that would happen yet he could not help himself to double check.

Then, he watched himself transition to phase one and then back to normal. It was just as easy as breathing. He then transitioned to phase two and even though he could feel the chimera's intensity dwelling inside of him, it was nothing compared to how it was before he turned to stone. Owen felt in full control, and with that, he couldn't help but smile after he transitioned back to normal. Owen contemplated transitioning to phase three but the fear ingrained in his mind from the facility about performing such a task overwhelmed him. Still, he wanted to try. He had to know what his mind and body could handle and if he truly had full control over his transitioning. If what he was told was true then in theory, he could transition to phase three and not be at risk of fully transitioning into the chimera.

"I really hope a chimera doesn't bust out of this bathroom," Owen muttered to himself. He took a few quick breaths while shaking his arms and tilting his head back and forth to loosen his neck. Then, he transitioned quickly to phase two and moments later pushed it to phase three. "Whoa!" Owen shouted in a loud, animalistic voice. He was caught off guard by what was looking back at him in the mirror.

"Everything okay?" Marcus called out.

Owen quickly transitioned back to normal and responded, "Yes…everything is fine. Sorry…just checking out some stuff." Owen slapped his forehead for in hindsight, his response was not the best one due to his current location.

"Such as?" Marcus inquired from outside his door.

"Such as he probably just scared the heck out of himself by testing his transitioning limits," Livia called out from her room.

"Yeah…she is right. Sorry to disturb everyone," Owen said as he peaked his head outside the bathroom door.

"Told you," Livia remarked from her room.

"How did it go?" Marcus asked.

"I just transitioned to phase three and I'm here talking to you now as a normal human so I am guessing it went well," Owen responded with a relieved smile on his face.

"Outstanding but next time you want to test out a theory, maybe try it in a less populated area. At the very least go outside," Marcus suggested while giving Owen a quick wink.

Owen lightly chuckled, "Understood." He then closed the bathroom door and went back to the mirror.

With more confidence behind him now, he smiled and transitioned back to phase three. This time, he was ready for the image he would see. His body was covered in golden fur and his claws and fangs were slightly bigger and denser. Also, his muscles appeared to be a little larger than before. He then noticed that his feet were hard like the hooves of a goat, but not in the shape of them. Then, Owen's eyes widened as he whipped his body around so his back was to the mirror. He looked over his shoulder and to his relief, he did not see any evidence of a tail. Owen presumed the larger fangs would produce more venom, maybe even more potent than before.

He turned around to face the mirror and stared at what caught him off guard before, his facial features. It was like his face and the face of a lion had morphed into one. At this point, the chimera's presence was quite evident in his mind. He could feel the personality, memories, and instincts of the chimera entering his mind. What Owen enjoyed the most was that even with the instinct of wanting to kill everyone in the house to provide himself with food and safety, he was able to suppress it. However, he could tell the longer he stayed in this phase, the more effort it took to suppress the new feelings he was experiencing. He didn't think he would lose control but to be safe he transitioned back to normal. He also knew at that level of transition; the chimera could easily drive his actions if he let it.

Owen's smile went from ear to ear as he became overjoyed by what he was now able to do. The constant struggle he felt to transition back and forth, or just to stay in his normal state, had vanished. Even if it took some effort to keep himself under control if he was deep in transition, he would gladly take that over how he felt in the past. He wasn't sure what other things he would find out about himself down the line, good or bad, but for now, he would take the win.

Owen came across a set of clothes that someone must have left out for him while he was in the bathroom. Before Owen headed back to bed, he figured he would get in a quick round of meditation. As Owen was walking off to find somewhere quiet to meditate, he realized that he didn't have to. He was so used to meditation being part of his daily routine that he forgot that the internal conflict he felt had vanished. With a sigh of relief, he smiled and headed back out to the main room to just lay down instead.

The sofa bed was more comfortable than he imagined it would be. While laying down and tuning out Bailey and Michael's reactions to their games, Owen reminisced about the good times at the facility with his friends, before everything became crazy. While he did that, a stray memory popped into his head from the chimera. It was from when it was hunting the random animals that were led into the mountain to feed it. Owen blinked hard to get the image out of his head and decided to hold off on reminiscing until another time. Instead, he cleared his mind before closing his eyes and drifting off to sleep.

Owen yelled as he woke up. The first thing he saw was Livia, Michael, and Bailey sitting over him. Each of them stared at him with worried eyes. Owen quickly sat up in the bed right as Marcus and Isaac came into the room.

"Is everything okay?" Isaac asked, but then he stopped and just stared at Owen with his mouth partially opened.

"Sorry, I must have been having a nightmare. I didn't mean to disturb the entire house," Owen replied while still breathing hard and slightly perspiring. He then scanned the room and noticed there was a faint light coming through the window which indicated that dawn was approaching.

"Calm yourself down. Take deep, slow breaths," Livia slowly and softly said. Owen did what she requested and his breathing slowed down to normal and the sweating ceased.

"I feel better. Thank you," Owen commented back to Livia. He then noticed everyone was still watching him. "Okay…it was just a nightmare…let's not make a big deal out of it. They are quite common. I bet even more in our line of work."

"It is not as simple as that," Isaac politely countered.

"Why's that?" Owen inquired. His brow crinkled from the confusion he was feeling from everyone's continued reaction.

"Because your eyes are still in transition, yet you feel normal," Livia added.

Owen's jaw briefly dropped from shock but then he did a long, hard blink and when he opened his eyes, he could see everyone do a sigh of relief.

"Better," Livia commented as she smiled at Owen.

"Sorry. I didn't even realize it. Did I make that much noise that you heard me from your bedroom?" Owen asked Livia.

"No, we went ahead and got her," Bailey interjected. Owen's eyes narrowed as he stared at her. Once again, he was confused.

"You were tossing around and grumbling in your sleep. Then, Bailey and I heard a low growl come from you. That is when we noticed your claws emerge, but only temporarily. It was then that Bailey went and grabbed Livia," Michael said as he turned his head toward Bailey and Livia.

"I figured she was the one that would understand the most about what was going on inside of you," Bailey added as she turned her head in the direction of Livia.

"I normally don't invade people's dreams because I feel it is an invasion of privacy; however, with your complexity and how you were acting while asleep, I peered into your mind. Sorry," Livia said as her lips pressed together and her eyes drifted away.

"No, it's okay. I understand. You needed to make sure I wasn't going to set the place on fire or turn into the chimera," Owen replied with an embarrassed half-smile.

"I wanted to make sure you weren't suffering but yes, those other things crossed my mind too," Livia added as a faint smile returned to her face.

"I can kind of remember bits and pieces. I feel like I was fighting something. What did you see?" Owen inquired.

"You were right. It was a nightmare…the chimera's nightmare. It can be hard sometimes to remember your dreams, even for humans. From what I could see, you were fighting off humans yielding swords and shields. It seemed like you were protecting other chimeras, even smaller ones. The more you killed the more that showed up. Your attacks became more frantic and when it got to the peak of it all, that is when you woke up," Livia responded.

"Great. Is this one of the unforeseen things you discussed with me yesterday? Is this what I have to look forward to?" Owen asked. His words were laced with defeat as his shoulders slumped forward.

"Not so much unforeseen. Remember, we talked about how the two minds are as one. You may have control, but the other mind is still quite present. You will share aspects of its personality and memories. Like anybody else, those memories may carry over while you sleep. You don't always have nightmares so I would think the same for the chimera. In time with meditation and just getting used to your new hybrid self, you will regain even more control," Livia reassuringly said as she put her hand on his shoulder and smiled. Owen returned the smile but inside he was kicking himself for tossing aside the meditation the night before.

"Would the chimera now have his memories as well?" Bailey inquired.

"Yes, but I don't think it will mean much. The chimera's mind would be in control during a full transition and honestly, I don't think the beast would have the complex thinking to rationalize everything.

I presume it would go off instinct and see you as either food or a threat if your paths ever crossed," Livia explained. Bailey nodded her head while Owen's head sunk and his eyes drifted to the floor. He wished the answer Livia gave would have been different because if so, he would not have to worry about killing one of his friends or even innocent people if he ever turned.

"I guess I'm not riding the chimera into battle any time soon," Michael jested, causing the entire room to laugh.

At that time, Duncan and Anders walked into the cabin. They both seemed confused as their heads tilted and their eyes narrowed. "Did we miss something?" Duncan asked.

Isaac chuckled, "Yep. Good timing as always. I will catch the two of you up later."

"Everyone is in one piece so we could not have missed much," Anders remarked.

"Okay, the show is over. Everyone, please do whatever you need to get ready for the day. We will all meet later to talk about the next steps," Marcus directed. Everyone dispersed and followed his command by cleaning themselves up and having breakfast, which consisted of eggs, bacon, sausage, bread, and an assortment of jellies, jams, and marmalades. Owen ate his usual amount but he still felt hungry so he went back for another round of food. After he scarfed down another plate, he began to eyeball the remainder of the food.

"Dang, are you still hungry?" Michael asked. His eyes were wide with disbelief as he examined Owen's empty plate.

"Not really, but I could maybe go for a little more bread or something," Owen replied. He too was amazed by how much he ate.

"Your metabolism is higher now it seems. You can thank the chimera for that," Isaac nonchalantly commented as he was walking past the table.

"I guess you will have to eat more calories for the chimera to burn," Michael said while he smirked.

Bailey rolled her eyes. "Big surprise. A man gets to eat more

46

food to maintain or lose weight while us women can't even look at a cookie without gaining ten pounds."

"Don't blame me. The doctor says I need to eat more. It will be tough but I will manage," Owen teased as he gave Bailey a wink. She smiled as she shook her head and left the kitchen. Owen decided to forgo a third breakfast and assisted Livia in cleaning the kitchen. After that task was complete, he then helped Michael convert the bed back into a couch.

"Now that everything is completed, can you please gather the others that made their way into the barn?" Isaac politely asked Marcus.

"Not a problem. It appears it will be Duncan, Anders, and Bailey. I'll have them back momentarily." Marcus responded as he exited the cabin. Owen left the cabin shortly after Marcus, but he did not follow him. Instead, Owen stayed behind to relax on the porch. He rested his hands upon the rail while gazing off into the distance. Owen took in a deep breath of the fresh clean air while enjoying the slight breeze. He was thankful for the clear, blue sky which allowed the warmth of the sun on his skin to make him feel more relaxed. Marcus returned with the other three about fifteen minutes after he entered the barn. Owen thought to himself that it was a good thing that they showed up when they did. Any longer and the relaxation would have dwindled any remaining motivation he had to be productive today. Owen followed behind the group as they all walked back inside the cabin.

"Everyone, please take a seat," Isaac requested while he stood near the fireplace. Owen felt a little anxious over what Isaac was going to discuss. In particular, the part that involves him reuniting with Hailey. He sat at the end of the couch, with Bailey sitting next to him, and then Michael sat on the other side of Bailey. Owen's leg began to bounce with anticipation of Isaac's speech.

Bailey leaned over toward Owen and whispered, "Calm down or else you are going to lose the leg."

"Sorry," Owen whispered back as he ceased bouncing his leg. He felt embarrassed and to a degree, silly. Here he was with all this power and yet he was afraid of running into, or even worse, talking to Hailey. Owen took a deep breath to calm his nerves. Once everyone was seated, Isaac began to speak.

"Here is the latest intel that I received as of this morning from the scouts at the facility. There are at least now a dozen people that have been spotted around the area of the headquarters. It seems they haven't found the cabin yet, but they are a couple of miles away and spread out around the cabin itself. Either that or they know where the cabin is and have created a perimeter. These people are new so the creatures that they harbor are currently unknown to us. As for Hailey and Avery, they have been living in the metropolitan areas of New Jersey for the past month. The attacks have not been as frequent due to the area being very populated. Previously they were going to start in the Appalachian Mountains in New York and hike their way down, but the attacks almost tripled so they had to abort. My guess is that this person wants the gem but doesn't want to attract too much attention. With that said, the last couple of attempts at the gem has been bolder."

"How are they holding up?" Owen inquired.

"They are currently handling everything just fine but with the pressure increasing, we need to get Hailey and Avery to the facility. As good as they are, they can only handle so much. I instructed them to at least make their way to any of the bigger cities in Pennsylvania that is closest to the facility. That way they are getting closer to the facility but still not out in the open," Isaac replied.

"Can't Hailey just fly the gem into the facility or at least fly into the area of it and sneak her way in?" Owen eagerly asked.

"You would think that would be an easy solution but of course, it's not," Isaac politely rebutted. "The opposition has flyers of their own, as well as snipers from what has been reported. Hailey is strong but she is not invincible. Also, if she leaves now then some of the forces will go after her. Unfortunately, that means some will go after Avery and I fear for her safety. She is not as strong or as mobile as Hailey. Besides, I am trying to keep the facility location a secret, or at least a secret for as long as I can."

"Understood," Owen responded. He was bummed from Isaac shooting down his idea, yet kept his composure.

"I thought the plan was to hand the gem off to Owen and have him bring it the rest of the way in?" Anders inquired.

"It was, but I am nervous that they will figure out the switch sooner, rather than later," Isaac replied. Owen felt a weight lift from his chest as he let out a quiet sigh of relief. Isaac must have understood his concerns and will now allow Owen to help clear the way for Hailey and Avery instead.

"Then, what is the new plan?" Anders asked.

"The same as before. I am just altering the handoff location," Isaac responded.

"Of course," Owen mumbled to himself as the knot returned to his stomach. "What are the details behind this plan now?" Owen asked.

"All of us, except for Livia and of course Duncan, will go back to the States. Marcus, Anders, and I will head to the facility and start clearing out the new threats. Our goal is to have the area secured so we can get the gem back to the facility. As we are doing that, Bailey and Michael will meet with Hailey and Avery and pretend to be their support. I say pretend because also around that time, Owen will arrive and retrieve the gem. At that point, Owen will head to the facility while Hailey and the rest of her group will also do the same, but will take the scenic route. My hope is that all eyes will be on them which will allow Owen to make it to the facility unchallenged or if he is, then we can be his support. It will look as if we are just clearing out more of them like before. If the plan works, the gem and everybody else will be safely within the facility," Isaac announced to the entire room.

"That sounds similar to your previous plan," Anders remarked.

"It is similar, but one of the key differences is where Owen will receive the gem. I'm going to instruct Hailey and Avery to head to the closest metropolitan area to the facility. It will not only allow more opportunities for Owen to get the gem, but it will also give our enemy less time to figure out what is going on," Isaac explained.

"There is a problem with that plan," Owen casually added.

"Owen, if it involves your concerns about how you will act in your new state of mind or even about Hailey, let me reassure you that we would not ask this of you if we didn't think you were capable of handling the task," Marcus responded while he stood up and walked toward Isaac.

"It's not that. I already got the impression that I am just going to have to work through those concerns, but thank you for the sentiment. However, my concerns deal with something else," Owen countered.

"What are your other concerns?" Isaac inquired.

"The main one is how will I get the gem from Hailey and Avery? I presume our enemy always has their eyes on them, so they just can't hand it to me or leave it under a rock for me to retrieve. How am I supposed to get the gem from them?" Owen asked as he too stood up. At this point, everyone rose from their seats.

"A valid point and my response to that is to be creative," Isaac replied while he shrugged and smirked.

"Creative?" Owen asked with a furrowed brow as he tried to figure out what Isaac meant by his response.

"Yes, creative. There is no clear-cut way to get it so you will have to find a way before you reach Hailey and Avery. At the end of the day, not being noticed is key. We are relying on the rest of the world thinking that you are dead for this to work. If needed, you can communicate with Bailey and Michael since they will be near Hailey and Avery. Then, when the time grows near, they can help set up whatever you need to make this happen," Isaac explained. He appeared relaxed as he talked, which kept Owen from freaking out. Yet, Isaac's demeanor made him wonder if he was truly not concerned or if it was thousands of years of practice of not conveying stress.

Owen scoffed. "I guess I will figure it out when the time comes but while I am asking questions, does anyone have a plan to figure out what is inside this gem? That and to find out who this person is that is bound and determined to steal it from us?"

"That is something that everyone will be trying to figure out while this plan is in motion," Marcus responded.

"Unless everybody wants to live in the facility for the rest of their lives, I presume we need to find out before we all walk through those cabin doors." Everyone seemed caught off guard as they glanced around at each other with their eyes widened regarding Owen's snarky remark. At first, the room was quiet, but then Anders broke the silence.

"The kid has a point," Anders responded in his usual deep voice as he stared intensely at the group. He then turned his attention to Owen and gave him a small nod, which Owen returned.

"Owen's point is valid," Marcus said as he turned to Isaac.

"Indeed," Isaac said with a grin. "Since it will be difficult for my group to gather intel unless we can get it out of one of the people stalking the facility, that will leave Bailey, Michael, Hailey, Avery, and Owen to see if they can somehow gather the information needed. I would reach out to my contacts that could do this easier but everyone is being watched and I don't want anyone else being attacked. Even if I wanted to, with our resources spread thin, I can't even ask members of other facilities to assist in our endeavors. I would rather them safeguard their own headquarters and safe houses for now."

"I can also see what I can find out from my contacts. They are not really associated with yours so they may have better, and safer, luck." Livia added. Both Marcus and Isaac smiled and nodded in agreement with Livia's proposal.

"When do we leave?" Michael asked.

"I need some time to make the arrangements so a few days, but Owen will leave the next day after we leave," Isaac replied. Michael's brow crinkled after Isaac's comment.

"It will draw attention to me if I tag along with the rest of you," Owen commented, which seemed to clear up Michael's confusion as he nodded his head while his brow eased. "Do you think anyone has seen me here?" Owen inquired.

"I don't believe so. Once the gem left here the people that are after it seemed to care a lot less about the cabin. We sometimes will catch a stray person on the outskirts of the perimeter here but that is about it. I have a feeling that once we make it the rest of the way off this mountain, the eyes will be more on us," Isaac answered.

"I guess all that is left now is for me to find a mask or a hood for me to wear and I will be all set," Owen sarcastically said, causing the rest of the room to giggle.

"I have never seen such a relentless pursuit over one gem. It is imperative that it does not fall into the wrong hands. Please, everyone, be careful out there. Now, if there are no more questions or comments, I suggest we go about our normal daily routine and most importantly, get some rest. After a few days, you are going to need it." Isaac paused for a moment to see if anyone had anything else to say or ask. The room remained silent as people glanced back and forth at each other. "Okay then, class dismissed." Isaac smiled as he walked into the kitchen. The rest of the group slowly dispersed afterward.

The next few days seemed to drag for Owen. Since everyone had their assigned tasks and routines that they were used to, it was hard for Owen to help as much as he would like to have done. He was at least able to help at random times with the cabin chores or by helping Duncan out in the barn. He assisted in grooming the horses, as well as cleaning out the stalls. He wanted to go out and help patrol or hunt but Isaac denied that request for fear that Owen may be spotted. Besides those few tasks, Owen didn't have much to do. He decided to take his free time and use it as a combination of meditation, naps, and relaxation. Owen's free time became more useful than he realized. The additional rest and meditation helped him make more sense of the emotions and memories that the chimera brought to the table. As much as the self-awareness helped Owen, there was still much to be worked out, which only time and practice could accomplish.

Owen also used his free time in trying to figure out how he could retrieve the gem from Hailey and Avery without the transaction being witnessed. He became frustrated as only a few ideas came to mind and unfortunately, those ideas Owen was able to find flaws with them. His only hope was that he would figure something out when the time came. It was a gamble but it was his only move at the moment. Besides, Owen felt he needed to have another plan for what he would say when he finally would meet up with Hailey and Avery. That too was going just as well as his other plans, to the point that some made him cringe. It seemed like all his plans ended with him having to figure it out when the time arrived, which didn't sit well with him. In any case...the gem must be retrieved by him, the identity of the leader and the creature within the gem must be revealed, and hardest of all...he will have to meet Hailey and Avery again.

CHAPTER 4

Owen awoke to the sound of people talking outside but he didn't mind. He was just happy and relieved that he didn't have another chimera nightmare. He looked around and noticed Michael and Bailey were gone. Owen lied there for a minute and wondered what was going on before it dawned on him. Today was the day that everyone was going to leave to head back to the States. He quickly sat up and put on his flops before heading outside.

When he walked onto the porch, he could feel the cool morning air rush over his body. Owen squinted momentarily as his eyes adjusted to the sun. It seemed to be another nice day with blue skies and only a few puffy white clouds scattered in the sky. The beautiful, relaxing mornings were something that he knew he would miss once it was his time to depart. In front of the cabin, Owen noticed five horses, from the corral, and each of them had a satchel filled with supplies. Along with the satchel, there was a large backpack near each horse. Duncan was managing the horses to make sure they did not wander off. Just off the porch, he saw everyone congregating.

"Was everyone trying to sneak off without saying goodbye?" Owen playfully asked.

"Well, we thought about it but no one wanted to volunteer in fear of being eaten," Bailey responded while smiling as giggles could be heard throughout the group.

Owen chuckled. "Well, it's good to know I can strike fear into the hearts of people while I am just sleeping." Owen then turned his attention to Marcus. "Really, you are going to ride a horse in a suit?" Owen was flabbergasted.

"It's an older suit that I don't mind getting dirty," Marcus retorted as he had a slight grin on his face.

Isaac approached Owen, "Don't forget, you will leave tomorrow and I left your itinerary with Livia. Even though it's urgent that we secure the gem, don't rush through this assignment. However long it takes as long as we do it right. We will all have our phones on us and will be communicating with each other so that everyone is on the same page. Everyone's part in this plan is crucial, but Owen, yours is even more important. Everything will be based on your progress. Once you get the gem, consider us your support team until the gem is safe from the others who want to possess it."

"No pressure," Owen sarcastically commented after a quick raise of his brow.

"None at all," Isaac quickly countered as he winked.

"I feel like everyone should be bringing more stuff," Owen remarked as he observed their belongings.

"You would be surprised what you can fit inside these backpacks. Besides, the rest of our stuff is in a room at that inn you stayed at when you first arrived at the base of the mountain," Michael answered while walking up to Owen.

"I bet your game is with you as well," Owen commented.

"No, it's not with me. I don't just live to play video games," Michael resentfully replied with an ill look on his face.

"Seriously?" Owen said as he lowered his brow in disbelief.

"Nah, it's in the satchel. It was one of the first things I packed on my horse," Michael replied as his face lightened up and a large smile appeared on his face. The two laughed right before they gave each other a few strong pats on their arms.

"Be safe," Michael said to Owen before he walked to his horse.

"You too," Owen called out to him. Then Isaac, Marcus, and Anders approached Owen and each of them exchanged handshakes with him before they headed back to their horses.

"You know I don't do goodbyes so I am just going to say good luck," Bailey commented from behind Owen.

"Yeah, your distaste of anything sappy kind of gave it away," Owen responded as he grinned and looked over his shoulder. "Good luck out there and be safe," Owen added. The two nodded at each other as Bailey walked past him. As Owen began to turn to face the rest of the group, Bailey stopped. She turned around and briskly approached Owen and gave him a big hug. "No more death scares," Bailey whispered as she released herself from the hug. She then followed the hug with a punch to his shoulder.

"I know, I know…I deserve that," Owen remarked as he rubbed his shoulder, even though it didn't hurt. "Don't worry, I'll try to keep the death scares down to a minimal, acceptable level," Owen jested. Bailey smiled and gave Owen a slight nod before she headed over to her horse. Even though she punched him, Owen was surprised that Bailey hugged him again. It was out of character of her to do so but he didn't want to make her feel awkward by drawing any attention to it. Owen presumed her memories of his demise still lingered in her mind.

At this point, everyone had grabbed the reins of their respective horses. At first, Owen couldn't understand why they haven't mounted their horses yet until it dawned on him. They must walk their horses through the vegetation until they reach the trail. Once they are on the trail, then they will be able to ride the horses. Owen respectfully nodded to the entire group that was about to leave. In return, they nodded back and then turned their horses around and began to slowly walk them out of sight.

"Wait!" Owen called out. Everyone stopped and turned around. "Don't tell Hailey or Avery about me yet. As much as I rather have someone else tell them about me, I think it would be best if it came from me."

"Yeah, we all discussed that earlier, and we already agreed that we would save that fun for you," Bailey sarcastically replied.

"Yeah, loads of fun. Thanks," Owen said as he lightly chuckled. "Everyone, have a good journey." The group smiled before returning to leading their horses across the field and into the bushy area, eventually slipping out of sight.

"I wonder if I will see any of them again," Owen muttered.

"I'm sure you will. You just need to stay hopeful," Livia gently said to Owen. He tried to be hopeful but at the same time, there was doubt. In their line of work, anything can happen to anyone at any time. His first mission taught him that all too well.

"What do I do now?" Owen asked Livia and Duncan.

"As much as I would love to give you a list of chores to do around here, I will give you a pass today. Take advantage of the free day and relax. I'm sure starting tomorrow you won't get that luxury nearly as much as you will need it," Duncan responded.

"I agree. I will give you the itinerary later," Livia added.

"I think this is one of those times where I should just follow orders and not question them," Owen joked as everyone smiled at each other. He then proceeded back inside the cabin.

Owen spent the first part of the day relaxing, both inside and outside of the cabin. However, as much as he tried to relax, it didn't last long. Physically, he was quite relaxed; however, mentally he felt exhausted from all the various thoughts that bombarded his mind. One, of course, was what he would say to Hailey when he finally saw her again. He thought of multiple ways to react and what to say depending on how she would react. That alone stole a good portion of his mental capacity, but there was more. He was still racking his brain on how he would gather any intel on the gem or the person who desired it. Where would he even begin? If the others that have hundreds and even thousands of years of experience over him are having trouble, then how can he make a difference?

Before he let his anxiety take full control, Owen decided to pack for tomorrow's adventure. Unfortunately, that did not take long since he did not have many possessions at the cabin. As Owen stood by the couch staring at his backpack, the door opened.

"How's everything going?" Livia asked as she stopped near the couch.

"Peachy," Owen responded with a slight grin.

"That bad, huh?" Livia commented as a small grin appeared.

Owen scoffed. "Are you back in my head again?"

"No, I'm just a human with two eyes. It doesn't take a psychic to see that obviously, something is bothering you," Livia responded.

Owen sighed. "I wouldn't even know where to begin."

"From the beginning," Livia said as she sat on the couch. She then patted the cushion next to her.

Owen sat down next to Livia and took a deep breath before speaking. "My mind has been everywhere. If it is not on how Hailey will react when she sees me, then it's on my response to her when she does. Then, if I manage to not think about those two things, my mind is then trying to figure out how to gain any knowledge of the person who wants the gem or what's inside of it." Owen hung his head while he rested his forearms on his knees, frustrated.

"I would say to stop worrying about what will happen between you and Hailey since it is out of your control and you will drive yourself insane, but we both know that will not happen. That's just a part of your nature. All I can say is that you have already thought of everything and probably even rehearsed it in your head all day so let it be. Just tell yourself that when those thoughts enter your mind again that when the time comes, you will know what to say. Remember, regardless of what happened at the mountain or even with Joshua, you two have a lot of positive history together. Believe it or not, that goes further than you think. I am a woman…I know these things," Livia said as she winked.

Owen smiled. "I guess I should listen to the spokesperson for all womankind," Owen teased as he smiled after he raised his head. Livia chuckled as she shrugged her shoulders. "Seriously though, I understand your point and you are right. I will need to keep that in mind or else I will go insane thinking about it. Being distracted helps too, so all this sitting around isn't helping. With that said, if there is anything you want to talk about, mission-related or not, then I'm all ears," Owen added.

"When you arrive in the States and especially your final destination, I would take the time to explore your surroundings. Day and night. You will have time because it will take Hailey and Avery a lot longer to reach their own destination due to all the obstacles they will have in front of them. You may find clues or even people that may be willing to open up to you. At the very least you can observe what is going on around you. Think about it. You will see an influx of people, that work for this person, come into your area and they will not know who you are. You can observe what they do and where they go. That alone may shed some light on what is going on," Livia suggested. Owen sat back on the couch as his eyes drifted into the air.

"I like the idea but I'm confused. How will me doing recon in a random city be of any use to anyone?" Owen inquired.

"It's not some random city. You are headed to a city that is one of the few metropolitan areas that are anywhere close to the facility. It would be a good stopping point for anyone before heading to the mountains. Also, once the attackers analyze Hailey and Avery's path, then more and more of our adversaries will make their way to the same city that you will already be in. Trust me, there will be more recon and action than you realize," Livia replied with a slight grin.

"I didn't think about that. In that case, your idea is excellent. Thanks!" Owen said energetically as he smiled and perked up in his seat. Livia's reply made him think of all the potential his assignment now had.

"I'm glad I could help," Livia replied as she stood up. "Duncan is going to grill some venison in a little while so when you smell something good, then make your way outside," Livia said as she smiled and exited the cabin. Owen smiled as well, for that thought alone made his stomach grumble. He wasn't smiling solely because of that. He was also smiling because he felt he now had a plan of action once he reached the States. He was also going to take her advice and not burden himself with the constant worrying about how Hailey will react. Livia was right with everything she said and he was grateful for her wisdom and kindness.

Sure enough, not too much time passed before Owen smelled Duncan cooking the venison. He strolled outside and over to the grill, which was on the side of the cabin.

"All this time, I never knew the grill was right over here. The venison smells good," Owen commented.

"I used to have it closer to the barn since that is where I have my own little butcher area where I process the meat, but I moved the grill. I didn't want the horses to think they may end up on the menu." Duncan's comment made himself, along with Owen and Livia, chuckle at his response. The combination of smells from the venison steaks, charcoal, and the smoke from the hickory made Owen's stomach growl. To the point that he started to glance around to see if anyone could hear it. With not a moment to spare, Duncan was done cooking the steaks. Each person got a hefty-sized piece of steak, along with a vegetable medley. Everyone went inside the cabin and into the kitchen to enjoy their food. No one really spoke, minus the occasional small talk. When everyone was finishing up their food, Duncan spoke.

"Owen, if I had to give you any advice for your next assignment, it would be to trust your instinct. If you go on this mission doubting yourself or your decisions and not trusting anybody but your current friends, then you will end up failing. Don't get me wrong, be smart and cautious, but also take some risks. Go with your gut instincts. It's not foolproof, but it will get you further than what you think."

"I just have to trust myself first. Easier said than done," Owen countered.

"True, but think of everything you have accomplished in such a short time. Think of how you were able to save your friends while completing the mission. Regardless of the choices and the actions that had to be done, at the end of the day…you did it. You may doubt yourself but when the moment arrives, you always find the right action to take. At least that is what I've heard," Duncan replied while he grinned.

"Hopefully that streak continues," Owen replied.

"Also, don't forget that you are in charge…not the chimera. Take advantage of the new partnership that you have with it. Just remember that its instincts and personality can still pierce that veil, to the point that it could alter your decisions," Livia added.

"I thought I was in charge?" Owen inquired with a worried look.

"You are, but as I mentioned before, you still share a mind with the chimera. As time goes on, the more you will be able to manage yourself and the chimera. It's just in the beginning, as you adjust, that you will have to be more mindful. You just need to focus and you will be fine." Livia said with a reassuring look.

"I hope so. At this point, I feel like I just need to get out there and go for it…handle things as they come. All this waiting and thinking has me feeling anxious and a little on edge. Like I am some caged animal," Owen said as his knee began to bounce.

"That would be an example of the chimera wanting to take action, so before you cause an earthquake with your leg bouncing like that, read this." Livia handed Owen a folded piece of paper. Owen reached over and gently took the paper from her hand. He unfolded it and it was the itinerary for his trip. He reviewed it and it appeared that his flights would end in Pennsylvania. From there, he would take a car that was already parked in the long-term parking lot, with the ticket hidden under the floor mat. Owen also read the note following the itinerary that mentioned that the car had a tracking device on it so if he needed to just leave the car, it could be found. There was also a small map of safe house locations marked on it, which he already knew he would have to memorize since he could not take the map with him. Luckily, he only needed to focus on the one that he was going to stay at. He hoped it would be well-stocked and have a comfortable bed.

"Thanks. If you don't mind, I am going to finish getting ready and study this some more. I think I may even meditate for a while to get my brain back in the game. I am guessing bright and early tomorrow?" Owen asked.

"Yep, because you will have to stop by the inn before you go and it will take time to get there, as well as the airport too. I say once the sun is up, you should be up and ready," Duncan suggested.

"I can do that. Thank you, everyone…for everything, including helping me to stop bouncing my leg. I appreciate it," Owen said while he smiled and stood up.

"Of course. Please let me know if there is anything else you need or would like to talk about," Livia gently said while smiling.

"No problem and I will have your horse ready by the time you are up. I'll make sure it's the most stubborn and mean one we got," Duncan joked.

Owen chuckled. "You're too good to me."

Owen left the table and entered his room to wrap up a few things for the trip tomorrow. The advantage of the group leaving meant that he got his own room besides having to sleep out on the fold-out couch again. Once he was done, he spent the rest of his time meditating. He wanted to get a good session in since he preferred to have his mind strong before he started the day tomorrow. Hours passed before he came out of his meditative state. During that time, he felt as if he had not only cleared his mind but the chimera's mind as well. He felt more refreshed than he had felt in a long time. Owen debated about walking back into the main room of the cabin or even outside, but due to how late it was, he decided to just call it a night.

His alarm went off early the next morning. With a good night's sleep under his belt and a renewed mind, Owen sprung out of his bed. He took a quick shower and got himself ready for the journey that awaited him. He felt more motivated, almost eager, to get started. Once he finished, he went into the kitchen and grabbed some protein bars from the pantry so he could have a quick bite to eat. He even packed a few extra protein bars and water bottles for him to take on his trip. With the light now shining through the blinds, he knew it was time to leave.

Owen grabbed his backpack, along with some items for the satchel, and walked outside. Of course, there was Duncan tending to the horse near the front of the cabin. Livia was standing on the front porch watching Duncan until she saw Owen.

"Morning! Let me take those for you," Duncan energetically said as he briskly walked up to Owen and grabbed his backpack and other items. He then took them over to the horse to get everything situated.

"Thank you!" Owen called out as Duncan walked back to the horse. He then turned to Livia, "I also want to thank you again for everything that you have done for me. I really appreciate it."

"You're welcome. Have a safe journey and good luck. Be careful," Livia responded as she smiled and gave Owen a long hug. He smiled along with her as they hugged, for her words and gestures during his entire stay seemed so genuine.

Once they released from their embrace, he walked over to Duncan and extended his hand. "Of course, thank you too for everything you have done as well. You're a good man," Owen said as he smiled and gave Duncan a hearty handshake, along with a pat on the arm.

"I appreciate it and you too. Remember, you will travel the same way that you came to my cabin all those months ago. There is a trail guide if you need it with your itinerary. Don't forget to stop at the inn before you head to the airport. The spare key is in your papers and you can just leave the key in the room and I can get it later when I go to retrieve the horse. Have a good trip," Duncan said as he patted Owen on the back as he walked past him.

"Will do. Thanks," Owen responded as he picked up his backpack and strapped it onto his back. He then grabbed the reins, waved goodbye to Livia and Duncan, and led the horse out of the field and into the brush.

Once Owen cleared the brush, he found himself back on the path. The weather was cool but warm whenever the sunlight hit his body through the openings within the leaves in the trees. There were clear blue skies with only a slight breeze that gently moved the green leaves populating all the trees. He could even hear some faint sounds of birds chirping off in the distance. If Owen didn't have the flight leaving today, he would have found a spot to relax and take in the scenery.

He turned to his horse and took a moment to admire its smooth golden-brown coat as he gently rubbed its neck. Duncan sure knew how to take care of his horses, Owen thought. The horse was already at ease so Owen decided to mount it while the horse was calm. He fidgeted in the saddle for a moment to get comfortable and then with a flick of the reins and a few clicks from his tongue, the horse trotted down the path.

As Owen rode down the path, it began to seem familiar to him. Even the area where he, Hailey, and Avery all stopped and took a moment to admire the beauty and the magnitude of where they were. Similar to the way up the mountain, Owen used the same method of descending by changing up the speeds of the horse from a trot to a run and then back to a walk. He was also mindful about taking breaks whenever he or the horse needed one. Since Owen did not take any long breaks, he was able to make it down the mountain by lunchtime.

He dismounted and walked his horse over to the corral. Once the horse was secured within it, Owen strolled over to the inn itself. He pulled out the key to see the room number. Once he entered the inn, he went directly to the staircase and up a flight of stairs, and then he proceeded down the hall until he found the room. It had a privacy sign on the door handle so he knocked just in case someone happened to be inside. There was no answer so Owen decided to cautiously enter the room.

Once he entered, it appeared to be more of a supply room than anything else. The sign must be to keep the room attendants and other employees out. There was a variety of everything from clothes to camping supplies to various sundry items. The only item that the room did not have were any weapons, which did not bother Owen since he himself, was a weapon. He figured the absence of weapons was because the room wasn't fully secured. Owen unloaded his camping supplies and gathered more clothes for himself. The rest of the items he needed were already included in his backpack. Owen even had money that came along with the paperwork he received last night. He checked the time and he had at least an hour before the car would arrive to bring him to the airport. He decided to use that time to relax a bit in the room.

Owen's relaxation was cut short when he began to feel hungry. He decided to go downstairs to the little marketplace they had next to the lobby and grab a sandwich and a drink. He could have eaten a few sandwiches but he just wanted enough to last him until he arrived at the airport. Then, Owen could at least eat more there and during the flight.

"Would you like to charge that to your room?" The clerk politely asked.

"Sure," Owen hesitantly responded. He wasn't sure if he was supposed to but no one said to not do it so why not? Owen went outside to sit down on a bench and eat his food while enjoying the peaceful and beautiful weather one last time. He noticed a black vehicle pull up to the curb he was sitting nearby. The driver got out of the car, "Owen I presume?" He asked as he approached Owen.

"Yes sir," Owen responded with a grin as he stood up and discarded his trash into the garbage can near the bench.

"Good...good. Do you need me to take your bags?" The driver asked.

"Nah, I got it. It's just my backpack and this one carry-on," Owen responded as he lifted the two bags and placed them in the car himself.

"Very good. I should have you at the airport on time. Let us get moving," the driver said as he smiled. The two of them then got into the car and left.

The drive to the airport was uneventful, which Owen was thankful for. It was also quiet, except for the Italian opera music that the driver turned on at a low volume. Owen enjoyed the music genre selection as he stared out the window and took in the final views of the Alps and Italy before reaching the airport. He could have used the time to think more about the mission but instead, he decided to keep his mind clear. He had plenty of time to think about the mission on the long plane ride home.

Minus some delays due to the vast amount of people within the airport, Owen was able to reach his gate with time to spare before he had to board the plane. He even had time to stop at an airport restaurant to grab some chocolate pastries to snack on while he waited. It felt weird to be traveling alone, which was ironic since before he was recruited to the facility, he traveled alone for years. Now, he felt alone without his friends. There were no familiar faces around and no one to talk to. He couldn't even text or call anyone since Isaac mentioned keeping the communications on an as-needed basis only. Owen had a feeling that this mission will be lonely for a good part of it until he met up with Bailey, Michael, Avery, and Hailey. He just didn't realize he would feel the weight of that so soon.

He pondered if maybe the loneliness he felt was stronger because of the chimera. If the chimera was used to being a part of a pride, then being alone would make things worse. "We will be okay. We are in this together," Owen muttered to himself while trying to stay positive. He was attempting to not only make himself feel better but the chimera as well. Owen's thoughts were disrupted by the beginning of the boarding process.

After a long flight that mainly consisted of eating, sleeping, and going over the mission. After that and a short connecting flight, Owen eventually reached his destination. Since he didn't check any luggage, he was able to quickly weave his way through the airport and into the parking garage. He located the car that he was supposed to use and it wasn't much. Just a basic four-door silver sedan, but it would suit his needs. Besides, he didn't need anything flashy if he was to remain under the radar.

Owen put his bags into the trunk and got into the car. He turned the key to start the car but he didn't pull out of the spot afterward. Instead, Owen sat in the seat as a wave of tiredness engulfed him even further as his eyelids became heavy. Between the early start, traveling, and time zone changes…Owen was now exhausted. However, he needed to push forward if he was going to make it to the safe house. That, and he needed to get back on track with the new time zone. Owen rubbed his eyes, switched on the radio, and turned up the air conditioning to keep the car nice and cold. Anything to help keep him awake. He even debated about getting a soda or a coffee but he didn't want to have to stop to use the bathroom.

Owen finally pulled out of the spot, paid for the parking, and drove off. He couldn't tell if his driving skills were not as good as they used to be because he was either that tired, that out of practice, or both. He drove carefully to compensate and felt very fortunate that there was a GPS in the car directing him the entire way to the safe house. Hours passed and he finally made it to his destination just before nightfall. The safe house was located on the outskirts of the city, and the city itself was one of the last larger metropolitan areas before reaching the mountains. Anything after that was the countryside or small towns. The safe house itself was a condo located on the top floor of a twelve-story building. Owen grabbed his bags and made his way up to his new, temporary home.

As he entered, he could see it was a small, but adequate two-bedroom, one-bath condo that had a kitchen and a family room. The walls and furniture were all neutral colors consisting of whites, tans, and grays. Owen walked past the family room to a door that led to a small balcony. The view itself didn't offer much except for the tall illuminated buildings of the city off in the distance. He headed back inside to put his bags into the master bedroom closet before exploring the rest of the condo. It was stocked with non-perishable foods, drinks, and your typical kitchenware items.

The second bedroom was where the extra supplies were, which were similar in nature to what he saw back at the inn, minus the camping supplies. This time, he did find some weapons ranging from pistols and revolvers to handheld combat weapons. These weapons ranged from daggers, knives, brass knuckles, and even small maces and throwing axes. He even found a couple of small crossbows. Of course, there were ammo and sharpening blocks for everything as well. Owen presumed there were not any large weapons since they were more difficult to conceal within the city. He spent some extra time in the supply room to get a good idea of what he had to work with before heading back to the bathroom located in the master bedroom.

On his way back, he discovered a washer and dryer tucked away in a closet in the hallway. When he made it back into the master bedroom, Owen took a moment to sit on the bed. He smiled, for the mattress slightly sunk in, and it felt as if he was sitting on a cloud. Owen pried himself off the bed and made it into the bathroom, which he noticed already had some extra toiletries and towels. For a small condo, he was delighted that it was both well-stocked and comfortable.

Owen decided to take a shower to wash away the day's journey.

Once he was done, he still felt tired but at least clean and refreshed just enough to have a small snack before going to bed. He debated if he wanted to watch TV, but his mind was mush and his eyelids were heavy, so he finally dragged himself to bed. Sleep swiftly captured him.

The sound of Owen's phone vibrating is what finally woke him up around mid-morning. He missed a call from Bailey so he listened to the voicemail. *"Hey it's me. You should be in the same city as us by now. The other two with the package are delayed due to other interested parties. Keep you posted."*

Owen understood the message but still chuckled over how she left the message. She sounded weird in her attempt to talk like an undercover agent. It needed some work, Owen thought. He hoped Hailey and Avery didn't run into any trouble they couldn't handle. He felt it was wrong that no one else was allowed to help them. Isaac and his team were already in the mountains while Bailey, Michael, and himself are in the same city…just waiting and doing recon. At least Isaac's team was going to be busy with the important task of clearing the way for the gem and keeping the facility hidden. Owen had to make sure his recon work was just as productive and useful to the mission. Still, he didn't feel right about his current task.

He sat on the edge of the bed with his mind torn between sticking exactly to the mission or going against orders and assisting in killing off the opposition that stood in Hailey and Avery's way. He had to think of something. It was a waste to have three people doing recon on a city, regardless if people know them or not, he thought. Owen began to think of a way where he could feel and be more useful without breaking any orders.

The safe house he was at now was relatively new. One that Isaac set up after the gem was found so it was off the radar to a lot of people. The original safe house was located on the other side of the city where Bailey and Michael were staying. That would mean if anyone was going to get the jump on them at the original safe house, they may have to come through his part of the city first.

"Received message. Stay on your side of the fence and I will stay on my side. Cover more ground that way," Owen texted Bailey. He got a quick response, *"Agreed."*

As much as Owen wanted to do more, he decided to stick to the original plan. He knew the importance of the information that was needed. At least this way, they would cover more ground in their reconnaissance by splitting up the city. Now, if he happened to get attacked then he would have no choice but to defend himself. If the result ended with him capturing or killing someone because of it, then well how could he be faulted, Owen pondered with a smirk on his face. He used the time during the day to review the map of the city to see where he would begin.

Each night, Owen went to one of the designated areas that he wanted to stake out but each night it was a bust. He tried walking the streets and even alleyways in hopes he would either see something going on or someone would try to attack him. He even visited some of the local bars and restaurants but again, he did not see anything suspicious. After three nights of constant walking and surveying, Owen became frustrated. He started to doubt his decision to stick to the original plan. Owen felt so frustrated that he went back to the condo sooner than planned because he could feel his rage starting to get the upper hand. He used the extra time when he did this to meditate.

On the fourth night, he tried an area that he picked out that was further away than the others he already checked out. The area he was in now was a more high-end, low-crime area versus the previous areas he surveyed. Ironically enough, even though he strolled around the crime-ridden streets the previous nights, he came across no issues.

After a quick bite to eat, Owen stayed around to have a couple of beers to blend in to see if he could see anything out of the ordinary, but once again, nothing. He huffed as he stood up and exited the establishment and decided to walk the streets for a few minutes before calling it another lost cause. It was late and dark outside so there were not a lot of people around. As Owen walked past an alleyway, he heard a noise that caught his attention.

CHAPTER 5

It sounded like a bottle was broken and he was going to dismiss it and move on, but then he heard some form of a struggle. Owen paused and surveyed the area while listening and that is when he heard a man scream. He bolted down the alleyway and around a few corners until he slid to a stop when he saw what was causing the commotion.

Owen witnessed three men in suits, minus the jackets, attacking a woman in ripped blue jeans and a black crop top. The men, who seemed to be in their thirties and forties, appeared to be quite strong by the appearance of their muscles bulging through their button shirts. On the other hand, the woman seemed to be around Owen's age and at best, her body appeared to be toned, but she didn't seem to be in distress.

Before he could react, Owen witnessed the woman elbow one of the men attacking from the side in his nose, causing him to stumble back. She then sent a side kick to the man attacking from the opposite direction. Her foot slammed into his chest which made him fall back onto the ground. The third man attacking from in front of her was able to punch her across the face. Her head whipped to the right from the impact but she immediately followed back with a backhand, catching the advancing man across the chin. As he stumbled back, she followed up with a slash across the man's neck. Blood squirted from his neck as he grabbed it and fell against the wall behind him. He slowly slid down the wall and fell to his side. The man was now lying dead on the street in a growing pool of blood.

Owen's eyes squinted to see what she used to slice the man's neck wide open. That is when he could see the blood dripping from her claws as she turned to face the other two men that were back on their feet. Owen then noticed the men's eyes were not human. He could not see the woman's eyes since her dirty blonde hair, which came a little past her shoulders, was obstructing his view. It didn't matter…the claws were evidence enough. Did he just stumble on some hybrid war and if so, were any of them involved with the unknown person who wants the gem? Owen's question caused him to hesitate. His initial reaction was to help the woman since she seemed outnumbered but now, he didn't know what to do, except observe.

He heard growls, rumbles, and snorts as the battle continued, but it was short-lived. As the two men converged on the woman, she moved toward the man on her right, ducking under his slash. She popped up from behind him and quickly snapped his neck. The other attacker stopped as he watched his fellow comrade crumble lifelessly to the ground. At this point, no one knew Owen was standing in the shadows watching.

Owen could see the fear on the man's face as the guy's eyes widened and his jaw slightly lowered while he stared at her. As soon as she took her first step toward him, he turned and leaped high into the air and grabbed onto the ledge of the building, and pulled himself up. The woman followed him by leaping onto the building and quickly scaling her way to the top. She used a combination of her claws and took advantage of the imperfections on the walls. Owen knew he couldn't let these two out of his sight so he transitioned and followed the pursuit. He scaled the building using the same method as the woman. By the time he reached the top, he could see the man had already jumped to the next building with the woman not too far behind.

Owen sprinted across the top of the building and leaped from the ledge and to his surprise, he made it to the other rooftop without having to grab onto the side of the building and scale his way up like the others had to do. He would understand if the buildings were closer together but not for the large gap that he just sailed over. Owen quickly understood why he was able to as a smile formed on his face after he realized another benefit of his new hybrid self.

He continued his pursuit of the other two and he was gaining on them more quickly than he planned since he did not have to stop to climb up any of the buildings. However, he also felt the chimera's predatory instinct shining through as the pursuit continued. It was like the two in front of him were his prey and he needed to catch them. As much as that instinct commanded that he kill them once he caught them, Owen had to suppress that urge and ensure that it stayed that way until he at least had more information.

As he grew closer, he could see the woman glancing over her shoulder. She must have sensed he was close behind her. She turned her head and stayed focused on the other guy, which the distance between them narrowed with each building they leaped to. Owen wanted to throw the woman off guard so he changed tactics and leaped to the adjacent building and kept moving forward. He needed to get in front of them and stop them both to get a better idea of what was going on.

Owen transitioned more and with that, he gained a lot of momentum. He leaped from building to building effortlessly and immensely faster than before. Within moments he was a building ahead of the man. While having the advantage, Owen leaped onto the building that the man had just leaped onto himself, causing the guy to stumble to a stop. As Owen was about to speak the man pulled out a dagger and swung wildly behind him but it was too late. The woman was already in position behind him and was able to grab the arm with the dagger. In one fluid motion, she twisted his arm and drove the hand that held the dagger into his chest. With the man holding his chest and slightly bent over she grabbed his back and tossed him off the building. The man screamed on the way down until Owen heard the body slam into one of the garbage dumpsters on the street below.

For a moment, his jaw dropped and his brow raised in shock. He didn't expect that to happen and he wanted to try to talk to them both but now it was just the two of them. Owen composed himself and redirected his focus on the fact that she was able to kill three other hybrids. This meant she was either a skilled fighter, had a rare creature inside her, or both. He knew he had to proceed with caution, especially since he did not know what side of the good versus evil fence she was on. To lessen the intensity of the moment, he transitioned back to normal and took a few steps forward, while trying to keep a calm facial expression. As he did, the urge to kill her from earlier after that pursuit vanished. She slowly turned her head to look over her shoulder. He finally got a good look at her eyes as a pair of amber-colored lion's eyes stared him down.

Owen's mind was filtering through the creatures that had lion-like eyes but there were so many. He needed more to go on. She slowly turned to face him. He could see and feel her intensity as she breathed heavily while her blood-soaked claws trembled not with fear, but with power. A small, sinister smile appeared which allowed her fangs to show as she glared at him.

"Did you not learn anything from your buddies?" The woman grumbled in a feminine, yet raspy voice.

Owen quickly shook his head in both disagreement and confusion. "My buddies...no. I don't even know them."

"Oh, so you just happened to be in the area when this went down?" The woman asked as the smile left her face and was replaced with an accusatory look while she slowly approached him.

"Actually yes. I have been surveying this city for days in search of some answers and heard the commotion. Do I even look like one of them?" Owen asked as he gestured to his clothes. He tried to remain calm even while she was slowly approaching him.

"Well, it seems these people come in all sorts of forms so your attire doesn't mean much to me. Besides, why didn't you help me when the other three were attacking me?" She said as she stopped a few feet from Owen. She was not breathing as hard and the intensity was not as fierce but her claws and fangs were still visible while her amber eyes watched over him.

"It all happened so fast and I didn't know the story behind it all. Besides, if anything the men appeared to need the help, not you." Owen responded while he smirked.

She smiled with a quick raise of her brow. "Now that part I do believe. So, were you chasing me or that last guy then?" The woman asked as the smile left her.

"Both. My goal was to figure out what was going on and to get some answers. Such as, who was my enemy and who was my ally," Owen answered.

She slowly approached him again and stopped within inches of him. The woman grinned as she whispered, "Which do you think I am? Friend...or foe?"

Owen lightly chuckled, "I have a feeling I am going to find out in just a moment."

The woman's smile grew as she took a few steps back, "I'm still trying to find out if you are either that cocky or that stupid to be this calm and not in transition," she calmly said. Owen simply shrugged. Then, without warning, the woman's smile vanished as she sent her claws slashing toward his chest. Owen countered by grabbing her wrist.

"Maybe, it's just confidence," Owen replied while he had a smug look.

The woman struggled to rip her arm away from Owen's grasp but failed in her attempt. "How are you able to hold me and not even be in transition? What the heck are you?" The woman asked as she continued to struggle. She then slashed at Owen with her free arm, which he caught that wrist as well. He was able to hold her in place but it became harder to do so when she pushed herself deeper into transition, as the fur began to become more prevalent on her skin. She snarled as she tried to jerk her arms away from Owen while even snapping at his arms.

Owen's brow lowered, his nose wrinkled, and his eyes narrowed as he began to put more effort into holding her in place. It was now becoming harder to hold on with the additional struggling and her transition, so he used his current leverage and swung her around. As he let go, her momentum slammed her into the side of an HVAC unit, and then fall to the ground. She shook her head as she slowly pushed herself to her hands and knees but the impact seemed to just anger her more.

"I'm just a guy trying to find some answers. Let's not do this," Owen sternly said. The woman growled as she rose to her feet. Her claws were stretched out as her shoulders raised up and down from her heavy breathing. "I guess we are doing this," Owen muttered to himself. Even though he knew she was about to attack he did not transition. He was hoping the less he provoked her and the more on the defensive he was, the better chance she would see he just wanted to talk. He just didn't know how long he could do that before the chimera had enough.

She lunged forward and sent her claws toward Owen's head. He was able to duck under her first attack with ease but just barely avoided the second swipe of her claws as he leaned up and away. She then sent a forward kick directly at his chest, but Owen was able to cross his arms in front of him to block the attack. Even with him successfully blocking the attack, the impact slid him back a couple of feet. She followed up with a roundhouse kick to his head, which Owen swatted away, causing her to stumble back. Owen did not advance. Instead, he remained where he was with his hands in front of him in a gesture to calm her down.

"Fight me!" The woman yelled.

"I just want to talk," Owen gently replied.

The woman took a few deep breaths and with that, she transitioned back to normal. Owen released a deep sigh of relief that he finally got through to her. He too, dropped out of transition as she approached him. It was the first time he saw her in human form. She smiled gently at him as she gazed upon him with hazel eyes. She stopped within just a foot of him.

"I'm sorry. It's just every new person I have encountered lately has been out to kill me or up to no good. That tends to make a girl keep her guard up," The woman said with a crooked smile while slightly shrugging her shoulders. Her voice was as gentle as she was at that moment.

Owen lightly chuckled, "I guess a girl can't be too careful these days. No worries."

"Thank you," The woman said as she held Owen's hand and raised it to his chest level, smiling as she did. "I'm sorry. You seem like a nice guy." Owen crinkled his brow in confusion. Then, before he could react, she slipped back into transition and pulled his arm with both hands toward her mouth. In the same fluid motion, she sunk her fangs into his arm. She released her bite as he pulled his arm away from her. The pain caused him to grasp his wound as the blood trickled down his arm.

"But a girl can't be too cautious. At least this way we will be able to talk. You see…" She was interrupted when Owen surprisingly backhanded her across her cheek, causing her to lift into the air and land hard on her back. At this point, Owen fell into transition without any thought, for that attack on him provoked the instinct of the chimera. He let out a large growl as he pounced.

The woman was still shaking off the hit but was able to roll off to the side to avoid Owen's claws. She stumbled to her feet and sent a wild swing toward Owen, which he blocked with his forearm and quickly grabbed her throat with his other hand. In the same motion, he drove her back into the brick-covered stairwell. The impact was hard enough to cause the pieces of the brick to flake off when she slammed against it. The intense urge to rip her to shreds coursed through his veins.

While she was still dazed, his claws began to pierce her neck as his grip tightened. She began to choke while he rose his other hand in the air, which the moonlight highlighted his dark, razor-sharp claws. Her eyes widened in fear. Then, Owen gained enough control to use his hand that was around her throat to jerk her forward. As he did, he drove his fangs into where her neck met her shoulder. She screamed up until Owen released his bite and tossed her to the ground. She winced in pain as she grabbed her neck, with the blood slowly oozing between her hand and her neck.

"Now maybe your stubborn self will stay still long enough to listen to what I have to say!" Owen snarled at her while still in transition.

"How are you still moving?" She asked while she unsteadily rose to her feet.

Owen's brow furrowed as his head tilted, "I can ask the same." He couldn't comprehend how she could still be moving after he pumped her full of venom.

"I guess your confidence and your performance are not at the same level," she mocked as she smiled through the pain until she gasped when she looked at him.

Owen scoffed. "I doubt that." He then paused while he slowly walked toward her. "Why did you ask me how I was still moving?"

"It can't be," the woman muttered as she slowly walked toward Owen as well. Her head was slightly tilted and her brow knitted from her curiosity. As she came within a few feet of Owen, he growled at her as he stopped. He didn't trust her after the last time she got close to him. His reaction caused her to halt, so she raised her hands up to show she meant no harm. Regardless of her actions, Owen's guard was still up as he glared at her.

"Our eyes are the same and we both are confused as to why our bites didn't work…I wonder," she said as she slowly moved her hands off to either side of her. Owen's jaw dropped, as well as his guard when he saw flames ignite around her hands. Owen, who was speechless, mimicked her gesture. The woman gasped as she saw the flames around Owen's hands.

"You are a chimera?" The woman asked rhetorically as she transitioned back to normal.

"I am," Owen replied as he transitioned back to normal as well. "Isaac mentioned he knew of only one other chimera. I'm guessing that is you."

"That would be me but how can you be a chimera as well? Sure, you have the same abilities but you're different at the same time…stronger too," the woman responded as her eyes scanned Owen.

"Yeah…that's a long story of its own, which I wouldn't mind discussing it with you provided we can talk without you trying to kill me," Owen said, followed by a slight smile.

The woman lightly chuckled. "Fair enough. How about you and I grab a drink? I know a place not too far from here that isn't so…uptight."

"A stranger that tried to kill me not too long ago now wants me to follow her to some unknown location. Yeah, I feel all warm and fuzzy about that," Owen said sarcastically but then grinned afterward.

The woman smiled as she walked closer to Owen. He was surprised he wasn't nervous due to what happened the last time she was so close to him. If anything, he felt very at ease with her. He couldn't explain it, he just…was.

"Abigail…and you are?"

"Owen. Is it okay if I call you Abby?"

"Not if you want to keep breathing," Abigail responded as she winked.

"Well, I really enjoy breathing so Abigail it is," Owen responded while he smiled and quickly raised his brow.

Abigail laughed. "Well since we aren't strangers anymore Owen, follow me," she said as she turned around and proceeded to the edge of the roof. Owen paused as he was pleasantly surprised by her witty yet bold demeanor.

Abigail winced and stopped walking. "I almost forgot that you bit me pretty good there. I'm not used to being on the receiving end. Give me a moment and don't freak out," Abigail said while touching her neck again. She then transitioned deep into phase two and held it for a couple of minutes.

"I need to at least stop the bleeding until I can fully heal it later," Abigail mentioned in a grumbled voice.

"Good idea," Owen added while he held his arm from her bite. He was going to transition to phase three but he didn't want to alarm her so he kept it at phase two. Owen could see his wound close but the damage was still there.

"Don't forget to wash your hands," Abigail said as flames appeared around her hands. Owen smiled, for it was a good way to get the blood off his hands so he copied Abigail's actions. It didn't take long before Owen transitioned back to normal. Not too long after Abigail did the same.

"See, now I just fix my hair, and there you go. It's like we never had our playdate," Abigail jested as she positioned her hair to help cover her wound. Owen felt her response was fake from her decline in playfulness.

"I know how it is to come back from a chimera transition. If you need a few moments to calm yourself then please do. I understand," Owen suggested. He remembered how difficult it was for him in the past to calm down even from a phase two transition.

"I appreciate it but I have been around long enough to be able to handle it. Nothing like a little workout can't fix. Try to keep up," Abigail said and then winked right before her eyes transitioned. She then turned and jumped off the roof. Owen smiled with her playful comment as his eyes transitioned. He ran and jumped off the roof and onto a smaller building. He could see Abigail jumping from rooftop to rooftop, using her claws to grasp onto any buildings as needed for leverage. Owen smiled and followed suit. Even though she had a head start, it didn't take long for him to catch up to her. He then jumped to the next building and turned around and waited on her, confidently smiling with his arms crossed as he did. Abigail leaped onto the building and approached Owen.

"I guess I caught up to you," Owen said with a smug demeanor.

"Yeah, I guess you did. You're really going to have to explain how you are pulling off this super chimera thing you got going on," Abigail responded as her brow knitted. Owen's abilities bewildered her. She then smiled as she passed him while gently grazing her hand across his arm. "It's not too far from here. I guess we can walk the rest of the way like two normal human beings."

The two jumped down from the roof and Owen transitioned back to normal but Abigail's eyes remained the same. His brow lowered and his head tilted from confusion.

"Your eyes are showing," Owen joked as the two began to walk down the sidewalk.

"They are, aren't they," Abigail responded in a carefree manner as she smiled and continued to walk forward.

"You may draw some unwanted attention," Owen loudly whispered as he nervously scanned the area.

"I can sense Isaac is still firmly parked in your mind. I need to loosen you up," Abigail commented as she smiled and put her arm around the crook of Owen's arm. She then leaned toward him to speak softer, "Go ahead...try it. You would be surprised how little people pay attention to their surroundings anymore." Owen nervously smiled while still looking around.

"Oh, come on. You can do it. Don't worry. If anything bad happens, I'll protect you," Abigail said with a playful smile.

Owen took a deep breath to compose himself and then transitioned his eyes. Abigail smiled as they continued to walk. Owen then saw a couple walking toward them on the same sidewalk. He began to angle his eyes away from them.

"No, no, no…eyes forward," Abigail said as she squeezed his arm with her own. Her confidence and smile made Owen trust her enough to look forward. As they passed the couple with no reaction, Owen chuckled to himself out of disbelief.

"See…didn't it feel good to live on the edge?" Abigail asked with the same playful smile as before.

"Yeah. Sadly enough, that was a rush," Owen replied, smiling as he did. He then noticed another couple walking toward them, which they were occupied by looking at the same phone as they strolled down the sidewalk. As Owen and Abigail grew near, Owen spoke. "Good evening." The couple lifted their heads and shifted their eyes enough to reply, "Evening." There was no frightened reaction. No hysterical cries of a monster. Just a faint smile as they walked by and then refocused their attention back to the phone.

"Well look at you go. There may be some hope for you yet," Abigail remarked as her brow raised and a large smile appeared on her face.

"I'm a fast learner," Owen playfully responded.

"Always a good trait in a man," Abigail commented as the two of them laughed.

They eventually reached the bar, which seemed to be located on the outskirts of the nicer part of the area. As they reached the door, the two of them transitioned back to normal. Once they were inside, they found a table near the back corner of the room. The inside was not large and between the music and the décor, it favored rock. The music was loud but bearable and the place itself was not crowded. As they sat down, the waitress came over and they both ordered a beer. Not too long after that, they both received a large mug of beer.

Abigail took a gulp from her drink. "Okay…story time. How did you reach super chimera status?"

Owen's head briefly tilted before taking a swig from his drink as well. "I will give you the condensed story. We were on a mission to stop a group of people from getting their hands on a gem deep within a mountain in the Alps. It was intense. They had a small army and some people like us that were not afraid to fully transition. On top of that, they were ready for us since they had a man on the inside."

"Who?" Abigail asked.

"Not sure if you heard of him or not, but his name was Klayden," Owen replied.

"Yeah, I heard of him. His ego holds no bounds," Abigail responded sarcastically as she rolled her eyes. "I thought he and Isaac were close?"

"The closeness apparently was one-sided. Anyway, in the end, we ran out of options after he fully transitioned into a manticore..." Owen said but was interrupted by Abigail.

"Manticore! Wow...impressive. How did everyone escape?"

"Not everyone escaped," Owen solemnly responded before his eyes drifted down.

"Sorry, I didn't know," Abigail softly replied as her face winced from guilt.

Owen shrugged off his sad memories and moved on. "It's okay. Anyway, there was no way we could make it out of there or give the manticore a chance to free itself. So, without any other options available, I transitioned into the chimera. Obviously, the chimera won."

"Obviously, but it still doesn't explain how you are a chimera on steroids. I have never seen such power from someone not in transition, nor have I seen such control over the creature inside someone before," Abigail countered as she leaned forward in her seat.

"An almost fully transitioned gorgon giving just the right amount of her gaze for just the right amount of time, plus a fully transitioned chimera that has a magical gem inside of it equals…me," Owen said as he held his hands out to either side with a slight smirk.

"What…how? Enough with the summary…I want all the details," Abigail said while she arched her brow.

"You asked for it," Owen countered as he shrugged. He then proceeded to tell her some more details about the mission, his time spent inside the mountain after he turned to stone, and then the events after he left the mountain. This also included everything that Livia explained to him. He spoke freely and without fear that he could be talking to a member of the opposition. He had an unexplainable trust in her. The entire time Owen spoke, Abigail appeared to be quite captivated by his words as she leaned in and listened intently.

"Wow…that's insane, yet good to know. For a moment, I thought I was losing my touch. Also, for someone who has only been in the game for a short time, you sure racked up some experience," Abigail commented as she sat back in her chair and took another gulp of her drink.

"I aim to please," Owen jokingly responded. "How long have you been doing this?"

"You're a curious one, aren't you," Abigail responded as she smiled.

"Well, I figured since I just poured my soul out to someone I just met, it would be nice to know a little more about the mystery girl whose name I am not allowed to shorten." Owen followed his reply with a crooked grin.

Abigail grinned and then nodded in agreement. "A couple of hundred years, give or take a decade or two. Marcus was the one that actually found me in a small town out west, where I was living at the time. I had a variety of odd jobs to make ends meet but I wanted more than to just survive from day to day, so at night I found another way to make money. I stole it." Owen's eyes widened with her comment.

"Don't judge me. Back then there were not as many opportunities for women as there were for men," Abigail defensively added as her eyes narrowed.

"No judgment from me. I was more surprised by your honesty. It's refreshing," Owen commented.

Abigail smiled. "Well good because you will get a lot of that from me. Anyway, one night I picked this man's pocket and as I turned the corner, I saw him. He confronted me and before I could respond he rolled up his sleeve to reveal something glowing. That man was of course Marcus and as they say…the rest was history."

"So did Isaac assign you to the same mission as me?" Owen asked as he took another sip of his drink.

"See that's the thing. I used to do missions for him but it got old. It was like a job that you had to go to all day, every day. I don't know if it was because of my personality or the chimera or what, but it took its toll on me after some time," Abigail replied.

"So, you quit then? I didn't know one could do that," Owen commented as his brow arched.

"I didn't quit. I just found another role within the organization," Abigail responded but her answer only caused his brow to lower due to his confusion.

"Now I roam where I please. I rarely check in with Isaac or Marcus…or even visit that facility. My job is to keep the underground scene in check." Abigail raised her finger in a gesture to silence Owen before he could ask what that meant.

"You see Owen, there are rogue hybrids all over the world. Some are good…some are not so good. There are even mythological creatures that roam this Earth still. Some because they never vanished and some because someone touched a gem that they had no business touching and the creature won. That kind of stuff needs to be kept in check but it is hard to find such things because most of the time, it happened off the radar. Isaac only sees the large-scale issues happening so he and his recruits deal with that. I, along with others spread all over the world, deal with the rest."

"That is impressive but it still seems like an all-day, everyday job," Owen retorted.

"Not exactly. I'm not on the clock all the time. If I see something I will check it out but if not, I am living my life. I have seen and experienced so much while doing this over the past fifty to seventy-five years that I can't imagine doing anything else. I also don't have to live with and follow, the black-and-white rules that Isaac holds dear to him. Don't get me wrong. He is a good man but there is just so much gray out here that you must make your own decisions, because the cookie-cutter ones don't always fit."

"Understandable. In that case, what brings you out here then?" Owen asked.

"I have been in this area for a good ten years now. The longest I have stayed in one place for who knows how long. I know some good people here and I like the after-hours nightlife here as well. It is both fun and it keeps me busy. With that said, I have noticed a lot more traffic come through here over the last month. Even more this past week. None of them are friendly and some are just reckless, hence why I didn't believe you before. This gem you mentioned earlier must be something for the amount of time and effort it is taking me to fend them off," Abigail mentioned as she slowly shook her head and rolled her eyes before she took another drink of her beer.

"Speaking of which, should we clear those three bodies off the street?" Owen suggested.

"If I didn't have to chase after the last one then I would have, but by now the bodies have been discovered. Especially with all that commotion from the fight. I purposely killed them in ways that didn't seem unnatural or too weird. With everything that I have seen they, like other cities, will just either not report it or it will be another animal attack, mugging, or something else that will just be pushed under the rug," Abigail answered.

"That's comforting," Owen sarcastically remarked. "Maybe we can team up and see what we can do to end this. We can solve your problem of the extra work lately and my problem of finding out what is in the gem and who wants it. Maybe you can even help me get the gem secured once we figure out everything else."

"Tempting. I will have to think about it," Abigail responded as a hint of a smile appeared. "What's your number? I will text you where you can meet me tomorrow. Then, we will see how truly ready you are and how I may be able to help." Abigail's smile grew and became more mischievous.

Owen lightly chuckled. "Nothing like a good cliffhanger to get me motivated."

"Well, a girl has to keep some mystery about her, doesn't she?" Abigail responded as she playfully smiled and then winked.

The two exchanged numbers and finished their drinks, which Owen had to drink faster since Abigail was further along with her drink than he was. The two left the bar around midnight and began to stroll back the way they came but ended up stopping not too far from the bar.

"Well, this is where we part ways for now," Abigail commented as she walked toward the side of one of the nearby buildings.

"I'll see you later. It was nice to meet you," Abigail gently added.

"It was nice to meet you too. Have a good night," Owen responded. Abigail smiled as she transitioned. She then leaped onto the wall and scaled the building with ease and disappeared once she reached the rooftop.

"It's such a long way back to my car," Owen muttered to himself. He then looked all around him and sighed. "Which way is my car?" Owen muttered to himself again.

He picked a direction and like Abigail, he transitioned and scaled the building. From there, he was better able to get his sense of direction. As he moved from building to building, he thought about

Abigail. He pondered why he was oddly at ease with her and how it was different from how much he felt at ease with Hailey back at the facility. It was a different type of connection that he had to figure out what the meaning was behind it. It was more than just her free-spirited and daring nature…or even her personality and appearance. He was quite intrigued about how their next encounter would go.

CHAPTER 6

Owen woke up later than he planned due to his late night and realized it was already close to noon. He darted up and leaned over to check his phone on the nightstand but he didn't see any messages. Owen let out a sigh of relief fearing that he may have missed Abigail's text. He figured their next encounter wouldn't be until tonight but he still wanted to be ready in case it happened sooner.

After finding some food in the condo to eat for lunch, he went to the bathroom to get himself ready for the day. Once he was done, Owen found himself sitting around and checking the phone every so often. He needed a distraction or else he would drive himself insane thinking about his next encounter with her.

Owen first texted Bailey, *"Working on a lead. Will update once I learn anything of interest."*

She responded back, *"Okay. No leads here but we are keeping an eye on some people that may want what we have."*

Owen sent a quick text back, *"Okay everyone be careful."*

"Be careful too," Bailey texted back.

Once Owen was done texting Bailey, he decided to watch some television. He hoped there would be something to distract him while he patiently waited for Abigail to text him. Owen debated about texting her first but he held off. He didn't want to appear needy. Luckily, Owen found some shows that kept his mind occupied to pass the time.

A couple of hours later, Owen heard his phone ding. It startled him since he was concentrating on the show he was watching. He fumbled around with the phone for a moment until he got it steady.

"Dress fun because we are going to a club tonight. Meet me at nine and I will send you the address soon."

"Will do and I will dress as fun as this safe house will allow me," Owen texted while he smiled at the phone. After a brief pause, she responded.

"I'm sure you can find something there that doesn't scream boring. See you soon."

Owen was about to respond but then another text came through with the location and a note saying that they are meeting at a place near where they were going. He decided not to text anything else since it seemed like the conversation was over. A club…is she just wanting to dance and have fun or will I find out anything about my mission, Owen wondered. His curiosity grew when he thought more about the vagueness of her text.

He searched the internet for places around that address but he was confused about the results his search yielded. He could not find a club near the meeting place. It was near the outskirts of the district he was paroling the previous night, so there were some restaurants, bars, and office buildings in the area, but that was about it. As much as he trusted her for reasons he still wasn't fully sure about, he needed to proceed with some form of caution until he learned more about Abigail and her intentions. His mind then drifted to how he thought it was cute that even though she was slender, yet toned, her cheeks were ever so slightly puffy. He shook his head vigorously to regain his concentration.

Owen spent the next few hours eating dinner, meditating, and getting ready to go out. He searched the wardrobe for something that would be acceptable to wear out to a nightclub. He eventually was lucky enough to find a dark button-down shirt with a gray and black checkered pattern on it. It was a long sleeve shirt so he rolled the sleeves past his elbows and kept the shirt untucked. He found some black pants and shoes to go along with them. Owen left the condo around eight to give himself enough time to drive, park, and walk to where Abigail requested he meet her.

It was dark, yet people were still roaming the streets as he arrived a few minutes before nine. He stood near a bench and waited for her. Just a couple of minutes later, he heard her speak, "I like a man who is on time," Abigail said as she smiled and approached Owen. She was wearing an upper-thigh length frilly skirt with a tight, black top that was low cut, accompanied by a few dangling silver necklaces. Oddly enough what really caught his eye were the black combat boots she was wearing with the outfit, along with the many black bracelets that she wore on each arm. She really pulled it off as it matched her personality, he thought as he had to divert his eyes from staring.

"I hate to keep a lady waiting," Owen responded as a crooked grin formed.

"Well, I never did claim to be a lady," Abigail playfully responded.

Owen chuckled. "You said it, not me. Anyway, you look very nice," Owen commented while he smiled.

"Thank you. You cleaned up well yourself. I see you were able to find an outfit that wouldn't be something that Isaac would wear," Abigail replied as she grinned and moved a little closer to Owen.

"Yes, thanks. I was going to wear that same skirt that you wore so I am glad I changed, or else this would be awkward right now," Owen jested.

Abigail laughed, "Never…if anything that would have been a fun outfit to see you in!" She then glanced at Owen's legs.

"Are you picturing me in a skirt right now?" Owen asked while he laughed.

"Hey, you started it. Now I have this mental picture in my head," Abigail responded as the two of them laughed. She then turned to stand by his side while tucking her arm around his, "Let's go."

The two walked a few blocks and around some corners until she stopped him in front of a rustic brick Italian restaurant. From a glance, there seemed to be a decent crowd inside.

"I thought we were going to a club?" Owen asked.

"We are. Follow me," Abigail replied as she directed him to the side of the building. She then turned to Owen as they stopped in front of a door on the side of the restaurant.

"Is this the side entrance that employees use?" Owen looked perplexed at this point as his face crinkled.

"You of all people should know that looks can be deceiving," Abigail commented as her brow arched.

Owen smiled as he slowly shook his head, "The restaurant is a front."

"Very good. Don't get me wrong. The food here is excellent, but the actual private club is underneath. You can only enter if you know the code. Even then, you must pass through security before you can enter the club itself," Abigail responded.

"This should be interesting," Owen commented as he began to walk forward, but was stopped by Abigail. "What is it?"

"Before you go in there, you need to leave Isaac at the door," Abigail directed.

"What do you mean?" Owen inquired.

"What I mean is that you will see and be exposed to a lot of things down there that Isaac would not approve of and cannot know about. Our kind is the only type of people that can enter and it is a haven. A place to do as you will…within reason of course. A lot of them haven't even heard of Isaac." Abigail pulled Owen closer to her and stared into his eyes. "Promise me you can not only be cool with

93

this but also keep it a secret."

"You're putting a lot of trust into a man you just met," Owen responded.

"I tend to be a good judge of character. Besides, trust works both ways," Abigail answered.

Owen lightly smiled, "I promise."

A large smile appeared on Abigail's face, "Great, let's go!" The two of them walked up to the door and Abigail punched in the code. Owen could hear the mechanical locks unlock as the door opened. A metal staircase illuminated in front of them that led down beneath the restaurant. The two descended for quite some time until they reached the bottom, which led to another entrance. This time, it was a red curtain that draped down from the ceiling within the doorway.

Abigail turned and whispered to Owen, "When he asks for identification, just show him your chimera eyes and you will be fine." Owen nodded in agreement. He was nonchalant, but it was an act. He was both excited and nervous to know what world he was about to enter. Just the few things that Abigail mentioned about the club had his mind racing with imagination.

Abigail pushed the curtain aside and the two entered a medium-sized room with both the ceiling and walls painted black. Even the few leather chairs scattered in the room were black. This drew Owen's eyes to the red carpet that they were now standing on as they passed through the curtain. The carpet was just wide enough for two people to walk side-by-side, and it led all the way to a red door on the other side of the room. Standing in front of the red door were three overweight, yet muscular tall men, and they too were dressed in black. They even wore red neckties to work with the theme of the room.

Abigail and Owen followed the carpet down to the man in the center, who happened to be behind a stanchion. The other two men were off to the sides of him and were armed with semi-automatic firearms and broad swords sheathed on their backs. Owen then

94

noticed that they even had silver and wooden stakes on their belts. From their appearance and stern facial expressions, they took the security here seriously.

"Identification please," The middle bouncer said in a deep voice. Owen did what Abigail requested and transitioned his eyes. He could see Abigail do the same as she quickly glanced over to Owen. The large man undid the latch and pulled the velvet red rope aside as he moved away. "Enjoy," the man said as the two of them passed him. Owen noticed her eyes went back to normal so he followed her lead. Abigail grabbed the handle and turned her head and he saw her cute, yet devious smile. She then pulled the door open and the noise from the club hit Owen like a wave. Everything must have been soundproofed since he was caught off guard. They both strolled into the club.

Owen maneuvered around the chairs and tables as he followed Abigail through the crowd. There was so much to see that Owen's eyes were bouncing around from one thing to the next. There were at least one hundred people if he had to guess, which was more than what he anticipated. The club itself had a new age gothic vibe to it between the sleek modern furniture and design of the club. The design consisted of dark colors and gothic designs used throughout, such as black drapes and chains that were hung over and around the rails that surrounded the large dance floor. The area itself had to be at least half the size of the main room at the facility.

However, as Owen was walking through the crowd, his chest began to feel tight and his breathing increased. He felt a wave of panic come over him as he started to look around at the vast number of strangers around him. He then felt a hand on his chest. His head whipped up as he growled to see who it was. It was Abigail.

"Are you okay? What's wrong?" Abigail loudly asked due to the music blaring. Her brow was knitted due to her confusion.

"I don't know. Just so many people. So many threats," Owen responded as he breathed faster while his eyes drifted from one person to the next.

Abigail gently laid her hand on the side of Owen's face and slowly pulled his attention back to her. She stared into his eyes and smiled, "You will be okay. No one in this club will hurt you or anybody else here. It is against the rules. Just focus on me and take a deep breath. Calm yourself and transition back to normal."

Owen didn't even realize he was in transition but he could tell once Abigail pointed it out. He took a few deep breaths while concentrating on her. The anxiety faded away as he transitioned back. He quickly nodded his head, "I'm good. Sorry, crowds have never bothered me before."

"They may not bother you but they may bother your other half. It's all good though. You gained control back and composed yourself. This might be one of the things you have to adjust to," Abigail mentioned as her hand returned to Owen's chest.

"I guess so. Thank you," Owen responded as he put his hand on her shoulder.

Abigail's smiled as she nodded her head, "Well we got some time to kill before we meet up with my friends. Let's go have some fun," she said with a lively smile as she grabbed Owen's hand and led him to the dance floor.

They made it to the middle of the crowded dance floor. She then turned around and they began to dance. The rock-styled music had a good rhythm to it, Owen thought. He just hoped he didn't embarrass himself in front of her.

Abigail danced close to Owen but then leaned forward and spoke loudly into his ear, "I see I am going to have to remove that Isaac-sized stick from your butt." Owen lightly chuckled to himself. Then Abigail put one of her arms around Owen's neck while the other arm was in the air, bouncing to the beat of the music and occasionally using it to play with her hair. Her body was only inches from Owen and at times, even slightly rubbing against him. Owen became more relaxed as the world around him melted away. He put one of his hands on her hip and found the same rhythm as her as the two danced away. He felt relaxed as he enjoyed dancing with Abigail. The burdens he carried were gone and at that moment, he felt happy and carefree. A few songs passed before the tempo transitioned to a slower, more romantic vibe.

"I think this is our cue to take a break," Abigail mentioned as she headed off the dance floor. Owen was a little caught off guard by the abrupt stop but could understand how a slow song would maybe be too intimate.

"This way. The people I want you to meet should be here by now," Abigail said as she motioned for Owen to continue to follow her.

"Will these people be able to help me…us?" Owen inquired.

"They should be able to help or at the very least find someone who can," Abigail responded.

Owen nodded as the two walked down the side of the room. While he walked, Owen noticed individual rooms lining the perimeter of the room in both the first and second levels of the club. Some of the rooms upstairs even had a balcony.

"What are these rooms for?" Owen asked.

"They are private rooms that people own or rent. In there you can do whatever it is that pleases you," Abigail responded.

Some of the rooms that they passed had the same vibe as the club, but not all of them. Owen noticed a variety of different styles within each of the rooms, even some that were the opposite of the club itself. He could also see many people being free with their transitions. As he walked, Owen observed an array of creature eye types, along with some using their special abilities for fun. He even saw one man who climbed halfway up to the second floor using something that looked like suction cups on his hands and arms. Then, there were a couple of people on a balcony that was jointly using their abilities. One woman created an assortment of flowers from seeds that a man poured into her hands. She then tossed the flowers in the air while the other woman was able to blow the flowers across the dance floor with just the air she blew from her mouth. Owen watched as the flowers gently fell onto the people dancing like rain. He could not help to smile at how much at ease everyone was. It was liberating in a way and he could see why people like him would flock to such a location. Abigail stopped and turned at one of the metal-grated staircases that led to a room that had a balcony.

"I own this one upstairs. Everyone should be there by now," Abigail commented as she turned and proceeded upstairs. Owen followed her while he glanced around at the many spectacles the club had to offer. As he got to the balcony, he happened to notice another door at the back of the club. At first, it appeared to be the exit but it seemed odd to Owen that the steel door was also reinforced with steel bars and had a couple of people guarding it. Before he could ask Abigail what that door led to, she tapped him on the arm and motioned for him to keep following her. He holstered that question for now.

A vast majority of the noise from the club disappeared as the door shut behind them, leaving only a faint sound from the music playing outside. The room itself was almost as big as the room they first entered that had the three security guards inside.

In the back corner of the room was a small kitchen, and the rest of the room was filled with couches, oversized chairs, and stools that were lined around the long island near the kitchen. He noticed a door partially opened in the back of the room that led to a bathroom. However, the décor of the room caught Owen off guard. He was expecting the room's décor to be similar to the kind he saw in the club, but this was not the case. Sure, the furniture was black, and there were even some deep purple accents, but the walls and ceiling were a combination of light grays and shades of white, which seemed to lighten up the room. The floor was a faux grayish-brown wood and the walls were decorated with mainly abstract paintings. Owen also happened to get a glance of the corner of the room to the side of the door they just entered. To his amazement, it was a curio cabinet that housed various animal figurines, as well as, some other smaller antiques, beer steins, and even an autographed signed baseball.

"It looks like we are still missing one but we can get started. Everybody, meet Owen," Abigail announced to the two other occupants within the room. A woman wearing a long purple dress that covered most of her sleek figure stood up from her chair and walked over to Owen. She had fair skin, dark brown eyes, and dark hair that was cut in a bob fashion. If he had to guess, this woman had to be a couple of years younger than him. She smiled as she extended her hand to Owen.

"Nice to meet you. My name is Selena," she said as she gently shook his hand and smiled.

"Nice to meet you too," Owen responded as he smiled as well. He got a pleasant vibe from her just from their short exchange.

"The sociable one leaning against the wall in the kitchen is Caine," Abigail playfully remarked as she nodded in Caine's direction. The man nodded his head, with a faint smile, as he took a sip from his glass. Owen returned the acknowledgment with a head nod of his own.

"It's a nice, yet interesting room," Owen commented as he glanced around at the room again. "Especially the paintings and even more…the items on the curio cabinet over there. I say that with respect. It's just probably one of the last things I expected to see in this club." Owen then strolled toward the display.

"Typically, that is what people say about me," Selena said as she giggled. Owen lightly chuckled as Selena walked to the side of him. "First off, bonus points for even knowing what type of cabinet this is."

"My parents used to collect antiques, figurines, and even other items such as shells and trinkets whenever we would travel. Ironically enough I even remember my dad having a signed baseball on display as well," Owen added as he leaned closer to the display to get a better view.

"That is sweet and without you knowing it, gave you some culture and respect for cherishing moments. Every piece on that cabinet has a special meaning to me," Selena responded as she too leaned forward.

"What's the story behind the baseball?" Owen asked as he leaned in even closer. "It even has scuff marks on it."

"That is the only piece on there that doesn't belong to me," Selena responded.

"It actually belongs to me," Abigail added. "I caught that home run at a baseball game that I went to a handful of years ago. Everyone around me was amazed that not only had I caught it, but also that it didn't even hurt me. Between that and the fact that I didn't even spill a drop of the beer I had in my other hand, the player that hit the home run was impressed and signed my ball after the game. Selena let me place it there since not only was it just cool to catch a home run in the stands, but it also makes me smile thinking of all those men's reactions to how a girl was able to pull that off," Abigail laughed as she walked up to them.

"How does that not surprise me," Owen said as he laughed. He then turned his attention to the paintings. "Did you collect these as well? I like them. They are quite impressive."

Before Selena could respond, Caine spoke in a firm voice from across the room. "They're mine."

Owen turned his attention to Caine who was pouring a dark mahogany liquid from a fancy glass container into another glass. He then approached Owen while holding two glasses. Caine had slightly pale skin with blue eyes and short, light brown hair that was slightly curly. He also had a thin layer of stubble on his face. As the man stood in front of Owen, he appeared to be of normal build and was a few inches taller than him. It was difficult for Owen to gauge his age but he figured maybe a few years older than him. Caine wore black jeans and a lightweight long sleeve gray shirt that had just a few buttons near his neck.

"You collected these?" Owen inquired.

"I painted these, though I do like to admire the works of other artists," Caine responded as he turned and observed the paintings along with Owen.

Owen's eyes widened, "Wow…they look good."

"What do you like about them?" Caine asked with an intrigued expression on his face as he slightly turned his head toward Owen.

Owen approached the paintings on the wall. "They are really expressive and eye-catching."

"What do they express to you?" Caine asked as he stood to the side of Owen.

Owen glanced over the paintings. He noticed that a lot of dark colors were used, with hints of brighter colors such as red and off-white. There were not any clean lines and a lot of layers and textures were used. The paint strokes themselves appeared aggressive.

"Darkness and agony mainly. There are some that show the same thing but with some hint of hope," Owen casually responded while still staring at the paintings. In a way, they spoke to him.

"Impressive…especially from someone whom I presume is not an art critic or even in the art scene," Caine replied. As Owen turned to look at him, he saw a small smile form on Caine's face before he spoke again. "When one identifies with another's work it means they have experienced what the painting is projecting." Caine raised his hand to offer Owen the other drink, which he accepted.

"I've had my fair share," Owen replied with a reluctant half-smile before taking a large sip of his drink. It was a good, yet strong, bourbon. Owen did his best to hide his reaction from how strong it was.

"Do you paint often?" Owen inquired.

"Only as needed. Therapy…in a way," Caine replied while he grinned. He then strolled over toward Selena and Abigail.

Owen smiled before he redirected his attention from the

paintings to the rest of the group. "I guess it's better to put your pain onto a canvas versus taking it out on someone."

"Not always," Caine responded as a devious smile formed on his face.

"And on that delightful note, have you been in town long Owen?" Selena inquired. She was smiling but not before she glared at Caine, who paid no attention to her reaction. She seemed almost embarrassed that he made that remark. Owen wondered if she didn't want him to joke around in that manner in front of someone new…if it was a joke at all.

"Just a few days. I know this is your room Abigail but with the mixture of Caine and Selena's stuff in here, have you guys known each other long?" Owen asked.

"I have known these two, individually, for a long time. Once I procured this room, I informed them about it. I figured they would enjoy it too. Besides, owning a room like this with no one to share it with gets boring after a while," Abigail responded.

"Even though Abigail has known us for a long time now, Caine and I have only known each other for a handful of years since coming to this establishment. I like to think my kind nature is starting to chip away at his ruthless, yet charismatic self." Selena winked at Caine with a hint of a crooked smile after her comment.

Owen chuckled. "I see. What about you Caine? Has any of your personality rubbed off on Selena?"

"I sincerely hope not," Caine responded as his eyes quickly shifted away while he took a sip of his drink. If Owen didn't know any better, it seemed Caine didn't want any of his darkness inflicting the sweet gentle nature of Selena.

"Tell us about yourself, Owen," Selena requested as she sat down on one of the couches.

"I figured Abigail probably already filled everyone in," Owen commented as he looked over toward Abigail.

"It wasn't my place to do so," Abigail responded as she

shrugged.

"Well in that case…" Owen was interrupted by the door opening and the sudden burst of music from the club. A woman, maybe his age or slightly older walked through. Her build was average but hard to tell with the loose-fitting black dress that came down to right above her knees.

"Sorry, I'm late. I was doing all that double back stuff that Caine taught me to make sure I wasn't being followed," the woman announced. Her ice-blue eyes then locked onto Owen.

"Hi. My name is Olivia. Nice to meet you," she said as she walked up to Owen and shook his hand. She moved a strand of her wavy light blonde hair away from her face, which her hair itself came to around the upper part of her back. Her smile was warm and instantaneously contagious.

Owen smiled, "Nice to meet you too. My name is Owen." Olivia continued to smile but seemed at a loss for words.

"Good timing. We were just about to begin to get to know each other even more," Abigail chimed in, breaking the awkward moment between Owen and Olivia as they just stared at each other, lightly smiling.

"Glad I didn't miss anything," Olivia said as she sat down on one of the chairs. Everyone else followed suit and found a seat.

Owen then began to talk about himself and his time before, during, and after the facility. He didn't go into as great of detail as he did with Abigail, but enough for everyone to know about him, his creature, and his current mission. Owen only gave up this information so freely due to the trust he had in Abigail. He was also mindful of not unleashing too much of his emotional baggage.

"Now I understand why you were able to identify with my paintings," Caine commented in a low tone of voice. Owen simply nodded his head slowly.

"That's amazing about the change you went through after you were turned to stone. Anyway, I bet you are happy to find another

103

chimera, aren't you?" Olivia asked.

"Happy, lucky, grateful…any of the terms will work," Owen responded as he peered over to Abigail who gave him a quick wink.

"Same here, but he is on a totally different level than me. His power and control still both baffle and amaze me," Abigail responded.

"It's not all glitz and glamour," Owen countered.

"Nothing ever is but I'm sure it will work itself out," Abigail added in a carefree manner.

The room was quiet for a moment before Selena spoke up. "I guess I will go next," she said while she smiled and placed her hands on her lap as she sat back on the couch.

"Since seven hundred years is a long time frame to talk about, I will just do my best to summarize. Even though my family did not have much, my childhood was a good one. Full of love and fond memories and I wouldn't have traded it for the world. When I was older, I helped my family with their business in order to support all of us. However, around that time, the Black Death was spreading through Europe. People who had enough money tried to outrun it but we did not have enough. The wealthy, who had more than plenty to assist others in trying to escape, cared only about their riches. We did our best to prevent the plague from entering our home but eventually, it did. I watched each of my family members die until only I was left." Selena paused as her eyes became glassy but then she composed herself by taking a deep breath and quickly wiping her eyes before continuing.

"As the world around me was slowly fading away, I remember someone in a hood and a mask that came into the house. I couldn't see what this person had in their glove but I could see it glowing. As the person looked in my direction they asked if I was the only one alive. Their voice was muffled so I couldn't make out if it was a man or a woman. I nodded since I was too sick and weak to speak. The only other movement I was able to do was to shiver from the fever. I saw the person take out an emerald the size of a golf ball and then place it into my hand. The person told me that they knew what resided inside the gem and that I would feel pain, and then pain again in three days. After that, I would be either dead or alive. Not just alive, but alive and cured. The person then added that some chance of survival was better than none. After that, I felt the pain shoot up my arm as I screamed and then I passed out."

"The person knew what was in the gem?" Owen blurted out. His eyes were large with hope.

"Yes. There are ways to peek inside," Selena replied. She seemed patient with Owen's interruption as her facial expression did not change.

"Anyway, I remember nothing until I went into transition on the third day. The pain was immense but short-lived. Once that ordeal was over, I felt better. I wasn't sick anymore and I even felt stronger and healthier than ever before. The person stayed to observe the outcome of my transition and since I survived, they then proceeded to tell me about the new life I was entering and what I was. This person then stuck around long enough to teach me how to survive and cope with all the changes I went through. After that, I never saw that person again. I never even found out the identity of the person who helped me in so many ways. I'm still not even sure if the person was a man or a woman. I guess the person wore the mask to not get sick or to keep their identity a secret or both. Sometimes I even wonder if it was another creature under that mask," Selena commented as she shrugged.

"How did you survive and not get sick again? I guess we may have higher immune systems but still…how did you not die even with the creature inside of you? Maybe if you fully transitioned, I could see that but you didn't. Also, there is the fact that partial transitions only heal physical injuries so how did you pull it off?" Owen asked. His brow crinkled while he tried to figure it out.

"The creature I inherited saved me. Call it luck, fate, destiny, or whatever...but that was the only thing that saved me," Selena replied.

"Do you feel comfortable telling me what your creature is?" Owen politely asked.

Selena smiled, "Of course. My creature is a unicorn."

A look of enlightenment came over Owen's face as he smiled and his brow raised. "That makes sense. There is some lore out there that says the unicorn can heal, take away sickness, and even make poison vanish. It's also rumored that it cannot die from old age. You hear more about its ability to take away poisons but here you are...alive and well over seven hundred years later. When you transitioned, its abilities erased the illness from you. With the unicorn's essence inside of you, it kept you healthy."

Selena smiled and nodded to acknowledge Owen's correct statement but her smile slowly vanished. "True, and I have those abilities, but I haven't noticed any of the other magical abilities it supposedly possesses. Either the lore is inaccurate or it's because I haven't transitioned that deep to be able to discover any more abilities," Selena said as she slightly shrugged.

"Maybe someday you will discover more abilities but even if you don't, the ones you have now are very impressive," Owen remarked.

"Thanks, but it is more than that. I just wish I would have honored the unicorn's virtuous nature quicker than I did. Instead, I used the power and speed that it also possesses to keep itself from being captured or killed in an impure way." Owen tilted his head, for he was perplexed at her statement.

"In the beginning, I used my newfound strength and speed to locate and kill all the rich noblemen that turned my family and me away when we needed their help. However, in time I found peace by accepting my past and focusing on a more tranquil existence. By doing so, I was able to honor not only the unicorn but my family as well. Over the years, I visited many places and forged many great relationships but I never met or dealt with the person you mentioned…Isaac. My journey did lead me to this place and to all of you and I'm grateful. So far, no one here has given me a reason to feel differently…yet," Selena said as she winked at Caine. In return, he partially smiled while he shrugged his shoulders.

"Your story is amazing. I know there are some aspects during your journey that you wish you could take back but it has made you the person you are today. It's inspiring," Owen added with a gentle smile toward Selena.

"That's sweet of you to say. Thank you," Selena replied as a large smile appeared on her face.

"Well before this gets too mushy, I will go next," Caine mentioned as he took another sip of his drink and then leaned back in his seat before he continued.

"If seven hundred years is too much to go into detail then nine hundred would be even worse. Before I turned into the being I am today, all those centuries ago, I was a butcher. My skills were so respected that I was hired to bring my high-end cuts to the royal families across the city. Then, during one of my deliveries, I got caught in the middle between an upper-class family and a mob of lower-class citizens that felt they had been wronged. After taking a pitchfork to my stomach, I managed to drag myself away; however, I didn't get far. I ended up in some random alleyway bleeding out. Then, a person approached me and as he grew near, I drew my butcher knife. I was caught off guard because the person simply smiled and kept approaching. When he was within range, I slashed at him but he easily deflected the blade away from me. He then said he admired my will to fight, even with death's grasp upon me. One thing led to another and I went from human to a monster."

"A monster?" Owen said as he tilted his head.

"Yes. In the beginning, I hid my identity and used my new powers to secretly dispose of the human filth that littered my streets and preyed on innocent people. They would take their money, beat them, or kill them simply because they were not high enough up the social ranks ladder. It didn't take long for that to stop after one by one, they would flee the city as I left the head of their comrades at their doorstep. People began to realize it was me doing it and I received an immense amount of praise for my actions. Then, people started to put two and two together. I was able to yield so much power, my wounds were short-lived, and I couldn't be a butcher anymore."

"Why couldn't you be a butcher anymore?" Owen asked.

"Being around blood all day was hard for me to handle, especially being so new to the game," Caine responded as his eyes briefly turned blood red. Owen remembered seeing those same types of eyes with Joshua and Michael.

"Your creature is a vampire," Owen said as he sat back in his seat. It was all starting to come together now. Caine didn't respond to Owen's remark and just continued with his story.

"Once my fellow friends and acquaintances realized I had…changed, I went from hero to monster. Regardless of my efforts to alleviate their concerns that I was not a threat to them, they didn't care. They sent their warriors and hunters after me but my powers far exceeded their skills and weaponry. In the end, there was one hunter that finally realized he was outmatched so instead, he laid a trap to capture me. His plan worked and I was in prison for many centuries." Caine paused for just a moment as a faint grin appeared on his face.

"Finally, a man hiking through the mountainside came across my prison. He unknowingly unleashed me, which was to his own peril. Filled with rage, I spent a few centuries killing across Europe and Asia before coming to America. There, I continued my rampage until one day I came across a woman that was able to show me there was another way. Each day, I find another sliver of my humanity and it's all because of her," Caine said as his eyes drifted toward the floor while he pressed his lips firmly together.

"That's impressive you were able to find your way back from

the darkness, but that wasn't all because of one woman. You must give yourself some credit too," Owen commented. Caine responded with a quick, fainted smile. "Regardless, you must be thankful for the woman who helped you."

"More than you or her will ever know. Selena's friendship is one of the most valuable things I have been honored enough to receive," Caine replied as he glanced over at Selena. The two of them smiled at each other.

"The woman was Selena!" Owen exclaimed in astonishment as his brow raised. He then composed himself and calmly added, "I can see that."

"If anyone can help return a vicious killer's humanity, it would be her. No offense," Abigail said with a half-smile toward Caine.

"None taken. If anything, I take it as a compliment," Caine responded with a devious grin.

"I now understand the inspiration behind your paintings," Owen commented.

Caine's face grew cold, "You may recognize it and even understand it, but you will never understand it to the depths of what I have experienced."

"I understand it more than you realize," Owen countered softly.

Caine scoffed. "Why, because you had a rough few months, or is it because you think the few number of years that you have walked this Earth have been that tough? It doesn't hold a candle to what I have been through."

"Yeah, exactly for those reasons. You don't have to live for hundreds of years to be allowed to know what pain and heartache feel like. Besides, it's more than that. Since the chimera and I are now one, I feel any sorrow it has felt as well." Owen's tone was direct when he spoke to Caine.

"I'm sure the beast doesn't have complex emotions," Caine casually responded while he grinned.

Owen's eyes transitioned as he shot up from his seat and took a few steps forward toward Caine before Abigail was able to stand in front of Owen. "The chimera has emotions!" Owen yelled as his eyes blazed with anger. "It felt happy, safe, and love when it was with its pride and did anything it had to in order to make sure they were safe. Then, a large group of soldiers ambushed the pride from different angles. Regardless of the efforts, the chimera had to watch its pride…its family, be slaughtered. Trust me when I say it felt pain…it felt sorrow…and it felt anguish. Before it could tear the remaining soldiers to pieces, an arrow with a sapphire attached to it was sent soaring toward the chimera."

Owen paused as his eyes began to well up. "Regardless if I truly experienced it or not, I feel it all." His voice was gravelly and his fangs and claws were now showing. At this point, hair encompassed most of his body as he went deeper into transition. Yet, with all the rage Owen felt at that moment, the pain from the memories cracked through as tears ran from his eyes.

"There's the reaction I was looking for," Caine responded with a crooked smile. His comment caused Owen to pause as he was confused by Caine's comment. "That anger-filled, emotional response said more than words could ever do. My apologies. Apparently, you do understand my paintings," Caine sincerely replied, unfazed by Owen's rant.

"Calm down. Remember you are in control," Abigail whispered to Owen. He took a deep breath and transitioned back to normal.

"Thank you," Owen whispered while placing his hand on Abigail's shoulder. "Sorry, everybody. Still trying to get used to the new type of residency I have going on in my head," Owen announced to the group.

"Each of us had to get used to having a creature within us. You are just having to go through it again due to your unique situation. It's quite understandable," Selena replied with a warm smile. Owen nodded and smiled in return. Her comment appeared to be shared by the room as he did not notice any negative vibes from the rest of the group.

"Well, it will be hard to follow that but I guess I'm the last one to go. At least my story isn't long because there isn't much to tell," Olivia said as she eased back into her seat after the excitement ceased.

"Long story short, I had a great relationship with my parents until I became older and their work was apparently more important than their own daughter. In a pathetic attempt to gain more attention from them, I even worked in the same field. I tried to be innovative and the best in my field, but even that couldn't divert their attention to me. Then, to make matters horrifically worse, my mom died. If I didn't feel alone before, I certainly did then. I not only lost my mom but my dad as well since he decided that the best solution to deal with his emotions was to become extensively more involved with his work." Olivia paused for a moment as she wiped a tear from her cheek. "So, I left him and everything else behind and have been living for myself."

"How did that work out for you?" Caine rhetorically asked.

"You of all people would know," Olivia replied with a half-smile. Owen crinkled his brow since their exchange confused him.

"A couple of months ago I was pulled into an alleyway by some people and they just started to beat on me for no reason. I screamed, even more, when their faces turned into monsters, but it was short-lived as I became dazed from the beating I was taking. To this day I still don't understand why they did that to me. Anyway, just when I thought I was going to die, this man jumped in and saved me. The group turned their attention to him as he was slaughtering them left and right. Still, I wanted to help since I felt he was outnumbered regardless of how well he was doing."

"For the record, I had it under control," Caine added as he smirked.

"You saved somebody," Owen blurted out.

"It tends to happen on rare occasions," Caine casually responded with a faint smile.

"I know. It surprised me too," Abigail added as she winked at Caine. His smile grew with her comment.

"Anyway…I picked up a knife that one of them had dropped and stabbed one of the attackers in the neck. He fell to his knees and turned his body to face me. He then did the weirdest thing and smiled before tossing this emerald, which had to be no bigger than a half-dollar coin, before he fell to the ground. Out of instinct, I caught it and a few seconds later I realized why he smiled. I felt this intense pain shoot up through my arm and throughout my body. The next thing I knew I was in the back room."

"The what?" Owen asked.

"Sorry, the back room is another part of the club. It's where people can spar and even fully transition if needed or they just want to. A lot of stuff happens back there," Olivia replied. Owen's brow arched with curiosity.

"To fill in the voids in her memory. I saw the guy toss her the emerald and before I could tell her to not touch it…she caught it. I then saw her writhing in pain on the ground. By the time I reached her, the emerald had disappeared and she was unconscious. Knowing what would happen in three days and not knowing what the creature was in the gem, I brought her here. For a moment I thought she was going to fully transition on that third day. She was so close and with how long she was experiencing the pain I thought she would turn, but she didn't. She's fortunate I had enough patience to wait and not just kill her when I thought she may fully transition," Caine added as he took another sip of his drink.

Owen nodded as the story began to make more sense between Olivia and Caine's recollection of that night. He also held back the snarky comments in his head about Caine's patience. He had a feeling his definition of patience and Caine's were not the same. "I'm glad it all worked out. What was your creature if you don't mind me asking?"

"I'm also a vampire," Olivia replied as her eyes turned red and her smile revealed her fangs.

"We all have been helping her adjust to her new life and of course, Caine has pitched in extra since he can relate," Selena added.

"It's definitely been an adjustment but I'm getting there," Olivia said as she reverted to her normal state.

"It does take time but you'll get there. My friend Michael is just as new as you and he too is a vampire so he could help you as well. One new vampire to another. I'm sure you are in capable hands here but if you need anything, then please let me know. I'm new as well…twice oddly enough," Owen said with a soft chuckle.

"Thank you. I may take you up on that someday," Olivia mentioned as she smiled.

"We are just hoping she doesn't gain any of Caine's wonderful personality traits," Abigail teased.

"If only anyone had as much character as me," Caine replied with a crooked grin. The group laughed and then the room was silent. At that time Owen noticed something wasn't right. He stood up and as Abigail went to speak, Owen raised his index finger to signal he needed silence. He slowly walked around the room as everyone watched him, bewildered. Owen's face then became stern before he spoke.

"I thought we were getting to know each other, yet now I feel like I am being deceived."

"What do you mean? We have been honest with you," Abigail replied, perplexed by Owen's comment as his brow knitted.

"Maybe, but everyone has conveniently left something out it seems," Owen replied with a stern tone and his eyes narrowed. Abigail pressed her lips together as she turned her head. Owen scanned the room and noticed Selena had the same expression as Abigail; however, Caine was still nonchalant. Olivia seemed to be the only one confused as her eyes and brow were lowered while she scanned the room.

113

"That's what I thought. If I can't trust you then I don't need to be here," Owen sternly mentioned as he began to head to the door.

"It's not our place to say," Abigail muttered.

"That phrase is becoming too convenient now," Owen coldly countered.

"I must be missing something so you will have to fill me in. What's wrong?" Olivia asked.

Owen stopped and turned around, "The question you should be asking is why are you hanging out with a bunch of people that have been lying to you as well."

"What do you mean?" Olivia asked as she stood up and walked toward Owen while she nervously looked around.

"I will answer your question with a question of my own. Why do I only hear three heartbeats out of the four other people in this room?"

CHAPTER 7

Owen's eyes drifted past the wide-eyed expressions of the females in the room over to Caine, whose devious smile grew as he stared at Owen. He was still relaxed in his seat, not fazed by Owen's comment, as he took another sip of his drink and placed it on the table. Then, in the blink of an eye, Caine sped from his seat and grabbed Owen's shirt near his shoulders with both hands, and drove Owen into the wall behind him. Owen, who was caught off guard by the speed and brute force of the attack, shook his head. As he focused, Owen saw the blood-red eyes of Caine intensely staring back at him. His face was merely inches from Caine's.

"Everyone was getting along just fine until you had to come along and stir up trouble. I have done nothing but try to do the right thing for quite some time now and yet here you are only seeing a monster. It is exhausting in moments like this when you feel all your efforts are for nothing so how about I show you what a real monster looks like," Caine said in a stern voice as his eyes narrowed. "I wonder what chimera blood tastes like," Caine added as he raised his lips to expose his fangs.

Owen could barely keep him away and he knew Caine would be able to kill him at this point so he had to react. A low growl came from Owen as he quickly transitioned deep into level three. With his added strength, he was able to hold Caine from advancing. While Caine was caught off guard by Owen's deep level of transition, he sent his forehead crashing into the bridge of Caine's nose. Caine stumbled back as he held his face. Owen proceeded further by shoving Caine back to give himself more distance between them. Caine stumbled back a few more feet but was able to keep himself from going any further or even falling from the impact.

"Oh, it's time to play now. I wonder how long it takes to fully cook a vampire," Owen snarled. His voice was barely human at this point. Owen showed his fangs while the flames danced around his claws.

"Owen, don't!" Abigail yelled. Owen's eyes stayed fixated on Caine as the fire dissipated. Caine's sinister smile grew as he took a few steps toward Owen; however, he stopped his advance. Caine's eyes widened at what he was witnessing. The fire didn't go away, it only relocated. Caine's eyes fixated on the orange glow from Owen's partially opened mouth as flames flickered past his fangs. Owen took in a deep breath and as he was about to unleash his fiery rage, Abigail stepped in between him while Selena stepped in front of Caine.

"Owen, please," Abigail pleaded. Even though Abigail was in a low level of transition, Owen could see the concern behind her chimera eyes. Then, her body tensed and her face crinkled from the fear of being burned alive. He didn't want to hurt her or Selena but he couldn't contain the flames any longer. He turned his body and spewed the flames coming from his mouth onto the floor next to him. The stream of flames lasted just a few seconds but ended up leaving a scorch mark on the floor. Luckily, there was nothing else in the area for the flames to ignite.

While breathing heavily, Owen slowly turned his head back toward the rest. He could see Abigail smile as her eyes transitioned back to normal. He then noticed Selena, who was facing Caine but had her head turned to see him, was in transition. Her pupils remained black, but the rest of her eyes, including the sclera, were a light brown while the skin around her eyes was pure white. She too smiled as she transitioned back to normal.

"How dare you threaten the lives of everyone in this room, especially Selena's. I will rip you to pieces and use your skull as my new goblet," Caine furiously yelled at Owen. As he started to move, Selena put her hand on his chest to stop him.

"You will do no such thing," Selena said with a direct tone. Caine began to talk but was silenced when Selena put her finger on his lips. "He didn't hurt any of us. If anything, he impressively restrained himself and if memory serves me correctly, the violence didn't start until you rushed him. I understand your fears but you need to calm yourself, please," Selena calmly requested. With that statement, he reverted to his human form, yet he still looked at Owen with disdain. Feeling the room become more at ease, Owen took a deep breath and transitioned back to normal.

"Okay, now that everyone is calm let's discuss this in a civilized manner," Selena added.

"No…not everyone is calm," Olivia commented from the corner of the room, near the curio cabinet. Her voice trembled as she spoke while she had her hands nervously stretched out in front of her. Olivia's eyes and mouth were still wide open from the confrontation.

"It will be alright," Selena softly said with a gentle smile as she slowly proceeded toward Olivia.

"No, no, it will not be alright," Olivia quickly responded by moving one of her raised hands toward Selena to signal her to stop, which Selena respected her wishes. "Are you trying to tell me that Caine is an actual vampire? My mind can't even process that and then you add how close Owen came to a full transition. He didn't even look human," Olivia frantically snapped back at Selena. Then, her eyes turned red. "Why are my eyes changing? I didn't even mean for them to change," Olivia said as her voice cracked and strained from becoming upset. Owen could see a tear about to roll down her cheek before she pressed her hands against her eyes.

"Olivia…" Abigail began to speak but was interrupted by Olivia.

"I can't," Olivia muttered before storming out of the room.

"I will go talk to her," Abigail said as she quickly went after Olivia. Once the door closed and the music from the club ceased, an awkward silence filled the room.

"And you wonder why I keep my true nature a secret," Caine remarked without any expression on his face.

"I understand why you don't announce it to the world but why not Olivia…or me?" Owen asked. His tone remained passive due to his belief that Selena would keep everything calm in the room.

"As you can see, she wasn't ready to be bestowed that knowledge. Besides, I wasn't sure how long her time with us would be once she was trained and had full control of herself and her abilities. I prefer to keep my personal life contained to my trusted inner circle," Caine replied as he remained by Selena's side.

"What about me?" Owen inquired.

Caine began to slowly approach Owen, "What about you? Let's see…we could revisit my inner circle comment or we can discuss Isaac's views on what happens when a person fully transitions on that faithful day three," Caine replied before stopping within a few feet of Owen, his demeanor switching from expressionless to controlled anger as both his face and voice were strained.

"Your story. The person in the alleyway was a vampire that turned you and then the townspeople rebelled against you once they figured out you were a vampire." Owen paused for a moment while Caine just stared at him. Then, another realization came to be. "Your prison was the gem, which that hunter put you in. Then, the person that stumbled across that gem did not survive the day three transition." Owen was more talking out loud to himself than he was to Caine.

"Look at you putting all the pieces to the puzzle together. Now, what is Isaac's rule about the fate of the creature on day three?"

Caine coldly questioned Owen.

"The creature is to be killed," Owen replied as his eyes briefly drifted away from Caine.

"To be killed...that is correct," Caine quickly repeated. "Can you now understand why the vampire that fits this description did not want to open up about his nature to one of Isaac's people?" Caine sarcastically asked.

"I do understand but even though I work for Isaac, it doesn't mean I don't have a mind of my own. Besides, why didn't you just explain it to me like you just did versus attacking me?" Owen asked.

"It wouldn't have been as fun is what his next response would be," Selena commented from the background.

Caine smiled. "She knows me all too well."

Owen lightly chuckled. "Fair enough and your secret is safe with me. Curious though...how do you know about Isaac?"

"I have been around long enough to hear about him, as well as, run into some of his fellow students that did not share your...understandings. Also, there is obviously Abigail who is associated with Isaac," Caine replied and as he finished, Olivia and Abigail came back into the room.

"Sorry. I just needed some time to process everything," Olivia addressed the room. She still seemed nervous by the way she was not making direct eye contact as she fidgeted in her spot. Still, Owen could tell she was a lot calmer than before, and at least not in transition.

"It's quite alright. What is second nature to us is still new to you. Embrace the fact that you had the strength to come back into this room afterward," Selena remarked while gently smiling as she laid her hand on Olivia's shoulder. Owen could see the confidence flow back into Olivia as she stood up straight and smiled. Owen admired Selena's calm and innocent presence about her, which definitely helped Olivia.

"Wait a second. It literally just dawned on me that fire just came out of my mouth," Owen remarked with a half-smile.

"Oddly enough I was standing here thinking about how you can hear heartbeats besides thinking about the flames that just shot out of your mouth," Abigail responded as she lightly shook her head in disbelief.

"The hearing thing I already knew about but the fire coming out of my mouth is a new one," Owen replied.

"Well, I know I can't so that must be another new and cool super chimera trait you got going on," Abigail responded with a slight smile.

"Quite a useful weapon to have in your arsenal. Very few people with creatures within them can have their special powers originate from their mouth. Consider it another secret weapon at your disposal," Caine's brow arched with interest.

"I need to test this out more," Owen commented as his face lit up with glee.

"Yes, but maybe do it in a safer place…preferably not in this room," Selena suggested with a warm smile.

Owen laughed. "Of course." He was excited about his discovery. Being able to redirect the fire from his hands to his mouth had many possible uses in battle. He even wondered how much more control over his fire ability he may have.

"Anyway, now that we are all better acquainted," Owen announced as he winked at Caine and gave him a couple of strong pats on his arm. Caine simply smirked. "Does anybody here know how we can figure out the identity of the person who wants this gem and what is inside of it?"

"Well, finding out what is inside the gem shouldn't be that hard. We just need either a witch or maybe even a very powerful psychic. With all the people in this club I'm sure someone knows somebody," Abigail replied.

"Do any of you know anybody?" Owen asked.

"I personally don't know of anyone," Abigail replied.

"The few that I know are too far away to help," Selena responded.

"I drained the ones that I met when they became of no use to me," Caine responded, nonchalantly. Selena sighed loudly after his comment while she slowly shook her head. "I'm a vampire...a vampire that was also going through some dark times. What did you want me to do? Hold their hands and frolic through a field of daisies?" Caine sarcastically rebutted. Owen couldn't help to snicker at his comment.

Abigail moved to the center of the room, "As for knowing who is after the gem...that will be trickier but I know someone that may be able to help. This person also probably knows someone that can identify what creature is within this gem. We just need to have a little field trip to the back room."

"That place always makes me feel uneasy," Selena commented after she sighed.

"Come on. It will be fun. What could go wrong?" Caine's smile was carefree as he responded.

"If it will get us closer to the answers we need then I'm game," Owen said as he headed toward the door.

The group gathered and proceeded out the door and down the steps to the club floor. They then proceeded to weave their way through the crowd. The closer they got to the door that led to the back room, the fewer people there were. As they approached the door, one of the security guards acknowledged them as he opened the heavy metal door.

"Remember, the rules of the club are more suggestions once we pass through this door," Olivia whispered to Owen.

As they entered the room, Owen was taken aback; however, he tried to remain calm and not gawk at everything he saw. The room itself was bigger than he imagined it to be, even with it being half the size of the club. With the size of the room, Owen was surprised there was only a fraction of the number of people in this room versus the club itself. At the same time, due to the nature of this room, he could understand. There were a handful of smaller caged arenas scattered throughout the room. Each arena had two people sparing, which seemed intense as each person was not wearing any protective gear and they were in transition. From what Owen could tell, they didn't seem to be going easy on each other from the impact of the hits and the blood on the fighters.

Each fighting arena had its own spectators while other people were just roaming around. Owen also noticed a few people off to the side of the room practicing their skills against targets on the wall. He saw a variety of special attacks from fire, ice, wooden spikes, and even people just using throwing-style weapons.

"It's like an entirely different world in here. It especially seems like a good place to train or blow off steam. Where does that extra fortified door over to the left go?" Owen asked, for even that door stood out from the rest of the room.

"That leads to an area underground which is used for people that want to transition or may have no choice, like Olivia a couple of months ago," Abigail responded.

"Wow," Owen responded, but that was all he could say. The thought of creatures on the other side of the door was both intriguing and slightly off-putting. He could only imagine how Isaac would react if he knew of the existence of such a place. "Can it hold many creatures and is it actually that secure?" Owen had to ask to help ease his mind.

"There are three spots downstairs that can hold a creature. The ceiling, along with everything else, is lined with steel and even if it got past that, there is the sealed door you see. That too is lined with steel and heavy bolts as locks," Abigail responded, unfazed.

"What if the creature is rare or just enormous or something?" Owen inquired.

"Then I guess we will have some excitement then," Caine replied from behind Owen. He turned his head to view Caine who gave him a half-smile.

Owen lightly chuckled. "Who is going to help us in here?" Owen asked the group.

"The Yeti," Abigail mentioned as she pointed in the direction of a group of men sitting on the bleachers next to one of the fighting arenas. They seemed to be watching the fighters closely. "He's the big guy in the middle."

"They call him that because he is that big?" Owen inquired with a puzzled look.

"They call him that because his creature is a yeti. His actual name is Cedric," Selena added.

Caine leaned toward Owen, "It's also because he is that big," he said with a grin.

"He has numerous connections and is very well respected not only in this club, but the entire city," Abigail added as she led the group toward Cedric. When they neared the other group, two men stood up and approached Abigail and put their hands on her shoulder to stop her from getting any closer. Before she could say anything, Owen stepped in front of Abigail while pushing the other two back in one fluid motion. Owen then growled at the two men as the chimera's eyes momentarily flashed at the men. The two men's eyes transitioned but then quickly went back to normal when Cedric bellowed, "Stop!"

Cedric slowly turned his head to speak to Owen directly. "You must be new here, boy. If not, you would have more respect knowing what I, and my friends, are capable of doing," Cedric said in a deep voice. At this point, the other two men that were sitting next to Cedric stood up as well. All of them were glaring at Owen with discontent.

"I was just protecting my friend. All I want are some answers to my questions and I was told you are the person that could help me. After that, I won't be a bother to you anymore," Owen responded calmly regardless of his stern facial expression.

"After your act of disrespect, you will have to earn it from me now," Cedric replied in a slow, deep voice, and his face was expressionless.

"Okay, and how do I go about that?" Owen asked while he shrugged and his brow was knitted.

"If you can last one round with me in that ring, I will help you. Deal?" Cedric proposed. The men around him began to smile.

Owen chuckled, "Just one round. Yeah, no problem. If anything, you should be the one that should be worried." At that time, Cedric stood up and slowly walked down the short set of bleachers. The closer Cedric got to him; the wider Owen's eyes became. When Cedric was only a couple of feet away, Owen had to tilt his entire head back in order to look into Cedric's brown eyes. His facial expression seemed as hard as steel.

"I doubt it," Cedric muttered as he turned and walked into the arena. Before he stepped in, he took off his jacket and handed it to one of the men that stood behind him.

"Inform the fresh meat what the rules are," the man that held Cedric's jacket mentioned to Abigail before he walked off.

"You tell him, Caine," Abigail annoyingly directed to Caine as she began to storm off.

Owen gently grabbed her arm to get her attention, "What's wrong?"

Abigail yanked her arm away from Owen and got in his face. "What was that back there? Hmm? I don't need a bodyguard! I can handle myself. Now, besides getting the information that you wanted in a civilized manner, you will now have to go and earn it." Abigail's brow was lowered and her eyes were narrow, yet wild, as she was obviously angry at Owen. Before Owen could respond, Abigail marched away.

Owen turned to the rest of the group with a furrowed brow while he shrugged his shoulders. "I wasn't trying to be her bodyguard. I would have done the same for any of my friends. For some unknown reason, I guess I took it to another level. Still, I meant no harm."

"When this is over, I will talk to her. That's a sensitive subject for Abigail. I would go talk to her now but you may need some healing after this fight," Selena said with an apologetic smile.

"Yeah, back to that. Did that guy eat the yeti or something? I mean look at him. His muscles have muscles. He is basically the size of the yeti without being one," Owen commented while turning his attention to the fighting arena. He was still in awe of the tall, muscular man but his nerves were quickly settled when Owen remembered that a chimera outranked a yeti. If anything, he could just send waves of fire at Cedric to last the round.

"And you are almost the same thing as a walking chimera so calm yourself," Caine replied while stepping in front of Owen's line of vision. "Here are the rules whenever anybody fights in these arenas. You can transition and use whatever tactics you can to either make your opponent submit or become unconscious. However, in order to keep the match fair, no special abilities can be used."

"What?" Owen exclaimed. He could feel the sweat begin to form on his forehead as he now felt the fear return as his main advantages had been stripped from him.

"Yep, that means no venom and no fire. Also, no killing on purpose but accidents do happen. One other thing, I am not allowed to fight in these matches or interfere. Cedric knows what I am, but not the others, so out of mutual respect and usefulness to each other, we have that rule in place," Caine added as he turned to the side to allow Owen to walk to the arena. "Chin up and use the power that the chimera has gifted you. You are a true hybrid. Use it."

"Thanks for the advice, although I am surprised you are giving me any. I figured you would want Cedric to win," Owen responded.

"Who says I don't want him to win," Caine replied as he winked. Owen scoffed and looked over his shoulder at Olivia and Selena who both nodded and smiled with encouragement. Owen returned the gesture, took a deep breath, and proceeded to the arena.

As Owen entered, he could feel the chimera churning inside of him, which boosted his confidence. Not only did his confidence grow but his aggression started to simmer as well. He felt like a caged animal, ready to attack at any moment as he began to pace back and forth.

"Announce your creature, then begin. You have three minutes," a voice called out from the audience.

"Yeti," Cedric said while he glared at Owen.

"Chimera," Owen replied as his eyes narrowed in on Cedric and his breathing became heavier. At this point, Owen felt the ferociousness of the chimera was about to boil over. Cedric didn't seem fazed by Owen. Instead, his eyes transitioned from brown to black as white fur appeared over the dark brown skin around his eyes. Cedric balled his fists, which caused his already bulging muscles to increase even more.

"Don't you think you should transition, boy," Cedric suggested as he quickly came across the ring at Owen. He then drove his fist down toward Owen's head, which Owen used both of his hands to grab. It took a lot of effort but Owen was able to stop the powerful strike from Cedric.

"You are not in transition. How is this possible?" Cedric inquired as he strained to drive his fist forward. In that brief moment, Owen pushed Cedric's hand up in the air, which caused him to take a couple of steps back. At that point, Owen sent a front kick to his chest, which made Cedric grimace and stumble back. Owen couldn't make out what the crowd was saying or their reactions but he could tell they were already into the fight due to the loud yelling.

Cedric growled before he charged and when he reached Owen, he grabbed him by the shoulders and drove him back. Owen tried to defend himself by grabbing both of Cedric's arms but his power and momentum were too great. As he drove Owen back, his claws sunk into his shoulders. Owen yelled in pain as Cedric rammed him into the metal fence that surrounded the ring. The attack from Cedric

126

caused the chimera to come forth. Owen transitioned deep into level two and let out a loud roar before he knocked Cedric's hands away from him. Owen quickly followed up with a couple of slashes that tore through Cedric's chest. He grabbed his chest but the pain was only visible on Cedric's face for a moment.

He retaliated by grabbing both of Owen's arms and tossing him into the metal fence again. While Owen was on the ground, Cedric sent a heavy kick into Owen's midsection. The impact was hard enough to lift Owen's entire body slightly into the air. If Owen didn't know any better, Cedric's foot was made of iron. He made it to his hands and knees before turning his head to glance up at Cedric, but it was too late. Cedric's fist was already coming down toward Owen. His fist crashed into Owen's face, which sent him hard onto the floor again, where Owen lied motionless.

Cedric raised his hands in a victorious manner as he began to walk around the ring. However, it was short-lived when he heard a low growl come from Owen. Cedric turned his head and his eyes opened wider in shock as he saw Owen's head slowly turn to look at him.

More fur grew on Owen's body and his facial features became more animalistic, while his muscles twitched with intensity. The attack caused Owen to just barely enter a level three transition. The blood trickled down Owen's face where Cedric's claws must have cut him from his previous attack. Owen got to his hands and knees again before darting toward Cedric. He then stole a move out of Cedric's tactics and shoved him into the fence. There, Owen went into a frenzy with his slash attacks. From the power and speed of Owen's attacks, Cedric's blocking was becoming ineffective quickly as Owen continued to tear through his flesh. Cedric's arms eventually dropped from weakness due to the volume of lacerations on his arms. That didn't stop Owen's fury of attacks as he began to rip the flesh from Cedric's chest. The blood was pouring down his body as he dropped to his knees. Cedric's head and body were wobbling at this point. Owen sent another claw attack at Cedric, which slammed against the side of his head. The impact caused him to fall to the ground and lay flat on his stomach, motionless.

Owen grabbed Cedric by the shoulder and abruptly rolled him onto his back. Cedric had blood running down the side of his face and was dazed as his eyes tried to focus. He could see that the blood originated from his last hit to Cedric's face, for it left a serious bruise and laceration around his temple. Even seeing this, Owen wasted no time grabbing Cedric's neck and raising his other hand in the air to bring down another vicious blow. Cedric was still too dazed to defend himself or even realize what was about to happen. Owen, who was still breathing heavily from the intensity he was feeling from the battle, began to grind his teeth as his lip raised. If Owen were to continue, Cedric could easily die, but the rules state the fight wasn't over yet. At this point, Cedric's eyes became wide as now he too realized the same thing as Owen, but he was still too hurt to defend himself.

His arm began to tremble as there was a power struggle between his humanity and the chimera's rage. Owen lifted his head and let out a roar that filled the entire room, causing everyone to turn their heads in the direction of the noise. He then whipped himself away from Cedric and took a deep breath before transitioning back to normal. He then stood over Cedric and offered his hand. Cedric's brow lowered due to his confusion.

"I have no quarrel with you and I am sorry for any disrespect I have displayed," Owen said while keeping his hand extended. He was still trying to catch his breath and he used his smile to mask the pain his body was feeling.

Cedric slowly transitioned back to normal. As he did, he pressed his lips firmly together and his face crinkled from the increase in pain. Luckily, Cedric was a strong and sturdy man. Owen extended his hand and Cedric stared at it, bewildered before he grabbed it. Owen hoisted him to his feet. Cedric seemed a little unsteady at first but gained his balance quickly. He gave Owen a small smile and a nod before turning his head to the person keeping track of the time.

"I believe it has been three minutes," Cedric mentioned. The man, who was motionless and whose eyes were wide open with shock, finally clicked the timer without even looking at it.

At that time, a few other men walked into the ring and none of them appeared to be happy as they approached Owen. He looked at them and then glanced over to Caine who simply smiled and shrugged. Owen rolled his eyes and turned his attention to the small mob that was forming.

"You got some explaining to do! No one has defeated The Yeti in the arena like this! How dare you," one of the men in the small group yelled. Before Owen could react, Cedric bellowed out, "Enough!" This caused everyone in and around the arena to become silent.

"This man doesn't owe any of you an explanation. He has won fair and square and on top of that, showed me true respect. No one is to harm this man without my consent and he is to be treated with respect. Do I make myself clear?" Cedric announced loudly to the room. Everyone within Owen's eyesight nodded their heads in agreement, including the men in the ring. The small mob then turned and walked away.

Cedric leaned over to Owen, "With that said I wouldn't mind knowing how you fought the way you did." His deep voice was low so others wouldn't hear him.

"Of course, but I have a question. How are you not sore? Even I am feeling like you ran me over with a car, then backed up again for good measure," Owen inquired.

Cedric chuckled, "I feel like the same vehicle ran me down too. I just hide it better." The two smiled as they exited the arena. "I do have some vampire blood on hand that you are more than welcomed to have."

"Is it Caine's blood?" Owen asked.

"No. He is very particular about letting others drink his blood. Besides, I would be too afraid I would catch something from it." Cedric's joke caused Owen to burst out into laughter while holding his side from the pain. At that time, Caine, Selena, and Olivia approached them.

"Impressive," Caine commented.

"It was more than that. You kicked some butt out there!" Olivia added but then her smile quickly vanished. She realized that her comment implied Cedric was on the receiving end of the beating. "Sorry, I didn't mean it that way," Olivia began to fumble over her words until Cedric raised his hand to stop her.

"It's okay and he did kick some butt out there," Cedric said with a reassuring smile, causing Olivia to let out a sigh of relief.

Selena put her hand on Owen's chest, "I could heal you if you like?" Her gentle smile and warm touch put Owen at ease.

Owen put his hand on top of Selena's and smiled back at her, "I appreciate it but Cedric and I have some vampire blood lined up for us already. I should stick to that commitment." At a quick glance, he noticed Caine seemed bothered by Selena and Owen's interactions but was tolerating it as he rolled his eyes and looked away.

Selena's smile grew as she nodded her head. "In that case, I will go find Abigail and try to at least heal that wound. I don't think she realizes your protective instinct was triggered by her being a chimera as well. Lions, like chimeras, are protective of their members once they are accepted into the pride. With your new state of mind, you acted on that. You probably didn't even realize it. Going off your interactions, it would also explain why you trust her and even feel more at ease around her."

"I didn't even think about it but I guess that makes sense," Owen replied. Her explanation finally shed light on why he was able to open up to her as quickly as he did. Owen now wondered how much of what he felt when he was around Abigail was chimera related versus how he truly felt. Either way, he was just delighted that there was some reason behind it all.

"Now that you realize it, for your own health, I would try to be mindful of it when around Abigail," Selena said as she winked. She then turned around and began to make her way out of the room.

Owen followed Cedric off to the side of the room while Caine and Olivia wandered off together. Everyone continued their normal routine but only moments later, that changed.

Owen could hear muffled screaming that no one else seemed to hear except for Caine, which Owen noticed he was looking around trying to locate the sound as well. Caine narrowed in on the noise before Owen…it was coming from the transition room. At that time, the door swung wide open as a couple of people ran out screaming in terror. A third person began to exit the room but tripped. A second later, something grabbed a hold of the guy's foot and yanked him back into the room, leaving only the claw marks on the floor from where the man tried to save himself from being taken. A blood-curdling scream could be heard from within the darkness of the room. It was quickly silenced at the same time a large spray of blood projected from the darkness and splattered across the floor.

CHAPTER 8

At that moment, most of the people began to scream and panic as they ran for the exit. Owen called out to Caine, "Close the door!" Caine nodded at Owen as his eyes turned red. He briskly ran to the door, but to mask his true nature, he did not run at his full vampire speed. He slammed the door shut but before he got a chance to seal it, a large roar bellowed from behind the door. The door then slammed back open, smashing Caine against the wall before it toppled to the floor. Caine slid down the wall and plopped onto the ground. He had patches of blood around his head and body and even though he still seemed coherent, he was too weak and injured to move. Any other person would have died from the impact, but being a true vampire saved his life, Owen thought. The area around the door was now cracked and even slightly bent which left just enough room for the beast to burst from the darkness.

It resembled a hyena, but a lot larger and stockier. Its shoulders stood about five feet from the ground and its back sloped down from there. Its reddish-brown fur was shaggy around the shoulders and became less furry the further down its back until it was almost a thin layer of fur.

"Nandi bear," Cedric yelled. At that time, it stood on its hind legs and raised its claws into the air. It then let out another roar through its blood-soaked fur and fangs as it landed back on all fours and charged. For a beast its size, it was able to move fast. From what Owen remembered from his studies, the beast seemed slightly larger and had a lot more muscle mass than what the lore described.

A couple of people rushed toward the rampaging beast and tried to stop it. The Nandi bear swiped at the first person, slashing through her with ease. As she fell to the ground, the other person was able to stab it in the shoulder. The Nandi bear barked as it turned around and chomped its fangs into the head of its attacker. Using its immense strength, the Nandi bear crushed the guy's skull. As the man fell to the ground, the Nandi bear slowly turned its head toward the next two people closest to it…one of them was Selena.

It darted toward them, trampling the first person who was trying to run away from it. The Nandi bear didn't even break its stride as it continued toward Selena. She raised her hands to shield herself while turning her head and screaming in terror. Even with her in transition, she knew the Nandi bear could still kill her or at least make her wish it did. Caine yelled from the other side of the room, "No! Selena!"

Owen quickly transitioned and sprinted toward Selena. Between his transition and his focus on Selena and the Nandi bear, the pain he felt melted away with each stride he took. The Nandi bear went to pounce on Selena and as its claws neared, Owen tackled her out of the way. The two rolled across the ground, with Owen using his hand to cradle her head for protection. The two came to a stop with Selena on top of Owen. She looked at him and while out of breath said, "Thank you."

Owen smiled and went to respond but instead, he used his left arm to fling Selena off him while using his right hand to send a burst of flames at the Nandi bear that was about to bite her. The Nandi bear reared its head back to avoid most of the flames while Selena tumbled away. Seeing the Nandi bear staring him down and raising its lip, Owen knew he had to go deep into transition if he had any chance of surviving. As Owen transitioned further, the flames grew larger around his hands. The two began to snarl and raise their lips at each other, exposing their deadly fangs. There was no fear in Owen, for the chimera's confidence and determination replaced it.

Owen was the first to charge, which triggered the Nandi bear to do the same. He raised his hands and sent streams of fire at his attacker but it didn't slow the beast down this time. Instead, the Nandi bear leaped through the flames and collided with Owen. He felt as if a wrecking ball had hit him as he fell to the ground.

He tried to quickly get up but the Nandi bear sent its heavy paw at Owen and its claws sliced through his upper chest and left shoulder. Owen was anguishing from the pain that was now pulsating from his wound. The pain was intense enough to make it difficult for him to move his left arm. While Owen was on the ground, the Nandi bear stood over him and snapped at his head. In defense, Owen slapped the beast's face away and then sent a burst of flames from his mouth that covered the Nandi bear's face. It bawled in pain while it lumbered off Owen and then he harnessed the chimera's will to push past the pain and make his move.

He gritted his teeth and lunged at the Nandi bear and slashed its front leg and then again across the side of the beast. When the Nandi bear countered by snapping at Owen, he tumbled forward and sunk his fangs into the hind leg of the Nandi bear. He injected as much venom into the beast as he could. The Nandi bear shook Owen off but it was too late. It had trouble pursuing Owen and to his surprise, his venom paralyzed not just the leg he bit but the other one as well. His venom must be more potent now due to his new hybrid status, Owen concluded.

The Nandi bear was still able to take a swing at Owen, which he ducked and then he drove his hand into the chest of the beast. As his hand broke through its chest, he sent flames through the same hand that was buried inside the Nandi bear. Owen removed his hand as the beast squealed in pain before it fell to its side. He could then see smoke venting from the Nandi bear's mouth, as well as smoke and blood pouring from its chest. The beast then became silent and motionless as it lied on the floor, dead.

Owen collapsed to his knees. He was exhausted from fighting Cedric and then the Nandi bear. He began to feel light-headed from both exhaustion and the blood loss he was experiencing from the Nandi bear's slash. He put his hand over the wound to slow the bleeding down but the area was too large for him to cover with just his hand. Owen began to transition back to normal but was unable to because the more human he became, the more the pain increased. Even his wound seemed to become worse as the blood started to escape faster. Instead, Owen transitioned further knowing he could control himself from fully transitioning into the chimera. However, he wasn't sure for how long he could do this, especially with his injury. He fell to his side, from his knees, and lied on his back as he tried to hold on both physically and mentally.

At that point, Selena rushed over to Owen and knelt by his side. His vision was blurry, but it seemed as if she was in transition. She placed her hand on Owen's wound, which hurt at first, but then the pain began to slowly go away. Within moments, Owen's vision was restored as the immense pain, as well as the wound itself, had disappeared. He transitioned back to human as he sat up and turned his head toward Selena. He noticed she was taking slow, deep breaths before she returned to her human state.

"Thank you," Owen gently said to Selena while moving his left arm around to release some of the stiffness he felt. Selena leaned toward him and gave Owen a hug.

"No, thank you," Selena said before releasing her hug. "You saved my life. I healed that nasty slash you took but I don't know how I could ever repay you." Owen could feel the sincerity emanating from her as she gently smiled at him while she held her hand over her heart.

"Tack on talking with Abigail later to smooth things over and we are even," Owen replied and then gave Selena a quick wink.

Selena chuckled, "I'll see what I can do." Owen stood up and then helped Selena to her feet as Cedric approached them.

"Once again you have earned even more of my respect, as well as everybody else's respect. Thank you. Still…I don't know how you did it. In all my years I have never seen a person so in tune with their creature and have such control. It is like you are a human chimera," Cedric remarked as he passed a vial of vampire blood to Owen.

"Because I am," Owen replied after he chugged the contents of the vial. He then let out a sigh of relief as he could feel the rest of himself that Selena didn't get a chance to heal became rejuvenated.

"Excuse me?" Cedric questioned after he drank his own vial. His head was slightly tilted and his brow was knitted.

"I can tell you the details later but essentially a series of events led to me going through a change. A change that has turned me into a true hybrid. The chimera and I are one true being now and not two beings held together by a mystical gem," Owen responded nonchalantly.

"That explains a lot," Cedric replied as his eyes briefly widened and his brows eased. Cedric briefly peered over Owen's head. "I need to go over there and pretend to give Caine some vampire blood in order to keep up his charade." Cedric patted Owen on his shoulder as he walked past him.

Owen noticed Abigail from his peripheral vision. He turned to look at her and could see she had recently walked back into the room and was in shock from the sights of everything. He then noticed Selena walking in her direction. He hoped she would be able to smooth things over with Abigail, for he did not want her upset at him, especially over something that he didn't have any control over at the time. As his thoughts dwelled on Abigail, Cedric and Caine redirected his attention to them.

"Nice to see that the vampire blood healed you," Owen mocked Caine who in return rolled his eyes at Owen. The dried blood on Caine masked his injuries that healed long before Cedric ever made his way over to him.

"Gentlemen, I hate to interrupt but do any of you recognize this man?" Cedric asked as he pointed to the deceased man where the Nandi bear used to be.

"I have no idea who he is," Owen responded.

"He is unknown to me," Caine replied.

"I don't recognize this man either and I make it my business to know everyone coming in and out of this club, especially this room. So how do I not know him?" Cedric asked while waving over one of his associates that were standing by him earlier. "I want you to find out everything you can about this person and get someone to clean and fix all of this up. I want it done as soon as possible," Cedric directed. The man nodded, "Yes sir, right away," and then scurried off.

"I think I had enough fun for one night. I am going to head out," Owen said, but as he began to turn around, Cedric grabbed his arm.

"What did you want to ask me earlier?"

Owen paused, for it took a moment before he realized what Cedric was referencing. "My friends are in possession of a gem that somebody is going through great lengths to acquire and we don't think their intentions are good. We are trying to get it to a secure location but we can't with all the added pressure and bodies this person is throwing at this gem. We need to figure out what creature is inside this gem and who wants it so badly," Owen answered.

"Where was the gem discovered?" Cedric inquired.

"Deep inside a mountain in the Alps within a magically sealed box," Owen replied.

"I will see what I can find out but it may take some time with everything else that just went down," Cedric mentioned as he surveyed the room.

"Any help is much appreciated," Owen replied with a hint of hope in his voice. Cedric gave Owen a quick smile as he shook his hand. The two then exchanged numbers before Cedric walked away to help direct the current clean-up efforts of the room.

"Owen, one moment please," Caine requested, causing Owen to pause again.

"Tonight, you saved Selena…a person that is very dear to me. For that, I am in your debt." Caine's face was stern with how serious he was with his comment.

"It's okay. We're good," Owen replied with a quick smile but Caine quickly rebutted, "No, we are not good until I repay you for what you have done here tonight. This is non-negotiable."

"Fine, you owe me one but please tell me…what is it between you and Selena?" Owen asked.

"As you already know, she was the one who found me and that has made me feel more human than I have felt in ages. She is the beacon of hope that keeps me on the right path. I fear if I ever lose that light, I will fall into a place that will be darker than where she found me originally," Caine replied and to Owen's surprise, there was a hint of emotion in Caine's eyes as they became glassy. Without Caine knowing it, Owen gained a lot of trust in him for how he allowed himself to be vulnerable and honest.

"I had that once but I, unfortunately, lost it. Luckily, I had my friends to pull me quickly out of the dark hole I fell into. I will do my best to make sure that doesn't happen to you," Owen replied while extending his hand. Caine proudly shook Owen's hand and gave him the numbers of everyone else in the group before the two parted ways.

Even though Owen was completely healed, he was mentally exhausted from the night, and with the rest of the group gone, he decided to go home. The entire drive home he didn't think or even listen to music. He needed silence to give his mind a break. Once he arrived at the safe house and showered, he lied on the bed and tried to go to sleep. That sleep he desperately wanted now eluded him since the thoughts he suppressed before began to pour into his mind like a flood.

He replayed the entire night in his head, thinking once again about Abigail and how horrible he would feel if things weren't the same after tonight. Within his thoughts about Abigail, he tried to figure out how he truly felt about her since now his feelings for her were clouded by the pride concept that Selena mentioned before.

On one hand, it would explain how he became so trusting and protective of her, but on the other hand, he was fond of her personality. She was easy-going, fun, and carefree, yet she was smart and quite able to handle herself. Those feelings he felt were his own but even then, he had doubts. This would be a great time to talk to Avery about this, Owen thought. After dueling back and forth in his mind, Owen came to the conclusion that for now, he wouldn't actively pursue Abigail in any type of romantic relationship.

First, he wanted to talk with Hailey to see where they stood before he entertained any kind of relationship with anyone else. He knew they were not together anymore but he still wanted to talk to her to see how she felt. Also, deep down, a part of him hoped they would get back together. The talk would bring either closure or a relationship, which anything was better than the limbo he was trapped in.

Second, he wanted to confirm which feelings were from the chimera and which feelings were from himself before he ventured down any path that had himself and Abigail becoming closer. Lastly, as playful and flirty as she could be, he wasn't picking up any vibes that she wanted to take it further. The more he thought about it, the more he could picture her as a close friend and nothing more just between their interactions thus far. He would feel content if that was the case since being friends with her has gotten him more out of his shell.

Owen's mind then jumped to the others in the group. It was a rough start but not only does he better understand Caine, Owen felt he is now more on his side after saving Selena. Of course, Selena was on his side and her sweet, pure nature was a huge breath of fresh air. Then, there was Olivia who he couldn't wait to introduce Michael to her. He thought Michael would truly be able to help another newbie vampire like herself. The two of them would be able to relate more to each other because of that. As for Cedric, it was another rough start for him but after the events from tonight, Owen felt he earned the respect of another powerful ally.

Owen's mind drifted to the Nandi bear, and he pondered what truly happened to ignite the series of events that led the Nandi bear to escape. If he didn't hear Cedric's reaction to the stranger, Owen would have presumed it just simply escaped. What were the stranger's intentions, Owen wondered? Regardless of the concerns that he had; Owen did feel more at ease. This was because he knew that he now had another group that not only would be able to help him but also that he could call friends…even Caine. His brain finally grew tired enough for him to finally go to sleep.

It was late in the morning when Owen woke from his slumber. He sat up in the bed and rubbed his eyes to clear his morning vision.

"Morning sleepy head." Owen let out a quick gasp as he jerked his head in the direction of the voice.

"It's about time you woke up. You must have been exhausted. You barely moved all night," Abigail said with a playful smile while laying down to the right of him.

"How…how did you get in here?" Owen asked.

"You left the balcony door unlocked. You should be more careful. You never know what creatures may wander in here," Abigail replied as she sat up in the bed with a devious smile.

"Why are you here? Wait…is that one of my shirts you are wearing?" Owen asked with a knitted brow. He was confused, yet his voice was calm since he was not mad at her intrusion.

"Most men would enjoy waking up to a woman in their bed," Abigail teased.

Owen smiled. "It's just after last night I was afraid I wouldn't see you any time soon and especially not in a good mood."

"Selena talked to me last night and she explained everything. I may have overreacted so I wanted to come over to apologize. Also, you don't know why that chivalrous type of behavior bothers me so much, so it's unfair for me to get upset at you. I figured you were at this safe house so I decided to see you sooner rather than later. I would have caught up to you before you went to sleep if I didn't get detoured." Abigail's face became more serious as her smile faded away.

"How so?" Owen inquired.

"Apparently, there were a couple of people watching over your condo so I handled it," Abigail responded as she smirked.

"Handled it?" Owen cautiously asked.

"Yep. Handled it," Abigail said as the chimera's eyes flashed before Owen.

"Ah…got it. Thank you but I'm curious as to why they were out there. How could they have identified me?" Owen questioned.

"Maybe whoever is after the gem knows about this safehouse and was staking it out or you were tailed from somewhere. I doubt they know it's you. They probably thought it was just another hybrid to watch," Abigail responded.

"Hopefully so," Owen added.

"Anyway, I managed to get in here and then decided to change since my clothes were bloody and torn. Since you were already asleep…I figured I would join you. Now that you are awake, I wanted to tell you that I am sorry for how I acted. I should have explained myself besides just running off. It's just I had many men over the years act like they are my white knight in shining armor and they ended up being just smoke and mirrors. For as long as I can remember, I have made it a point to not let men treat me like I am a damsel in distress or like some object. I feel fortunate to be able to tell you that now because from what I hear, I may not have gotten the chance with you playing hero and such. You know…the hero doesn't always win," Abigail responded. He didn't pick up on any playfulness or contempt as she spoke. However, he detected concern in her voice as he heard a slight tremble within her words at the end.

"I don't know about the whole hero thing. I wasn't trying to be one. I just reacted to the situation. However, I do appreciate what you shared and all the help that you have given me so far. Just your company alone makes me happy…most times. It's kind of situational now that I think about it," Owen playfully responded.

"Good, and you can repay me by letting me use your shower," Abigail said as she perked up and then gave Owen a quick, hard kiss on his cheek…close to his lips. Owen, who was caught off guard by the kiss, noticed when she stood up that she was wearing just his shirt and it only came down to her upper thigh. She made her way to the bathroom and before she closed the door, she turned to him. "Me showering is not an invitation for anything." She then winked at Owen before closing the door.

Owen was at a loss for words and once he heard the shower turn on, he got out of bed and put on a shirt since he was wearing only his mesh shorts to bed. He then grabbed some food from the refrigerator and went out to the balcony to enjoy his meal as he waited. As he ate, Owen thought about Abigail and how grateful he was for her sharing what she did and for not still being mad at him. He kept his thoughts solely on that and not on her actions while in the condo.

Owen's mind ceased its thinking when he heard the bathroom door open. Moments later, Abigail exited his room wearing only a towel that covered from the top of her chest to her upper thigh. Her hair was wet and curly from where she did her initial drying with the towel.

"The bathroom is all yours. I am going to get some water and raid the closet. Hopefully, I'll find something that doesn't look like it would belong to Isaac's mother," Abigail mentioned as she walked past Owen. She grabbed a water bottle from the fridge before going into the other bedroom.

"Good luck with that," Owen replied as he headed toward the

bathroom while removing his shirt. After only taking a few steps into the bathroom, he heard a knock at the door.

"I got it!" Abigail called out from the other room. Owen's heart dropped into his stomach as he felt all the air leave his body. His eyes grew wide in fear of his friends, especially Hailey, showing up and being greeted by a half-naked strange woman. Before he could say anything, he heard the latch and the door handle turn. After that, he only heard rumblings of people talking. Owen froze at first but then slowly made his way to the bedroom door.

"Your friends are here," Abigail casually mentioned as she headed back to the closet. If Owen didn't know any better, he felt even the chimera was scared at this point. Owen felt he hadn't breathed since he heard Abigail answer the door so he took a deep breath and walked out of the bedroom.

He turned his head and saw Bailey and Michael at the door. He felt a rush of relief swarm over him as he smiled. Bailey had an accusatory expression on her face while her arms were crossed. Michael was smiling as his eyes kept drifting around Owen to watch Abigail while she made her way to the closet. Bailey's eyes never left Owen.

"It's not what it looks like," Owen stammered.

"Of course not. Just a wet, half-naked woman and a half-naked man by themselves. What's next…you are going to tell me the two of you were up knitting all night and morning?" Bailey responded as she grinned while her brow arched.

"I would knit with her any time," Michael softly blurted out which was swiftly followed by a quick elbow to his midsection by Bailey. He grimaced while holding the area she hit. Owen, realizing he was shirtless again, quickly ran and grabbed his shirt to put it back on him. At that point, Bailey and Michael entered the condo.

"Seriously…nothing happened. She needed a place to crash after fighting off some of the henchmen or whatever we are calling them. Heck, I didn't even know she was here until I woke up," Owen loudly whispered to them.

"Relax, I believe you. It still doesn't explain why you went radio silent. It's the reason why we are here. That and to let you know that Hailey and Avery should enter the city either today or tomorrow," Bailey informed.

"Is everything okay?" Michael asked.

"Sorry and yes, everything is fine. It was just crazy last night between meeting new allies, having to prove myself in a fighting arena, and then ending the night by having to kill a Nandi bear that got loose. The good news is that I think I found someone that can help us in finding out what creature is inside the gem and maybe even who is behind it all," Owen said with a hint of excitement as he perked up.

"I don't even know where to begin with what you just said," Michael commented as he quickly shook his head.

"Same here, but that's good news about finding people that can help us. Good job but now we are going to need some details about last night," Bailey added.

"Which I can fill in while you get cleaned up," Abigail said as she placed her hand on Bailey and Michael's shoulders and smiled. Owen noticed that Bailey side-eyed Abigail; whereas, Michael smiled.

Owen paused as once again; he was at a loss for words before mumbling out, "That's comforting." Owen then turned around and headed into the bathroom. He didn't take too long in getting ready since he was eager to see how the three of them were getting along. When he walked back into the living room, he noticed the three of them sitting down around the table. Each of them was talking and laughing which made Owen feel better.

"Hey, hero. Glad you can join us," Bailey jokingly mocked Owen. He rolled his eyes at her response as he sat down next to Abigail on the couch, across from Bailey and Michael who were sitting in the chairs.

"I'm guessing you filled them in without any embellishments," Owen asked Abigail.

"I did but I am not sure if they bought the part that your hair was blowing in the wind as you fought the Nandi bear," Abigail replied with a playful grin.

Owen softly chuckled. "You weren't even in the room when that happened."

"Not exactly, but I did see the footage after Selena talked to me. Quite impressive," Abigail responded as she winked.

"She mentioned we can stop by the club later to meet everyone and check out the place," Michael added.

"Yeah, but until then I think we need to compare notes to see if we can figure anything new out," Bailey chimed in.

"Sounds good but I'm pretty sure that Abigail mentioned whatever I was going to tell you. The rest you will find out at the club later," Owen commented.

"Not a problem. It's easier for me to fill you in on everything versus me trying to text in code," Bailey replied and then rolled her eyes. "From what Michael and I have seen during our recon of the city, there are agents...henchmen...whatever you want to call them, everywhere. It's as if all their forces are converging on this city. They must have figured out where Hailey and Avery are headed but there are still enough people to attack them as they travel here."

"Do we need to help them?" Owen inquired.

"As much as I would like to, Isaac wants us to stay here and be prepared for them when they arrive, especially with them being so close," Bailey replied.

"They handled themselves this entire time so they should be able to make it," Michael added. To Owen, it sounded like Michael was saying it more to convince himself.

"I hope you're right," Owen commented.

"We have enough going on here with all the extra people filtering into the city. At first, I didn't think any of them noticed us, but now we have caught a few tailing us and we even had a few encounters ourselves. As for Isaac, Marcus, and Anders, they are still dealing with the remaining people around the facility. The original plan was to clear the area and then Anders would stay behind in case anybody else tried to take a position near the facility, while Marcus and Isaac ventured over to this city. They planned to arrive here around the same time as Avery and Hailey but now it's unknown when they will be able to show up," Bailey added.

"The objective is still the same. Isaac just feels we need more focus here since he underestimated the amount of attention this gem is receiving. It's the same reason why they are now unsure if they can get here at the same time as Hailey and Avery. Isaac underestimated the extent to which this unknown person will go to retrieve this gem," Michael commented.

"The more help the merrier. As much fun as it is, I am starting to grow weary of this daily battle. I even lost one of my favorite outfits last night due to those thugs outside this condo," Abigail mentioned in a carefree manner.

"Wait, outside of this condo?" Bailey asked as her brow furrowed.

"Yeah…why?" Abigail questioned with the same expression as Bailey.

"Because I thought this condo was one of the unknown locations that Klayden would not have known about, so why are they now staking out this place?" Bailey replied.

"Maybe Klayden knew more than what everyone realized. He was a very clever and intelligent person who always thought a few steps ahead. Either that or maybe Owen was followed when he left the club," Michael suggested.

"I wondered if he was followed too. There are people that survey the perimeter of the club but it's always possible since they can't watch everything all the time," Abigail added.

"This is getting more and more complex with each passing

moment. We need to start making bigger strides in accomplishing our objectives or else we are going to become overwhelmed," Owen suggested as he leaned forward and rested his elbows on his knees, deep in thought.

"Could we hide the gem in the club? It seems like a secure area and it would buy us some time," Michael asked.

"No can do. The gem...and even Hailey and Avery, would not be allowed anywhere near the club. There are too many people that use the club as a sanctuary and a place to be free and open and that gem would jeopardize all of that. Sorry." Abigail was direct in her response but softer when she apologized.

"That's okay. Hailey and Avery can stay in the city. With the extra civilians around I am hoping that will lessen some of the fighting and pursuing. By then, hopefully, that guy...Cedric will have some answers for us," Bailey responded while she leaned back in her chair. She rubbed her face in what seemed to be an attempt to wipe away the concerns she had.

"In that case, I am going to be on my way. You kids have fun. Owen, I'll text you later and we will all meet up tonight. Nice meeting everyone," Abigail cheerfully announced while she placed her hand on Owen's leg as she got up to leave. Once she left, Bailey and Michael just stared at Owen and smiled.

Owen scoffed. "Seriously, nothing happened." The two said nothing, yet continued to smile. "You two need help," Owen said as he smiled while he shook his head. Bailey and Michael finally cracked a grin after his comment, which turned into laughter.

Bailey and Michael stayed a few more hours to have lunch with Owen and reminisce. They talked about their time at the facility and even some of the more pleasant times after they left. He even discussed more about his time at the club and the new friends he met. It was a welcomed break from all the chaos that was going on around them. Not too long after lunch, Bailey and Michael left to take care of a few errands and to get ready for tonight. Once they left, he used

147

the remaining time he had before he had to get ready to decompress. Owen wasn't sure what the night would bring, for it could be filled with a fun night out with his friends, serious discussions about the gem, or another night filled with blood. Only time would tell.

CHAPTER 9

Bailey, Michael, and Owen rendezvoused with Abigail at the same location where she told Owen to meet her the other night. The group walked to the club and both Bailey and Michael were given the same preparations as Owen before he entered the club for the first time. As they entered the club itself, Owen noticed both Bailey and Michael looking all around them as they weaved their way through the crowd.

"This is crazy!" Bailey yelled into Owen's ear while she smiled with her eyes wide open in amazement. Michael had a similar reaction but was speechless. They eventually made it to the stairwell that led to Abigail's room. As they walked up the steps Owen noticed yellow tape across the door to the back room, which also had a few extra people guarding the entrance. As they entered the room, Selena, Olivia, and Caine were already present. Selena stood up from the couch and gave Owen a hug before introducing herself to Bailey and Michael. Both Caine and Olivia nodded at Owen to acknowledge his presence but only Olivia smiled. The two grabbed their drinks from the bar and strolled over to introduce themselves as well to Bailey and Michael.

"I will let you all talk. I'm sure you will hear everything that I heard yesterday and I don't want to take anything from that," Owen announced to the group. He was happy that everyone was there and he was glad to see them too but at the same time, he felt he needed a little space. His mind was cluttered with thoughts about the mission, Hailey, and even Abigail to some extent. Thoughts that may have been alleviated if he would have meditated besides watching television earlier. Besides, he had already heard everything and wanted them to bond with his other friends.

"I'm sure they won't hear everything from last night," Caine casually commented with a hint of a smirk.

"Of course," Owen responded. He realized Caine did not want to divulge his secret to Bailey and Michael and wanted to honor that. "Have fun," Owen added with a half-smile before leaving the room. The volume of the music had lowered, making it easier for Owen to lean forward on the railing and glance over the crowd without feeling as if his brain was pounding to the beat. His mind began to wander back to all the things he wanted to not think about earlier in the day. Before he went too deep down that rabbit hole, he heard the door open behind him.

"Do I dare want to know what's on your mind?" Abigail asked with a hint of a smile as Olivia followed behind her.

Owen scoffed. "There isn't enough time in the day for that," he responded with a fake smile.

"Stop worrying about everything. You have done enough of that already. We are all here to help. This isn't Owen against the world. You have all of us. Well…most of us and maybe Caine," Abigail commented as she nudged Owen and smirked. Her response made him laugh.

"Also, don't forget, you are a chimera. Even more in that sense of the word than I am. Use that power and confidence that is dwelling inside of you, along with your humanity and the bonds that you forged with your friends, to help guide you along the way," Abigail calmly said with a reassuring smile.

"Trust me, I wish my mind would just shut off and I didn't dwell over the same thoughts over and over, and then find more things to worry about on top of that. You are right though and I'll bear that in mind. Thank you," Owen responded as he grinned. He agreed with what she said but at the same time, it was stuff he already knew. Not only did he know about it, but he also tried and failed to implement that reasoning within his mind; however, he did appreciate the gesture.

"Of course I'm right," Abigail playfully said while giving Owen a quick wink and peck on his cheek before she went back into the room. Owen chuckled lightly to himself.

"Her words deflected off you like water against a rock, didn't they?" Olivia commented while she smiled and handed Owen a beer.

"Was it that obvious?" Owen responded while staring at the door that Abigail just walked through.

"I don't have to be a psychic to see whatever burden you are carrying is still with you after you gave Abigail that fake response," Olivia replied while she leaned against the rail next to Owen. The two of them were facing away from the crowd below. "So, why are you putting up this front with her, especially when you like her?" Olivia asked as the two turned to face each other.

Owen smiled followed by a quick raise of his brow. "Wow…I guess I am more of an open book than I realized." Olivia simply shrugged with a crooked grin.

"A few reasons. First, there is the fact that I don't know how she feels about me and I'm not even sure how I feel about her. Abigail is hard to read at times and besides, I am still trying to decipher if what I am feeling is originating from the chimera versus myself. Then, sprinkle on top of that, me wanting to talk with my ex-girlfriend Hailey to either get closure or maybe get back together with her," Owen responded nonchalantly as he took another sip of his beer.

"Wow…way to overthink a situation," Olivia responded, followed by her giggling.

Owen laughed along with her. "Yes, it's what I do best. The sad part is…those aren't the only thoughts in my head. On top of that, there is the bigger matter of this whole battle for the gem. I lost too many people and saw too many of my friends get hurt during the last mission and I don't want that to happen again. I'm stronger now so I must do whatever it takes to be able to make sure we get the gem back to the facility as smoothly as possible. Then, once I find out who wants the gem, I can stop that person so that my friends will be safe. I just hope I can accomplish all of this. My friends' safety and well-being depend on it."

"Wow…that sounds like a lot to have on your mind. Good luck with that," Olivia casually responded.

Owen was so caught off guard by her comment that he laughed as he was taking another sip of his beer. He had to press his lips tightly together to keep from spraying his drink all over Olivia before eventually being able to swallow his beer. Owen let out a small cough and cleared his throat before he wiped his lips and spoke. "That's your response! Nice."

"How do you want me to respond?" Olivia asked as she laughed. "There is nothing that I or anybody else can say that will make you stop worrying or thinking too much. Oh, it may help for a moment but your thoughts will return. Don't take this the wrong way but it's just who you are."

Owen scoffed. "Ah…so I'm hopeless and I need to accept it."

"I didn't say that. I'm telling you to embrace who you are. From your actions yesterday in the back room to what I have heard about you from others, and just simply talking to you now, I can tell you are a good person who has a lot of admirable qualities. Even though I am young, I have been all around the world. I've met a lot of people and it's rare to come across someone like yourself. I'll repeat myself…embrace who you are. If that constant thinking becomes too much to bear then take a break from it. Meditate, spend quality time with your friends, or just keep your mind busy by focusing on the details of whatever mission you are on. Use that overthinking for some good. Just live your life with no regrets. You'll sleep better at night if you do," Olivia said as she smiled at Owen before taking a sip of her beer.

"After that speech, I now have another thing on my mind and that is if you like me and if we should date," Owen teased Olivia which caused her to laugh and spit out a portion of her drink. The two laughed even harder after that. "Joking. Sorry, I couldn't help it. Seriously though for someone who is young, you do have a lot of wisdom. I do need to embrace all the aspects of myself…the good and the bad. It's who I am so why drive myself and others around me insane? Thank you. I appreciate it. This time I mean it," Owen smiled and gave her a side hug which Olivia returned.

"You said you traveled a lot?" Owen randomly asked.

"Yes…before this whole vampire thing I did a lot of traveling. Now I spend my time training and taking orders from Caine," Olivia replied as she rolled her eyes.

"I bet you wish you were traveling again," Owen commented.

Olivia chuckled lightly, "You have no idea." Olivia's expression became sullen. "Honestly, I would wish for a lot of things. For starters, to be who I was before I inherited the vampire. Also, to be able to go back to how it was with my parents and me before things changed. Heck, to have my mom be alive again. I don't know…some wishes are just too far-fetched." Olivia stared off into the distance after she finished.

"I'm sorry. They all sound like good wishes. It can be unfair…trust me I know. Unfortunately, all too well. You just have to be happy with not only who you are, but also what you have today. If not, you are strong enough to make a change in order to be happy," Owen commented while giving her a gentle nudge.

Olivia shook her head. "Yeah, or I can just wish for a ton of money or something fun like that. What would you wish for?" Olivia asked as she smiled. Owen knew it was just an attempt to change the subject so he went along with the ruse.

"Wow…umm…so many things. To have both of my parents alive. For Joshua to be alive and not possessed by that vampire Warrick. For Hailey's brother to be alive. That's sad that my wishes involve bringing people back from the dead." Owen paused for a moment as he realized how serious he was becoming. "Or just go with an obscene amount of money and the ability to not care and overthink so much," Owen added with a quick tilt of his head and a grin.

"You are just as damaged as I am," Olivia nonchalantly remarked. Owen laughed out loud at her comment, which his laughter caused Olivia to laugh as well.

Owen then raised his beer toward Olivia, "To us. May people not ever truly know how deeply damaged we are."

"Cheers," Olivia said as the two clanged their bottles together and finished their drinks. At that time, Abigail stuck her head out and waved the two back inside. As they both entered, the rest of the group was huddled around the center of the room.

"I just received news that Hailey and Avery have entered the city. They are going to stay in one of the hotel rooms deeper within the city itself. They already felt the pressure ease up the further they entered the city so that's a plus. As for Isaac and Marcus, they are still dealing with everything," Bailey announced to Owen while holding her phone up.

"We should make our way over there," Michael suggested.

"No, we shouldn't," Owen softly replied. Both Bailey and Michael looked at Owen, and each other, with crinkled brows since they were confused by his statement.

"Hear me out. They have been fighting every step of the way and now as soon as they get to a place where they can actually relax, we are going to make them move and fight again. Let's give them a day or two to relax and build their strength. Besides, it will also give Cedric more time to find out the information we are looking for. Not to mention, also giving Isaac and Marcus time to sort things out,"

Owen explained.

"As much as I want to call you out for wanting to avoid Hailey, that makes sense. I will relay that over to the others so they know," Bailey mentioned as she began to text.

"It makes sense except for one thing. Marcus and Isaac are not your only support. You have all of us in this room and I bet if you asked Cedric, he and his people would assist as well," Abigail added while she took a few steps forward. Both Olivia and Selena were standing right behind her in support of her comment.

"I don't remember volunteering myself to help in whatever war they have going on," Caine frustratingly said as his eyes flared. Before Owen could mention how Caine owed him one, Selena spoke up.

"Their war is our war or have you not noticed the increased conflict, battles, and general nuisance lately? Wouldn't you like for things to return to as they once were before all this chaos began?" Selena politely, yet firmly, asked Caine.

"And as an extra added bonus, Michael can take me off your hands and train me. It would be beneficial for me to learn from another vampire that is closer to my vampiric age than you," Olivia added while putting her arm around the crook of Michael's arm as she smiled. Michael, who at first flinched because he was caught off guard, then smiled along with Olivia while he nodded his head and became more at ease.

Caine let out a large sigh as he clenched his eyelids. He then opened his eyes to address the group. "Fine. If it means getting everything back to normal and allowing me freedom from training then so be it. I will assist as well but mark my words if any harm falls upon any of the original occupants of this room, then I will make sure it is revisited to our guests tenfold." Caine's eyes were stern and his face was cold as he delivered his speech. There was a moment of awkward silence within the room.

"That is his polite way of saying he would be honored to help.

155

Be grateful, what he said was nicer than what I thought he was going to say," Selena commented while she slowly turned her head to look at Caine. Then, a crooked grin appeared on her face. Caine did not respond. He only took a sip of his drink and walked to the other side of the room.

"Thank you. I speak for everyone that we really appreciate the gesture. At this point, we need all the help that we can get. With the extra added numbers, this could actually make our mission a success," Owen said with a smile that was built on hope.

"How do you think Isaac will react when he sees you guys helping us? I say that because you are not a part of the global facility," Michael inquired.

"He's not stupid. Isaac is aware that not all of our kind are members of the organization. That is one of the things that I am tasked with. To make sure these non-members stay in line," Abigail responded with a slight smile.

Owen laughed, "That's convenient. Now, tell me again how he knows about this club?" Owen playfully asked.

"Well, he doesn't need to be in the know for everything," Abigail responded with a devious grin. Owen rolled his eyes while he smiled at her response.

Everyone in the room spent the next couple of hours talking and joking around. Toward the end of everyone talking, Owen noticed the dynamics of the room beginning to change. Olivia and Michael were talking more with each other and eventually left the room. Then, there was Caine who began teaching Selena some of his painting techniques. To Owen's surprise, he saw Caine laugh along with Selena.

"Do you want to check in with Cedric to see how things are coming along?" Abigail asked Owen and Bailey.

"Sure. That's a good idea. Let's go," Owen responded as the three of them exited the room and made their way to the back room. The guards moved out of the way when they saw Abigail approaching but then they reached out and patted Owen on the back and even shook his hand. Owen heard responses such as "good to see you" and "glad you're back" to which he thanked everybody for their kind words. As they entered the back room, he looked at Abigail…dumbfounded.

"After your heroics last night, you are well respected around here now. Even a hero to some so enjoy it while it lasts," Abigail commented and then gave him a quick wink.

"Great…if his head wasn't big enough already," Bailey joked. In response, Owen playfully smacked her on the arm. He then noticed Cedric leaving the transition room so he made his way toward him.

"How's everything going?" Owen asked as he extended his hand.

"Slow, but going," Cedric responded as he shook Owen's hand. "We at least cleaned up the mess and scheduled funerals for the ones that perished. The repairs should be completed this week or next. As for the mystery guest and your request about the information surrounding that gem and the one who seeks it…I haven't been able to put my full attention on it. Sorry, but my resources are now spread thin with this mess, but I was able to get at least a couple of people started on the investigation."

"No problem. I know you are a busy man so any help is much appreciated at this point," Owen responded. Then, his brow raised. "Oh, sorry…this is Bailey. She is one of my good friends from the facility. The same with Michael even though I believe he is still with Olivia somewhere."

"Pleased to meet you; however, I do find a werewolf and vampire duo to be humorously ironic," Cedric said as he shook her hand and grinned.

"Nice to meet you too but how did you even know about us?" Bailey inquired as she slightly tilted her head.

"I had one of my men follow up on Owen, which included the company he kept. I wanted to make sure he was as honorable as he appeared," Cedric responded.

"Did I pass?" Owen asked.

"You wouldn't be standing here if you didn't," Cedric quickly responded with a serious face. He then patted Owen on the shoulder as his face lightened. "Chin up. You did, so no worries. Now if you will excuse me, I have some matters to attend to. I will let you know as soon as I find out any pertinent information." Cedric then turned around and left to talk to a few people with clipboards. Owen glanced around the room and it was busy as usual, minus fewer crowds of people watching from last night.

"If I knew more about this back room I would have dressed differently. I could go a few rounds just for fun," Bailey commented as she lifted her knee quickly toward her own chest and then again with the other knee, indicating her tight jeans may cause her to have less movement.

"You have been fighting for days now and you want to fight some more? Why?" Owen asked with a crinkled brow yet he smiled, for he found it amusing.

"What can she say, the girl has needs," Abigail commented as she put her arm around Bailey's neck while she smiled. Bailey stood there with a smug look on her face. "What you have on is fine, so let's see how we can remedy your problem."

"Sounds fun," Bailey responded as the two of them walked off toward an open arena. Owen thought about pursuing them but decided to let them bond over whatever violence they were going to partake in. As Owen left the back room and into the club again, he noticed Michael and Olivia dancing together. That image brought a smile to his face for it filled him with joy to see Michael happy…even Olivia. He figured Selena and Caine were still painting upstairs and that is when he realized that he was the odd wheel. Without wanting to intrude on anybody, Owen decided to leave the club and head back to the condo. He wasn't upset since everyone else was having a good time.

Owen hadn't walked too far from the club when he heard someone shout his name. He turned to look and saw Cedric briskly walking toward him.

"Hey, I just got some news that I wanted to share with you. The guy from the other night...the Nandi bear...that was his first transition. When I say first, I mean the third day after touching a gem, first transition."

"Really? Well, that would explain why you didn't recognize him but how do you know it was his first transition?" Owen asked.

"Once we were able to identify him, we were fortunate enough to find a camera from a local establishment that happen to have the angle to the front door of his apartment. The man had a routine he stuck to every day, until a few days ago when some hooded intruders entered his apartment. Then, two and a half days later the man, along with the hooded intruders, left the apartment. The intruders went somewhere off-camera but that man came to the club and went into the transition room. Later that night the Nandi bear appeared," Cedric replied in a steady voice.

"It wasn't an accident," Owen softly said as he peered off to the side, in thought.

"No, it wasn't. It was a calculated move. Think about it. Sending in someone that already had a creature in them would be too risky since they may have been identified and the plan would have been stopped. Also, a regular would have been smart enough to know that their plan would have ended in their death, either by someone here or by me. That fear alone would have made them inform me about it but sending a new person in...now that was smart. They could fill his mind with whatever they wanted to make him go through with it." Cedric paused while he briefly rubbed his chin before he continued.

"It was even more calculating to convince him to enter the transition room and not do it within the club around a group of people, since the initial transition would take too long. All that screaming would have cleared the room and one of the guards would

159

have killed him to protect everyone else if it came down to it. Instead, the man was aware enough to go to the transition room since no one would hear or even see anything. He never entered the cages or went to speak to anybody about securing himself since the cameras would have caught it. The guy, knowingly or not, went on a suicide mission," Cedric added.

"It wouldn't surprise me if he was misled as to what the end result would be. He could have been fed a bunch of lies or something. Either way, something was said and done to make him go to the club of his own free will. I don't know what worries me more. Everything you just mentioned or the bigger unknown…how did he know the layout of the club and how everything worked? An even bigger question…how did he get past security or even past the coded outside door?" As Owen finished speaking, he could see Cedric's face harden as his eyes narrowed.

"It was an inside job. The insider used his code to help him gain access and it seemed to be the same man who opened the door to let the monster out into the open. His death by the Nandi bear, unbeknownst to him, was part of the grand plan I bet. Works for me. It saved me the trouble of killing him myself. As for getting past security, he used special contacts. It's an old trick and I had a long discussion with the guards that I replaced after that discovery," Cedric sneered.

"I wouldn't want to be in those guards' shoes after that but the scary thought that just entered my mind makes matters even worse. Whoever gave that man the gem knew what monster was inside of it. The gems are becoming weaponized and that's not good," Owen said in a loud whisper due to a couple walking past them.

"None of this is good and it needs to be stopped. I just don't understand why the club was attacked. The gem was nowhere near it," Cedric questioned out loud as his brow crinkled.

"There have been some reports of locations being attacked or staked out if it was believed it could aid Hailey and Avery in any way. Maybe the leader thought your club could provide enough backup to become a concern," Owen suggested, masking the high level of his concern. Owen already knew how determined this person was to get the gem and even how resourceful the person was, but this took it to an entirely different level. Nothing was safe…anywhere.

"I need to inform the others," Owen said as he grabbed his phone and began to walk back to the club, but Cedric grabbed his arm to stop him.

"I already have my men on it. I just wanted to personally tell you," Cedric said.

"The king doing peasant work. Look at you getting your hands dirty," Owen jested.

Cedric chuckled. "See that's the thing. I want to get my hands dirty. I didn't build my empire by just sitting on my throne. I had to fight for it with all my blood, sweat, and tears. Now, I have people to help me with everything as I sit back and enjoy the spoils. Unlike others, I can only do that for so long before I grow bored. That is why I started to fight in the arena. Also, you truly don't know what is going on in your kingdom unless you get out there and see it for yourself."

"I can respect that and it makes total sense. Thank you. I should be on my way now," Owen commented as he shook Cedric's hand.

"Same here. I am going to patrol the area for a while. See if I run across anything fun," Cedric winked as he turned and walked away.

Owen still sent out a mass text to give the highlights of what Cedric informed him as he made his way back to his car. The group seemed to have the same concerns as him.

As he drove back to the condo, he reflected on how well Bailey and Michael fit in with the new group of people and even more, how Michael and Olivia appeared to have bonded quickly. Being such a close friend to Michael made Owen glad to see him happy and with someone. As for Bailey and Abigail, they both were strong women so he could only imagine what they did to blow off steam. He laughed to himself as he could see a tall order of vampire blood being needed. With Cedric and what he conveyed to him, he could only imagine how large his organization was and how strong of a leader Cedric was to run it.

Owen finally pulled up to the condo a little after one o'clock in the morning. While making his way to the building, he stopped before he could get out of the parking lot. Whispers hidden within the darkness around him caught his attention.

"It's late and I'm tired so either go away or make this quick," Owen huffed as he rolled his eyes and turned around. At first, there was no response. Then, he saw one figure walk into the light from the street lamp.

"Don't you know you shouldn't walk around by yourself at night," the man said with a strained, aggressive voice. He slowly lifted his head and looked directly at Owen with his pale-yellow eyes. The man also had a disturbing grin that showed a line of sharp teeth and fangs. If Owen had to guess what his creature was, it was a werewolf. That is what he hoped since he knew Anders's creature had a similar appearance but was much stronger.

"Well, technically I am not alone," Owen casually responded while he grinned. He then flashed his chimera eyes at the stranger. "You are outmatched. How about you tell me whom you are working for and what is inside that gem that your boss so desperately wants and I'll let you live." Owen took a few steps closer to the stranger as he made his proposition.

The man smiled as he raised his hand, which was followed by eleven more people that filtered out of the darkness and surrounded Owen. Between how they carried themselves, along with having a similar appearance to the people he faced at the mountain, they appeared to be mercenaries.

They were about twenty feet away from Owen as he glanced around. Even when a handful of them drew their handguns and pointed them at Owen, his fear quickly melted away and was replaced with the rage and confidence of the chimera. Owen's upper lip raised and without turning around to view the rest of the attackers, he simply turned just his head and glared over each shoulder before focusing his attention back on the original person.

"Do you care to retract your statement?" The stranger asked with a smug expression.

Owen knew his only chance would be to maneuver his way, quickly, to a set of mercenaries that were not carrying any guns. Even though the ones without guns did have knives and brass knuckles, he would be too close to them for the other mercenaries that did have guns to fire their weapons without shooting their fellow companions. Another advantage was the fact that only the original person had a creature while the rest of them were human. On the other hand, a significant disadvantage for him was that he didn't want to use his flames or his venom for fear that it would give his identity away. Owen transitioned further into phase two before he bent his knees slightly and raised his claws...ready to pounce. At that moment, he heard a grunt from behind him.

Owen turned his head and saw one of the mercenaries, that had a gun, laying on the ground dead. It appeared his neck was snapped by how his head was unnaturally laying on the ground. Then, another grunt as one of the nearby female mercenaries, that also had a gun, was heard as she fell to the ground with a broken neck as well.

The remaining few that held a gun began to fire blindly into the night at any hint of a sound or figure. Luckily, between the guns having silencers and the condos being made of solid brick, along with being located across the street from the parking lot, there would not be any attention brought to them. Owen turned to see the next mercenary lying on the ground with his heart lying next to him. Then, a man's head rolled across the ground as the next gunman fell to the ground. Only one gun-yielding mercenary was left and she was trembling in fear. Her eyes were wide open as she looked all around. Her gun was empty so she tossed it to the ground. "See, no gun. I am out of bullets," she exclaimed as her voice quivered. None of the other mercenaries, or even their leader, would go near her. Instead, they all slowly shook their heads and backed up. She stood alone, asking for help. Then, Owen saw the brutal assassin. It was Caine.

He stood behind the woman with his blood-soaked hands and a sinister smile as his red eyes stared at her. She slowly turned around when she noticed all eyes moved from her, to behind her. When she saw Caine, she punched him in the face but it didn't faze him. "My turn," Caine said before he pulled her close to him and then drove his fangs into her neck. In a matter of seconds, he released her bloodless body onto the ground.

Caine used his forearm to wipe the blood from his lips before he addressed everybody. "Now it's a fair fight. You may continue."

"Thanks, but you are not even going to help with the others?" Owen asked as he stood up straight and shrugged his shoulders.

"I already killed five of them for you. There are only one, two, three…seven left. Come on now. You are the great hybrid. This should be easy for you," Caine sarcastically replied as he leaned against a tree and smiled at Owen.

"Thanks," Owen responded while he rolled his eyes and shook his head in disbelief. He then turned to his opponents, who at this point had regrouped and were standing in front of him. Owen's eyes narrowed while he squared off against them.

The first person rushed Owen and slashed at him with his knife but he was able to grab the mercenary's arm and thrust his other hand into his chest. Not realizing his own strength and intensity, Owen's hand made it through the other side of the mercenary, besides just stopping at his heart. The other mercenaries took a step back since from their angle, all they could see his Owen's hand holding the man's heart outside of his own body. Owen pulled his arm out of the person's body and let him fall to the ground, twitching for a moment before he died in a pool of blood.

Owen didn't waste any time. He growled and then tossed the

heart at the group. As they moved away from the man's heart, Owen dashed toward them. He used the distraction to his advantage as he slashed the first woman's throat and then followed up with another slash to the chest of one of the male mercenaries. With his claws tearing through the flesh of each one, they dropped to the ground instantly. The next mercenary drove his blade down toward Owen, which he grabbed and redirected the man's arm to drive the dagger into the heart of the other attacker next to Owen. Then, before the mercenary could realize what just happened, Owen snapped his neck.

The last human mercenary was trembling but she still attacked. She swung at Owen with her brass knuckles which landed across Owen's cheek, which caused him to be dazed for only a moment. As she brought her arm back for another swing Owen charged her and dug his claws into her shoulders as he drove her back into the tree. The impact from the tree caused her to stop yelling in pain since she was now barely conscious. He then yanked her forward and drove his fangs into her neck and pumped her full of venom. Moments later her body became rigid and she toppled over. Between her bluish skin and her eyes that rolled back in her head, Owen could tell that the venom had killed her. At this point, he wasn't worried about anyone finding out his identity, for probably the same reason as Caine. Owen knew that none of his opposition would leave there alive.

The last man growled as he charged Owen. His first slash cut Owen on the arm that he used to block the attack. He winced but could not retaliate since the man followed up with a front kick to Owen's midsection. He grabbed his stomach as he stumbled back a few steps. The man sent another kick toward Owen's head which Owen aggressively swatted away as he grunted. The stranger fell to the ground and held his leg from where Owen's claws gouged him.

"Who sent you? What creature is inside the gem?" Owen loudly asked.

The man did not respond. He simply snarled and went on the offensive again. He went to tackle Owen but he used the man's momentum to hip-toss him to the ground. Then, Owen jumped on top of the stranger and held him down while the stranger tried to snap at Owen with his fangs. Owen took in a deep breath and yelled into the guy's face. As he yelled, flames shot from his mouth and began to burn the man's face. The man's high-pitched screams were loud and agonizing but short-lived, for it did not take long for the continuous flames to char the man's flesh right down to his skull. Owen let out a loud roar before pushing himself up and off his last victim.

Caine approached Owen, clapping as he did. Owen slowly came out of transitioned and turned to him. As he did, his breathing became steady as his intensity decreased.

"That was an impressive demonstration of violence, and that is saying a lot coming from me," Caine said with a crooked grin.

"I'm glad you approve. I guess your debt is paid in full now," Owen responded as he examined his wounds.

"No, it's not. That was fun for me and you probably would have still found a way to win. I take my debts seriously," Caine replied.

"Suit yourself. In any case, thanks. Any chance you can spare some of your blood? This one slash mark is a little nasty," Owen asked.

"No!" Caine spat back at Owen as his eyes turned red for a moment. "I'm not some fountain for people to drink out of as needed. Blood sharing is personal for me," Caine sternly voiced.

Owen raised his hands up, "My bad. I didn't know. It's all good. I will just walk it off. Maybe a few transitions will do the trick. At the very least, help me with the mess."

Caine nodded and the two of them gathered the bodies and placed them in a nearby dumpster. Once they were piled inside, Owen set the bodies on fire to burn whatever evidence could be found. He knew the fire would draw attention, so he quickly turned and patted Caine on the shoulder. "Thank you," Owen said. Caine nodded his head as he turned around.

"Are you just going to run all the way back?" Owen asked.

"Run…no. I am going to drive my much nicer than your vehicle back home. This is the modern age. Come on now," Caine responded as he smirked before he walked away. Owen softly chuckled at his response and headed back to his room.

Once Owen was inside the condo, he went straight into the shower to clean all the blood, dirt, and sweat from his body. Before he turned the water on, Owen examined the dried blood on his hands. Knowing it would take a while to scrub it off, he decided to take a shortcut and transitioned to let the flames cover his hands. It only took a few seconds before he transitioned back to normal and his plan worked, for the blood had burned off.

As Owen showered, he thought about the events of the night. Caine's assistance was very helpful but then Owen thought about the attackers themselves. All but one was human. That had to mean that the leader didn't have an endless army of hybrids at their disposal. It was a similar technique at the mountain during his previous mission by using an increased level of humans compared to the few hybrids scattered in. It made Owen wonder if this person's forces were starting to finally dwindle for that tactic to be used again. He then thought about how much easier it was for him to not only defeat all his opponents but how easy it was to transition back to normal after all the violence. In the past, it would have taken him a lot longer to fully recover. It was a relief for him and the thought was only interrupted by the pain he felt when he cleaned his wounds.

After his shower, Owen was able to examine his injuries closer since all the blood was cleaned off. A couple of the claw marks seemed worse than the others so he went into transition. "This is going to take forever," Owen mumbled to himself as he stood there but then he had an idea. He went deep into transition, to the point that he almost didn't recognize himself. He held it for a few minutes before returning back to normal. To his delight, Owen's plan worked and all his injuries had fully healed. Owen was still feeling exhausted after all the events of another long night so he decided to go to bed, but was detoured by the sight of blue and red lights.

Owen stepped out onto the balcony to see a handful of police cars, a couple of fire trucks, and a few ambulances. There may have been more, but from where his room was, he could not fully view the area of the parking lot or the dumpster from where he was standing. Still, he didn't want to be seen trying to look, so Owen went back inside, locked the balcony door this time, and went to bed.

Owen woke up late that morning and to his surprise, there were no messages or visitors. At first, he was concerned as to why that was the case, but then he presumed that no news was good news. After lounging around for over an hour, Owen finally received a text message from Bailey.

"*Entire group from the prior night to meet within the city tonight at nine.*" She then texted an address, which Owen looked up and it was a restaurant deep within the city itself. He figured that Avery and Hailey had to be in one of the larger hotels within the area of the restaurant.

Owen also noticed that the group text message consisted of Bailey, Michael, Abigail, Olivia, Selena, and even Caine. He presumed the late time was suggested by someone other than Bailey or Michael due to Caine's unhealthy reaction to sunlight. He wondered if he should invite Cedric to come along as well but then realized Cedric would not have the time due to how busy he was.

Time moved slowly as Owen couldn't help but watch the clock. With each passing moment, Owen's mind dwelled on him finally seeing Avery and Hailey, especially Hailey. As much as he tried to force it out of his mind and focus on the mission details, he was unsuccessful. It was midafternoon by the time Owen couldn't handle it any longer. He decided he was going to drive to the city now to beat the traffic. Once he got there, he figured he would eat and have a couple of drinks to ease his tension. Owen changed into a pair of jeans and a dark-gray t-shirt and left for the city.

The closer he drove to the city the more butterflies entered his stomach. When he finally found a place to park, it was around five o'clock. Owen walked inside a restaurant within a few blocks of the meeting location and went straight to the bar and asked for a couple of shots. He received them and he downed them quickly.

"You seem nervous. Did the shots help?" The male bartender asked.

"Not as much as I hoped but nothing a cheeseburger and fries, with water and a beer, couldn't fix," Owen responded with a half-grin.

"One nervous remedy coming up," the bartender exclaimed. Owen was relieved the bartender didn't want to play therapist and instead, tended to his other customers. The food arrived quickly which Owen scarfed down and washed the rest of it down with his drinks. He felt a little more at ease and told himself that once he got past this, good or bad, it will be better since all the wondering will finally be over. He sat there for a little while longer and watched a variety of random sports on the wall-mounted televisions, while he enjoyed some of the funny comments he heard from people sitting around him.

Owen paid his tab and then wanted to make a stop at the restroom before he left. As he made his way to the restroom, he figured with the extra time he had to spare, he would survey the area to make sure everything was safe once he left the restaurant. As Owen was walking back down the hallway from the bathroom that was in the back of the restaurant, he stopped dead in his tracks when he heard, "Owen?" The gentle voice sounded familiar to him as his eyes widened and his jaw dropped, while he quietly gasped.

CHAPTER 10

Owen took a deep breath and slowly turned around and his suspicions were correct…it was Avery. Her eyes began to water as her jaw slightly lowered while she exhaled quickly and loudly. She stood there, motionless except for the slight quiver of her lips. She stood only a handful of feet away from Owen. Regardless of how much he was caught off-guard to see her, he still smiled. He forgot how happy Avery made him and how much it filled his heart with joy to see her again.

"Hey, little sister. It's been a long time," Owen softly said. Avery's eyes immediately turned sky-blue as her brow lowered. She then gritted her teeth and charged him. The move surprised Owen as she grabbed him by the front of his shoulders and forced him out the back door. She continued to push him across the alleyway and into the next building. Owen grunted from the impact while Avery held him against the wall.

"How dare you say that to me! Is this some trick to get the gem? Who are you?" Avery bellowed as her body and voice trembled from anger, yet her eyes remained glassy.

"You know who I am. I just need a moment to explain," Owen replied as he grabbed her arms and slowly, yet forcefully removed them from him.

"You are not Owen! First off, Owen couldn't remove me from him without even transitioning, and second off…I watched him die," Avery countered as her voice cracked at the end from the emotions that overwhelmed her. "I should just kill you now and be done with it," Avery added, coldly.

"Call Isaac," Owen quickly said while he raised his hands up in defense to help calm Avery down. He was doing his best to keep his voice and demeanor calm to not only help put her at ease but also to avoid having to hurt her if she attacked.

"What?" Avery asked. Owen's words sidetracked the overflow of emotions she was feeling as her brow crinkled.

"Call him and ask about me," Owen responded. Avery reached into her pocket and pulled out her phone and clicked a few buttons. She raised it to her ear while she kept an eye on Owen.

"It's me. Do you have something to tell me? Specifically, about Owen?" Avery asked while she attempted to suppress how furious she was. Owen could hear Isaac speaking but he could not make out what he was saying due to the street noise off in the distance. After just a few seconds, Avery hung up the phone while Isaac was still talking. She looked at Owen and her eyes transitioned back to human and as her sky-blue eyes vanished, a river of tears formed as she approached Owen with her arms out. As the two embraced, Avery buried her head into Owen's chest and began to bawl. Owen held her tight while one of his hands rubbed her back. Shortly after, he kissed the top of her head and rested his own head on top of hers while she continued to cry.

"If this continues, I am going to have to go home and change into a dryer shirt," Owen whispered to help cheer Avery up.

"Shut up," Avery chuckled as she backed up a couple of feet from Owen while wiping his chest and then her face. "How…how is it possible? I watched the chimera turn to stone."

"It's a long story that I would love to go back inside and tell you about provided you won't try to crush me again," Owen teased.

Avery smiled while Owen put his arm around her shoulders as the two walked back inside the restaurant. Avery led him to her booth in the back corner of the dining room. There, Owen filled her in on everything from the mountain to the present. The talk was all one-sided as Owen detailed everything out as much as he could. Avery only sat there and slowly nodded her head while her facial expressions showed a wide array of emotions. After he caught her up, Avery was silent while she stared at her drink.

"You must have something to say after all of that," Owen added to break the silence. He began to fidget as he became more nervous. Thoughts dwelled in his mind as to how Avery would accept the information he just told her.

"It's a lot to take in. I don't know where to even begin," Avery responded with a quick shake of her head to snap out of her trance. She seemed calm which Owen felt was a good sign. "Let me just start by saying words cannot express how ecstatic I am that you are alive," Avery said with a joyful smile. Her smile began to fade as she asked, "Why did you not tell me sooner?"

"Something of this magnitude I wanted to do in person for both you and Hailey. With that said, please don't tell Hailey. I rather do that in person, especially how things were left between us," Owen pleaded.

Avery sighed. "I understand and I will keep your secret but please don't make me keep something like this from Hailey for too long. She of all people would want to know that you are alive."

"I planned on doing it today when everyone met. How is she doing?" Owen asked.

"Not well at first. Heck, none of us were. For the things left unsaid and for simply just having someone close to us yanked from our lives as we watched you die. It wasn't easy. Words cannot even begin to do any justice to how I felt. Hailey mourned but then I think she buried her feelings and used this mission to distract herself. She has become the perfect little soldier as she follows orders and doesn't allow herself any free time. She has become focused and determined on returning the gem to the facility. To the point that she has become colder and colder each day. She has also become harsher and deadlier in battle. We use to be able to talk about anything but now it is more just about the mission. Even now she is scouting the area to make sure everything is secure while I am finally taking a break. I am just hoping she is using this mission as a distraction and will become more the Hailey I knew once it is all over."

Owen could see the concern on Avery's face as she spoke. He too, hoped this wasn't the new Hailey for it would be a shame for her to lose herself, especially because of him. At the same time, he probably would have used the same tactic to distract himself.

"I can only imagine how tiresome this past month has been for you, or really the past few months once the gem was found. Hopefully, now that the reinforcements have arrived, you two won't have to carry this burden alone anymore," Owen added. Even though Avery appeared to look the same as the last time that he saw her, he could tell she was worn out. It appeared that she may have lost a little weight, in addition to the dark circles around her tired eyes. If that wasn't enough, even her demeanor indicated that she felt defeated as she talked with her shoulders slumped forward.

"It would be a nice change of pace from just Hailey and me constantly on the move. Having to battle each day and sleep in shifts, with the constant stress if you are going to live to see the next day," Avery said as a single tear ran down her cheek before she wiped it off. "So yeah, it weighs on you, so having a team of people again would be wonderful. Last night was the first night that I was able to get a full night's sleep, well, full for me at this point. My body wanted to keep waking up since it was not used to all the extra sleep and comfort. Ironic isn't it," Avery added as she rolled her eyes.

"I will make it a goal of mine that you finally get some real sleep," Owen said with a sympathetic smile. He then moved to sit on the same side of the booth as Avery, putting his arm around her as he sat down. Avery laid her head on the side of his chest.

"I missed you," Avery said after a few moments of silence.

"Who wouldn't miss me, I'm awesome," Owen joked, causing Avery to giggle while she playfully punched him in his stomach. Owen then laid his head on top of Avery's head and whispered, "I missed you too." The two sat in silence as they enjoyed the moment.

"Care if we join you?" Owen's eyes drifted up to see that the voice belonged to Michael and next to him was Bailey.

"Hey!" Avery called out as her joyful smile returned. Owen left the booth to allow Avery to greet them. She, of course, gave them both a huge hug. As always, it made Owen smile to see Bailey tolerating the hug from Avery. It seemed some things didn't change.

"Did you guys just happen to run into each other?" Bailey inquired.

"Pretty much. It caught me off-guard but it worked out," Owen replied.

"I wish I could have seen the look on both of your faces when that happened," Michael added.

"Well, she didn't think it was me at first, so her face was more of an I'm going to end you while mine was more ouch, ouch, ouch," Owen said, jokingly. Avery simply smiled and shrugged her shoulders. The group laughed and chatted for a bit as Bailey and Michael caught Avery up on everything with them.

"Sorry everyone, but I need to get moving. I promised Hailey I would sweep this area before we meet up with everyone else later," Avery informed.

"Wait, do you have the gem with you now?" Michael inquired.

"Nope, Hailey has it. Her thought process was if we were to get ambushed, she could just fly away," Avery responded.

"Do you want me, or any of us, to come with you?" Owen asked.

"Thanks, but I got this. The threat decreased dramatically once we arrived in the city so it was more to put her mind at ease. I'll catch up with you later," Avery said but she didn't get a chance to say goodbye. She was distracted by the parents at the booth a couple of spots away trying desperately to find something to light the candle for their daughter's birthday. The child seemed young, maybe four years old, and was beginning to pout as her eyes started to water. The waitress was apparently off trying to find a match or a lighter.

Owen put his hand on Avery's shoulder and whispered, "I'll be right back." He then strolled over to the booth and in a very pleasant and polite tone of voice, asked the parents, "May I help you with the candle?" They both responded in desperation, "Please! Thank you!" Owen then turned his attention to the little girl. "Wow, that candle says you are going to be five years old. You are becoming a big girl now. Do you want to use magic to light the candle?" Owen nicely asked the girl. She wiped the tears from her face and smiled while she nodded.

"Are you sure you want to do magic now, Owen?" Bailey called out.

"It will be fine. Don't be jealous because you can't do magic," Owen replied and then winked.

"I will only need one thing," Owen continued as he glanced around. "Ah, may I borrow your sunglasses?" Owen asked the mother. She agreed and handed them over. The mother's brow was arched and she grinned with anticipation as to what Owen was going to do next.

"Those are girl glasses," the little girl said while giggling.

"I know. It's just for a moment in case the light gets too bright for my eyes but you are a big girl now so you will be fine," Owen replied while he put on the sunglasses. He then placed his finger on the candle wick. "When you are ready, I want you to touch my hand and say the word fire. You must yell it so that your voice is strong enough to make my magic work. Okay?" The girl smiled and nodded her head again. She then put her tiny hand on top of Owen's and said "fire" but nothing happened. She looked at Owen and began to pout.

"Remember, you have to yell it for my magic to work," Owen reminded her. She smiled as her eyes narrowed. She then yelled "fire!" As she did, Owen transitioned and had enough control to only transition his eyes while in phase two. With the sunglasses masking his transition, he used that same concentration and was able to send fire to just the one finger that was needed. As he did, the candle wick was lit.

"Wow!" The little girl said with her eyes and mouth wide open in astonishment. The parents had similar reactions. Owen then heard applause from behind him. He turned his head and noticed that all the customers in the area, including the staff, had turned to watch. Included within the staff was the waitress who returned and was holding the requested lighter.

"Ouch. This is hot. Can you blow out my finger before you blow out your candle?" Owen asked as he turned back to the little girl and pretended the fire was hot. The girl's eyes widened and her smile grew before she blew on Owen's finger with all her might. As she did, the flame vanished as Owen transitioned back to normal. "Yay!" The little girl yelled out as she smiled from ear to ear while she clapped her hands.

Everyone around them began to applaud again for both the little girl, as well as Owen. As he glanced around, Owen noticed Avery, Michael, and Bailey were slowly clapping but their eyes and mouths were wide open with shock. Avery's face finally converted to a smile as she began to clap faster. Owen then heard some clapping that was louder than the rest. He turned his head in the opposite direction and saw Abigail and Olivia both clapping and smiling; however, Olivia's eyes were tearing up. Before Owen could walk away, everyone sang happy birthday to the little girl. She then blew out the candle and her attention was solely on the cake now.

"Thank you," the girl said as she quickly glanced over to Owen before she began to run her finger along the side of the cake to get a tasty sample of the chocolate icing.

"You're welcome," Owen replied to the girl and as he was about to take off the mother's sunglasses, Abigail swooped in and flung her arm around Owen's neck, and pulled him closer. "I definitely need a picture of this," Abigail said as she raised her phone in front of them. She then snapped a picture of them while they both made goofy faces. He then returned the glasses and parted ways with the family.

Owen turned to Olivia who seemed to be slightly more upset. "Are you okay?" Owen inquired.

"Yeah, it's just dusty in here, or my allergies or something," Olivia stuttered as she turned and left the room. Both Owen and Abigail looked at each other with crinkled brows before they both shrugged their shoulders and headed over to the rest of the group.

"Kind of a bold move, don't you think?" Bailey addressed Owen with a stern look.

"It will be okay. I had sunglasses on. Besides...people do street tricks that are leaps and bounds more magical than what I just did over there. Live a little," Owen nonchalantly replied as he winked. Bailey simply shook her head.

"It was for a little girl's birthday. I know you got a heart somewhere deep in there," Owen playfully added. Bailey scoffed but smiled right after.

"It was a bold yet sweet gesture," Avery commented as she nudged Owen and smiled.

"Yes, it was, but it was also smooth. Imagine lighting a woman's cigarette using that move. It's a sure win to get her number," Abigail added as she smiled and moved closer to him.

"Where did you think I got the idea from," Owen said while turning to look at Avery. At first, Avery looked at Owen with a crinkled brow until she realized what he meant.

"Oh my gosh, you remember that?" Avery responded as her face lit up.

"How could I forget? It was when we were hiking through the Alps during the last mission," Owen responded as he smiled.

"Is this...Hailey?" Abigail asked while slightly tilting her head as her eyes drifted over to Avery.

"No, sorry...Avery, Abigail...Abigail, Avery," Owen said while gesturing back and forth between them. The two of them smiled and shook hands.

"Sorry. The way you two act together just made me think otherwise," Abigail added with a crooked grin as she turned her attention to Owen.

"Oh...we are just close," Avery stuttered.

"Yeah...we're just close friends. That's all," Owen stuttered as well.

"Hmm...I see," Abigail replied. She then pressed her lips tightly together to hold back a large smile as she continued to stare at him. Owen briefly smiled but then scoffed and looked away.

"Well, I should go check on Olivia. It was a pleasure meeting you, Avery. See you all soon," Abigail said as she smiled at Avery and then briefly touched Owen's arm before leaving.

Avery turned to Owen, "Abigail, as in the chimera, Abigail?"

"That would be her," Owen responded.

"You failed to mention how beautiful she is...and friendly too," Avery said in a deadpan manner.

"I didn't think it was relevant and don't forget, Olivia was here too. Olivia, the vampire," Owen said in a nervous attempt to change the subject. Avery only responded with an arch of her brow.

"Nothing happened between her and I. Just two fellow chimeras. Besides, I'm still trying to figure her out and I'm not going to start anything with anybody until I have talked with Hailey," Owen quickly added in defense.

"Even when she showered at his place, nothing happened," Michael added.

"Seriously! Not helping," Owen loudly whispered while slowly turning his head toward Michael with his eyes wide open. Michael just stood there and smiled. Owen turned to Avery and her eyes widened and her arms crossed with the comment.

"Yes, even when she took a shower at the condo, nothing happened. I saw nothing...I did nothing. They were there too and can confirm it," Owen briskly said while pointing at Bailey and Michael.

Avery busted out into laughter. "I'm just messing with you. I trust you, Owen. I just wanted to see how flustered I could make you." Owen lowered his head and chuckled to himself.

"I really need to get going. Bye, everyone!" Avery energetically replied. She then gave Owen a quick peck on his cheek before leaving.

After Avery left, Owen turned to Michael. "Gee, thanks for the help."

"Anytime," Michael replied as he laughed and patted Owen on the arm. Owen couldn't help but laugh along with Michael. Moments later, Abigail and Olivia returned.

"Sorry about that," Olivia casually said as she put her arm around Michael's shoulders, causing him to smile and place his hand on her lower back. Owen enjoyed seeing how great the chemistry was between them.

"We got a couple of hours to kill before we meet up with everyone. Let's do a quick sweep of the area just to be sure we don't walk into an ambush," Abigail suggested.

"As much fun as that sounds, Avery and Hailey are already doing that," Bailey countered.

"Then we expand the area. Search outside of their radius just in case reinforcements are on their way," Olivia added.

"That's not a bad idea. Besides, I need something to distract me," Owen said as he stood next to Olivia, Michael, and Abigail.

Bailey rolled her eyes, "Sure, why not? I didn't want to relax anyway."

The group paid their bill and left to scout the area. They figured Avery and Hailey would have a search perimeter of about one mile from the rendezvous so the group decided to start two miles out and work their way in. They walked up and down the side streets, alleyways, and even the main street and nothing seemed out of place.

It was dark now; however, the lights from the main street and the tall buildings made it seem earlier than it really was. At this point, they were all walking down the main street. There was less traffic and people on the main street, but not few enough for someone to easily try to make a move on them. Each step Owen took made him feel more and more anxious. It was to the point that he heard the rest of his friends talking but their words may as well have been in a foreign language. His mind was racing with thoughts of what to say when he finally saw Hailey.

"Look, there is Caine and Selena up ahead," Olivia mentioned as she waved. Those words were powerful enough to snuff out the oxygen around Owen. He nervously glanced up and sure enough, he saw Selena waving back while Caine slightly smiled, but that is all that he saw. He felt relief for just a moment before his brow crinkled. Owen began to wonder why it was just Selena and Caine there. Everyone came together and exchanged pleasantries.

"Where are Avery and Hailey?" Michael asked while he looked around.

"I don't know. We are a few minutes early so they may be here soon," Selena mentioned. The group randomly chatted for the next few minutes as they waited. During that time, every female face that resembled anything close to Hailey's made Owen's eyes dart toward them in fear.

"It's now thirty minutes past the mark and no sign of them and they are not answering their phones. Something is wrong," Bailey commented.

"I agree. We need to search the area. It is later now and the crowds have thinned even more. Maybe someone made a move on them," Owen suggested as his mind switched from fear to worried.

"We should split up to cover more ground faster," Abigail suggested. Everyone agreed and split into groups which consisted of

Caine and Selena; Bailey, Michael, and Olivia; and Abigail and Owen. The groups then fanned out in all directions in search of Hailey and Avery. More time passed as Abigail and Owen walked further away from the main street. Both were now using their chimera eyes to scan for them but even with the clearer vision, there was still no luck.

"Where can they be?" Owen frustratingly muttered.

"They have to be somewhere," Abigail replied but her response trailed off as she put her hand abruptly on Owen's chest to stop him from walking. Her eyes were fixated on the top of a nearby skyscraper. "What were Hailey's unique abilities?"

"Flying and lightning, why?" Owen asked as his eyes followed her line of sight to the top. His eyes then squinted to try to reveal what Abigail was seeing. Then, he saw a quick arc of electricity at the top of the building, causing his eyes to widen. He then looked back at Abigail.

"Well either the building has a short or we just found your friends," Abigail commented as she looked at Owen.

"We've got to go! Now!" Owen spurted out as he extended his claws and squared off to the wide-based building.

Abigail grabbed his arm, which caused Owen to look back at her and slightly growl. "Easy there. We can't scale that entire building. It's too tall and the glass windows add an additional challenge. Even if you made it to the top with your heightened abilities you would be too tired and worthless to help." Owen's face became stern as he looked back and forth between Abigail and the roof. "I know they mean a lot to you but we have to be smart about it," Abigail added but then her brow arched. "I have an idea. Tuck your chimera away and follow me." As much as Owen wanted to rush to their aid, Abigail was right. He followed her lead as they ran to one of the nearest doors.

The two rushed into the lobby, causing the security guard to abruptly stand up and put his hand out. "Whoa, slow down. This building is closed. Only authorized personnel can be in here," the guard said loudly. The two slowed down in response to the guard.

"Sorry, it's an emergency. We are trying to get in touch with somebody," Abigail said in a scared, frantic voice.

The guard became more relaxed, "It will be okay. Tell me their name and I will see if they are still here or not."

"Yes, thank you. Her name is Selena Caine," Abigail responded in the same frantic tone of voice while Owen stood behind her trying to mask his bewildered look.

"I don't see that name in the system. Are you sure she works here?" The guard inquired as he looked up from his computer screen.

"Oh, my phone is buzzing," Abigail said as she quickly took out her phone and looked at the screen, which Owen could see was blank. "It's her! This is the wrong building and she is actually looking for us. I'm so sorry. I feel like such an idiot," Abigail said while holding her head and putting her phone away.

"Not a problem. Glad it worked out," the guard added with a hint of a smile and a small pat on her shoulder.

"Thank you anyway," Abigail said while giving the guard a hug before turning around and leaving. Owen followed her but was perplexed about what that scene was about. When the guard's back was turned, Abigail darted around the corner with Owen right behind her.

"What was that about?" Owen loudly whispered.

"That was about me getting the access card for the elevators," Abigail replied while she dangled the card in front of Owen.

Owen lightly chuckled, "You picked his pocket. Nice. I bet your friend Selena Caine would approve."

"I'm sure she would," Abigail said while winking. "Now, let's go help your friends." The two took the furthest elevator from the guard all the way to the top floor. Luckily, the elevator moved fast and there were no stops with the lack of people in the building. Even with the quick ascent, Owen was jittery with anticipation of whatever battle they were about to walk into to save his friends. Not just friends, but two people that meant so much to him. While in the elevator, Owen remembered to text his other friends with their whereabouts for them to assist. The elevator door finally opened and the two ran to the nearest stairwell and followed it to the roof. They reached the top but the door was stuck so Owen kicked the door wide open before the two walked onto the rooftop.

The roof was just as wide as the base of the building, with a flat gravel surface. At a quick glance, Owen could see a few HVAC units located throughout the rooftop and lights that surrounded the edges of the roof, which seemed to be more decorative since the roof itself was not well-lit. However, Owen did notice a handful of dead bodies scattered about. Then, Owen's eyes were redirected to the fighting that was going on in different areas on the roof.

To the left of them, near the far side of the back corner of the building. There appeared to be someone but Owen couldn't tell who it was since they were pinned face-first on the ground by six other individuals. This did not last long for Owen saw a flash of light, followed by sparks that sent most of them tumbling off the pile. It was obvious at that point it was Hailey, whom Owen could see her straining to push herself off the ground with all the weight on top of her. More sparks flew which illuminated her area, allowing Owen to see that a heavyset man was doing most of the work of holding her down. The flashes of light revealed his skin to have a gray, rigid tone to it and the bolts from Hailey were not doing much against him. From Owen's viewpoint, it was difficult to ascertain what type of creature the man was, but it was obvious that Hailey was in trouble.

Owen then quickly turned his attention to the commotion on the opposite corner of the roof, which involved Avery and another handful of attackers. What made Owen nervous was how dangerously close she was standing with her back to the edge of the roof. Avery sent her fist hard into the throat of one of the men, causing him to stumble back and then fall to the ground. He rolled around for a moment while holding his neck before becoming still.

With Avery out of position from attacking the other person, one of the assailants took the opportunity to send his fist slamming into the side of Avery's face. The impact caused her body to turn but she immediately retaliated with a strong backhand. The back of her fist landed right under the man's chin and it sent him flying backward into the side of the small three-foot wall that lined the rooftop. His head smacked the edge of the wall, which caused him to go limp as he toppled over to the ground. The blood splatter from the impact turned a nearby light from white to pink. At that point, the remaining three rushed Avery. All three of them grabbed her and began to push her back and with the gravel, it was difficult for Avery to hold them back as she slid.

"She's in trouble," Owen quickly commented to Abigail as he sprinted toward Avery. He knew both Hailey and Avery were in trouble, but Hailey's creature was more powerful and even more, could fly. As much as he wanted to help them both, they were too far apart.

"I'll help Hailey," Abigail called out to Owen as she darted toward Hailey.

Owen heard Abigail and felt relieved she would help Hailey but it was only for a moment, for his concentration was refocused back to Avery. As Owen ran, he transitioned to give himself more speed and better footing on the gravel. Every second counted at this point and he also needed to be ready to fight as soon as he got to Avery. The need to help and protect Avery grew stronger with each step.

Avery slid far enough back to where her backfoot was now against the wall, which in a way, helped since she now had enough footing to use her strength again. She used her new advantage to send a headbutt to the person in the middle. The impact caused the attacker to release her grip and take a few steps back while she held her head. She then shrugged the other two off her and in time, the female attacker shook off the headbutt and came after Avery again.

As the woman sent her fist at Avery, she grabbed her wrist and sidestepped out of the way. Avery used the attacker's momentum to her advantage by pulling her wrist with one arm while shoving her in the back with the other arm. This jolt sent the woman screaming over the edge.

Before Owen could enjoy the fact that Avery took out another attacker, his eyes grew wide and he gasped as the other two attackers whom she shrugged off, charged at her again. He was thirty feet away and could not run any faster and Avery was too close to the men for him to use his fire. Both men rammed their shoulders into Avery, sending her plummeting over the edge.

Owen unleashed an angry roar while he flung his hands in front of him and projected fire toward the two men. The flames engulfed them as they flailed about and yelled in agony. Owen didn't slow down but he did increase the length of his strides the closer he got to the ledge. The only thought that was on his mind was to save Avery at all costs. That thought stayed with Owen as he leaped from the roof's ledge in a swan dive fashion.

CHAPTER 11

As Owen was in midair, it felt as if time had stopped. He looked down and could see Avery's terrified facial expression as she flailed her arms about and screamed as she plummeted. Everything then sped up as Owen started his descent and that is when he quickly realized that his momentum was leading him into the adjacent building. He had to think quickly or else he would slam into the glass head first or even worse, break through the glass and lose all hopes of saving Avery.

When Owen was close enough to the glass, he tucked his body and used every muscle he had to perform a somersault in the air. The move was successful for now his feet were about to hit the glass but he still feared he would go through it. Owen felt he had to do more so he spaced his feet apart to distribute the weight of the impact. He hoped between that and losing some momentum from the somersault that he would not break through the glass. He knew the glass on these types of buildings would be sturdy, but it could only handle so much. In addition, to lessen the impact he knew he must not lock his knees. Instead, he needed to bend his knees to absorb more of the impact to save himself from a serious injury and to decrease the likelihood of him fully breaking the glass.

Owen smashed into the glass, causing it to crack in several

places but luckily it did not shatter completely. He used every ounce of power to propel himself from his crouched position as soon as he hit the glass. He was now soaring toward Avery like a bullet. She was falling flat with her back facing the rapidly approaching ground. He reached out to Avery to grab ahold of her but she was still a few feet out of range. Her eyes widened and she stopped screaming once she saw Owen come within range of her, but the look of terror was still evident on her face. Fear filled Owen from the thought of him not being able to save her but he kept his arm stretched. Avery stuck out her hand…their fingertips were merely inches away.

Finally, he was able to grab her hand and yank himself toward her, embracing her as he did. A new problem now presented itself in the form of the stone bottom section of the building quickly approaching. "Hold on!" Owen yelled, causing Avery to wrap her arms around him tightly and bury her head into his chest. He placed one of his arms on her back while using his hand from that same arm to cradle her head. There was no easy way to slow down their momentum besides trying to use the chimera's climbing ability and dexterity to survive the fall or at least allow Avery to survive. In order to do this, Owen had to take the brunt of all the impacts. He knew her creature was tough but he didn't want to take any chances. He went deep into transition in hopes that it would save them both.

As they were about to crash into the stone wall of the building, Owen observed imperfections, cracks, and small ledges under the windows. He twisted his body around just as they slammed into the building. This allowed him to use his free hand to grab anything that he could use to slow their descent. The initial impact knocked the wind from Owen, as the pain from the impact itself coursed throughout his entire body. It felt like he was hit by a car and from the pain, he knew he had to have broken a few bones in his ribs, arm, and shoulder. He gritted his teeth and endured the pain because he had no choice but to push through it. Owen hit the building hard enough to damage the few things that he planned to grab onto. This caused him to continue to fall at an alarming rate. Dazed from the impact, Owen had enough sense that he was close enough to the building to dig his claws into the side of the building as they fell. The screeching from the claws scraping along the stone was quite audible but mild compared to the searing pain he was feeling in his fingertips. Owen clenched his teeth before he yelled and growled from both pain and determination.

He was slowing down, but not fast enough. During this, Avery stayed glued to Owen with her face still buried into his chest as he continued to hold onto her. To keep Avery's arms from being scraped along the building like Owen's body was, he had to contort his back just enough to keep her from harm. Regardless of the dizziness and excruciating pain he was experiencing, his will to not give up remained strong. Owen caught a glimpse of a ledge slightly off to the right of him that if he could make it over to it, could possibly help stop their fall. He had to chance it.

Owen used his feet to push himself in the direction of the ledge which he succeeded; however, that moment of joy was short-lived. He grunted from the pain that shot through his legs from absorbing the force of the impact. Not only that, but the ledge also began to crumble so Owen had to think quickly for the few seconds he had left. His only option now was to leap toward the alleyway that was around forty feet away. It was a risky move because of the pain and injuries he already sustained.

As Owen began to push off the ledge it fully gave away, which caused him to only have a partial push off from the ledge. Now, there was no way he could land on his feet. As Owen plummeted, his only course of action to protect Avery was to wrap both his arms around her and try to maneuver himself enough so he would take the full impact of the fall. Owen held onto her tight and as they were about to crash onto the ground, Owen twirled his body in order to hit the pavement first. Owen slammed into the ground and the two of them tumbled, while still holding onto each other, another handful of feet before finally coming to a stop.

Avery, who ended up on top of Owen, rolled off him as his arms flopped to each side of him. Besides the wounds she had from the battle on the rooftop, Avery only sustained a few minor scrapes and bruises from the fall itself. On the other hand, Owen's injuries were substantially worse.

His vision was blurry but from what he could see were many large cuts, scrapes, and bruises. They were especially worse on the side that took the brunt of the slide down the building. He could barely move his hand and even when he tried to move it, he was in severe pain. It appeared some of his claws were also broken, along with his fingers. That was his guess since it was hard to even notice anything with his hand covered in blood, loose skin, and fur. He tried to roll over to his side but grimaced and stopped as the pain coursed through his body. Owen presumed he must have broken even more of his bones when he hit the pavement. It was difficult to pinpoint where the broken bones were since the pain radiated all over his body.

He was deep into a level three transition, so he figured he transition down some to take the edge off being so close to a full transition. When he did, the pain became immensely worse so he had to hold his current state of transition. Owen became fearful. Part due to his current condition but the bigger part was how long could he sustain a deep level three transition without turning into the chimera.

Owen could see Avery talking to him but her words were muffled. He could barely tell it was her due to his frosted vision, which was now becoming more tunnel-like. He turned his head away from Avery to cough up blood. Then, he turned his head back to see Avery look up at something that caught her attention. At first, she seemed as if she quickly raised her fist but then lowered it just as fast. It then appeared she was talking to someone and then nodded her head as she wiped her eyes and backed away. Owen could feel the chimera gaining more and more control.

"Run…can't hold. Kill me," Owen weakly said as it took a lot of effort to push those words past his lips. At this point, he saw no other option but to kill him now before the chimera had free reign of the city or even worse, kill any of his friends. He then saw what appeared to be Selena's face appear from behind his head. Her head was mirrored over his own while it hovered just a foot above his. She gently smiled as she placed her hands on the sides of his face. Even with his blurred vision, he could still make out that her face and hair became pure white as she lowered her head toward his. When her forehead touched Owen's, he saw nothing but a bright white light. He could then feel his pain melting away and the chimera becoming more at ease. He couldn't tell how much time passed before the light vanished and it was just the night sky above him.

Owen slowly sat up and quickly examined himself. He was not in transition anymore and not only were all his wounds healed, he didn't even feel sore. He glanced off to the side and noticed the attacker that Avery threw off the roof was lying on the ground in an unnatural way. He was glad that he and Avery did not share that same fate.

Owen rose to his feet and turned around to see Avery, Michael, Bailey, Olivia, Selena, and Caine. All of them were standing in awe of what just occurred except for Selena and Caine. Selena was on one knee with her hair half white and half dark and her fair skin had returned minus some white blotches. Caine was kneeling beside her with his hand on her back.

"She just needs a moment. She had to go deep into transition to save you," Caine said as he glared at Owen.

"Which, I'm grateful for her help," Owen responded before he turned his attention to Avery. "Are you okay?"

Avery nodded her head as she approached him and gave him a big kiss on his cheek before she wrapped her arms around Owen and squeezed. While returning the hug, Owen whispered, "If you keep squeezing me like this, I will need Selena to heal me again."

Avery chuckled, followed by a sniffle before she took a step back from Owen.

"Are you okay?" Avery asked.

"Yeah...actually, never better," Owen replied while looking over himself again. His torn, blood-soaked clothes reminded him about how close he came to dying.

"Good," Avery paused a moment before she began to slap Owen a few times on his chest and arm. "You can't fly, Owen. Why would you do that?" Avery frustratingly asked Owen with her brows knitted and firmly pressing her lips together after she spoke.

"Gee, Owen...thanks for saving my life," Owen sarcastically responded.

"Owen!" Avery exclaimed.

Owen sighed. "Because I care about you. So yeah, I will do whatever it takes to keep you alive and if you are mad at me about it then fine. I rather you be mad and alive than dead," Owen frustratingly replied. He paused to compose himself and before Avery could respond, he continued in a calm tone, "I don't know what I would do with myself if it was the latter."

The tension in Avery's face eased. "I get it and don't get me wrong...I am thrilled to be alive and there is no amount of me saying thank you that will cover what you did for me." Avery paused. "I just care about you a great deal and I don't want to be the reason why you are dead," Avery responded with a gentle voice.

"Then I guess to move past this crossroad we just don't die. Fair enough," Owen commented with a hint of a smile and a wink.

"Deal," Avery lightly chuckled as she hugged Owen. He looked over and noticed that Selena had fully converted back and was standing next to Caine. Owen mouthed the words, "Thank you," to her which she replied with a smile and a small nod. Michael and Bailey seemed to be still in shock from the events that just unraveled as they stood there, speechless.

"Impressive," Olivia commented while she smiled and held

Michael's hand. Owen smiled and shrugged his shoulders the best he could while he continued to hug Avery.

As Owen and Avery finally released from their hug, he gasped before saying, "Abigail and Hailey are still fighting on the roof." It slipped his mind with everything he just went through.

Michael's eyes grew wider, but not at Owen, but at what was behind him. "I don't think they are on the roof anymore," Michael said calmly and slightly under his breath.

Owen's eyes briefly widened after Michael's comment. His eyes then drifted to Avery who whispered, "It will be okay," while she grinned and placed her hand on his chest. He was surprised she didn't comment on how hard his heart was beating. Owen quickly smiled at Avery and took a deep breath. It was now finally time to face Hailey.

Owen turned around and the instant he did, Hailey stopped dead in her tracks. Her jaw dropped and her eyes both widen and became glassy as she put one hand on her chest and the other shakingly pointing at Owen. "It's impossible. That can't be you. Who are you!" Hailey screamed as her eyes emanated a fierce white glow and thunder shook the area. Owen could see Abigail behind Hailey glancing up into the sky.

"It's Owen. I already confirmed it with Isaac," Avery hastily called out while stepping to the side of Owen.

"How did you do that so fast? Also, how are you not even fazed by his presence?" Hailey asked as she tilted her head and her brow crinkled while her eyes transitioned back.

Avery hung her head for a moment before she looked back at Hailey, "Because I already saw him earlier today," Avery's voice was solemn.

"Excuse me. You knew and you didn't tell me. How could you do that?" Hailey asked as her voice trembled. Owen could hear the pain in her voice.

"I asked her not to tell you. I wanted to do it in person," Owen blurted out. Hailey looked at Avery and Owen and merely shook her head as she raised her hands up. She then turned around and began to walk away.

"Hailey, stop. Let's talk about this," Avery called out while she walked after her. "Hailey!" Avery called out again, but louder. She didn't respond or look behind her. Instead, she darted into the sky and vanished.

"Not fair!" Avery yelled into the night sky.

"I didn't mean to upset her," Owen quietly said.

"She is probably madder at me than anything else. I will text her everything and once she reads it and calms down, she will come around. Then, I will hopefully be able to talk to her some more and you will be able to chat with her as well," Avery responded while she grabbed her phone to text Hailey.

Owen didn't know how to feel. Part of him felt horrible for upsetting Hailey, while another portion of him felt hurt by her reaction. Even if she was upset at them, she could have stayed and talked it out, especially under the circumstances. Owen began to wonder...was she not at least a little happy that he was alive? He stared into the sky until Abigail broke his concentration.

"Sorry, not the best timing but we need to go. A lot just went down and this place will be swarming with police, news people, and everyone else." She lightly touched the side of Owen's arm and had a sympathetic face. Owen nodded and the group left the scene. They didn't go directly to the main street but instead, took a few side streets until they reached a different section of the main street. The group then proceeded to the hotel.

"Why don't you stay with us for a while?" Bailey offered to Avery.

"Thanks, but going off their behavior this past month, after an attack like that, they won't try anything until they gather more forces. Besides, the hotel is safe...for now at least. Isaac is bringing some fresh supplies and should be here hopefully soon so once Marcus and

Isaac are here, we will have even more backup. Besides, I should wait for Hailey," Avery replied while the group followed her to the hotel.

"Well, then I guess I am getting a room at the hotel tonight as well. Sorry, but I'm not leaving you alone. You need all the support you can get and what if they decide to change it up and send in a second wave," Bailey countered.

"She makes a good point so count me in. I will stay at the hotel tonight as well," Michael added. He then looked over to Olivia who smiled and gave him a side hug as they walked.

"I already know arguing will be pointless so I will just say thank you," Avery added with a hint of a smile.

"I would stay too but until things with Hailey and I cool down, it will probably be best that I give her some space. I can continue to work with the others in finding out what is inside that gem and who is after it," Owen mentioned with a hint of defeat in his voice.

"Be careful," Avery said while giving Owen a hug.

"You too," Owen replied as Avery smiled and turned around, and walked into the hotel. Owen turned to Bailey and Michael. "Keep her safe."

"Of course, and what's that…you want us to be safe too. How sweet," Bailey sarcastically responded. A smirk then formed on her face.

Owen lightly chuckled. "Your safety is important to me as well. Both of you." Bailey nodded before she turned around and entered the hotel. Michael gave Olivia a hug before patting Owen on the arm and entering the hotel as well.

"He'll be okay. We have been through a lot in a short time frame and Michael has survived and thrived," Owen commented to Olivia after he saw her staring at Michael as he walked away.

"I know…especially with the group of friends he has in there. The bigger concern is Hailey," Olivia replied.

"What do you mean?" Owen asked as the question caught him

off guard.

"She has the gem and is currently emotionally flying around somewhere in the city. That can't be safe for her or the gem," Olivia answered while turning to face Owen.

"She has a point," Selena added as the group huddled off to the side of the entrance to the hotel.

"Any idea where she would be?" Olivia asked.

"There is nothing in the city that has any significance to her so she could be anywhere. My guess is somewhere not accessible unless you can fly so she could be alone to collect her thoughts. At the same time, she may be a totally different person by now and be in a bar somewhere for all I know," Owen replied.

The group then discussed the possible locations of where Hailey could be; however, he did not add any input. Instead, he began to ponder how different she may be. Many months have passed since he last saw her and she could have easily changed during that time, being her feelings toward him or just her personality in general. It was hard for Owen to accept this since to him; it was like the events at the mountain just happened not too long ago.

"Owen!" Abigail yelled while grabbing his arm. He shook his head to regain his attention. "Earth to Owen, are you still with us?" Abigail asked.

"Yeah…sorry. It's just been a mentally exhausting day," Owen muttered as he turned around and began to walk away.

"Where are you going?" Olivia asked.

"Back to the condo to end this day and start fresh tomorrow," Owen replied but then stopped and turned around. "Thank you for all of your help back there on the roof," Owen gently said to Abigail who smiled and slightly nodded her head in return. Owen then turned to Selena, "Thank you again for healing me. I don't know what would have happened if you didn't."

"It was the least I could do to honor your heroic act to save Avery. It would have been a shame for you to go through all of that for it to end badly," Selena replied as she grinned.

Owen smiled. "Have a good night, everybody." With that, Owen left.

As he walked down the main street, he revisited the alleyway with Hailey over and over in his mind. Then, he was startled by a figure that was standing next to him and that came out of nowhere. It was Caine.

"You should be more mindful of your surroundings," Caine casually commented to him while he matched Owen's pace but kept his eyes forward.

"So I've been told. Do I even want to know why you are here?" Owen asked while he looked around for the others, but he did not see them.

"Merely here to inform you that I applaud your efforts in saving, what's her name…Avery. I haven't seen an act of courage to that extent in a long time. You must care for her a great deal," Caine said while still looking and walking forward with Owen.

"Thanks, but I would have done that for any of my friends," Owen replied. In his mind, he was trying to figure out Caine's motives since this was out of character for him.

"I doubt it. At least not to that extent," Caine countered with a quick glance toward Owen.

"Okay, you got me. If you fell, I would have just let you fall," Owen rebutted but with a hint of a smile when Caine looked over at him. Caine smirked at his response.

"As I just said, you must care a great deal for Avery. I can respect and identify with that. You would stop at no lengths to protect her," Caine remarked.

"True, like how you would for Selena," Owen replied and then stopped to face Caine.

"Exactly. She is the shining light in my eternal darkness. Without her, who knows what evil I would be capable of performing," Caine replied with a devious grin. Owen felt quite sure that Caine would hold true to his word. Caine continued, "Selena may not have any quarrel using her powers to save you but I will if I feel it begins to become habitual."

"I'll try to be more mindful of keeping my near-death experiences down to a minimal amount," Owen sarcastically responded. "Besides, why didn't you save me? It would have taken care of that debt you owe me," Owen inquired. He asked in hopes that it would change the topic.

"First off, as I said before, my blood isn't on tap for people to use. Second, there were too many eyes around for me to risk exposure. Finally, I was curious to see what would happen if no one assisted you," Caine answered with a large grin and a quick arch of his brow.

"At least you're honest," Owen replied as he shrugged his shoulders and began to walk to his car again. "So, when do you think Cedric will have the information I need?" Owen asked but did not hear a response. He turned to look and Caine had vanished. Owen quickly looked all around and didn't see anything. "Well, I guess it will be a quiet rest of the trip home," he mumbled to himself.

As Owen predicted and wished, the rest of his trip was quiet, minus the thoughts in his head about Hailey. He hoped that Avery would be able to talk to her and make her understand that no one was trying to emotionally harm her. He wanted the opportunity to talk to her again, but now Owen was uncertain if Hailey would want the same. Of course, he could not help but reminisce about their time back at the facility and even on their first date once they passed the test with Marcus. It made him smile and those memories were what he focused on and not the negative ones from Joshua's death and forward. He hoped they would be able to make more fond memories.

Owen awoke early the following morning and was surprised he was up so early. After everything he went through the night prior, he thought he would end up sleeping most of the day. He didn't know if it were the continuing thoughts about Hailey or Selena's healing powers that revived him more than he imagined. Either way, he was up and wide awake so he decided to get ready for the day since he wasn't sure what it would entail and when it would start.

As Owen was wrapping up, he heard a knock on the door. He froze, anxiously wondering if it was Hailey. He heard the knock on the door again but louder this time so he took a deep breath and went to answer it. Owen figured the talk had to happen sooner or later so why not get it out of the way. At least he would know where they both stood. He opened the door and saw Abigail leaning on the door frame dangling a brown bag in one hand and holding a drink tray with two coffees in the other, smiling as she did.

"Your balcony was locked," Abigail teased as she walked into his condo.

"Good morning to you too. What brings you here?" Owen curiously asked.

"It was going to be breakfast in bed but since you are the early bird today it will be breakfast on the couch. Hope you like bagels and cream cheese," Abigail commented in an upbeat tone as she made her way to the couch.

"That actually sounds really good right about now. Thank you, although I am curious as to why you are bringing me breakfast," Owen replied as he sat down and took a sip of his coffee before he prepped his bagel.

"Can't I just do something nice for a friend?" Abigail responded. Owen countered with just a side glance. Abigail sighed, "Okay, okay…after last night with Hailey I wanted to make sure you were good. Sue me."

Owen smiled over Abigail's frustrated look at being caught. "I'm good if I am distracted. If not, then my mind just dives right into the world of Hailey."

"I can imagine. In my opinion that wasn't the best move for her to just leave you hanging like that. Kind of selfish to be honest," Abigail commented before taking a bite of her bagel.

"She just got overwhelmed plus Avery's prior knowledge about me didn't help either. I probably should have found a way to tell Hailey sooner," Owen rebutted and then began to eat his bagel as well.

"You defend her because you still love her and have hope that you two will reunite again. Just don't let it cloud your judgment of what's best for you. Occasionally, you need to think about your feelings too," Abigail replied while she had a hint of a smile. Owen shrugged and continued to eat his food. What Abigail said was true but it was not easy for him to do.

The two finished their meals and cleaned up and began to chat about random subjects. Owen welcomed the distraction and the fact that Abigail always knew how to make him at ease. During the conversation, Owen heard another knock on the door. Both Abigail and himself looked at each other with crinkled brows, wondering who it would be. There was another knock on the door, followed by "Owen, it's me. Can we talk?" The voice belonged to Hailey. Owen's heart dropped to the pit of his stomach as the two of them looked at each other with their eyes wide open.

"Should I answer the door?" Abigail playfully whispered.

"I was thinking more about you leaving through the balcony," Owen hastily whispered as he stood up.

"I'm not scaling a building in broad daylight and it will become suspicious if you leave her out there for too long, so what do we do?" Abigail quietly asked.

"Go into the supply room. She shouldn't have any reason to go in there," Owen suggested. Abigail rolled her eyes and walked into the other room, closing the door behind her as she did.

Owen's heart was racing. This was it…the talk that he wanted to have yesterday, the one that he wanted to have for a long time now, was about to happen. Owen felt excited, but fear was the dominant force due to last night's events. He took another deep breath and walked to the door; his heart pounded as he opened it. As soon as he did, Hailey entered the room and gave Owen a long hug. During that moment, Owen could feel his concerns and stress melt away. It was the first act of affection that he had received from Hailey since the facility.

"Sorry, I should have done that yesterday," Hailey said as she slowly stepped away from Owen and smiled.

"Better late than never," Owen teased which caused Hailey's smile to grow.

"I'm a little wired so bear with me. I didn't sleep well last night so I am running off an obscene amount of coffee. After I flew away, I took some time to clear my head, and afterward, I returned to the hotel and cleaned myself up. Then, Avery and I had a long chat. She filled me in on everything so I am up to date and Avery and I are good. I just still can't believe you are standing here right in front of me," Hailey said as she glanced Owen over.

"Well, you are still smiling so I am guessing the talk went well," Owen commented with a crooked grin.

"Well, I don't hear any thunder so that's a good sign as well," Hailey jokingly replied which caused Owen to smile and nod his head before he continued to talk.

"I know Avery explained everything but still…I wish I could have told you sooner. Sorry. Honestly, I also wanted to see where we stood, since the last time we talked it was under…unusual circumstances. I wasn't sure if you would be happy to see me or not." Owen slightly frowned as his eyes drifted away from Hailey.

"I understand and of course, I would be happy to see you. I'm so sorry that I led you to believe that you were some monster because you are anything but one. That has been a constant regret that I have been trying to live with ever since the mountain," Hailey responded as her eyes began to swell up.

"Well, that's good to know I'm not a monster. Here's to second chances," Owen gently said with a hint of a smile and caring eyes as he moved closer to her. The news that Hailey didn't see him as a monster was a huge relief for him because he truly felt that is how she viewed him since the death of Joshua.

Hailey's face winced as she turned around and walked a few steps back before she turned back to face Owen. "I have a lot to get off my chest and I know I won't say it correctly. I'm sure I'll fumble about as I talk but I need to say it and it won't be easy. All I ask is that you just listen." Hailey said as she fidgeted in her spot while she rubbed and squeezed her hands. Owen, who suddenly became nervous about what Hailey was about to say, did a quick nod and remained silent. He could feel the butterflies in his stomach.

Hailey took a deep breath, "You wanted to talk and I kept avoiding you, and then I ended up regretting it when you died that day inside the mountain so here it is. When we were in the facility, I didn't just love you…I was in love with you. Everything about us just felt right. Then, when you had to kill Joshua, I wasn't sure what to think anymore because I didn't know if you were the same Owen I knew. I struggled between the love I felt inside of me and the fear of what monster you had become." Hailey paused while she cleared her throat and wiped a single tear from her cheek.

"Even when I came to terms with why you had to kill Joshua, the internal struggle inside of me continued. If anything, it became worse because I started to wonder if any of us, even our friends, were the same person anymore. Either way, I was stubborn and wrong to not talk to you before we left for the final journey to the mountain. For that, I am truly sorry. We should have talked. Regardless, I paid for my stubbornness when I saw you die. Even worse, I was punished with the knowledge that you died thinking that I thought you were a monster. It devastated me." Hailey rubbed her face to wipe the tears that began to roll down her cheeks. Owen was about to speak but Hailey continued.

"After that day at the mountain, I did nothing but meditate to try to get past the regret and remorse I felt. Even then, the images of the stone chimera haunted me. Then, an opportunity came once they found that gem. A chance to not only consume myself with protecting the gem and getting it to the facility but to also make sure that you didn't sacrifice yourself for nothing. Not only did it work, but it also opened my eyes to something. A realization that this job…this new life we all have now, has changed all of us…especially me. To the point that how can I have a relationship in this new life, or even experience true joy for more than a fleeting moment? I don't know how anyone like us could but for me, the answer is…I can't," Hailey said as her eyes narrowed and her posture straightened while she took a deep breath. Even with her brave front, Owen could tell it still bothered her since her eyes were still glassy.

"That's not entirely true," Owen blurted out. "Sorry, but I don't agree with everything that you just said. I do agree that for better or worse, we all have changed. What I don't agree with is what you said about the joy and relationship part. Yes, it may be harder for us but if you love someone enough, then it's worth it and can be done. As for joy…remember what I told you about finding happiness in the small moments? Sometimes that's all anyone can do, but those small moments are what stick with us and keeps us going and happy…human or not. Heck, it's no different from couples or families out there who are with someone that has a dangerous job. They make it work," Owen added calmly while he took a couple of steps forward.

Hailey raised her hand to stop him. "And there are some people that can't."

"Or don't want to," Owen was snarky in his response as he sat on the couch. He could see the direction the conversation was going and he felt Hailey had already made up her mind. At this point, his objective changed to controlling his emotions as he stared in front of him.

"It's not like that. We work in a dangerous field and I just can't handle losing someone that I am in love with at any moment. Wondering if our current conversation will be our last," Hailey calmly countered.

"Yeah…it's called life," Owen coldly commented while he continued to stare in front of him. Hailey ignored his response and continued.

"There's more. They said with time, the internal conflict between us and our creatures becomes easier, which it seems that way for the rest of us. I understand that for the people who have a rare creature it can take longer, but maybe mine is too rare to ever get to the point where the conflict eases up. You lucked out with your change back at the mountain but my conflict has not gotten any better. Not one bit. There are days that I think it's getting worse. I have tried everything that Isaac and Marcus have suggested and nothing has worked. There is no relief Owen and I'm tired…tired of the endless struggle of staying in control while this powerful creature is constantly leaning on the door," Hailey explained and then sat on the couch next to Owen and rested her head in her hands.

"Maybe Isaac can find a place for you to transition to take the edge off. Either back at the facility or some remote place where the thunderbird could roam free and not be seen," Owen suggested as he turned his head to Hailey. She rubbed her face from what Owen presumed was due to the mental exhaustion she felt.

"There is no such place. That's the problem. Everyone knows the thunderbird is a massive creature but no one knows to what extent since it is so rare. That room we transitioned in back at the facility may not even be able to contain it. As for a remote location…sure, there may be a place but there is one minor problem…the thunderbird can fly and cover great distances quickly. What if it flies away and makes it to a town or a city? That, or it gets spotted on the radar due to its size. Then what happens?" Hailey asked. Owen could hear the frustration in her voice even though her demeanor remained calm.

"I'm sure Isaac must have some plan because at some point, even if it's not until many years into the future, you will transition,"

Owen replied.

"Maybe, but until then I will live in fear of losing control. In the beginning, I felt that having all this power would help me make a difference in this world. I was even honored to have such a sacred creature within me. Now, when I think back to the time that Marcus offered us the choice to cross the threshold of that door, I wish I would have rejected the offer. Who knows…maybe if I received a lower-level creature I would not feel this way. I know it sounds bad but please understand, you haven't done anything wrong," Hailey pleaded. Owen heard what she said but he knew it still wasn't going to change the outcome.

Owen scoffed. "Are you really giving me the 'it's not you, it's me' speech." His head then slowly turned back and he continued to stare in front of him like before.

"Owen…" Hailey started to talk but was interrupted by Owen.

"So, you are never going to fall in love again and just constantly work? To never enjoy life and just keep going until you collapse? Not even try to work with Isaac on your issues? That doesn't seem like a life. It sounds horrible."

"I don't know but I had months to think about this and live that life and so far it's working for me, minus the mental fear and exhaustion of dealing with the thunderbird. Someday, I would like to have those things you mentioned. I just don't see it happening any time soon." Hailey kindly responded.

"I could wait for you so when you are ready, I will be there for you," Owen softly spoke as he glanced at Hailey. He was doing his best to swallow all his emotions that were wanting to come out so he wouldn't break down in front of her. Even though his comment sounded pathetic when he heard the words come out of his mouth, he had to at least try everything so he would not question himself afterward.

Hailey smiled as a tear ran down her face. "I know that you would and that would be wonderful if in the future we did find our way back to each other. It's just unfair of me to ask that of you or even to let you do it. So…this is me…setting you free. Live your life to the best that you can and be happy. In return, that will make my heart full to see you truly happy again," Haley said with a shaky voice as she talked and smiled through her tears. Owen could feel his eyes begin to water but he held his emotions back. He paused for a moment to regain his composure before he replied to Hailey's statement.

Owen turned his head fully to see Hailey, who still had tears rolling down her face. "Answer me one question. Are you still in love with me?" Owen's voice cracked from the emotion that leaked through.

"I still love you, Owen," Hailey replied as she wiped the tears from her face and tilted her head slightly while a hint of a smile formed on her face.

"But are you in love with me," Owen asked with a slightly sterner voice.

"Owen, please," Hailey pleaded as she slowly shook her head.

"I need to know. Please," Owen begged.

Hailey lowered her head and quietly muttered one word, "No." She then began to sob. That one word hurt Owen more than the fall from the skyscraper itself.

"That's all I needed to hear. You can go now," Owen quickly said as he turned his head and stared in front of him once more.

"Owen, we can talk more," Hailey responded while she continued to cry. She wiped the tears from her face and then put her hand on his arm.

"Why, so you can find more creative ways of hurting me. Thanks, but I'm good," Owen coldly countered. His face was now without any expression regardless of how devastated he felt. He refused to look at her or even respond to her touch.

"I don't want to leave things between us like this," Hailey pleaded.

"Hurts, doesn't it," Owen responded.

"Owen..." Hailey softly spoke. Her voice was laced with sorrow.

"Just go," Owen said while he continued to look straight ahead and not at Hailey. He still did not show any emotion minus one single tear that ran down his cheek. Owen didn't hear anything else from Hailey except for the door closing as she walked out.

Owen sat quietly on the couch as silence filled the room. He felt like an empty shell, for his heart was broken.

CHAPTER 12

Owen sat on the couch while resting his elbows on his knees, in silence. No tears…no thoughts. The empty shell that was Owen began to fill with anger, which was fueled by the anguish he was currently feeling. He didn't know how much time passed after Hailey left before he heard Abigail's voice. With what just happened between him and Hailey, he forgot she was still in the condo.

"Owen, I'm sorry. Do you want to talk about it?" Abigail gently asked as she sat down next to him.

"What's there to talk about? I wanted to find out where we stood and she told me," Owen slowly responded without expression. He didn't even turn his head to look at Abigail when he responded.

"Obviously there is more to it so talk to me. You can't bottle this up," Abigail replied.

"Why, because it's a healthy thing to purge one's thoughts. Sure, let me lay down on the couch and we can get started with the therapy session," Owen sarcastically responded as he finally turned his head to look at Abigail. He could feel himself becoming more agitated by the moment.

"Well, yeah there's that but I was going to say so that you give the chimera any more fuel with all of your negative thoughts and energy," Abigail calmly replied.

"Sorry if I'm not a big ball of sunshine riding a rainbow at the moment," Owen snapped at Abigail as the chimera's eyes briefly glimmered. Immediately after that, Abigail's eyes widened as she slowly moved over on the couch. That is when he realized that he was uncontrollably taking his anger out on Abigail, which only made him angrier at himself. Owen abruptly stood up and kicked the oversized chair across the room as he yelled, which his scream had a hint of a growl within it. The chair tumbled across the floor and crashed against the wall. The impact from the chair was strong enough to leave cracks in the wall that fanned out.

"Sorry," Owen commented with his back to Abigail and his head lowered.

Owen felt Abigail hug him from behind while she rested her chin on his shoulder. "Don't be. The woman that you love just told you that she doesn't want to be with you and even worse, doesn't feel the same about you anymore. That hurts, and the type of creature that we have inside of us makes any emotion we feel more intense." Owen didn't respond. He only stood there with his eyes narrow while pressing his lips together to hold back any further outbursts.

"Now, I don't agree with what she said and I think she is acting more out of fear and exhaustion, but the only way you will get past this is if you look at it from a different viewpoint," Abigail added.

"What do you mean?" Owen inquired.

"Hear me out. You have to at least give her credit for being strong enough to tell you, in person, how she feels. On top of that, she is not asking you to wait for her, which is not an easy thing to tell someone. Especially knowing that she may lose you to someone else. As much as I don't agree with what she said, I do believe deep down she cares enough about you to want you to be happy, with or without her. Remember…you oversee your own happiness."

"As true or not true as that may be, I'm done with her. I feel stupid for letting myself get attached to someone that was apparently the equivalent of a high school crush. I feel even more stupid for how

I allowed myself to go through so much emotional torment and even tried to change myself in order to win her back and it was all for nothing. Not only that, I then desperately threw myself at her by saying I would wait however long it took. You know, I told myself that no matter what, I would be happy just knowing, yet here I am allowing Hailey to make me feel pathetic. That stops now!" Owen said in a determined voice as his brow lowered while he shrugged Abigail off him.

He then thought back to the mountain when Hailey walked away after he pleaded to talk to her. Owen remembered how he lost control and it took a thump on the head from Avery to reel the chimera in and make Owen think straight again. In a weird way, Owen felt he was doing himself, as well as Avery justice for not fully losing it as he did before. He finally turned to face Abigail.

"Even though that is being derived from a place of anger and hurt, I do agree with the concept. Time to live life again, but first, you need to blow off some steam. Forget whatever gem duty you must perform for one day and take time to heal. Let's go out. Somewhere…anywhere. Just you and I," Abigail suggested as she stood in front of Owen with a perky smile while she held his shoulders.

Owen lightly chuckled, "That sounds fantastic but I must ask you one question and I need you to be honest. Why are you being so nice to me?"

"You know that sounds pathetic, right?" Abigail said while laughing.

"Well, you have fun," Owen dismissingly countered as he began to turn around but Abigail grabbed his arm to prevent him from going any further. She then repositioned Owen back so he was looking at her again.

"You want to know why I am so nice? It's because I like you and not in the sense of us becoming the next power couple. I'm still trying to get over a guy that was taken from me suddenly and that was over a hundred years ago. Why do I like you…it is because I can be myself around you while feeling safe at the same time. I don't know if it's just a gut feeling, or the chimera things we have going on, or the fact that you are truly a good guy. Annoyingly such a good guy that it makes me want to be a better person and I hate myself for just saying that out loud. I just know I'm happy and free around you and I would be perfectly fine if our relationship never went further than where it is right now because I'm happy. Besides…it also helps that you're cute," Abigail playfully said.

Owen tried to hold back his smile but failed. Her words had a strong impact on him and it was a relief to know how she felt and where the two of them stood.

"Same here, so where are we going?" Owen said as he smiled and gave Abigail a quick peck on the cheek as he walked past her. Even though he was fooling around with his response, he did enjoy being around her and Owen also felt she brought out the better qualities in him as well.

"Same here…really? I pour my heart out and that's what you come back with…same here?" Abigail responded, frustrated, but shook her head and smiled when Owen stopped and extended his hand, playfully smiling as he did.

Abigail took his hand, "Same here, huh? So, you too are still getting over a guy from a hundred years ago?"

"Okay, time to go. You made your point," Owen said quickly as he headed for the door.

"No, we should keep talking about our feelings. Come on Owen, purge. Was he cute?" Abigail teased Owen as she put her arm around the crook of Owen's arm.

"He was quite dashing," Owen jested, which caused the two of them to laugh.

Abigail and Owen spent the afternoon and early evening enjoying themselves around the city. After they ate lunch and had a couple of drinks, they ended up spending a large portion of their time at a fair that happened to be in town. It was set up in an open grassy area near a small lake. It was a nice, warm sunny day so the two of them had fun going on rides and trying some of the unique fair foods. Owen embraced Abigail's free spirit and didn't want to think about the mission…just for one day. Not just the mission, but Hailey as well. Besides, he had been going strong since he came back to the States and felt he deserved a mental health day.

As night fell, the lights from the rides illuminated the fairground. Owen and Abigail found a bench that overlooked the lake to sit back and relax while they enjoyed their popcorn and drinks.

"Thank you," Owen said while briefly rubbing Abigail's knee.

"For what?" Abigail asked.

"For today. It was nice to not think about the mission or Hailey, even though I can't believe I let you convince me to leave my phone in the car. I'm also surprised you were able to get me to come to the fair. I haven't gone since I was a kid," Owen replied as he grinned.

"You're welcome. You want in on a little secret?" Abigail asked with a playful smile and a nudge.

"What's that?" Owen quickly asked. His curiosity peaked.

"Do you feel calmer and more relaxed? Not just you, but the chimera too?" Abigail inquired as she turned toward Owen. He paused for a moment to think about her question.

"Actually yes, I didn't even notice it until you asked. The secret is chimeras like the fair?" Owen jokingly asked.

Abigail spit out some of her soda as she laughed. "No. A lot of creatures feed off our emotions. The less at peace you are feeling, the louder the creature within becomes. It's not foolproof but it helps."

"Then I guess I need to try to make more time for moments like this," Owen replied as the two of them smiled at each other afterward. "I'm glad our paths crossed."

Abigail's smile grew as she leaned toward Owen. He responded by leaning in closer, caught up in the moment as rational thought had left him. His lips began to pucker and right before their lips met,

Abigail whispered one phrase, "Same here."

Owen laughed out loud as he moved away from her. "I knew that was going to come back to haunt me someday."

"You know I had to say it," Abigail responded as she laughed along with Owen.

"I hate to break up this touching moment but your presence has been requested." The sarcastic voice sounded familiar. The two of them turned around to see Caine leaning against a nearby tree.

"How long have you been standing there?" Abigail rolled her eyes before she asked.

"Long enough for your sappiness to ruin the taste of popcorn for me," Caine responded with a deadpan expression.

Abigail shook her head in frustration as she and Owen stood up and approached Caine.

"What's going on?" Owen asked.

"Well, if you checked your phones, you would know that they have been blowing up all day from various people to the point that I was reduced to an errand boy since I could cover the most ground the fastest," Caine replied with a frustrated tone as he took a couple of steps toward them.

"You found us, so what is the big emergency?" Abigail asked and then shrugged her shoulders. Owen became nervous in fear of someone may have gotten hurt, or worse.

"It seems that our mystery adversary changed their tactics for some unknown reason and targeted their forces just on one person...Anders," Caine responded.

"Is he okay?" Owen frantically asked.

Caine grinned. "Oh, I believe Anders is doing quite well. From what I understand, he is resting."

"What? I don't understand what that means but we need to get back to the others and figure out how Anders is doing and why they would change up the game plan. It doesn't make any sense," Owen commented. He was unsure as to what could have provoked such a change in tactics and Caine's vague response was not helping.

"That is why I am here. To bring the both of you to the rest of the group so a meeting of the minds can occur," Caine responded, sarcastically.

"Well, it was almost a full day of no drama," Abigail mentioned to Owen.

Owen shrugged, "Let's go."

The two of them followed Caine's car to the hotel where Avery and Hailey were staying, to meet everyone else. During the car ride, Owen could feel the chimera stirring inside of him. He wondered if it was due to the sudden change of the added stress from the news he just heard from Caine's cryptic message. Owen had to keep his mind focused on the mission and hope for the best when it came to Anders. He didn't know Anders too well but from what he could tell and from what Bailey and Michael told him from their training, if anyone could take on a group assault against him, it would be Anders.

They arrived at the hotel and rushed to Avery and Hailey's room. As Owen entered the room, he could see everyone from Abigail's group to his own were already there, except for Cedric. The hotel room itself was a standard size room with two queen size beds and a small bathroom near the door, which meant the room was now cramped with everyone inside of it.

Avery briskly approached Owen and gave him a hug. "I was worried about you when you weren't answering your phone all day. I wasn't sure if something awful happened to you or if maybe you were too upset to deal with anybody after Hailey's visit," Avery said but she lowered her voice so that Owen could only hear the part about Hailey.

"Sorry, I was doing another recon of the city and I left my phone in the car by accident. I guess I had a lot on my mind," Owen replied to everybody and as his eyes met with Hailey, she awkwardly looked elsewhere. He knew it would be weird between them for some time but he had to push through it. Owen felt awful for lying to everyone about his true whereabouts but in fear of a negative reaction from the room for taking a day off, he decided it was the best course of action. He felt the guilt alone was punishment enough. He glanced over to Abigail, whose eyes quickly looked away as she kept her deadpan demeanor. Owen's eyes then drifted to Caine who simply smirked at him. He expected Abigail to not say anything but was surprised, yet appreciative that Caine remained silent on the matter.

"Understandable but don't let it happen again," Avery teased.

Owen smiled but that was quickly replaced with worry as he addressed the group, "How is Anders?"

"Anders…he's fine," Bailey answered.

Owen let out a sigh of relief, "That's good to hear."

"The Amarok is doing well too," Michael added.

"The what? The Amarok. Are you telling me that Anders fully transitioned?" Owen asked as his jaw dropped and his eyes widened from shock. He then turned to Caine. "That is what you meant by resting." Caine shrugged with a half-grin. He could also see Selena hold her forehead in disbelief.

"What's an Amarok?" Olivia inquired.

"Long story short, it's a powerful wolf from the Inuit mythology that stands around thirty feet tall," Michael responded. Olivia's brow raised with interest after Michael's description.

"Anders must have transitioned when the opposition switched gears and attacked him," Avery commented.

"Exactly. It was either that or die," Bailey added.

"With them being that deep in the Appalachian Mountains, he must have figured it would be safe to do so. With its solitary nature, it would remain in the secluded and cooler forest cover of the mountains," Hailey commented.

"In theory. What if the little doggie wants to go for a stroll or even better, finds some adventurous hikers to snack on?" Caine asked with a devious grin.

"That is why Isaac and Marcus are taking turns making sure the

214

Amarok doesn't wander too far. That and they are making sure it only sticks to animals and not people for food until whenever Anders transitions back to himself," Hailey replied.

"It should be full and tired anyway. From what I hear, the Amarok killed and even devoured some of the attackers that were nearby and chased some of them away," Michael mentioned.

"Their forces may have dwindled but that still leaves only one person guarding the facility. That explains why they all went after Anders. Either to kill him or to use his large, uncontrollable creature as a distraction. Either way is a win. There was no need to go after Marcus or Isaac. Marcus is too small of a creature and it would end up defending Isaac anyway, and Isaac is pretty much immortal so he wouldn't transition," Avery added. Owen chuckled to himself while he shook his head.

"I fail to find the humor in this," Selena commented.

"The Amarok is on their team now," Owen replied while he looked off into the distance. Selena's brow arched with curiosity.

"How? "Bailey inquired.

"Think about it. They have been trying to breach the facility for a while now with no luck and they need to do it in order to keep the gem away. If they can't gain control over the facility, what other better way to keep the gem away than to have a territorial Amarok nearby? If it's Avery's theory or mine…either way I hate to admit it, but it's a smart play," Owen addressed the entire group. Once he was done speaking, the room fell silent for a moment.

"Owen's right and in either scenario, they're going to need backup," Bailey said as her words sliced through the silence.

"True but the more people we send from our group over there to assist, the less guarded the gem will become," Michael added but then scoffed. "Which is probably part of their plan as well."

"So, what is the game plan then?" Avery inquired. There was silence for a moment as everyone tried to think of a solution.

"We do both," Hailey softly responded.

"How so?" Avery asked with a furrowed brow.

"I leave the gem here and go by myself to assist them at the facility," Hailey replied and as everyone began to disagree, she held her hand up to silence them. "It's the only option that makes sense. I can get there faster than anyone else here and with my rare creature, I should be able to level the playing field. With any luck, they may think that I am trying to get the gem to the facility which will divert their attention in the wrong direction. Meanwhile, the gem will safely be here, guarded by all of you."

"It's a good plan but who is the lucky person that gets the gem?" Olivia inquired.

"Owen." Hailey's suggestion surprised him. "The other side already knows Bailey, Michael, and Avery so they will be watching them closely. If Owen has possession of the gem our opposition won't focus on him as much because they will think he is just another hybrid from the club. They still think he is dead. Between that and Owen being even stronger than before, makes him the ideal person to handle the responsibility of carrying the gem. Also…no offense but I don't know the rest of you well enough to hand off the main priority of the mission."

"Her plan is sound," Caine added.

"And ironically what Isaac originally wanted," Owen added. He then smiled and shook his head because without being creative, he will have possession of the gem.

"I agree," Bailey remarked while the remainder of the group remained silent from the weight of Hailey's proposal. Owen didn't know about the rest of the group but he knew it was the best plan they had to work with.

"When will you leave?" Avery asked while her voice cracked and her eyes became glassy.

"Tonight. There is no time to waste," Hailey responded while she stood up. Avery nodded before her head sank forward. Owen could hear a quick sniffle from Avery while her head was down. As

Hailey approached Owen, he stood up. She reached partially down her shirt to pull out the anchor to her necklace…the pouch itself. The palm-sized tan pouch appeared to be made of leather, with leather strings keeping the gem sealed inside. She gently took Owen's hand and placed the pouch in it, using her other hand to seal his fingers around the pouch. Her hand remained on Owen's for a moment before she let go.

"Be mindful because if they realize you have the gem, they will become relentless in their pursuit of it. I'm not going to lie, even though I am headed into battle I feel a certain level of relief that the gem is no longer with me. Like a weight has been lifted from my shoulders," Hailey remarked.

"I will and as soon as the way is clear, just text us and we will be on our way to finally finish this," Owen responded as he shoved the pouch into his pocket.

"I will talk to Cedric to see if he can spare a few men to help keep watch over you, in addition to the rest of us," Abigail mentioned to Owen.

"Splendid. I went from errand boy to babysitter," Caine sarcastically muttered under his breath.

"Well, the bright side is that you will get to kill anybody you feel is a threat to the gem," Owen countered with a half-smile.

"That does sweeten the pot doesn't it," Caine responded as his devious smile grew. The group then conversed for the next couple of hours. The topics varied but were mainly focused on ironing out the details of the plan that Hailey proposed. Once that was done, everyone began to talk about random subjects to pass the time. Owen couldn't figure out if all the conversations were just distractions or if it was the group becoming closer…maybe both.

Abigail's group eventually said their goodbyes and left, leaving the rest to catch up even more with Avery and Hailey. Owen was glad that everyone was able to relax but at the same time, it felt weird. He wondered if everyone was avoiding the fact that Hailey was about to rush off into a dangerous situation. He knew everybody took risks just as equally as the next person during a mission, but this risk involved both the opposition and the Amarok.

Owen didn't speak too much to Hailey during his time there, but it was more because he didn't have anything he could talk about with her. All their positive memories were at the facility and he could not find an opportunity to talk about that. Also, he felt uneasy trying to make small talk after what happened between them earlier that day. During the times that he was silent, he pondered everything that both Abigail and Hailey said to him today. Owen was hurt by what Hailey said but he couldn't be mad at her for it. Instead, he concentrated on the fact that at least she was truthful and fair to him. His mind then wandered to the fun moments of the day with Abigail and how much he appreciated her for that plus all the advice she has given him.

It was shortly after two o'clock in the morning before Hailey stood up and began to say her goodbyes to everybody. He could see Avery was visibly upset between her tears and the multiple hugs she gave Hailey. As for Bailey and Michael, he didn't see any tears but he could tell it bothered them that she was leaving. Neither of them was as chatty as they normally were and their facial expressions were sullen. Once Hailey was done, she looked at Owen and gave him a quick smile before turning around to head to the balcony.

"Wait," Owen called out to Hailey as he followed behind her. She turned around to face him.

"I just wanted to say sorry for my behavior earlier today and to be safe out there," Owen said with a gentle smile.

Hailey smiled and gave Owen a hug. "Thank you and you be safe as well," Hailey replied as she let go of Owen and walked onto the balcony.

The group gathered in front of the balcony door, inside the room, while Hailey scanned the area to see if anyone would see her. At that time of the night and being on the top floor, Owen felt confident that she would be unseen. Hailey transitioned and started to slowly rise into the air as she moved away from the balcony. Then, she turned her head and smiled at everybody while her bird of prey eyes began to glow as a few currents of electricity bounced around her body. Then, without warning, she darted away and disappeared into the night sky, with only a faint sound of thunder to be heard.

Everyone stood there and gazed into the night sky. Michael and Bailey left the hotel not too long after Hailey left.

"I guess I should get moving as well," Owen said as he started to check his pockets for his keys.

"Please stay," Avery blurted out. Owen's brow lowered due to his confusion about why Avery asked him to stay.

"You shouldn't be walking around by yourself now, especially with it being late and you now have the gem with you. Besides, by the time you get home, you might as well stay up all night. You need your rest and you need to be alert...more now than ever before," Avery frantically added.

"Thanks and you're probably right but I'll be fine," Owen replied while giving Avery a quick hug before he turned around and headed to the door.

"Please, Owen," Avery paused as Owen turned around. She seemed more solemn. "I am worried for you and I honestly don't want to be alone tonight. You think after all this time of being attached to Hailey I would but not tonight, please."

Owen could see Avery was emotionally worn out so he nodded in agreement and stayed. The two talked briefly before they went to their separate beds and went to sleep. After the day he had, Owen felt relieved to not have to make the long drive home while also giving Avery the peace of mind she needed.

As Owen slept, his dreams this time were not of his own but of the chimera. Typically, the chimera's dreams favored pain, anger, and violence but this one was different. Images of other chimeras, even cubs, were present as they roamed the broad grassy valleys. Memories of them huddled around at night within the rugged mountains that lined the valleys filled his dreams with peace and joy. The dream even had chimeras playing around the edges of one of the lakes nearby their home. He could sense the unbreakable bonds of family and love in these moments.

Owen awoke and instantly smiled due to the peaceful sensation he was feeling from the chimera's memories. As he slowly turned around, he hit some form of a barrier. He turned his head to see what was stopping him and it was Avery's back against his. For whatever reason, she must have moved into his bed during the night, Owen thought. He wasn't sure why and he wasn't going to ask. If it helped her sleep then he was good with it but he now wondered if Avery triggered the chimera's peaceful memories.

From what he could tell, she too slept in her clothes from the night prior. Owen carefully slid out of the bed so Avery would not wake up and made his way into the other room. There, he sat down on the couch, leaned back, pulled out the pouch, and just stared at it. He slowly twirled the pouch between his fingers as he thought to himself that if such a small item is causing this much trouble now, then he could only imagine the destruction if the mystery person ever got their hands on it. What creature lies within this gem; Owen pondered.

"Have you been up long?" Avery asked as she entered the room.

"Not too long. Just sitting here thinking about this little troublemaker," Owen responded as he showed Avery the pouch before he put it back into his pocket.

"Little…more like a tremendous troublemaker," Avery replied as she rolled her eyes and sat down on the couch next to Owen.

"Hopefully this mission will be over sooner rather than later and when it is, I am going to suggest to Isaac that we get a long vacation," Owen remarked.

Avery smiled, "That would be a nice change of pace. Ever since the facility, it has been one thing after another."

"So, what is the plan now?" Owen inquired.

"The plan is for you to act normal and just go about your business. Michael, Bailey, and I will take turns indirectly watching over you in case something happens. Right now, they will think that Hailey still has it so we should be good for a while. Hopefully long enough for them to clear a path for you and to handle the Amarok situation," Avery responded.

"How do you know they will think Hailey still has it?" Owen asked.

"Because I had it for like a week and almost had it taken from me. Since then, Hailey has had it, and considering she has the strongest and rarest creature among all of us, that can fly as well, makes her the ideal person to keep it. Besides, seeing her head to the facility alone while I remain here unprotected will make them also realize that I don't have it," Avery replied without showing any concern on her face.

"I hope you're right," Owen said but the concern on his face was obvious.

"Of course I'm right," Avery perkily replied.

"Of course," Owen remarked and then laughed. "Anyway, I will talk to Abigail and see if they can take some shifts as well. With me hanging out with their group a lot lately, it would make it seem more realistic that I am with them and not you. I will also talk to Cedric to see if they will allow me at the club with the gem. Before it was a hard pass but maybe they will allow it now under these different circumstances," Owen mentioned as he took out his phone and began to text Abigail and Cedric to meet him at his condo later.

"You and Abigail seem close. Now that Hailey is out of the picture, do you think you two will get together?" Avery inquired.

"At first, the thought crossed my mind when we first started to hang out but honestly, I think we are just close friends for numerous reasons, one of them being the fact that she is a chimera as well. That's what I am going with. Trying to figure her out is harder than herding cats," Owen replied as the two of them chuckled before he finished his text.

The two chatted about random topics for part of the morning before Owen finally left to head back to his condo and get himself cleaned up before Abigail and Cedric came over. After that, Owen straightened up the condo but then he heard a knock at the door. Sure enough, it was Cedric and Abigail. He went over the plan with them and both Abigail and Cedric were more than happy to help watch over Owen while he had the gem. Cedric appeared to be the most eager to help and didn't even offer any of his people to watch Owen. He wanted to do it himself which Owen figured was his way of getting out of his castle to get his hands dirty. Also, after careful thought, Cedric even agreed to allow Owen to enter the club with the gem. The condition was that as soon as it seemed they caught on that Owen had the gem, then he would be banned from the club until the mission was over.

With that agreement, the next few weeks went as planned. The pressure from the pursuit of the gem vanished, minus a few henchmen from time to time, which Owen pretended to not notice them. He wondered if they decided to just keep watch for now since the last attack on Owen didn't end well for the others. As for Cedric, he eliminated any threat that came into or near his territory and since that was how the club operated, it did not appear out of the ordinary.

Caine took the pleasure of relieving some of the other henchmen of their lives if he was able to provoke them into making a move on him. The plan seemed to be working but it was hard to know how well the fight at the facility was going since Isaac, Marcus, and Hailey would only respond to their texts about once a week.

During this time, Owen did hang out with not only Michael, Bailey, and Avery, but also Abigail, Selena, Olivia, and even Caine. He worried at first that the opposition would put two and two together when Avery was with him but when nothing came out of it, Owen figured they must have been more focused on Hailey.

At first, Owen felt guilty when both groups would be at the club having a good time while the others at the facility were fighting, but he had to push the thought aside. The worrying would not solve anything. He had to keep up his end of the plan just as much as everyone else for it to work.

Owen enjoyed spending time with everybody, but especially Avery since he felt the closest to her. The two were able to talk freely about anything and he felt at ease with Avery. He forgot about how much she was always able to lift his spirits with her personality and how easy it was to talk to her. During this time, he also watched Olivia and Michael become closer. The two of them spent a lot of time together, to the point that sometimes others would have to cover one of their shifts since they could not make it to watch over Owen. He didn't mind since Michael was happy and he didn't want to take that away from him.

The entire group gathered at Abigail's club room one night after their usual activities of either dancing, sparing in the newly renovated back room, or just relaxing in Abigail's room. Due to the number of people, everyone would be spread out between the inside of the room and the balcony. This night, Selena, Caine, and Bailey were on the balcony whereas the rest were inside the room. Owen and Avery were sitting across from Olivia and Michael, and Abigail was at the bar area preparing a new mixed drink she has been wanting to try for some time now.

"They're a cute couple, don't you think?" Avery whispered.

"Yeah, and he must like her because I haven't seen or heard of a gaming reference in some time," Owen whispered back.

Avery's eyes widened, "Wow, it must be serious. He looks happy so that's always good to see."

"Okay everybody, the Abigail special is ready for tasting. I found a recipe and added a few things to make it my own," Abigail mentioned as she started to pour the light blue slushy concoction into the glasses.

"I can only imagine what mad scientist stuff you did to those

223

drinks," Owen said as he grinned while he stood up. "I will get the others from the balcony."

As Owen turned to head to the door, Cedric walked into the room with Selena, Caine, and Bailey behind him.

"What's wrong?" Owen asked as he could see the look of concern on Cedric's face. His question and Cedric's demeanor caused the rest of the room to stand up and gather around.

"My men have been trying to figure out the type of creature that is housed inside that gem and they have found a lot of information surrounding it and that mountain. Unfortunately, they haven't figured out exactly what is inside the gem. Therefore, I decided to assist them by piecing all their information together, along with what I found out on my own and I finally came across this small scroll," Cedric said as he showed the group.

"That doesn't look like paper," Avery commented as her eyes squinted. "Are those bones?" Her face squinched from disgust.

"Unfortunately, you are correct," Cedric responded as he unraveled it to show the group. "The paper is made from skin, which I hope that, and the bones, are not human. Same with the blood that was used as the ink to write the few words that are on here. I didn't have time to examine it in detail yet. Anyway, the language is some form of old Arabic and it loosely translates to a warning. A warning about the creature that resides in that gem," Cedric paused as he took a deep breath. "We have a problem."

"Why do we have a problem? What creature is inside this gem?" Owen asked as he pulled out the pouch and showed it to him. Cedric's reluctance to share what he knew made Owen become nervous about what the creature could be for Cedric to be that troubled by what he discovered. The entire room fell silent as they listened for the answer.

Cedric closed the scroll and viewed the entire group before his eyes drifted back to Owen. "The being inside the gem is a djinn."

CHAPTER 13

Silence filled the room, but only briefly. "A djinn! Like grant three wishes and all of that?" Bailey spurted out as her eyes flared with concern.

"The same," Cedric responded.

"I'm sorry, I must be missing something. Why is this a big deal? It's not like the gem is some lamp that a person can rub and summon the djinn. It's stuck in that gem or inside whoever touches it. Without a master, the djinn can't grant any wishes," Olivia commented and then shrugged.

"True, but a djinn without a master is dangerous enough as it is. If the person fully transitions then the djinn could have free reign and do whatever it pleases. If it is aware of its situation, it could unbind itself from the person that touched the gem," Selena responded.

"Or it can be free, simply if the person doesn't survive the third-day transition period," Caine added.

"This person is obsessed with this gem for a reason. Do you think a person that has the djinn within them could grant wishes, even minor ones?" Michael asked.

"That's a good question. Probably so, which alone could make them a real threat. I wonder if Isaac has any knowledge about someone who had a djinn as their creature," Abigail responded as she sat down.

"What are you thinking, Owen?" Caine inquired as his eyes narrowed.

"What if this person has found a way to bind the djinn in order to get their wishes," Owen responded as he rubbed the back of his neck. The room went quiet. "Yes, what everybody said before could be true, but whoever this person is has done nothing but pursue this gem with everything they've got. It just makes me wonder if they found a way to be granted wishes from the djinn." Owen surveyed the room. Apparently, his idea appeared to become worrisome for most of the occupants of the room between the silence and the lowered brows.

"You know there is some lore out there that says the djinn can't grant any wishes. That it's just an old wives' tale," Bailey commented.

"Maybe, but we have to presume that it does because, in the wrong hands, a djinn that can grant wishes could be devastating," Selena politely countered.

"I will text Hailey and the others what we just found out," Avery said as she took her phone out.

"Add Livia and Duncan to that text please since I know they are researching as well. They may be able to shed some light on the subject," Owen suggested. Avery nodded and continued to text.

"We should just find a way to destroy the gem or at least dispose of it someplace that nobody will find it. Throw it in an ocean or in a lava bed or heck, flush it down the toilet. Consider it a plan B if we can't get it to the facility," Bailey said.

"I am not aware of any method that can destroy the gem. Not saying it can't be done but it's not as simple as hitting it with a hammer. The gem's magic protects it," Abigail commented.

"And disposing of it doesn't mean that it is gone forever…only temporarily. Heck, someone sealed that gem inside the bottom of a mountain, and yet, it was discovered," Michael added.

"We may just have to make our way to the facility. Maybe with all the fighting, our combined efforts, and now the Amarok running loose, we can slip by. We can even prepare to leave in the next day or two," Owen said as he stood up.

"That could just work. Are we any closer to who wants the gem?" Michael inquired.

"We are closer but this person was quite thorough in covering their tracks. Luckily, I am very persistent and we have some fresh leads. I feel certain that we should have the identity of this person in the next few days, if not sooner," Cedric replied while beaming with confidence.

"Then it's settled. We make our way to the facility. It's late now so we can plan out the details and pack tomorrow and then leave the following day," Owen suggested. Michael, Avery, and Bailey all nodded their heads in agreement as they headed to the door. Owen did catch Michael giving Olivia's hand a squeeze as they looked at each other with great concern.

"No one here is obligated to assist us in this journey and I won't think less of anybody if they choose not to help, but with that said we can use all the help we can get." Owen's plea was directed at Selena, Abigail, Olivia, Cedric, and Caine.

"I will go with you," Abigail responded as she walked over to Owen and slung her arm around his neck. "I have been couped up in this city too long. I could go for some nature," Abigail added as she smirked.

"I will go with you as well. I believe my kingdom won't fall apart while I am off on an adventure," Cedric said as he winked.

"I'm not sure if us vampires will be of any use to you during the day so I guess we are staying here," Olivia said as she walked over to Caine.

"It will be okay. You must rely on your natural skills and if all else fails, have a vast amount of ammo and sharp weapons on hand," Michael countered as he smiled.

"I hate to be away from you but I am not sure if I am ready for this kind of situation and I don't want to be a burden. This is all still pretty new and bizarre to me. It still amazes me sometimes that I'm not just a plain human anymore. Also, I may have been in some scuffles but a full-blown battle…I just don't think I am capable of such feats yet. I will just hold down the fort and wait for your return. Besides, we have at least one more day together. Let's make the best of it," Olivia said with a gentle smile, which caused Michael to smile in return before he hugged her.

"I will go as well," Selena said as she stood up.

"You can't go. It's too dangerous and as much as I want to, I can't be there to protect you," Caine quickly rebutted as he stood up and gently turned Selena to face him. Owen could see the heavy concern all over Caine's face.

"I understand and I will be fine. I'm not as fragile as you think I am and with my power to heal, I can be a great asset to them. I handled myself for many centuries before I met you so just a week won't be the end of the world," Selena responded as she lightly touched the side of Caine's face. His only response was to gently place his hand on the side of her face before he nodded in agreement. Caine lowered his head while Selena walked over to the rest of the group that was going.

"Thank you," Owen addressed everyone that was willing to help. He then turned to Caine and Olivia. "I understand. No worries and I'll do my best to make sure everyone comes home safe," Owen added. It was obvious that Michael and Selena were on Olivia and Caine's minds, so he hoped his comment alleviated at least a portion of their concern.

Owen turned his attention back to the others. "Now let's get some sleep and take care of whatever packing and affairs you need to get done. Let's plan to meet at my condo later tomorrow morning to discuss the final details before we leave." Everyone agreed and began to disperse but before Owen could leave, he felt the tight grip of Caine's hand on his shoulder. Owen turned around to see what Caine wanted.

"I'm trusting that you will do everything in your power to ensure Selena comes back to me unharmed," Caine said with a quiet intensity.

"You have my word," Owen gently replied to Caine, which caused the grip on his shoulder to lessen and a slight grin to appear on Caine's face. Caine then turned around and walked to the bar area.

As Owen left the club, he felt both relieved and stressed. Relieved that the being inside the gem has finally been revealed and the person that has been pursuing the gem will soon be discovered. However, he was stressed at what was to come. Another battle in the mountains was coming and even though he had more allies this time, the forces against them seemed vast. At what cost would it take to get the gem inside the facility? That thought alone made him feel like he had a knot in his stomach.

When he arrived at the condo, Owen decided to do something that he hasn't done in quite some time now, and that was meditating. He needed to clear his mind and ease the chimera's restlessness as well. An hour passed when he completed his meditation and it was well worth it with how refreshed and calmer he felt. With a clear head, Owen came up with a few ideas of how to get the gem past all the forces on the mountain, including the Amarok. He wanted to share these ideas with everyone before they reached the edge of the mountainous terrain. Not too long after his meditation, Owen fell asleep.

The next morning, he woke up and quickly got himself ready for the day since he wanted to get started on packing. Owen also wanted to check out the supplies to see if there was anything of use for this last stretch of the mission. As he was wrapping up, he heard a knock on the door.

He opened the door to see Michael and Olivia standing in the doorway. "Hey! Good to see you two. You're early," Owen said as

229

he glanced at the clock on the wall.

"Traffic wasn't bad so we made good time. Abigail and Avery should be here soon. They went out to get coffee," Michael said.

"That's an interesting combo. Not sure if I should be nervous or not," Owen replied as he turned and proceeded to walk further into the condo. He smiled and he meant it as a joke but a small part of him was nervous. He wasn't sure about what the two would talk about or even how they would interact with each other after Avery's questions regarding Abigail the other day.

Owen turned back and both Michael and Olivia were still standing in the doorway. "Why haven't you two come in yet?" Owen asked.

Olivia sighed. "Because you haven't invited us in."

"Really? That's a real thing? You two aren't even full-blown vampires. Besides, you have been in here already Michael. Sorry, Michael and Olivia, please come in," Owen responded as he went along with the ruse.

"I have no idea if it's legit but a polite host would invite their guests into their dwelling," Olivia commented while she smiled as she and Michael entered.

Owen chuckled, "Fair enough. Come in and make yourselves at home," Owen said in a mock, snotty tone of voice. The three of them had a quick laugh before they all sat down. Once seated, the three of them gave each other a quick update on what they did this morning.

There was a moment of silence before Olivia asked Owen a question. "What would you wish for?"

"What?" Owen responded. He heard the question but it caught him off guard.

"You have a djinn in your pocket and you haven't even thought about what wishes you would make if you had the opportunity," Olivia responded in amazement.

"I guess I never thought about it," Owen replied as he leaned back and began to let his mind wander.

"We have some time to kill. What would you wish for? Just think of one and don't worry about how you would word it so the djinn couldn't find a loophole to mess with you. We kind of already talked about this at the club but now it's different. Now, the reality of your wish becoming true is real," Olivia added.

"I bet the djinn's wishes have restrictions," Owen commented.

"Probably so but there is so much lore out there as to what a djinn can or cannot do. Some say they can't do anything like grant infinite wishes, kill anybody, bring people back to life, or make someone fall in love with them. Those are the most common ones but who knows how true they really are and I am sure there must be a way around those things," Michael commented.

"Don't overthink it. Just pick whatever comes to your mind. That will most likely be what you truly want," Olivia added.

Owen's mind was filled with so many possibilities. He paused for a moment as he tried to filter through all the choices.

"Well…" Michael prodded as he grinned.

"It's difficult because all my wishes are based around bringing people back to life. I presume I'm not allowed to wish to go back in time and warn them or myself, so I'm not sure. I don't want to say the usual millions of dollars or some huge materialistic item, so I guess I would wish for this gem to be teleported right onto Isaac's desk in the facility. That way, no one else must get hurt or die and we can all finally take some time to ourselves."

"Your compassion holds no bounds," Olivia commented as she smiled. Owen smiled at the nice comment and at first, he said it to just give an answer but the more he thought about it, the wish seemed like something he truly wanted.

"What about you, Olivia," Michael inquired with a slightly lowered brow and a faint smile while he tilted his head.

"I would wish for a normal family life but I don't think any wish could make that happen so I would wish for the power to control people's minds," Olivia responded. Both Owen and Michael slowly

231

nodded their heads in agreement as they thought about her answer.

"Think about it. A person could do anything from bringing me a piece of chocolate cake to making someone spare another person's life," Olivia added as she leaned forward.

"Chocolate cake does sound good right about now," Owen commented as he became slightly hungry from the thought of that delicious dessert. Olivia giggled as Michael smiled and as he was about to make a comment, there was a knock at the door.

"I'll get it," Michael said as he stood up and walked toward the door.

"Wait, what about you? What's your wish?" Owen called out.

"That's easy. To get past this level that I am stuck on in my latest game," Michael responded with a quick raise of his brow as he turned back to open the door.

"Really?" Owen asked as he chuckled to himself. Olivia just smiled and slowly shook her head while she did a quick eye roll.

"Don't judge me," Michael commented as he smiled and opened the door. As he did, Abigail, Avery, and Bailey entered.

"We ran into Bailey on the way here," Avery commented.

"Why aren't we judging you, Michael?" Abigail asked as she gave him a pat on the back.

"We were all just talking about what wish we would ask the djinn for. I wanted the gem to magically appear on Isaac's desk to stop all the fighting, Olivia opted for mind control to get desserts, and Michael wants to beat some level on his game," Owen responded as everybody sat down.

"Of course," Bailey commented while she winked at Michael. Everyone had a quick laugh over Michael's wish.

"I would wish to eat whatever I want and not gain any weight," Abigail joked but got strong approvals from everyone else.

"I would wish to have full control over the werewolf whenever I fully transition. It would make any battle I'm in a lot easier to win. Imagine the face of my opponent when I transition into the werewolf.

Game over," Bailey said as she sat back with a smug expression.

"Avery would wish to be able to fly," Owen said as he sent a wink in Avery's direction.

"You know me all too well. I would love to be able to fly but Abigail's wish sounds very tempting," Avery said as she chuckled to herself. Owen couldn't help to smile at her as he pictured herself at a buffet with cake smeared all over her face.

"So, what's the plan?" Olivia asked the group.

"We pack light and head out shortly after midnight under the cover of darkness," Avery suggested.

"That would allow us to get out of the city easier and more quickly. Good idea," Owen commented.

"Is it though?" Olivia calmly blurted out as she winced from her own comment.

"Why do you say that?" Michael inquired.

Olivia adjusted herself in her seat. "Sorry, I know I'm not going but still. You are going to leave during a time when the other team is most likely to be on the lookout for you. Also, by the time you get there, the sun will be up…"

"And right into the enemy forces and the Amarok in broad daylight," Bailey added as she interrupted Olivia. She leaned forward and put her elbows on her knees as she pondered the words she had just spoken.

"Exactly," Olivia added.

"The Amarok will see us regardless of what time of day it is but still, she's right. We need to leave during the day and use the night as our ally to get as far as we can before we are seen," Bailey suggested.

"Then we leave around lunchtime tomorrow. That will give us time to get to the base of the mountain and take advantage of that small town that Marcus took us to for that celebration for passing the final test. Even from there, it will take a few hours to get to the facility and who knows what we will encounter. Either way, we will need to push through it. If the others receive our message in time

233

maybe they can help lure the enemy away long enough for us to make it through," Owen said with hope in his voice. His confidence was growing with each passing minute, which the others began to feed from that same confidence.

"Then it's settled. Someone needs to let Selena and Cedric know. By the way, where are they?" Michael asked as he looked around.

"Selena and Caine are helping Cedric narrow down who the mystery leader is, along with Caine learning some of Cedric's responsibilities so he won't come back to chaos. I will let them know since I need to swing by the club anyway," Abigail mentioned as she took a sip of her coffee.

"I guess we just go about our business until then?" Owen suggested.

"At this point, we shouldn't be careless and leave someone alone. We need to stick together until we leave," Avery suggested as she stood up. The rest of the group followed her lead.

"I can go with you," Owen offered as he turned to Avery.

"Include us as well," Michael added as he put his arm around Olivia.

"Do you want to accompany me back to the club? We can check on Cedric, Selena, and Caine and maybe even get a round of sparing in if we're lucky," Abigail suggested to Bailey.

"Why not," Bailey responded. Shortly after, everyone left. Once they left then Avery, Michael, and Olivia followed Owen to his car.

"Where to, my lady," Owen teased Avery as he buckled his seatbelt.

"Back to my apartment peasant to gather a few items to bring back to your condo," Avery mocked in a fake, fancy accent.

"Does that work for you two?" Owen asked Michael and Olivia who were both on their phones in the backseat. The two nodded in agreement.

As Owen drove, he chatted with Avery about random topics to

pass the time. He even commented on how Olivia and Michael were on their phones, sharing funny memes with each other. He and Avery smiled at their happiness.

The group entered the section of the drive that was the long stretch between where Owen stayed and the hotel Avery resided at. He knew this scenic route was a slightly longer distance to travel; however, at least Owen didn't have to worry about the stop-and-go traffic of the city. Also, the view itself was more pleasant with the vast farmland and sporadic houses and barns scattered throughout it. Eventually, the scenic route converted back to city life as the roads became more congested and the greenery all but vanished. The group arrived at the hotel and made their way to Avery's room. There, Avery gathered the belongings she wanted to take.

"You still have that?" Owen chuckled as he saw Avery pull the hammer axe from under the couch.

"You bet I do. I love this thing," Avery exclaimed as she examined it. Then, there was a knock at the door.

"Could that be the others?" Avery questioned. The rest of the group shrugged.

"That's too quick for them. Maybe it's someone that works at the hotel?" Olivia suggested.

"I'll take a look through the peephole," Michael said as he walked toward the door with Olivia not too far behind him.

"Something isn't right. Be ready with that toy of yours," Owen whispered to Avery. She nodded as she readied her axe. Both she and Owen started to head toward the door.

Then, without warning, the door was violently kicked open with enough force that the door itself flew off its hinges and slammed into Michael, causing him to fall back into Olivia. The impact resulted in Michael and Olivia laying on the floor dazed with a broken door on top of them. Standing in the doorway was one female, lean in stature, with short, spiked red hair and defined cheekbones. Her eyes were entirely green which between that and her display of brute strength, she most certainly had a creature within her.

As Owen was about to charge, he heard the balcony glass door smash as mercenaries, dressed in black, stormed the apartment with their handguns drawn. Owen noticed the hooks on them from where they used ropes to help scale the hotel, most likely from the rooftop to the balcony. The ambush worked for they were surrounded.

"You have two options. First, you can hand over the gem and get to live to see another day. Second, we kill everyone and take the gem anyway. Personally, I am fine with either option," the woman said with a cold expression, with just the faintest hint of a smirk.

"Well, I guess with those options we have no choice but to pick option three," Owen replied as he transitioned and sent a short burst of flames toward the men with the guns.

He needed enough to throw them off guard while not catching the room on fire. His plan worked as they turned away from the flame. Owen growled as he lunged forward but his eyes grew wide as one of the men was already back in position and aimed his gun at Owen. Between the short distance and the angle, the man had a life-threatening advantage over Owen.

The man jerked to the right as he fired and then held his shoulder. Owen could see blood seeping out from between his fingers. Another silent pop caused the man to grab his chest as he fell to the ground. Owen turned his head quickly to see Michael pointing his handgun, which was equipped with a silencer, toward the direction of the man he just killed. He winked before he began to open fire on the rest of the men. While the mercenaries were distracted by the gunfire, Owen took the opportunity to continue his assault.

He witnessed Avery charge toward the woman at the door, so Owen grabbed the office chair with one hand and flung it toward the group of men. As it bounced off a couple of them, he rushed the group and slashed the first man he reached across his chest. As he grabbed his chest and fell to the ground, Owen sent another slash with his other hand across the face of the man standing next to his fallen comrade. The man dropped to his knees as the blood flowed and the skin dangled from his face as he toppled over.

Owen turned his head in time to see Olivia take a backhand from the woman, which sent her flying across the room and slamming into the wall hard enough to send waves of cracks along the wall. Olivia slid down the wall while holding her head. When she reached the floor, she fell over to her side and appeared to be barely conscious.

By the time Olivia was on the floor, Avery finally got within range to swing her axe at the woman, which she caught with her other hand. The woman was holding the axe handle with the blade of the axe only a foot from her face. The fact that she was able to stop Avery's attack with one arm while Avery was in transition, was a testament to the woman's strength. Before Owen could react, Avery changed tactics and grabbed the lower end of the handle, and pushed it up and toward the woman. The speed and power behind Avery's surprise move allowed the handle to smack the woman on the chin. The attack caused the woman to let go and stumble back a few steps as she shook her head.

Seeing that Avery was handling herself well against the mystery person, he diverted his attention to the few remaining mercenaries that were still standing. With one on each side of Owen, he had to think quickly. He grabbed the arm of one of the men and pulled him toward himself while twirling around the attacker. As soon as Owen was in position, he sank his fangs into the man's neck. The venom coursed through the man's veins quickly as he became stiff as a board. Owen made sure not to kill him, for he had other plans.

He grabbed the paralyzed man and rushed forward, using him as a human shield. The last standing man sent an array of bullets toward Owen but none of them made it through his newly acquired shield. As he got closer, he pushed the now dead man at the last remaining intruder and as he shrugged off the dead body, Owen swatted the gun out of his hand and followed up with a slash across the man's neck.

Blood sprayed from his neck as he fell backward onto the floor, convulsing for a moment before death took him.

"Where is it!" the woman yelled at Avery while she pinned her against the wall with her own axe handle. The woman had it pressed against her neck as she leaned her body against Avery's. Owen could see Avery was grinding her teeth since she was using all her strength to keep from being strangled. He then noticed Avery's skin turning a light tan as she stared intensely back at the woman with her fierce blue eyes. With Avery deeper into transition she began to slowly push the axe back toward the woman. Just when Owen thought Avery had the upper hand, the stranger's skin began to form brown plates. Owen couldn't figure out what the creature was yet but whatever it was, it must have been stronger than the cyclops since

Avery couldn't push her off and Owen was running out of options. Olivia was still dazed on the ground and Michael was just now slowly getting up to one knee. Any gunfire or actual fire could hit Avery. He wanted to just ambush the woman but he didn't have the angle to make it effective and he didn't want Avery to pay the cost. He had to draw her attention away somehow.

"How many shots do you have left," Owen quickly asked Michael.

"One in the chamber and that's it," Michael responded after a quick check of his weapon.

"Make it count," Owen said to Michael. Then, he turned his attention to the woman and pulled out the pouch that had the gem inside. "Looking for this?" Owen rhetorically, and loudly, asked.

The woman looked over her shoulder and her eyes widened. She then sent a vicious headbutt to Avery, which caused her to crumble down the wall. With Avery out of the way, Michael took aim, but the woman noticed his intentions and threw the axe at him. He was able to get a piece of the door up like a shield just in time. The impact sent Michael back to the ground but as he started to get up the woman stomped on his chest. The impact sent him back to the ground while he held his chest and rolled to his side, trying to catch his breath as he did.

"You want this trinket so bad then come and get it," Owen provoked as he dangled the pouch in front of him. He then grinned before he stuffed it back into his pocket. He even reverted to his human form in order to entice her more.

"It will be my pleasure," the woman said after she deviously smiled at Owen. Her eyes flared a bright green glow as more of her skin formed into brown platelets. She then charged at Owen but he noticed her run and even her first couple of swings at him were slower than he imagined they would be and were easily dodged. She then sent a hammer-like attack down on Owen with both her hands, which he caught but had trouble holding the arms in his human form. The woman didn't seem to care that Owen was able to stop her attack while not in transition and continued to push her arms down toward him.

Owen gritted his teeth as his arms began to tremble under the unusually heavy and powerful arms of the attacker. As he held her arms, he realized it felt like he was holding a rock. The woman was deep in transition for Owen to figure out what she was.

"You're an earth elemental," Owen blurted out for the entire room to hear. She simply winked at Owen while continuing her attack. At that point, Owen transitioned. His chimera eyes peered directly at her green eyes before he growled and dug his claws into her rocky skin, but it did not cause any harm to her. He was strong enough now to hold her in place and as he did, he sent out a burst of flames from his mouth that landed on her face. More particularly, her eyes since she was not far enough in transition for them to be as protected as the rest of her body. She reared back in pain as she covered her face.

She lunged at Owen and her dense body ended up knocking him off his feet and sending him smashing into the desk. With him lying on his stomach, she dug her knee into his back while grabbing the

239

back of his neck. With her free hand, she began to dig the pouch out of his pocket. Owen growled and strained as he tried to push off the floor but he was only able to lift a few inches before falling back down. He repeated it a couple more times with no success. If only he could get more of his legs underneath him to have the power to shake her off him, Owen thought.

Then it happened…she pulled out the pouch from his pocket. Owen felt an instant fear fall over him at the sight of the pouch in her hand. Then, he heard a faint pop as the woman grabbed her arm and dropped the pouch. He turned his head and saw Michael lowering his gun. Owen quickly grabbed the pouch but the woman was now getting back into position on top of Owen again. He surveyed the room and noticed Michael was slowly rising to his feet but he still looked out of it. Avery was just now coming to as well. On the other hand, Olivia was now up and the most alert person in the room.

"Owen, toss it to me. I can get it to safety. We don't have much time. Trust me…let me help," Olivia pleaded with Owen. She was right, she was currently the only one that could leave the room the quickest and get the gem to safety. With that thought, he skipped the pouch across the floor to Olivia.

"Get out of here. Keep it safe," Owen yelled. Olivia grabbed the pouch and gave him a quick smile and a nod before she rushed out of the room.

"Shoot her!" Owen yelled.

"I'm out of ammo!" Michael exclaimed. Right after he made the comment Avery sprinted across the room and rammed her shoulder into the woman. The impact was strong enough to knock her off Owen and make her tumble over to around the balcony entrance.

"Michael, we got this. Find Olivia and help her protect the gem. Who knows how many others are out there," Avery exclaimed without looking back at Michael. Instead, her eyes were fixated on the woman who was now back on her feet.

"I'm on it," Michael responded before he rushed out of the

room.

Avery swung her axe down on the intruder who used her forearm to block it. Her axe glanced off the attacker's forearm but had enough force behind it to cut through her skin. If her attack would have hit more directly, she may have severed her arm.

The woman winced as Owen went deeper into transition and roared as he slashed at her. She used her other forearm to block the attack, but Owen was deeper in transition and had more power from the chimera behind his attack. With that additional power, he was able to tear past the semi-rocky skin. The pain from the injuries caused the woman to grab both her arms. As the blood trickled down her arms, she sent a front kick at Owen but he was able to dodge the attack by quickly shifting to the left. He sent another burst of fire at her which she deflected by crossing her arms in front of her face.

Owen's plan worked, for he was using his fire attack as more of a distraction to allow Avery to attack again. With the woman's back turned to Avery she yelled as she swung her axe down with all her fury. The blade broke through the stone and lodged into the woman's spine. The woman gasped for air as she immediately fell to her knees. She looked at Owen while blood began to pour out of her mouth and her head wavered about. As Avery pried the axe from the woman's back, Owen could hear the crunch of the bones as the blood splattered across Avery. Without hesitation, Avery screamed again and took another swing, this time her blade decapitated the woman's head. Her swing was hard enough to send the woman's head tumbling across the floor. The headless body tipped over to the ground as blood began to pour from her neck.

Even though he was happy that the woman was now dead, he became worried for Avery. She was deeper in transition than he thought. He could see the strain on her face while she was breathing heavily and staring off into the distance, grinding her teeth as she did. It seemed she was holding on to whatever humanity was left or else she would transition into the cyclops.

"Get out of here Owen. I don't think I can transition back to human," Avery pleaded with pain in her voice as she strained harder. A couple of tears ran down her cheek while she had a death grip on her axe.

Owen transitioned back to human and rushed over to her. He put one hand on her shoulder and the other he put under her chin and slowly lifted her face so she would look into his eyes. "I understand what you are going through. You can do this. Just concentrate on my face and my voice," Owen calmly said to her.

"I can't...I can't do it," Avery's voice cracked as she responded through her tears while she shook her head.

"Yes, you can. Just think about any good memory and then focus on that and only that," Owen said in a reassuring tone. Avery continued to panic for a moment but then her demeanor changed when she stopped panicking and a faint hint of a smile appeared. With that, Owen saw a ray of hope. "Good, now take slow, deep breaths and keep thinking about that good memory."

Avery's skin color began to phase back to her normal tone. That is when Owen was able to slowly take the axe and toss it to the side and he embraced her. After a couple of minutes, Avery backed away from Owen and he could see the smile on her face as she was fully back to human now.

"I could have killed you," Avery remarked as her smile vanished before she slapped him on the arm.

"You're welcome," Owen countered as he smirked. Avery partially smiled while she rolled her eyes.

"Thank you," Avery gently added as she lightly touched Owen's arm.

"We need to get out of here. I'm sure the entire hotel heard this battle," Owen hastily said as he briskly walked toward the door.

"Definitely, I just need one quick minute to grab the essentials and anything that identifies us," Avery replied as she grabbed her axe and strafed through the room. Owen stood at the door and kept an eye out while she did. Moments later, Avery came to him with a medium-sized backpack and a baseball bag that was used to conceal the axe. They started down the hallway, toward the stairwell, but were taken back when Michael and Olivia swung the door open.

"The place is crawling with cops and firemen and they are making their way up, floor by floor. It looks like the hotel heard the commotion and called them," Michael said between breaths. Owen and Avery looked at each other as Owen tried to think of an alternative route.

"How about the elevator shafts?" Owen suggested.

"You've watched too many movies. I say we go to the roof. There we can use the fire escape to make our way down. If anyone asks, we can just say we heard the alarms," Olivia countered.

"What alarms?" Avery asked as her brow knitted.

A crooked grin formed on Olivia's face. She then walked over and pulled the fire alarm lever. "That alarm."

"Roof it is," Michael chuckled as the four of them raced up the stairs to the roof. Michael kicked the door open and everybody rushed out onto the roof. Owen glanced around and didn't see any fire escapes.

"Darn it. I wasn't sure if there would be any fire escapes but I figured at least a ladder or something for the workers to use while they are up here. This building doesn't have anything," Owen commented. His lips were pressed firmly together to contain his frustration as he frantically looked around.

"We need to head back downstairs and just play dumb if the cops see us. If they don't believe us then we will think of something. One problem at a time but we need to move. Olivia, toss the gem back to me please," Owen directed as he raised his hands while he took a few steps toward the stairwell with Avery by his side. Michael started to follow but then they all stopped and their eyes narrowed as they stared at Olivia. Each one of them was confused as to why she didn't move.

She pulled out the pouch and smiled. "No, I think I will hold onto this."

"Not funny," Avery exclaimed.

"I wasn't trying to be funny," Olivia replied in a smug fashion.

"You must be kidding me! You're working with them? How did their leader even convince you to switch sides?" Owen asked as his eyes were filled with both hurt and anger.

A devious smile formed on Olivia's face. "Honey…I am the leader."

CHAPTER 14

Michael put his hand on his chest. "That can't be. That's impossible! Not everything could have been a lie. Not us. What we had…it felt real," Michael said as he grimaced. The internal torment he was experiencing from the bombshell that Olivia just dropped was all too much.

"If it's any comfort, you were quite helpful in gathering information and keeping the spotlight off of me," Olivia said nonchalantly while giving Michael a quick shrug.

"You don't mean that," Michael replied as he approached Olivia from her right side. Suddenly, Olivia sent a vicious elbow to Michael's chin while facing Owen and Avery. Michael's head snapped back before he landed on the ground, unconscious.

"Cute, but clingy," Olivia commented with a carefree attitude and a flick of her hair as she took a few steps toward Owen and Avery.

"You must be a decoy or something. Caine saw you touch the gem. He witnessed you go through the pain of that and the trials of the day three awakening," Owen remarked with his head slightly tilted and his brow knitted.

"Oh, you mean the…" Olivia began to pretend to be in pain as she yelled and convulsed. She then stopped and smiled as she deeply transitioned, and then began to mockingly yell while dramatically placing her hand on her forehead. Then, as quickly as she transitioned into her vampiric state, she went back to her human form. She then bowed toward Avery and Owen. Even though Owen was annoyed and angry at her display, he was amazed by the control of her transitioning.

"I really should have won an award for best dramatic performance and as for the gem, it was a fake. The person that tossed it to me was in on the plan and as for it absorbing into my hand, well that was just some good ole fashion sleight of hand," Olivia beamed with pride as she held up the pouch and quickly waved her other hand around it, making it disappear. Owen shook his head in utter disbelief.

"This entire time you were there, hearing everything we said. That explains so much now. Even the attack that just happened. Heck, even the fighting and injuries you sustained earlier were all staged," Avery commented as she still was trying to get over the shock of it all.

"Yeah, I don't know what was more ironic…you and the gang spilling all your plans in front of me or Caine teaching me how to be a vampire when I am actually older than he is," Olivia lightly chuckled at her own response. "I'm not surprised everyone fell for my superior acting performance, but I must admit, it was all I could do to stay in character when I saw you, Owen. Not much surprises me these days and yet, there you were…back from the dead and standing in Abigail's room. It took all my might to keep my jaw from hitting the floor."

"You knew about that?" Owen asked.

"Of course. I was there that day, in the mountain, and witnessed the entire event. You and the chimera were quite impressive and I was bummed to see it get turned to stone. So much potential wasted. Well, I thought it was wasted but apparently, I was wrong," Olivia added while she playfully smiled as she looked Owen up and down.

"Glad I didn't disappoint you," Owen sarcastically responded.

"Wait. Why did you wait so long to take the gem? You wasted a lot of time and your forces between us and your endless assault on the facility. Why?" Avery asked.

"I was already in with the group so the next step was to keep all the major players tied up at the facility so that the gem would be left with someone easier to take it from. Hailey's rare creature, and her ability to fly, made the confiscation of the gem difficult. The plan worked for the most part. I kept everyone away from the city and even got Hailey to give up the gem and head to the facility. The only part that I didn't expect was that you didn't follow her. I thought for sure the power couple would reunite and you would have handed it off to either Avery or Abigail and chased after Hailey. Once the gem was with you I either had to get it from you with brute force or with trust. As you can see, the latter worked," Olivia responded as she smiled and her brow raised slightly. Owen scoffed as he shook his head again in disappointment. How could he have been so blind to her true identity, Owen thought.

"Unfortunately, between Cedric becoming closer to identifying me and then your brilliant plan of bringing the gem to the facility, I had to act quickly. If not, my entire plan of divide and conquer would have been ruined," Olivia added as she placed her hands on her hips and slowly shook her head.

"Did your plan include getting stuck on a rooftop with us…in the daylight?" Avery rhetorically asked as she dropped her bags and marched toward Olivia.

"No, but I am not concerned with that," Olivia casually responded.

"Then you are not as bright as you make yourself out to be. If you don't hand over that gem right now, you will be as dead as that earth elemental chick I just killed," Avery added as her brow lowered and her lip raised in anger.

"She's dead?" Olivia asked in one breath as her jaw dropped and

247

her eyes widened.

"Yep. It seems they don't react well to hammer axes," Avery countered as she swung at Olivia. She caught Avery's fist and held it with a firm grip without even budging or showing any increased effort to stop the powerful punch from Avery.

Both Avery's and Owen's mouths were slightly opened while their eyes bounced between Olivia's face and her hand that held Avery's hand in place. How could she show such power while standing in the daylight, Owen wondered? Whenever Michael stood in the daylight, he was almost at human strength. That, and the fact that a cyclops is stronger than the vampire, made Olivia's strength perplexing. Owen became nervous with the facts leading to her possibly being an actual vampire that somehow had the power to be in the sunlight and not be weakened or killed by it.

"Big mistake! She was really the only good friend I had in my organization," Olivia angrily voiced through her teeth. She then sent a punch that smashed into Avery's temple, which sent her straight to the ground. Olivia stood over Avery and raised her foot to stomp on Avery's head. Owen roared as he sprinted at Olivia. She looked up in time to see Owen ram his shoulder into her and drive her back multiple feet before tackling her to the ground. He then lifted her up and slammed her against one of the HVAC units.

"Oh, kinky. I didn't know you had it in you Owen," Olivia said with a sultry expression on her face.

"If you like that then you will love what's coming up next. Give me the gem!" Owen screamed at Olivia as he transitioned. The chimera's fangs were only inches from Olivia's face while he screamed. As he yelled, Owen grabbed her forearms and pressed his claws into them, but the thing was, she was still smiling while looking at his claws. With a bewildered look on Owen's face, he glanced at her arms and his claws were not breaking through her skin. He took it a step further and flames engulfed both his hands and her forearms.

"You're hot Owen, but to get under my skin you will have to be a lot steamier than that," Olivia whispered in his ear. Owen couldn't figure it out. Even the chimera's flames should have hurt the strongest vampire. He pushed her back against the HVAC unit and while she was pinned against it, Owen unleashed the fire from his mouth directly over Olivia's face and neck area. After a few seconds, Owen let go of Olivia. He expected her to fall after the intense heat of his fire that was blasted all over her face. Even the earth elemental could not handle a fire attack to its face.

"I do admire the effort but you will have to try harder than that," Olivia said in a deep, raspy tone as she shoved Owen off her. The force of her shove was strong enough to send Owen sliding back a few feet. Olivia emerged from the black smoke that surrounded her but the smoke seemed to be only coming from the melted metal of the HVAC unit. Even more alarming was that the metal directly behind her was untouched. She patted the top of her shirt to snuff out the parts that did catch on fire and that is when Owen noticed it.

Her skin was green and full of scales and when she looked at him, he saw a pair of bright emerald green eyes with a thin, black horizontal strip going down the center of each eye. When she smiled, her fangs seemed thicker and longer than a vampire's fangs and she even had thick black claws. Then, with the blink of an eye, she was back to human form.

Owen slowly backed away from Olivia as she smiled and strolled toward him. "You're a dragon? How? I have seen your vampiric face," Owen questioned.

"Do you mean this one?" Olivia playfully asked as she flashed her red vampiric eyes at Owen.

"That can't be. How can you be a dragon and a vampire? Klayden told me, as well as others, that having two monsters inside you would mean certain death since the mind couldn't handle it," Owen said as his brow lowered. Confusion draped over him as he stopped and just stared at Olivia, who now stood just a few feet in front of him.

"Green dragon to be precise and it is possible if said person is also a powerful psychic," Olivia replied with a crooked grin and a quick raise of her brow. Owen's facial expression did not change since he was still trying to process what she just told him. "I don't have time to explain it all to you now. I've got things to do, especially since my life just became a whole lot more interesting," Olivia boasted as she revealed the pouch and waved it slightly above her head for Owen to see.

It was at that moment that Michael snuck up from behind and snatched the gem out of her hand. Olivia whipped around in time to see Michael toss it to Avery who was on one knee and already had her bags strapped around her back. She caught it and bolted toward the side of the building.

"No!" Olivia yelled as she went to pursue Avery but was tangled up by Michael who wrapped his arms around her. He was no match for her strength for she broke the hold. She then turned around and punched him in the chest. Michael grabbed his chest as he fell back to the ground, but it was enough time to give Avery the head start she needed. Avery did not slow down as she reached the ledge and with the momentum she had built up, she leaped from the rooftop.

"Avery!" Owen called out. He was fearful for her safety and hoped she had some plan in mind. Sure enough, he heard glass shatter off in the distance. His guess…his hope, was that she purposely jumped from the building to crash through one of the adjacent building's glass windows. There, she could find multiple ways to hide and escape with the added cover of the police and firemen to ward off any attempts by Olivia. With the gem and Avery now safe again, Owen decided to attack Olivia. He wasn't sure if he could win but he could at least buy Michael some time to escape as well.

"Michael, get out of here!" Owen yelled as he leaped onto Olivia's back. She reached over her shoulder and grabbed Owen and flung him off her. Owen landed hard on the ground but quickly got back up. He was further across the roof than he thought so he had to charge at Olivia to get close enough to attack. Michael was pushing himself off the ground when Olivia took her foot and stomped on Michael's back. He slammed back onto the ground and was pinned face-first to the rooftop while Olivia kept her foot on the upper middle part of his back. Michael hollered in agony as he struggled to get free but he was unsuccessful. Between the dragon's strength and the daylight, Michael had no chance of escape.

Owen charged Olivia and he knew his flames would be useless against her and harmful to Michael so he had to rely on his brute force, so he transitioned deeply to give himself some form of an advantage. At this level of transition, Owen started to show more physical characteristics of the chimera than himself between the fur, muscle mass, and more animal-like facial features. He was quick to reach Olivia and as he was about to lunge at her, she countered by sending flames from her hands at him, which he attempted to dodge as he tried to sidestep the blast.

The heat from the fire was intense, more intense than any other fire he has ever encountered. The flames hit the entire left side of Owen's body, causing him to tumble to the ground. He quickly patted himself to extinguish the few small fires on his clothes.

He could feel and see the burns he suffered on various parts of his body and even smelled burnt hair and flesh. He quickly glanced over himself and could see patches of hairless red blistered skin on parts of his arm and side. He tried to stand up but he couldn't put a lot of pressure on one of his legs due to the burns he suffered. The intensity and determination of the chimera, paired with his overwhelming desire to save Michael, outweighed the pain he felt as he hobbled his way toward Olivia. While Owen made his way toward her, Olivia blanketed the rooftop with her flames. Owen could not get over the intensity and distance of the fire projecting from her hands.

251

Owen had to stop his pursuit for he could not get past the flames that were now in front of him, especially with his injuries. Owen frantically looked around for another option, but there were none presenting themselves. He had to think of something before Olivia could hurt Michael even more…or worse.

"I lost a friend and the gem all in one day and as you can see, I'm not happy about it and I'm tired of waiting. So here is your homework assignment for today. I want you to find Avery and reclaim my gem. Then, you will hold onto it until I come and retrieve it from you. If you don't get the gem for me or try to delay in any way, then I will kill someone close to you. I will keep killing your friends and loved ones until that gem is in my possession. As far as I am concerned from here forward, any blood I spill is on your hands, not mine. Do I make myself clear?" Olivia's voice was absent of emotion as she coldly stared at him. Before Owen could reply, Olivia sent another quick stomp to Michael's upper back. He could hear Michael's spine and other nearby bones crack. Michael yelled again in agony as his squirming stopped.

"Stop! You're killing him. I understand what I need to do…just let him go," Owen pleaded.

Olivia slowly added pressure, to which Owen could now hear the slow cracks and pops coming from Michael as he screamed. "In hindsight, I should have worn my stilettos," Olivia added as she smirked. Owen transitioned down as much as he could before the pain became unbearable. He hoped the act would defuse the situation since he could not get any closer due to the flames. Even if he tried, Olivia had the advantage and could kill Michael before he reached them.

"Please, he is a good man. Don't do it," Owen begged as he reached his hand out to them. The internal fear he was feeling had now surfaced.

"I think what you meant to say, was…a good man," Olivia calmly replied and then smiled. Before Owen could counter, Olivia bent forward and projected an intense stream of fire from her mouth that covered Michael's head, neck, and shoulder area. He could hear him yell but for just a few moments before he fell silent. Even while he was silent, she kept the flames going.

"No!" Owen yelled as he watched helplessly as Olivia burned Michael alive. She then walked off Michael and let the flames follow her off, consuming the rest of Michael. The flames from her mouth ceased and then her eyes drifted up to Owen. A sinister smile then formed on her face.

"I'm so glad my green dragon's breath attack is fire. It's so much more fun and versatile than a poisonous gas that some of the other types of green dragons have. Now, get me my gem or else more of your friends will die!" Olivia exclaimed. The surrounding flames reflected off her dragon eyes before she darted into the air and disappeared into a cloud of black smoke.

Owen was in shock at the events that just occurred. The only thing he knew to do was to extinguish the flames on Michael and get him out of there. The problem was that there were too many flames to get to him and he couldn't find a quick way to put out the flames on Michael or anywhere else. He then heard voices coming from the stairwell. He was running out of time and had to do something.

Unfortunately, he only had one option available to him...he had to leave Michael behind and escape. Frustration and sorrow hit Owen all at once as he screamed from the pain of the loss of a close friend and for having to leave him behind.

"I'm so sorry, Michael," Owen muttered before he turned around and limped as fast as he could to the ledge of the rooftop. As he limped, Owen had to dodge the high, intense flames that were now beginning to spread throughout the rooftop. He could feel the pain coursing through his body but there was no time to slow down. There was a part of him that felt like he deserved to feel pain for not being able to save Michael.

He reached the ledge but Owen was in too much pain to make

the same leap that Avery performed earlier. While standing on the ledge, he could see the window that Avery crashed through. Owen's attention was then diverted to the voices of the first responders that reached the doorway but luckily for him, the black smoke concealed him from the others. He knew the smoke could vanish with just a strong gust of wind so he had to act quickly.

He climbed over the ledge and used his claws and footing to keep himself from plummeting to his death. Owen began to cough as the black smoke was now surrounding him, even when he was not on the roof itself. He thought about climbing down the rest of the way but now there were crowds of people lining the streets. He had to think quickly before he was noticed so he strategically fell to the closest balcony and entered the room.

It was vacant and the fire alarms were going off so he knew he could not just hide out in the room until everything blew over. Instead, he needed to exit the building like any other occupant but there was a problem. Owen was in transition and if he reverted to his human form the pain would skyrocket. Unfortunately, there was no other way around it. The silver lining was that he could hold off on transitioning back to human until he was around other people.

Owen snuck out of the room and into the stairwell and proceeded to go down the stairs, and not a moment too soon, for the fire from the roof had already made it to the floor below it. He made it all the way down to the third floor before he heard more first responders coming up the steps. Owen stopped and held onto the railing to brace himself for the pain he was about to experience.

"Hello! Are you okay? Hold on, we are coming to you," one of the first responders yelled as their pace quickened up the stairs.

Owen took three quick breaths and transitioned to human and with that, all the pain that it entailed. He instantly collapsed as the searing pain shot through his veins from the burns he sustained. His cough also became worse as he hacked while on his hands and knees.

The first responders reached him and wrapped him in a blanket and gave him a few breaths from their oxygen tank before escorting him the rest of the way to the ground floor. With his face shielded by the blanket, Owen took the edge off his pain by slightly transitioning. That was enough for him to be able to walk down the remaining set of stairs. Once he reached the lobby, the EMTs took over and led Owen to an ambulance. As they began to take the blanket off, Owen switched back to his human form and once they examined him, they went into action. They sprayed the burns with something that felt like a wintery blast hitting him. They then gave him a shot of what he figured was something for the pain. Before they could attempt an IV, they instructed Owen to stay where he was since they had to assist others.

Unattended, Owen looked around for an escape route, and time was now a factor since the pain meds were beginning to work. He could feel himself becoming light-headed and wobbly. With everybody's attention on the burning building, Owen slipped into a low-level transition. To his surprise, he felt less compromised from the pain medication. With his mind a bit clearer, Owen rolled up his blanket and let the hand that was holding the blanket become ablaze. Once the blanket was on fire, he tossed it in a nearby bush and watched it start to crackle from the slow burn it was experiencing.

"Fire," Owen yelled as he walked away with his head down. Now, the attention was either on the building or the small bushfire. As the crowds dispersed in different directions, Owen snaked his way around the oncoming people until he was cleared from the chaos of the large crowds and rescue vehicles. He made his way down a few alleyways until he knew he could not be found. Within the silence, the memories of Michael's death were louder than ever. He began to scream while punching the side of a brick building a few times before collapsing onto the ground.

With his bloody knuckles and mustering up just enough emotional strength, Owen took out his phone and sent a message to everyone.

"Olivia is not only a traitor but she is also the leader and more dangerous than you think. She is both a green dragon and a vampire. Olivia does not have the gem but knows where it is. Also, sorry to inform everyone this way but she also killed Michael."

Owen didn't have it in him to try to make the message hard to decipher and why would he have to anyway, considering Olivia has all the inside information anyway. He also hated the fact that he announced Michael's death via text but he feared if he didn't, then his friends might try to contact or search for him. He put his phone away, not worrying about the responses, and lowered his head and wept for the loss of his friend.

Hours passed before Owen heard footsteps nearby. "Whomever you are go away. I am not in the mood," Owen grumbled while he sat on the ground and against the wall.

"Not even for a fellow chimera?" Abigail inquired in a sympathetic tone. Owen turned his head to see her slowly walking toward him. He remained in his low-level state of transition as Owen responded with just a slight nod. She cringed as she grew near due to the sight of the burns on Owen's body before she sat down next to him.

"I'm sorry. I know you and Michael were close and even though I didn't know him as well as you did, from the interactions I had with him he seemed like a nice guy." Abigail added.

"Yes, he was," Owen responded with a soft, distant tone while he stared in front of him.

"The car isn't far from here. Everyone is meeting up where the farmlands and the edge of the city meet to discuss what to do now," Abigail mentioned but Owen didn't move or look in Abigail's direction. "Please," Abigail politely added as she extended her hand to Owen. He grabbed it and she helped him to his feet.

The two then walked down a few short alleyways until they arrived at a side street. Even with dusk approaching and being as far away from the hotel as they were, Owen could still see the smoke

256

from the hotel. The two got in the car and left. Owen stared aimlessly out the window while Abigail drove. The car ride was silent, minus the urge for revenge that was slowly germinating within Owen's mind. By the time they reached the other set of cars, it was nighttime. Everyone emerged from their respective vehicles when they arrived.

Owen hobbled toward the rest, refusing help from Abigail as he fought through the pain that was beginning to return from him transitioning closer to his human state. Avery ran up to Owen and went to hug him but stopped.

"Sorry, you look like everything on you hurts. I can't believe this is happening," Avery said through her tears.

"That makes two of us," Owen said, emotionless. Even the sight of Avery crying didn't faze him. He felt numb.

"How did it happen?" Bailey asked in a steady voice as tears rolled down her face.

"Just like the text said. Olivia, the one that has been with everyone this entire time, killed him. Slowly and brutally." Owen's voice became stern as his temper began to rise.

"I'm sorry, Owen. Let me heal you," Selena gently asked as she extended her hand toward Owen but he shrugged away from her.

"It won't take away the pain or the memories of Olivia burning him alive after she crushed his spine," Owen snapped at Selena. More tears appeared from Bailey and Avery as they covered their mouths from the disturbing details of Michael's death.

"Mind your tongue. She did nothing to deserve that outburst," Caine snapped back.

"You're right. It should be you. You were her mentor. How did you not see the conspiracy unless you were a part of it," Owen countered in a loud voice.

"You dare accuse me," Caine yelled at Owen as he approached him. Selena stepped in front of Caine to keep him from advancing. "I assure you that I had no part in her treachery and I for one do not like being a pawn in someone's game. She used me! Her deception will bring her nothing but pain and death." Caine's words were full of hate as he spoke.

Owen scoffed and turned his attention to Cedric. "I thought you knew everyone in the club. How could you not have seen her for the imposter that she was?" Owen angrily questioned.

Cedric's eyes narrowed in on Owen while taking a step forward. "Easy there, boy. Her background check was clean and with what Caine witnessed with the gem and the transitioning, there was no reason to look any further." Owen shook his head with frustration as he hobbled around the group.

"Owen, I may not be able to heal your emotional wounds but at least let me fix your physical injuries. You can't complete the mission and keep Michael's death from being in vain if you are not at your best. Please, let me help you," Selena pleaded. Owen nodded in agreement for he knew she was right. Selena gently smiled as she put her hand on Owen's shoulder. Her hand began to glow and a few minutes later, Owen was healed. With his injuries gone, Owen was finally able to transition back to his human state. Selena then walked off to the side to ease herself back out of transition.

"Thank you and I'm sorry, Selena. Sorry to everybody. You just don't know how upset…how mad I am," Owen said as he firmly pressed his lips together to help prevent any more emotional outbursts. "Let me get everyone up to speed."

The group gathered around Owen as he replayed the horrible events that took place from when Avery leaped off the roof to when Abigail found him afterward since Avery already filled them in on the events beforehand. However, Owen did have to fill in some of the holes for when Avery was out of it after Olivia's attack on her. Once Owen finished with all the details, he could see the shock on everyone's faces.

Avery was still upset and Bailey's grief appeared to have converted to anger as her face was stern and her eyes were narrow while she paced back and forth. Bailey and Michael had been partnered up since the beginning, so he could imagine how Bailey felt. Selena looked just as hurt as Avery but that too did not surprise Owen due to her empathetic nature. Cedric immediately went to his phone after Owen finished and began to push for answers. As for Caine, his lips were curled inward and his eyes were squinted as he balled his fists and paced back and forth. Caine appeared to be moments away from going on a raging killing spree.

Abigail, who seemed frustrated by how they were all tricked by Olivia, approached Owen. "What do you need us to do?"

"Help me hunt her down and kill her," Owen quickly responded without emotion.

"We need to think this through. I'm all for killing her but we need a plan. She is a vampire, a dragon, and a psychic. She…" Owen yelled from the spillover of anger he was feeling, which interrupted Abigail's calm retort.

"I don't want to plan. I'm tired of talking, thinking, planning, and waiting. It's time for action! We form hunting parties and go find her and end this!"

"Owen, do you think," Cedric began to talk but was interrupted by Owen.

"There's that word again. Think! Do you want to know what I think? I think that I could have somehow saved Michael from dying. I think I could have found some way to put out the flames to carry his body away and not leave him alone on top of some hotel. I think I really want to tear Olivia apart," Owen spat as his eyes became glassy.

"Owen, it's not your fault," Avery commented as her voice cracked.

"It is my fault!" Owen retorted. "I will have to live with it. I will have to live with the memory of a person that had a good heart and was a good friend, who is now dead. He didn't just die quickly. No…he suffered. She broke his spine and then slowly broke the surrounding bones before burning him alive. I have all those sounds and images etched into my brain now and I deserve it," Owen added as tears rolled down his cheek.

"I'm sorry you had to witness that but it's not your fault and she is the one who killed Michael, not you. I am not going to play the blame game anymore. You did all that you could. Now, before you get feisty, I know some people down at the coroner's office. I promise I will get Michael's remains back to you so he can be properly buried," Cedric mentioned with a slight grin and his hand on Owen's shoulder.

"Thank you. I appreciate it but that still leaves Olivia. Michael, along with all the people that have died and suffered in her pursuit of this gem, deserves justice. Speaking of the gem, Avery, do you still have it?" Owen asked. He was now composed but it was driven by his determination.

"I do. Here it is. Please, think before you act. I don't trust that look on your face," Avery gently said to Owen. He smiled as he took the pouch from Avery.

"Am I the only person that enjoys the idea of a hunting party?" Caine asked while he grinned.

"I like it too," Bailey said as she stood up. Like Owen, her tears had vanished and were replaced with determination and even rage as she mirrored Caine's earlier demeanor when he felt betrayed.

Owen approached Caine and presented him with the pouch. "Why are you giving me this?" Caine asked.

"Because I too like the hunting party idea and Olivia will think either Avery or I have it…most likely me, so I want to give it to the last person in the world she would think I would give it to. Besides, if there is an issue you are not afraid to get your hands…messy," Owen replied as he slightly smiled. He then laid the pouch down in Caine's palm.

"That's a lot of trust that you are putting into a person you accused not too long ago," Caine commented as he wrapped his fingers around the pouch.

"Don't make me regret it," Owen replied.

"I have some information that will narrow our search. We have her pinned to three different locations where she could be staying. One in the city, one near the club, and the last one is a farmhouse in the country area not too far from here. She may be in one of those but if not, then maybe we can find a clue to where she might be going next in one of those locations," Cedric said with a hopeful grin.

"Perfect. Thank you. We can divide up into teams to swiftly cover more ground. Avery and I will take the farmhouse, while Selena, Caine, and Bailey will take the one near the club just in case daylight comes and Caine needs shelter. Also, I added an extra person to your group to help guard the gem. Cedric and Abigail can take the one in the city. It will give you a chance to get your hands dirty away from your kingdom if you don't mind," Owen directed.

"I like how you think," Cedric responded as he smiled.

Caine approached Owen and put a firm grip on his shoulder and looked into his eyes. "Come on mate, let's finish this."

CHAPTER 15

Avery raised her hand right before she spoke. "How does one do that?"

"My guess is that we must strike hard while she is in human form or in the first stage of transition. That is when she is at her most vulnerable. Remember, a dragon isn't invulnerable or immortal and even though they may have a high resilience against fire, they are not fire-resistant. At least not a green dragon. You must strike hard with whatever weapon you are using because if she transitions deep enough, the scales will be nearly impossible to penetrate. I'm not sure where the underbelly of a dragon, where there are fewer scales, will be located on her. Just remember, between the timing and with enough strength and the proper weapon, man-made or from our own creature, she can be killed."

Owen paused as he rubbed the back of his neck and sighed. "The problem is, like me, she seems to be able to transition at will and without effort. That means she has more and quicker access to her creatures so once she is aware, don't continue unless you feel you still have the advantage. Remember, she is also a vampire and I have no idea if she has access to both creatures at the same time or not, so be mindful. Olivia has already made it clear that she will kill us if we don't give her the gem. Going on the offensive will provoke her."

Owen replied in a calm yet focused tone.

"And if we miss that opportunity?" Abigail asked.

"If you miss your chance and you can't find a way to immobilize or trap her, then retreat and contact the rest of us. Once we know where she is, then together, we may be able to take her out," Owen responded.

"Any information you can gather during this hunt may help either in how to kill her or how she plans to use the gem," Selena added. Owen nodded at her comment with approval.

"You think there is a special way to kill her?" Cedric inquired.

"What do you mean?" Bailey asked with her brows knitted.

"When we go in for the kill do we have to be mindful to strike an area that would also kill a vampire?" Cedric elaborated.

"Good question. Just kill her using a technique that would kill both a green dragon and a vampire. Cut off her head, rip her heart out, burn her alive, dig a hole in her chest and then jam a wooden stake in her heart. Have fun with it," Caine responded with a devious grin.

Owen lightly chuckled at Caine's response. "He has a point to some extent. Let's get moving before we lose any more time. After what happened at the hotel, I don't think she will be expecting a retaliation so swiftly," Owen added. He glanced around the room as everyone prepared to leave and was eager to begin the hunt.

"Owen, wait," Abigail said as she grabbed his arm, which caused Owen to face her. "Be careful out there and don't forget you are a chimera; however, don't just focus on the chimera's power. Not only do you have the predatory nature and stealth of a lion but you also have the sly, sneaky nature of a snake as well. Use that to your advantage when you are stalking your prey," Abigail commented as she stared fiercely into Owen's eyes.

"What...the goat can't be stealthy too?" Owen jested which caused Abigail to smile and shake her head. "I never thought I would hear a dragon be called prey," Owen added with a partial smile.

"Then you weren't around during the times when dragon slayers and knights hunted these creatures that threatened the lands, even the non-evil metal dragons. If you want revenge then I got your back but just be smart about it or else there will be someone else getting revenge for you," Abigail added while she put her hand on Owen's shoulder and smiled.

"I see your point and I will bear it in mind. Be safe," Owen said as he smiled and gave Abigail a hug.

"You ready to roll out?" Bailey asked as she was about to pass by Owen.

"Yes, I am," Owen replied but as he was about to walk away, Bailey tapped him on his arm.

"What's up? I'm surprised you aren't in the car already and trying to drive off," Owen asked out of curiosity.

"I just wanted to say thank you for bringing the fight to Olivia. We have been on the defensive for so long and we have struggled and lost so it feels good to be switching gears," Bailey responded.

"Anytime. Now let's make Olivia pay for her actions so we can have some justice and finally get that gem to the facility," Owen beamed with confidence as he replied to Bailey. The two fist-bumped before parting ways.

Everybody split up into their respective groups, swapped out supplies between their cars, and said their respective goodbyes before getting inside their vehicles.

The engines revved and before anybody drove off Owen honked his horn which caused everyone to look in his direction. Owen looked at each of their faces. As determined that he was to have Olivia dead, he still feared for everyone's safety.

"Good luck!" Owen called out before he pulled onto the road. Caine's group followed Owen while Abigail's group turned around and went back toward the city.

"Two questions," Avery said as she glanced over to Owen.

"Hopefully two answers," Owen jokingly responded.

"Why did you pick the farmhouse?" Avery inquired.

"Because I feel like there is a good possibility that Olivia is there," Owen nonchalantly responded.

"How are you so sure?" Avery questioned as her forehead crinkled.

"It's more of a hunch. She would want to be close to you and Hailey since that is where the gem was, but also be able to make it to the club and put on her charade for everyone to see. She was late when I first met everybody and her excuse was that she was covering her tracks to make sure she wasn't being followed. In reality, I bet she was driving into the area and got delayed. Think about it. She knew the city would be where you and Hailey would end up, so if she had a place in the city then it would be too obvious that she was the traitor because Cedric would have found out. Besides, staying in the middle also works out if the gem moved elsewhere." Owen responded while not taking his eyes off the road.

"Wow, that's some hunch," Avery commented. The two of them chuckled over her response. "It does make sense though. Why did you pick me to go with you?"

"Because no one else would want you on their team," Owen quickly replied while he grinned.

"Really! Shut up!" Avery loudly spoke as her eyes grew wide while she laughed.

"Sorry, couldn't help it. Honestly, there are a million reasons why I would want you on my team. Just to name a few…I trust you more than anybody I know. You are also smart and can handle your own in a fight. Most importantly, if you are near me, I know I can protect you if you ever needed it." Owen responded.

"Good to know I'm respected in battle. Back in the day, I was usually picked last due to my size and strength," Avery commented.

"It's more than just you being great on missions. I enjoy being around you. Your presence alone always puts me in a better mood. I cherish your compassion and humor and consider myself lucky to be as close to you as we are," Owen added with a quick glance over to Avery while he smiled.

She pouted her lips briefly before she smiled and gave his knee a quick rub. "Awe, thank you. I'm also happy we are as close as we are and there are a lot of things that I cherish about you as well."

"Like?" Owen playfully asked.

"I would but there are so many traits that it would take me too long to list them and I don't want to delay the mission," Avery mocked in a joking way. Owen laughed and nodded his head.

"So, what secret are you hiding?" Avery asked with an arched eyebrow.

"What are you talking about?" Owen asked. His brow lowered for he did not know what she was referring to.

"Back there, something with the exchanges between you and Caine," Avery responded.

Owen paused for a moment before he realized she may be referring to Caine's secret. It became second nature to conceal his secret that he didn't even think about it. "You already asked two questions," Owen countered, followed by a nervous smile.

"Oh, come on now. That second question was more like part of the first question. Just tell me. You know I can tell when you are hiding something and you know I can keep a secret. Spill it," Avery prodded with a quick tap on his arm.

Owen's lips pressed firmly together as he fought the urge to reveal the secret but Avery was right, he could trust her. "Caine is a vampire."

"Stop messing around. We all know he is a vampire. What's the real secret?" Avery asked as she half-smiled.

"No...he is an actual vampire, not a hybrid," Owen answered as he gave her a quick serious look to indicate he was not joking.

"Wait...what! Like a full-blown, drink your blood, shimmer in the daylight, kind of vampire?" Avery asked as her jaw dropped.

Owen began to laugh at the thought of Caine sparkling. "Yes, minus the shimmering and it would probably be best that you don't ask him if he shimmers."

"How is that even possible?" Avery asked.

"Long story short, he was turned into a vampire then someone captured him in a gem. Then, someone else found the gem and they weren't the right match so the person turned into the creature within the gem, which happened to be Caine. Back then, there was no facility where people picked the gems. It wouldn't surprise me if there are more creatures roaming free all over the world," Owen replied.

"I can't believe it," Avery muttered.

"Well, believe it, and please don't tell anybody, especially Caine, that you know. I told him I would keep his secret and if you haven't noticed already, he is not the nicest person around," Owen sarcastically replied.

"I promise I won't. Thank you for telling me. That's just amazing and it also explains why you were more concerned about daylight with him than you normally would be with Mi...any other hybrid," Avery said while she stammered toward the end. Owen could tell she was going to say Michael before she switched it to hybrid. "You know who would be head over heels excited about this?" Avery asked. He knew the question was a diversion tactic to focus the conversation anywhere else other than Michael but he didn't mind. If anything, he welcomed it.

After a moment, Owen thought of a name, "Amelia."

"Exactly. If she didn't ask him a ton of questions, she would be planning their wedding...maybe both," Avery said with an excited tone. Owen laughed and nodded in agreement.

As Owen drove, the two talked about a variety of subjects to the point the drive felt like a fun road trip and not a trip to do battle once again. This time, a battle against an opponent that far outranked each of them. Eventually, Owen could see the house far off in the distance. He waved at the group in Caine's car as he slowed down and shut off his lights. The group waved back as they sped away. A few minutes later Owen pulled the car off the road and parked it near a set of trees to help mask their vehicle.

"Okay, from here on we are on foot. We need to be able to sneak in and ambush her so stealth is key." Owen reiterated.

"I know and as much as you praise me, stealth isn't one of my strong skillsets and when you add a cyclops to it, you might as well just send a marching band across the field," Avery embarrassingly commented.

"True and bringing your hammer axe won't make it any better. You should probably put that back in the trunk for now," Owen suggested.

"You want me to leave behind my only means of killing her?" Avery asked with a dumbfounded expression.

"Hear me out. It won't work if she happens to be in a house since you will need a lot of space to swing the axe hard enough to even penetrate her skin. With your strength you can go for a neck snap or just knock her out and then kill her afterward," Owen responded.

Avery sighed, "Yeah, you are right."

Owen lightly chuckled. "Just follow my lead and you will be fine. Besides, I'm sure you and Hailey had to be stealthy while protecting the gem."

"More like hiding, being on the lookout, and fighting. Never had to ninja our way in or out of anything before," Avery countered.

"Well, I guess now you get to try this new skill on something easy," Owen joked which caused Avery to roll her eyes.

The two left the car and scurried between the bushes and trees as much as they could as they made their way to the farmhouse. Occasionally, they did have to cross a field but with the new moon phase, the area was quite dark. Owen, using the chimera's eyes, was able to see in the dark so he took the lead and let Avery hold onto his back whenever she needed to. They decided to go to the house first and then the barn second since the house was closer.

The style and wear of the two-story white house indicated it was built many years ago. If Owen had to guess, it was maybe around a hundred years old. Even though it appeared to be old, the house still had a warm, rustic feel to it between the white rocking chairs, a large wooden wheel propped against the house, and flowers sporadically planted around the house. There were steps that led to a porch that wrapped around the house itself, with columns every handful of feet to support it.

As they crept toward the house, the inside was dark. Owen wasn't sure if it was because no one was home, they were asleep, or it was a trap. The porch creaked with each step he took, which he cringed each time he heard the noise. He would hear the same sound again as Avery followed behind him. They continued along the porch and peeked through the windows in order to get a view of the darkness inside.

"I can't see anything. You?" Avery quietly asked.

"I can see but there isn't much to comment about," Owen whispered.

"Maybe we can find a quiet way into the house and search it to see if there is any sign of Olivia or what she is up to," Avery suggested. Before Owen could respond he was blinded by an array of bright lights. Avery and Owen shielded their eyes until they were adjusted. From what Owen could see, the lights were coming from the tops of wooden poles scattered around the house and the barn, and from the house itself.

"That can't be good," Owen muttered.

"We lost the element of surprise. Now what?" Avery asked as they both quickly looked around in all directions.

Owen turned to Avery. "I think we need to get away from this house before…"

"Owen, watch out!" Avery interrupted Owen as her eyes widened with fear as she looked behind him. Before Owen could turn around, he felt someone roughly put their hands on both of his temples. He yelled in pain, for it felt like someone put his brain in a blender. His vision became blurry, but from what he could tell, Avery started to come toward him but stopped. For what felt like a lifetime, but was only for a few brief agonizing moments, Owen was unable to move. Then, as quickly as the pain started, it stopped. He stumbled forward while he held his head until Avery grabbed his arms to keep him steady.

"Are you okay? What did you do to him?" Avery angrily asked as the blue eyes of her cyclops flashed at the person standing behind Owen. He turned around, with his hand on Avery's shoulder to keep him steady for he still felt wobbly and his head was still pounding. Once Owen was able to stand firmly on his two feet, that was when he noticed Olivia standing in front of them with a smug expression on her face.

"An insurance policy," Olivia replied with a quick raise of her brow.

"What do you mean?" Avery inquired with a furrowed brow.

"Do you remember when you told us the story about how Livia was able to restore order to your chaotic mind by giving you control?" Olivia's smile grew as her eyes drifted from Avery to Owen.

"What did you do?" Owen fearfully asked. It felt like the air around him was sucked away. He was scared to hear her response.

"Let's just say that with literally a snap of my fingers, you won't be the sweet, lovable Owen we all know," Olivia responded as she held up her hand with her thumb and middle finger pressed together.

"Please, don't! I won't have any control over my actions if the chimera has free reign within my mind. I could hurt or kill somebody. I can't go back to that. Just a short taste of it was too much," Owen begged as he took a couple of steps toward her. He dreaded the idea of his mind going back to what it was before Livia fixed it. Even worse, if Olivia snapped her fingers now then Avery potentially could be in danger or anybody else that was in his presence. The thought made him nauseous.

"Follow me," Olivia said as she smiled and walked past the two and toward the barn. Avery and Owen did as she requested and followed behind her. Olivia confidently strutted in front of them without looking behind her.

"How are you feeling?" Avery asked Owen as they walked.

"Not sure. The intense pain is gone but it now feels like my brain is vibrating. It's a weird sensation," Owen responded as he shook his head to clear his mind.

"You will feel like that until either I undo what I did or snap my fingers," Olivia commented without turning her head.

"Sorry, Owen. I tried to stop her but she said she would kill you if I came any closer," Avery remarked.

"She would have," Olivia said as she smiled over her shoulder.

"It's okay. We just need to find a way out of this or at least warn the others," Owen whispered.

"I don't know what you two are whispering about but any attempts against me or if you even touch your phones to contact your friends will earn Owen a snap," Olivia commented as she raised her hand with the same fingers pressed again.

"Maybe we can find a way to rip off both your hands so you can't snap," Owen grumbled. He then went to secretly extend his claws when he realized there was a problem, he could not transition.

"Well unless you plan on Avery attempting that without her trusty hammer axe, then you got issues because I'm sure by now you realize you can't transition," Olivia added.

"Is it true?" Avery inquired. Owen nodded.

"I knew I should have brought my hammer axe," Avery huffed. Owen could only shrug as a response for now he felt she was right.

They grew closer and closer to the barn. With all the lights, Owen could see everything as if it was daytime. The barn seemed to be your classic red barn with white trim and Owen could see the different corrals and pens surrounding it but oddly enough there were not any animals. Olivia opened the large barn doors and strolled inside as Avery and Owen followed behind her. There was enough light from outside shining inside the barn to keep it bright enough for everyone to see.

"Do I even want to know what happened to the owners?" Owen sarcastically asked.

Olivia turned around. "They got the news of a gas leak on their property so they, along with their smelly livestock, had to relocate until the extensive problem was resolved. So lucky for them that the inspector caught that nasty leak before it harmed anybody or any of their precious animals," Olivia mockingly replied.

"The inspector was working for you, wasn't he?" Owen asked.

"Of course, I've got people everywhere. Even someone to install all these lights for an occasion just like tonight when an unexpected guest arrives," Olivia replied.

Olivia then put out her hand, "Which one of you has my gem?"

"None of us," Owen replied.

"Now would not be a good time to lie to me," Olivia said as she rose her hand in the air and pressed her fingers together.

"He wasn't lying. We don't have it," Avery insisted.

Olivia walked closer to them as her eyes narrowed. "You two are telling the truth. Smart. Let's see if you can keep being smart. Who has the gem?"

"If you are such a powerful psychic then why don't you just read our minds and find out who has it. Even better, why haven't you already just made the person give it to you? I am wondering if you are as powerful of a psychic as you claim to be," Avery provoked.

"You are the last person to be trying my nerves little girl after you killed my close friend. You better start to appreciate how lucky you are that I am not at my full strength or else I would have made you do horrific things before killing you myself," Olivia's eyes flared as she spoke.

"Then you killed a close friend of ours so I guess that makes us even," Owen retorted.

"You barely knew Michael long enough to constitute him being such a close friend. I knew my friend way before you were even a sparkle in your parents' eyes," Olivia countered.

"Why aren't you at full power?" Owen inquired as he put his hand on Avery's shoulder and then took a few steps forward. He wanted Olivia to focus on him and not Avery since she seemed to be a sore spot for Olivia and he didn't want to provoke anything. He now hoped to see how much information he could gather while they could.

"It takes a lot of mind power to control two creatures. Even more when one of them is as rare and powerful as the green dragon. The best I can do now with my psychic powers are basic parlor tricks," Olivia responded.

Owen scoffed. "That's why you want to gem. Your question before about what we would wish for and you said to be able to control people's minds. You think the djinn can give you your full power back, but how do you think you can even control the djinn if it's locked inside the gem or even inside someone?" Owen asked.

"Is this the part where the villain reveals their diabolical plan to the hero so you can find a way to stop me?" Olivia sarcastically responded while she slowly approached Owen.

"Too obvious?" Owen responded after he gave Olivia a smirk.

A smile grew on Olivia's face. "Cute…I'll bite. You can't stop me anyway. The best you can do now is just to delay the inevitable." Olivia gently slid her fingers from Owen's left shoulder and across his chest as she walked off to the side of the barn. Owen pretended her touch did not make his skin crawl as he fought back the disgust he felt for her as he followed Olivia.

"What would you say if I found a way to transfer the djinn from the gem to a different vessel other than a human? A vessel that it can be summoned from," Olivia said as she turned around. Owen's eyes grew wide from the impact of what Olivia just told him. The possibilities were endless and scary with a djinn in her control.

"How?" Owen inquired. His curiosity was genuine at that point.

"With the correct ingredients you would be surprised what you can cook up," Olivia responded as she winked.

"If you found a way to do that then why not just remove one of your creatures from you back into a gem?" Avery coarsely asked. Owen turned his head toward her and his eyes widened. He was quietly indicating to her to not agitate Olivia.

"Oh, gee…why didn't I think of that," Olivia mockingly responded. "Maybe because I already tried and news flash, it doesn't work. The creature itself cannot be transferred back to the gem without breaking the person's mind. So, since I didn't want to be turned into a drooling crazy person like those poor souls that I used for that experiment, I decided to go a different route."

"You experimented on people?" Owen asked as his disgust surfaced.

"Don't you get all judgy," Olivia countered as her eyes narrowed. "Those people volunteered. They were so desperate to get their creature out of them that they didn't care about the consequences," Olivia nonchalantly added. As much as Owen wanted to debate the morals behind her comment, he chose to stay silent for fear of making her angry.

"What will your other two wishes be?" Owen asked to not only change the direction of the conversation but to also gather more information.

"I have some ideas floating around in my head. If I can't narrow it down, I can always make it up on the next set of wishes," Olivia shrugged as if it was not a big deal to her.

"It doesn't work that way. You only get three wishes…unless you figured out something with more of those ingredients you were telling us about before," Owen commented.

Olivia smiled as she took a few steps closer to Owen. "See…I knew you were more than just looks. The ingredients for this part are simple, and something I have an abundance of…people." Owen tilted his head and knitted his brow, unsure of what she meant by her comment. Seeing Owen's reaction, Olivia continued.

"Over the years, I have gained followers. At first, it was simply because I am a strong leader who is not only a psychic but also a vampire and a dragon. That alone looks great on a resume and will inspire people to follow you. As my reign continued, the word got out that one way or another, I will deliver on what I promised, so you can imagine the influx of followers that I gained when I said that I found a way to grant wishes to my most loyal of followers. Two wishes for me, which I will instruct them what to say, and one wish for them. I literally have a legion of people chomping at the chance to gain a wish." Olivia smiled as she gloated for a few seconds.

"With my psychic powers fully restored, I can ensure that a person won't change their mind and take all the wishes for themselves or use any against me. I could make them give all three of their wishes to me but instead, I allow them to have one wish for themselves. So you see, I'm not the villain here. Think of what you could do with a wish. At this point, I would be willing to allow you and each of your friends to have one wish each if you peacefully hand over the gem to me."

"Bargaining now. Someone must be getting desperate," Avery blurted out.

"Avery…" Owen turned and raised his hand to silence Avery before she said too much but she ignored his attempts to silence her and continued to talk.

"No, I'm not going to walk on eggshells in front of the self-proclaimed saint because she will allow someone to have a wish. It's just another form of manipulation to grow her army while she does whatever and kills whomever to get her way. You are no better than Klayden," Avery berated Olivia as she took a few steps past Owen. Avery's eyes were intense as she approached Olivia.

To Owen's surprise, Olivia didn't seem bothered by Avery's verbal assault. If anything, she chuckled lightly to herself. She then began to slowly circle Owen and Avery before she spoke.

"I never claimed to be a saint and as for Klayden, I am nothing like him. He was fueled by the desire to gain a wish in order to find some loophole to get his family back. I think that, combined with his dislike for Isaac, is what kept him driven to achieve my goal, no matter what it took. I'm not sure how he was going to reunite with his family since a djinn can't bring anyone back from the dead, but I was intrigued to see how he would pull it off."

"You found out his vulnerabilities with Isaac and his family and twisted it around and used it to gain Klayden as one of your minions. He was not perfect but you gave him just enough of a nudge to push him to become the monster he turned out to be in the end," Owen commented with a hint of disdain. He was trying to remain calm and gather as much information as he could, but it was now becoming difficult the more Olivia spoke.

"Anybody determined in accomplishing their goals can be viewed as a monster," Olivia countered as she shrugged. "Well, this conversation is beginning to bore me so I guess I will be on my way, but first, some last-minute business that still needs to be handled," Olivia added as she went to snap her fingers.

"No! Please, I can't go back to what I was before," Owen quickly spoke as he begged while extending his hands out, desperately hoping she would hear his plea and stop. Owen's anxiety was overflowing at this point as he began to breathe quicker.

"It's funny that you keep bringing that up but I never said that was what was going to happen when I snapped my fingers," Olivia replied with a devious grin.

"What will happen?" Avery slowly asked. Owen's eyes were intently on Olivia in fear of the unknown. Even his breathing went from quick to almost nonexistent.

"You see, I thought about undoing what Livia did but that

doesn't guarantee anything. Owen could still find the will to resist the chimera, especially with the help of sweet little, apparently walk-on-water-perfect Avery to assist him. Then, Livia could easily revert his mind to what it was before. Then, I thought about just killing one or both of you here and now, but that gets old after all these years. Same with the mind powers…at some point, it gets so boring knowing you can do whatever you want. Yes, trust me, I see the irony of me wanting my mental abilities back to full strength after that last comment. What can I say…they are handy to have at times. Anyway, one starts to find ways to add some spice to their bland ole life. I thought to myself…what could I do to make this night spicier while still achieving my objectives?" A crooked smile then formed on Olivia's face.

"What are your objectives?" Avery asked.

"One of them is to kill you. That should not be a surprise since I already told you that I would get you back for killing my friend. Of course, the gem is my top priority but as I said before, I make good on my promises," Olivia replied with a hint of a grin afterward.

"I will never kill Avery!" Owen blurted out as he approached Olivia.

"Once again, putting words into my mouth. I never said you were going to kill Avery." Olivia's smile grew even bigger now.

Owen gasped and his eyes grew wide as a wave of fear washed over him. He was only able to say a couple of words. "The chimera."

"Smart boy. Not only will the chimera have no quarrel killing Avery since well…that's what they do, but you will have full memory of it whenever you transition back. It accomplishes my goal, sends a message, and the way Avery dies will have more style than just killing her myself," Olivia bragged as she started to walk away.

"No, please, you can't! I don't have any control over the chimera. Even if you succeed, you will then have a chimera on the loose. What if it wanders into the city or attacks the other farmhouses in the area? Innocent people will be killed and it could lead to exposure which will put a damper on your plan real quick," Owen countered. He hoped that anything he just said would change Olivia's mind.

Olivia turned around, with a smile still on her face, as she slowly walked back toward Owen. "I know you don't have any control over the chimera and that's the point. As for it wandering into the city or any heavily populated area, I doubt it. The creature is smart enough to not draw attention to itself. As for the farmers around here, I am willing to take that chance if a few of them die. Wild animals do habit this area. Besides, there are hundreds of acres around here for it to roam around and hide. There is also enough livestock for it to feed on, provided it's still hungry after it eats your precious little friend," Olivia responded with a playful yet devious smile on her face as she stood within a couple of feet from Owen.

"Kill me instead," Owen blurted out.

"Owen, no!" Avery exclaimed.

Owen put his hand up to silence Avery. "Kill me and say it was to punish Avery. To make her suffering last longer than just killing her quickly."

"Impressive. I like the way you think, Owen," Olivia said as she approached him. "However, I like my plan better. People would not be surprised if you died and not Avery because regardless of what story I told, they would know you sacrificed yourself for her because that's who you are," Olivia replied as she laid her hand on Owen's chest. She then smiled and began to skip away. Owen's mind raced as he tried to think of anything he could do to prevent him from turning or Avery from dying but he couldn't think of anything. His stomach was in knots.

Owen quickly turned around to Avery. "Run! Go now. Get a head start!" Owen frantically said as he was in full panic mode at this point.

"No, I am staying with you. I am not leaving you and maybe I can help settle your mind enough for you to fight whatever hold she

278

has on you," Avery countered as she came closer to Owen and reached out to him but he backed away and held his hands up. He needed to keep his distance from her since he didn't know when Olivia would snap her fingers. He even thought about asking Avery to kill him but he knew she wouldn't and if Owen decided to run, Olivia would snap her fingers before he could even make it out of the barn.

"Turn into the cyclops. If you won't run and your plan doesn't work then it is your only chance at survival," Owen hastily suggested.

"The cyclops can't win against the chimera. Maybe if it had a weapon and somehow caught it off guard to get in the first attack, but even then, that is a big maybe. Me transitioning into the cyclops would just make me a bigger target for the chimera." Avery's eyes were glassy and her voice trembled but regardless of how upset and scared she was, Avery remained calm and didn't budge. Owen wasn't sure if it was for his sake or her realization of what was to come.

"If this doesn't go well, you must promise me that you will not blame yourself. Please Owen…promise me!" Avery added as tears began to roll down her cheeks.

"I promise," Owen lightly responded as a tear rolled down his cheek.

"Well, it has been fun but I must be moving. Even I don't want to be around for the chimera. I want its full attention on Avery and me being around may distract it, but Owen please feel free to find me later to tell me how horribly she died," Olivia said as she raised her hand and pressed her fingers together.

Owen's eyes began to water even more as he turned to face Olivia. "Please, don't."

Olivia snapped her fingers.

The vibration he felt in his mind vanished and was replaced with a barrage of the chimera's thoughts and feelings. Owen dropped to his knees in pain in the center of the barn as he fought the transition but he was losing the battle. His claws and fangs were forming while fur was beginning to cover his body and no matter how hard he tried, he couldn't stop it. Olivia smiled and waved before she darted through an open window and flew off into the night.

"Owen, look at me. Stay with me. You can fight this! You are in control of your mind, not the chimera," Avery shouted at Owen to reach his humanity that was quickly fading away.

"Avery, run! Please…I can't hold it much longer," Owen pleaded in a gravelly voice.

"No, I know you can do this. You just need to try harder. Think of all the good human thoughts you have of me and your friends. Use those thoughts to fight the transition," Avery exclaimed. Owen dug his claws into the ground and let out a roar. Then, he leaped at Avery but he was able to pull back his claws before they tore through her. He allowed his momentum to carry himself past her as he fell to the ground. It happened so quickly that Avery only let out a gasp.

Owen, who was now back to his hands and knees, looked up at Avery with his chimera eyes. His human features were becoming more animalistic. "Run, now!" His words were almost unrecognizable. At that point, Avery knew he wasn't going to be able to stop the transition, so she turned and rushed toward the barn door. As she reached the door, she heard a thunderous roar that shook the barn itself. She looked over her shoulder and saw all three heads of the chimera staring her down. Her eyes grew large as she turned and pushed open the doors and ran as fast as she could. She now feared for her own survival, for the chimera was in control now.

There was no way she could outrun it or even try to find a place to hide in the field for it would find her, so her only hope was to get inside the house. Her eyes narrowed and her brow lowered as she ran with all her might toward the house. She heard a crash behind her but she didn't turn to see what it was, for she knew it was the chimera that just escaped from the barn. She was getting closer and closer, maybe thirty feet away. She could hear the chimera's footsteps almost upon her while its breathing was becoming louder and louder as it grew closer. At that moment, she knew she wasn't going to make it. Avery took a chance and slid to a halt and then dove off to the side.

As she dove, she turned her head in time to see the chimera pounce on the very spot she was just at, as it slid on the gravel to a stop. The snake hissed at Avery as the other two heads turned and glared at her. It then turned itself around while Avery stood up. She locked eyes on the chimera and started to slowly back away with her arms extended. She was doing her best to not provoke the chimera but it began to approach her.

"Owen, it's me. Avery. You know me and I know you don't want to hurt me. I'm one of your closest friends. Come on, I know you are in there. Just walk away. I know you can do it," Avery calmly pleaded to the chimera. The chimera responded with a low growl as it raised its upper lip and exposed its fangs.

"I guess not," Avery muttered to herself as she began to tremble. There was nowhere else for her to go…nowhere to hide…and no way to defend herself.

The chimera grew closer to Avery…stalking her. Then, without warning, it lunged at Avery as it roared. She turned her head and raised her hands up in a desperate attempt to defend herself as she screamed in horror.

CHAPTER 16

Avery continued to scream until she felt something warm and slightly damp nudge her. Her scream faded away as she slowly opened her eyes and lowered her arms. She was startled at first, for the lion's head of the chimera was merely inches away from her. Then her fear converted to astonishment, for the chimera was gently nuzzling Avery with its nose.

Avery chuckled to herself. "I knew you were still in their Owen!" Avery exclaimed while she hugged the chimera and then gave it a quick kiss on its nose. She then took a couple of steps back. "Did you have to scare me like that? Olivia was gone so there was no reason to put on a show," Avery loudly voiced as her smile vanished. The chimera responded with a grunt as it quickly raised its lip.

"Whoa, okay...sorry. Wait...is that you in there Owen? Can you understand me?" Avery asked while the chimera just stared at her. "Let's test it out. Owen...sit." The chimera didn't react. "Sorry, I know you aren't a dog but it's the easiest command I could think of." The chimera turned around and began to walk off into the open field.

"Hey, wait! Stop!" Avery called out to the chimera but it did not react and continued forward. She began to slowly jog toward it. The snake hissed as it coiled itself into a striking pose when Avery got close to it, so she changed her direction and jogged along the side and a little further away. The chimera didn't break its stride but its snake tail did relax. As she passed the midsection of the chimera, she could see the goat's head turn and watch her. She was finally parallel with the lion's head before she was able to slow down to a walking pace. Avery had to keep her strides long and walk quickly to keep up with the chimera. The lion's eyes only glanced over at Avery as it continued its way toward the tree line.

"Thanks for waiting," Avery sarcastically commented. Once again, the chimera did not react. "Okay, so you didn't kill me but you aren't listening to me and not staying with me. So maybe the chimera senses from your newly joint mind that I am a friend and not food. That and obviously chimeras don't speak or understand English. It would explain all of this. However, if I'm right, then why did you attack me? Maybe with the chimera in control and me running away, I must have triggered your predatory instinct. I guess that would also explain why you didn't like my loud voice earlier. Maybe you took it as some form of a challenge. The question now is…what do I do with you?" Avery said to herself as she watched the chimera walk.

As the two walked side by side, Avery carefully began to slowly close the gap between her and the chimera. By the time they reached the tree line, Avery was within arm's length of the chimera. As they crossed into the wooded area, the trees were far enough apart for the chimera to be able to weave its way between them. It didn't go deep into the woods but instead walked just enough past the tree line to stay hidden.

Suddenly, the chimera crouched down low to the ground and began to crawl. Avery, not knowing what was going on, followed its lead and crawled on the side of it that was not facing the tree line. The chimera then stopped and peered out into the field. Even the goat's head and the snake were as low as they could go. Avery felt like she could see something moving but she couldn't figure out what it was.

A few minutes went by and suddenly the chimera silently dashed out from the tree line and began to chase something. Whatever it was, appeared to be randomly changing directions in an attempt to lose the chimera. The tactic did not work for the chimera stretched its claws out and tackled whatever it was chasing. Avery was astonished at how quick and silent the entire chase and takedown was. It then began to eat its prey. Avery shuddered at the thought of how that could have been her back at the barn and then hoped whatever it was eating was an animal and not a human. The chimera made short work of its food before it carried the remains back.

From what Avery could see as the chimera grew closer were the remains of what appeared to be a white-tailed deer. As she got a better view of it, the animal was a large buck from the number of points on its antlers. The chimera dropped it in the area of Avery before it walked further into the woods and lied down before it began to clean itself.

"Hmm…dinner and a show. How thoughtful," Avery responded sarcastically, even though deep down she oddly found the gesture to be sweet. She thought about trying to carve some of the deer meat away with her pocket knife and starting a small fire to cook it but she was nervous the fire would startle the chimera. She didn't know if it was expecting her to eat it so she faced the deer, which was more blood and bones than meat, and pretended to take some of the meat and eat it. She had her back to the chimera to help mask what she was doing. Her stomach rumbled but for the time being, she would have to hold out.

It then dawned on her that she needed to inform the others of what was going on. She decided to text a member from each team so she went with Bailey and Abigail. She thought about texting everybody but she was trying to keep the ruse going and was fearful that someone might accidentally indicate that she was still alive. Even then, she was nervous about sending the message out because there was no way to be vague about it. Feeling like she had no other choice, she got out her phone and began to text.

"No one must know I am texting or even alive except for our main group. Olivia was at the farm and made Owen fully transition. All under control. Since I am 'dead' come investigate why Owen and I haven't contacted you. Sneak some supplies in so I can keep an eye on the chimera. More details later."

Both texted back saying *"Okay."* Avery trusted Bailey and Abigail to follow her directions so now she had to focus on the chimera, which now was back up and moving back into the field. This particular area appeared to be a recently harvested wheat field, which provided no cover for them.

"I was hoping you would be tired after your meal but I guess not. Maybe we can get some sleep in a little while. It's been a long night," Avery suggested but the chimera didn't react to her minus a quick glance from the goat's head. "Oh yeah, that's right, you can't understand me," Avery added.

From what Avery could tell, the chimera was surveying the area…possibly looking for another meal. After some time, the chimera finally drifted back into the wooded area. Avery was pleased because not only did it get them into a more secluded area but she also hoped the chimera would stop soon. Her legs and feet ached and she was almost dizzy from being tired and worn out. Dawn approached as a hint of orange illuminated a small area off on the horizon. At that point, the chimera found an area and lied down in a half-moon formation as the lion's head laid on its front paws. However, the goat's head and the snake were still looking around.

The early morning air was brisk and Avery didn't want to lay down on the dew-covered ground so she took a chance and slowly approached the chimera. At first, she sat near its shoulder and the chimera did not react. She then took it further and laid her back against the chimera's shoulder and still, no reaction. Avery, exhausted, watched the sky slowly begin to transition from night to day.

"You want to know a secret. When I was grasping for any good

285

memory back at the hotel to keep me from fully transitioning, you were what entered my mind and saved me. Specifically, I remembered how peaceful it was when we were in the Alps and watched the sunrise together as we shared a blanket. I know we have had some dark moments, but we also had so many good moments as well. Even special ones like the sunrise I just mentioned. Those are the memories that I hold closest to my heart." The chimera's yawn broke Avery's thoughts.

"Sorry if I'm boring you," Avery said as she chuckled to herself. The chimera glanced at her before it continued to stare toward the open field again.

"You always make me laugh and I can be myself more around you than most people. I also feel so at ease when I am around you and I find myself wondering when I'll get to see you again whenever we aren't around each other. You even go out of your way to protect me when you can. Heck, you jumped off a skyscraper to save me and offered your life in exchange for mine earlier. By the way, don't let me forget to yell at you for that later," Avery softly spoke. She could see the lion's tired eyes now fixated on her as the other two heads were still on the lookout.

"You do all that but simultaneously, you don't make me feel useless. If anything, you make me feel special. You're such a wonderful person in so many ways. You really have no idea how lost and hurt I was when I thought you died in that mountain. All those months passed and the pain never went away. It didn't even dull. Then, when I knew you were alive, I was beyond happy. Words could not even begin to express the joy I felt. So much that I had to downplay it so I didn't seem like some crazy person. It made me think about why I felt like that and the conclusion I came to is that…I like you. As in…like, like you," Avery turned to her side to face the lion's head more. The lion's eyes drifted from Avery to the sunrise.

"That revelation both excites me and scares the heck out of me. It excites me because if we are this great with each other now, then it can only get better if we were a couple and we would grow even closer to one another. However, it scares me because I don't know how you feel about me and I am afraid of ruining what we have now. Then, there is a part of me that feels guilty…like I am cheating on Joshua or something. Yeah, I have moved on from him but I do get that rare guilt feeling at times. The guilt was worse when I realized that your death hurt me more than Joshua's. It made me wonder if I was a bad person or something, know what I mean?" Avery asked as she glanced at all three heads, with only the goat's eyes going back and forth from watching Avery to staking out the area. The other two did not pay her any attention.

"I'll take your silence as a yes," Avery joked. "You know I wanted so badly to blurt out how I felt for you right before she snapped her fingers, but I was afraid of how you would react and I didn't want your final memories of me to be tainted. Then, there is the girl code with Hailey. I know she said she wanted you to move on but I don't know how she would feel if you were to move on with me, and I don't want to mess up the close relationship she and I have. That leaves the big question…what's a girl supposed to do? My only response to that is to keep acting like I have been until some neon sign hits me in the head that shows me what to do next," Avery said as a smile began to form.

"Thanks for being the strong, silent type. It allowed me to get this off my chest; however, it's sad that I can talk about my feelings easier to a chimera than to you, Owen. Now, you know I must do what I am about to because how often does one get the chance to do this." Avery got out her phone and leaned toward the lion's head and snapped a quick selfie with the chimera.

"We will work on getting all your heads in the picture next time. Goodnight Owen," Avery said as she patted and rubbed the chimera's mane and shoulder before snuggling in. Between the body heat from the chimera, its gentle breathing, and her sheer exhaustion caused her eyelids to become heavy. She noticed that the lion's eyes closed and the goat's head laid on the back of the chimera. The snake slithered around Avery, enclosing her as it laid its head on the ground, facing away from the chimera. Avery shuttered, for the snake gave her goosebumps but at the same time, it did make her feel safer. After a long night and the sun fully breaching the horizon, Avery drifted off to sleep.

She suddenly awoke to the sound of the chimera growling as all three heads were alert and glaring down the field from where they walked the prior night. She narrowed her eyes to get a better view and to her surprise and relief, she saw Bailey, Abigail, and Selena. Her relief was short-lived as the chimera became more agitated and started to walk toward them. Avery was confused because the chimera recognized her as a friend but not the others. Regardless, she had to think of something quickly, or else the chimera would attack. Avery pulled out her cell phone and called Bailey.

"Hey there. We were just about to call you. We have been searching for a while now and we can't find you," Bailey said as they all continued forward.

"Stop! Everyone needs to stop walking right now! Take a few steps back as well," Avery blurted out.

"Why, what's wrong, and what's that sound I hear in the background?" Bailey asked as she signaled everyone to stop.

"That is the sound of a hostile chimera that is about to attack if you come any closer," Avery replied. She glanced over to the chimera which seemed less on edge as it went from growling and standing on all fours, to sitting down quietly and observing the group. "Okay, that seemed to have worked. It's calmer now," Avery added.

"Whoa! Thanks for the heads up. Where is it?" Bailey asked as she put everyone on speaker.

"I'd say around two hundred feet in front of you. Just past the tree line on your right," Avery responded.

"I think I see it," Abigail commented.

"Avery, where are you located?" Selena inquired.

"Right next to it," Avery casually replied.

"What! Don't move. We will distract it so you can sneak away," Bailey directed as they moved forward and began to yell random comments in the direction of the chimera, which caused it to stand completely up and snarl.

"Wait...stop! Are you crazy? You're making it angry again. I'm fine. It somehow recognizes me. Please, stop," Avery begged as she even tried to pet the chimera to help soothe it.

The group stopped again. "I'm sorry but are you telling us that you are hanging out with the chimera?" Abigail asked as her brow arched.

"Yeah, pretty much. I can send the selfie I took with it if you need more proof," Avery replied.

"Only Avery," Bailey remarked as she lightly chuckled to herself.

"Normally she would be dead by now. It must be because of Owen's unique hybrid dynamic," Selena commented.

"If it's fine with you, then why won't it let us get close to it? What's wrong? Owen doesn't like us or something?" Bailey scoffed.

"I doubt that is it. He must just have an even stronger connection to Avery," Selena responded.

"Well, he did think of her as his little sister back in the day," Abigail mentioned. Avery thought to herself about how what Abigail just said was another reason why she hasn't come forth to Owen about her true feelings for him.

"Maybe because you are all in a group. Try approaching one at a time," Avery suggested. Everyone shrugged as they all looked at each other to see who will take their chances first.

"He has known me the longest so I have the best chance," Bailey said as she began to walk forward after she patted Abigail and Selena on their backs.

"In theory," Abigail called out to Bailey. She looked over her shoulder and smiled at Abigail as she continued to walk.

The chimera growled as it continued to stand its ground while its snake tail was raised and coiled in a striking formation. "Stop!" Avery quickly said into the phone. "It's just Bailey. You know her. It's okay…she is a friend," Avery turned and gently said to the chimera while she rubbed the side of it. The chimera did not react to Avery. Instead, it continued to stare at Bailey while another low growl came forth.

"Sorry, Bailey. It's not going to happen. Go back to the others before it really gets mad," Avery suggested. She sighed as her shoulders lowered, for she thought the chimera would sense the strong friendship, accompanied by mutual respect, between Bailey and Owen.

"I'm not going to lie…that hurt a little," Bailey commented as she walked back to the others.

"I wouldn't take it personally," Selena said as she took the phone from Bailey and began to walk forward.

"What are you doing? If the chimera wouldn't let me get close, then what chances do you think you or even Abigail have?" Bailey asked with her brows knitted and arms raised out to either side of her.

"Maybe the chimera will sense the purity of the unicorn inside of me and not see me as a threat," Selena replied as she continued forward. She looked over her shoulder and winked with her unicorn eyes. She hoped that being in transition would help the chimera sense the unicorn's presence more.

Around the same area that the chimera began to become agitated with Bailey, the chimera reacted to Selena, but in a different manner. It crouched down and slowly started to stalk Selena from within the tree line.

"Selena stop and transition back to human! Then, head back to the others and whatever you do, don't run," Avery said as she started to walk behind the chimera.

"Why, what's wrong?" Selena asked as she took Avery's advice and headed back to the others. She was nervous about why Avery told her what she did as she kept looking over her shoulder.

"With Bailey, it acted like she was an intruder on its turf. With you, I think it sees you as its prey," Avery responded. Sweat formed on her forehead as she became more worried that the chimera did not stop its pursuit once Selena was human and back with the others.

"We…well you, have a problem. The chimera is still coming. You need to get out of here but if you run it will set it off and you will not be able to outrun it," Avery said in a panic.

"Can you reason with it?" Bailey asked.

"No. The chimera doesn't seem to understand anything that I say and it's not responding to my current attempts to calm it down," Avery frantically responded.

"What do I do? None of us can outrun or fight it. Even if we transition, Abigail's creature is the only one that can stand up to it, but do we really want to go that route? There is so much that can go wrong," Selena commented as she desperately looked for a solution.

"You just gave me an idea!" Abigail exclaimed as she transitioned and took out her phone to call Avery as she darted down the field. Bailey and Selena yelled for her to stop but she did not listen.

Avery put Abigail on a three-way call so the others could hear as well. The chimera stopped in its tracks and turned its focus, as it growled, to Abigail.

"Are you insane! What are you doing? You should be running in the other direction!" Avery yelled into the phone.

"If it senses that I am a chimera then it might be fine with me. I know Owen felt like he could trust me right away because of the chimera thing we have," Abigail responded as she slowed her pace down to a walk.

"That could work or it might think you are challenging it for its territory. Do you really want to gamble?" Avery asked. At this point, Abigail was only fifty feet away from them when the chimera emerged from the tree line and approached Abigail. Its lip was raised as it snarled at her. The snake began to hiss and there was even a hint of light from the goat's mouth as it prepared to spit fire at the intruder.

"I guess I am about to find out," Abigail responded and then hung up with everyone. She came to a stop and caught herself staring at the chimera. "So that is what I look like when I fully transition," Abigail muttered to herself. Her eyes were wide open as she breathed heavily in awe of the creature. The chimera grunted at Abigail and that was when she remembered she should not be staring at it. She didn't want it to think she was trying to be the dominant one, which could provoke a fight. She turned her head away and lowered it some to show she is being subordinate. Abigail only randomly glanced at the chimera to see what it was doing.

The chimera reached Abigail and slowly walked around her, occasionally sniffing her as it did. Due to the length of its tail, either the lion's or the snake's head was always in front of her as it circled. It was not growling, snarling, or hissing anymore and the light from the goat's mouth had vanished, but it still looked angry with its lip raised. Abigail tried to remain calm but the chimera loomed over her. Fear began to brew from within as beads of sweat ran down her face while she lightly trembled.

The chimera came to a stop right in front of her and lowered its head to stare into Abigail's eyes. She was not far in transition, just enough to make sure the chimera knew she was one too. She wanted to stare back but was afraid of provoking it. Therefore, she only looked at the lion's eyes for a moment before she turned her head slightly and stared off into the distance. She then pressed her lips firmly together as she braced herself in case her plan ended horribly. Finally, the chimera lowered its lip and walked away from Abigail and back toward the trees. Abigail let out a large sigh of relief as she wiped her eyes and face before she followed behind the chimera.

"You are one crazy, lucky person do you know that! You about gave Selena and me a heart attack," Bailey fussed yet both she and Selena had relieved smiles on their faces.

"How do you think I felt?" Abigail jokingly countered. At that point, the snake began to hiss.

"I think we should hang up before the chimera becomes more agitated again at me. One of us will text you in a bit," Abigail suggested.

"Sounds good," Bailey replied as everyone hung up their phones, which caused the snake to become calmer.

As they made it back into the wooded area, the chimera found a spot where the sun's rays had broken through and lied down. Avery ran up to Abigail and gave her a hug.

"I was worried about you. I wanted to come out but I was afraid Olivia may be around and find another creative way to try and kill me," Avery said before she released her hug.

"The gamble paid off even though I think I scared off a few years of my life," Abigail jested. "You don't need to be out here doing this on your own. As for Olivia, what's her deal?" Abigail inquired.

"She's mad because I killed her good friend when they attacked my room the other night," Avery replied.

"That's like me slapping you and then getting mad at you that my hand hurts," Abigail countered, which caused Avery to laugh. "Are you scared of her?"

"No, I am just trying to play it smart. I don't want to set the chimera off with any type of confrontation. Besides, I want her to think that I am dead so I can use that to my advantage when we go after her in the future," Avery responded as her brow lowered.

Abigail nodded in favor of what Avery mentioned and then she looked at the chimera. "Impressive. I still can't get over it. It's rare to see what your creature would look like in real life so this is blowing my mind." Abigail stood in awe of the chimera as she began to approach it to get a closer look and to even touch the beast. However, the chimera's snake tail raised from the ground and hissed at Abigail, which caused her to quickly take a few steps back. The snake then lied back on the ground but seemed to watch Abigail, along with the eyes of the lion and the goat, even though they appeared to be heavy with sleep.

"Can you get close to it?" Abigail asked.

"Yeah, it will let me touch it and everything. I think it's Owen's strong memories of me that are influencing how the chimera acts around me. For you, I think it senses another chimera. Think of it this way, would you let a stranger touch you? The same concept applies between chimeras," Avery replied as her eyes diverted from the chimera to Abigail.

Abigail scoffed. "True, but it's an intelligent creature. Surely it doesn't think I am an actual chimera."

"You're right, however, it does sense the chimera's presence inside of you. I think that is what saved you, yet it doesn't trust you. I have a feeling it will trust you over time once it sees you are not out to kill it or even try to be the alpha of the pride," Avery suggested.

"I don't plan on challenging it any time soon. So, what is the plan?" Abigail inquired.

"Right now...keep the chimera from killing anybody and making sure nobody sees it. I don't know how long Owen will be in this state," Avery replied as she glanced back to the chimera, whose eyes were now shut as it slept.

"So, it can't understand you?" Abigail asked and Avery just shook her head, indicating it could not.

"Well, unless you were a chimera wrangler in a former life, then I don't know how you will pull that off," Abigail commented.

"Well, at least it looks like it will sleep during the day and be up at night, so that will help mitigate the concern about making sure nobody discovers it. I can also adjust my sleep schedule to accommodate the chimera to help with that as well. The harder part is somehow making sure it doesn't kill anybody. Maybe we can redirect the chimera or devise a plan to get its unsuspecting prey to leave," Avery replied.

"Well, you have me now as a backup so you don't have to carry this burden alone. It will also play into your plan of pretending to be dead. Someone must keep the chimera from causing any harm so why not a fellow chimera? Olivia will buy that I bet," Abigail said as she briefly put her hand on Avery's shoulder.

Avery smiled, "Thank you. That would be very helpful and much appreciated. I feel like I can't do much as I watch over Owen…I mean the chimera."

"Then it is settled. I will go back to Bailey and Selena and inform them of the plan and I will also bring back supplies and camping gear. I should be back in just a few hours," Abigail replied.

"That works and I will get some sleep while the chimera sleeps. I presume Caine still has the gem. If so, I guess he can keep up with what he has been doing while the rest of the group keeps tabs on Olivia. I would say go after her but I feel we need more firepower first," Avery added.

"He does still have it and I agree. I will let the others know about the plan. I'll be back. Have fun," Abigail said as she winked and walked away. "See you later, Owen," Abigail said over her shoulder as she continued to walk away. Avery turned and noticed the chimera's eyes were open as it watched her leave. It then closed its eyes and huffed. Avery walked over to it and laid down against it again and went back to sleep. A few hours later, Abigail returned with two large backpacks that were full of supplies, clothes, tents, and even Avery's hammer axe.

Over the next couple of weeks, they took shifts watching the chimera. Their daily goal was to make sure it did not wander too close to a public area, kill any humans, or do anything that would draw attention to it. Since they could not tell the chimera what to do or physically have the power to stop it, they had to be crafty. Luckily, the chimera seemed to have claimed an area that was deeper within the vast sea of acres that had already been harvested, so there was less worry of the chimera running into humans or livestock. Luckily, there was enough larger wildlife for the chimera to hunt and a nearby pond for it to drink out of, which were helpful to keep it from roaming too far.

Still, there were a handful of times that hunters were in the area so Avery and Abigail used various techniques to divert them from the chimera. One method that made the two of them laugh was when Abigail transitioned and roared, which scared off a couple of hunters. Over this time frame, the chimera did warm up enough to allow Abigail to touch it but only for a short period of time before it began to growl.

Abigail and Avery also grew closer as time went by since they were always around each other. However, even with the tent, Avery only used it if it was rainy. The other times if both she and the chimera were going to sleep, Avery would lay next to it and talk about her day. She didn't feel weird about it since even Abigail would talk to it. They both used it to cope by pretending that Owen could hear and understand them.

As for the rest of their friends, they were on edge from Olivia's tactics. She wasn't attacking or sending others to get the gem. Instead, she was nowhere to be found and her followers were in a holding pattern in and around the city. Caine guessed it was to keep everyone contained in the city until they discovered who had the gem. At one point, Bailey wished they would attack because it was torture for her to just sit around and wait.

To help distract her from this, Bailey kept in contact with Isaac. She received a few updates from Isaac stating they were still under attack but not as much as before. However, they were still having to deal with the Amarok which was time-consuming, but they were developing a plan to contain the beast more efficiently. Isaac also relayed that things escalated when someone managed to get close enough to set the cabin, which was the main entrance to the facility, on fire. Everyone suspected it was Olivia who did a quick fly-by to keep them busy while she searched for the gem. Frustration grew because everyone knew what Olivia wanted but could not do anything to stop her. Cedric was working hard to find Olivia's new location since she abandoned her other sites, while the rest were trying to come up with a plan to stop her.

One day, Avery woke up around dusk and immediately began to panic, for the chimera was gone. "Abigail!" Avery called out as she spun around in a desperate attempt to locate the chimera.

"What is it?" Abigail asked as she poked her head out of the tent.

"The chimera is gone," Avery blurted out. "Do you have any idea where it could have gone?"

"I was taking inventory so I haven't seen anything. How do you lose a large creature such as a chimera?" Abigail exclaimed as she fully came out of her tent.

"I don't know. I guess I was just that exhausted," Avery replied as she continued to frantically look around.

"This is the day that the kindergarteners will be doing their field trip not too far from here. Of all days to lose that creature," Abigail responded with her eyes wide open and her arms spread out.

"Really?" Avery responded. Her eyes were now big too from the fearful thought of the carnage that may take place.

"Little kids are like the chicken nuggets of the mythological creature world," a familiar voice commented from behind Avery. She turned around to see Owen, back in human form, leaning against a tree with a devious smile. He was wearing a towel around his waist that came down to his mid-thigh and his special bio-shorts were sticking out above the towel line around his waist.

"Seriously!" Avery loudly voiced as she walked toward Owen and gave him a huge hug. Then, as she was releasing Owen from her hug, she slapped him hard on the arm. Enough for Owen to rub his arm from the sting. "Don't scare me like that!" Avery added. She appeared annoyed yet had a slight smile on her face.

"Sorry, he transitioned back like an hour ago and we both didn't want to wake you up. I filled him in on everything during his hiatus; however, the teasing you part was all Owen's idea," Abigail said as she smiled.

"Gee…thanks, Owen," Avery said as she rolled her eyes. She then glanced him over. "Did you work out or something since your return from the mountain?"

"Not really, why's that?" Owen asked as he tilted his head and knitted his brow.

"Then when did you get all those muscles?" Avery inquired, sharing the same expression as Owen.

"I just came out this way after the whole turned-to-stone metamorphosis thing," Owen responded while he shrugged.

"Getting turned to stone gave you abs?" Avery quickly asked.

Owen chuckled, "Yeah…I guess so."

"Well then you will have no trouble carrying all of this stuff as I take a break," Avery casually said as she winked and walked away.

"Welcome back. Good to see you again," Owen mocked to himself as he smiled.

Abigail walked over to Owen and stood side-by-side with him as they watched Avery walk off into the distance. Abigail then slightly leaned toward Owen and began to softly speak while continuing to watch Avery walk away. "Nice acting job. If you didn't tell me earlier, I would have never known that even though the chimera couldn't understand anything she said, you have access to its memories and you know and understood exactly everything she told it."

CHAPTER 17

A slight smile appeared on his face. "Thank you for not mentioning anything to her," Owen softly replied as he watched Avery walk away.

"It's not my place to say anything. Just know, the longer you wait the greater the chance she will feel like a fool and be hurt by you hiding such a big secret from her," Abigail countered.

"I know and it's killing me not to say anything for that very reason. On top of that, in this line of work, you never know if there will be a tomorrow. However, I need time to process everything," Owen responded.

"Do you like her the same way that she likes you?" Abigail asked.

Owen turned to Abigail, "At first, I did view her as my little sister and a very close friend. Now, after hearing what she said it made me think. Are my feelings for her more than what I thought? I think so. The more I venture down that path and allow myself to picture us together, it does put a smile on my face."

"You two would make a cute couple," Abigail added as she smiled.

Owen smiled, "I agree but like her, I have the same fears so I need to be sure. Besides, now is probably not the best time to approach that subject with everything else that is going on with this mission. What I am thinking more about now is how can you have brought all this stuff, yet forget to bring me a set of clothes to change into."

"It must have slipped my mind," Abigail playfully smiled as she winked. Owen shook his head and smiled as he began to help pack up the campsite.

It took a while, but Abigail and Owen finished clearing the site while Avery kept watching from the tree line for any of Olivia's people. The group waited until dark before they left the security of the wooded area to head back to the car. They then drove to the club where the rest of the group was gathered. Owen made a request to Avery and Abigail that they keep his return a secret, just so he could see the rest of the group's reaction. The two giggled and agreed and Abigail even had a plan on how to get around the extra security that Cedric put around the perimeter of the club. The security inside the club was even more strict, to the point that Cedric even put a ban on new members and first-time guests until the Olivia matter was settled.

Before they reached the club, Abigail stopped at a retail store to buy Owen some clothes to hold him over until he gained access to the rest of his belongings. Of course, she had to tease Owen about walking into the club, or even worse the retail store itself, in just his shorts and towel. Owen began to fidget in his seat until Abigail ensured him that she would not embarrass him like that, regardless of how tempting it was to her.

During the entire car ride, Owen sat in the back while Avery was in the passenger seat and Abigail drove. The conversation within the car was more about reminiscing about Owen's time as a chimera and catching him up on what was happening outside of the farm. Owen was confused as well about what Olivia may be up to, especially with her sudden disappearance, minus her fire attacks on the facility. It bothered him that their original plan to get the gem to the facility failed but there was nothing that could be done about it now. All they could do now is come up with another plan while they waited for her to make her next move.

Even with all the conversations in the car, part of Owen's mind was occupied with what Avery confessed to the chimera and how he felt toward her. He knew how deeply he cared for her and how much she meant to him. He even thought about all the times she was there for him and how she made him feel. Deep down, he knew in his heart that they should be together and he wanted to kick himself for not realizing this fact a long time ago. It was their wonderful friendship that built a strong foundation for them that enabled him to feel the way he did toward her, which he never had something like that before. Not even with Hailey.

Unfortunately, the common fears and obstacles they both shared made it difficult for them to act upon their feelings. He now felt like he was in the same boat as Avery, even down to the decision of either initiating the new relationship or burying his feelings deep down and continuing as he has been doing. It was a decision that he felt the two of them should make together but he needed to find the right time to talk about it with her. Of course, was there ever really a good time?

They finally arrived at the club and made their way up to Abigail's room. Abigail and Avery walked into the room first and Owen could hear the confusion and fear from everyone as to why they would let the chimera be alone by itself unless something bad happened. Then, Owen emerged into the room. Cedric, Bailey, Caine, and Selena's eyes all grew wide to the shock of Owen's return.

"Welcome back," Selena said as she gave him a hug while the rest of the group closed in around Owen.

"Good to see you aren't growling at me anymore," Bailey sarcastically remarked as she smiled. Owen slightly transitioned enough to growl at Bailey. "Nice to see some things don't change," Bailey added. Owen laughed and quickly rubbed her shoulder knowing that she wasn't the biggest fan of hugs.

"I presume you still have it?" Owen asked Caine.

"Of course. Was there any doubt?" Caine responded as he pulled the pouch from his pocket.

"Hold on to it for now. I still don't know what she is up to yet," Owen added before he turned to Cedric. "Do you have any idea where Olivia is?"

"Actually…as of last night I do and you will never believe where she is," Cedric responded.

"She's not at the club, is she?" Owen fearfully asked.

"Even better. She is at your condo and she is not trying to hide it. The only reason why it took so long to find her was that we didn't think to look there," Cedric replied.

Owen scoffed. "That's a bold move. I don't know if she is doing that because it was the last place we would look or because she is that cocky now?"

"Maybe she is waiting on you," Abigail suggested. Owen's brow knitted as he looked at her, perplexed by her comment.

"She may be right. Short of knocking at the club doors she wants to be found so she can figure out the gem's location. Olivia even said for you to come find her after you killed me so you could tell her about it. She may use your feelings on how you killed me against you," Avery suggested as she shrugged.

"Or she may want to also revel in your grief of brutally killing Avery. I know I would," Caine added with a slight grin.

Owen began to laugh until he realized that what everybody said, including Caine, could be the answer. "Maybe all the suggestions thus far could be what Olivia is feeling and planning to do. There is only one way to find out."

"I hope you aren't thinking what I think you are," Bailey blurted out.

"We don't know unless we ask, right?" Owen countered.

"Please don't tell me that you are going over there, by yourself, to confront her," Abigail commented as her brow crinkled. Owen slowly nodded his head.

"You're insane! You can't take her on by yourself," Avery exclaimed but as the rest of the room was supporting her statement, Owen's attention was drawn elsewhere. He moved forward and around Cedric and Selena to a small round table that came to Owen's waist. He heard people talking but it was muffled by what was on the table…an urn.

The room fell silent. "Michael?" Owen asked in a low tone and with mournful eyes before he turned around to look at Cedric for confirmation.

"Yes, it's Michael. I was able to get him cremated before he was returned to us since I didn't think you or anyone else would have wanted to see him in his current state. I hope that was okay?" Cedric responded in a sympathetic tone.

Owen nodded and then turned back to the urn. The urn was black with white engravings and as he looked it over, one engraved emblem stood out…a gaming controller. Owen's eyes became glassy as he ran his fingers across the emblem. "I'm sorry. You were a great friend and you will be missed. I hope you found peace and that you can beat all the levels now. Your death will not be in vain," Owen softly spoke to the urn.

Avery came to the right side of Owen and hugged his arm while Bailey stood to his left and put her hand on his shoulder. They stood there in silence before Caine chimed in, "Would you like a matching urn?"

"Excuse me?" Owen said as he turned around and took a few steps toward Caine.

Caine leaned nonchalantly against the bar with a slight grin. "Well, maybe not matching exactly. Besides some gaming device emblem, it could be a picture of an angry kitten or something."

Owen stood within inches of Caine. "Are you trying to provoke me or is this your usual charm?" Owen asked as the chimera's eyes flashed in front of Caine.

Caine was not bothered by Owen's actions. If anything, his smile grew. "That would be entertaining but what I am trying to provoke is some common sense. They are right. If you go up against her alone, the only thing you will achieve is getting yourself killed. At least with this team here, there would be a chance that we could kill her or at the very least restrain her. I would suggest waiting for the others at the facility to come join us but there is no telling when their schedules will be open."

"He's right Owen. As much as it kills me to say that, he is right. I know you want revenge for all the loved ones you have either lost or have been hurt but you need to play it smart, or else we will be avenging your death," Selena added.

"I can even grab some loyal men and women under my watch that can assist us as well," Cedric added as the entire room approached Owen.

"Face it…we are all going with you so the question is do we work together or separately?" Bailey rhetorically asked.

Owen sighed. "Fine. I guess I don't have a say in the matter so let's work together to end this once and for all." The group smiled but as they started to talk amongst each other, Owen interrupted them. "Except Avery."

"What?" Avery exclaimed as her brow creased. She was in shock at Owen's comment.

"Right now, Olivia thinks you are dead which makes you safe. Once she finds out you are alive, she will come after you again and this time, she may succeed," Owen explained.

"I can handle myself and I will be smart about it. Besides, there are more of us going so we will all have each other's back," Avery confidently objected.

"I know you can handle yourself but look what happened last

time we went after her. You only have so much luck before it runs out. As I said before, once she sees you alive then you are fair game again to her. I don't want to lose you…especially if it could have been avoided," Owen countered with desperation in his voice as he approached Avery.

"You are not the only one who has lost people close to you because of her. You of all people should know that. I deserve to be a part of this just as much as you," Avery's response was stern as she stared Owen in the eyes. He knew that there was nothing he could say that would change her mind. As much as he wanted to lock her in the lowest levels of the club and keep her safe, she was right and he had to respect it. With that, he nodded in agreement before lowering his head.

"It's settled then," Avery commented as she stormed off.

"What's the plan then?" Selena asked the group.

"I think we should hold off on that until we get there and do a quick survey of what we are up against. She is as smart as she is brutal," Cedric suggested. The entire room, including Owen, agreed to Cedric's idea.

"I don't know about the rest of you but I think drinks are in order before everyone leaves. Who's with me?" Caine announced.

"I like how you think…sometimes," Abigail teased.

Caine smiled, "I'll even play the role of bartender tonight."

"Look at you with the hospitality. I must be finally rubbing off on you," Selena teased, followed by a wink.

"That or I anticipated being asked," Caine responded with a crooked smile. Selena smiled yet rolled her eyes. Everyone came up to the bar and wrote down what they wanted and then went back to talking in general while Caine prepared all the drinks. Most of the orders were straightforward and acceptable to Caine; being either a beer, a glass of wine, or a glass of someone's favorite liquor, made either clean or on the rocks. However, the few mixed drink orders he received made him grumble. Not too long after the orders were placed Caine was already distributing them to each person.

"How about a toast to your good fortunes when you leave here?" Caine suggested as he began to raise his glass.

"You mean our good fortunes, right?" Bailey asked.

"I didn't think I would be part of this venture, seeing I am the keeper of the gem. It would be foolish to have the gem, the one object that Olivia desires the most, anywhere near her," Caine retorted.

"You never cease to amaze me, like how you think you are not coming with us as well," Abigail commented.

"Can't you just leave it hidden somewhere in the club?" Bailey suggested.

"And risk it being found by either an intruder or another inside person. No, it must stay with one of us," Cedric countered.

"Well, if you hang back while the rest of us go into battle, at night, then Olivia will be suspicious and figure out that you have it. You must act as you would if you didn't have the gem," Abigail added.

"Or at the very least fight but don't get too involved," Avery commented.

"Have it your way but if she gets a hold of the gem, then that burden is on you, not me," Caine's stern expression, yet calm voice, was still present as he first spoke to Abigail, but then redirected his comment to the entire room for the last couple of words.

"Then I guess the only thing left is a toast," Selena mentioned as she raised her glass, to which the entire room followed her lead.

"May tonight be victorious for all of us as we stand in triumph over Olivia's corpse," Caine announced with a devious smile.

"I like the sound of that," Owen muttered. "Cheers!" The entire room followed Owen's lead and each one of them quickly finished their drink before gathering to leave. While everyone was preparing to leave, Cedric made some phone calls to the people he had in mind that could come and assist in their plan.

"I have a dozen hybrids that will join us. They are all loyal and excellent fighters. This, plus the people in this room, should give us the numbers we need to win," Cedric boasted.

"Hopefully so. Thank you," Owen replied.

Owen then saw Avery sharpening her hammer axe in the opposite corner of the room so he decided to approach her. "Hey, I'm sorry about earlier. You are right about what you said. I just became extra worried for you because Olivia is such an adversary and determined to kill you," Owen calmly said as he stood near Avery.

"It's okay. I know you were just looking out for me. I didn't mean to snap at you, it's just I want her dead as much as you do," Avery replied.

"Please be careful out there. I care about you too much to lose you," Owen added with a sincere look.

"Same here. I care about you too," Avery responded but then she appeared to want to add something to it as her mouth opened but no words came out.

"Is there something else you wanted to say?" Owen asked in hopes that she would confess what she already said to the chimera.

Avery pressed her lips together firmly before she responded. "Nothing that can't wait." Avery then gave Owen a kiss on his cheek before she gave him a long, tight hug. Owen held her close as he kissed the top of her head before he rested his head on top of hers. The two embraced for a bit before Avery let go and briskly turned and grabbed her hammer axe before she exited the room.

"If there was ever a good time to tell her…that was it," Abigail whispered to Owen from behind him as he watched her leave.

"I'd rather not have her distracted with anything. I'm just glad there are not any harsh feelings between us and when this is over, I plan on talking to her then," Owen responded as he turned to face Abigail.

"You better, or else you will have me in your ear every day until you do," Abigail said as she playfully hit Owen in his shoulder and walked away.

"Have you heard anything from Isaac?" Owen asked Bailey.

"It's been quiet…more than usual. Nothing from him, Hailey, or Marcus. I hope they are okay. I have been sending them updates so if they are checking their messages, then they should be up to speed," Bailey replied.

"Something is keeping them from responding. I really hope as well that they are okay. As good as they are, they can only take so much," Owen commented. Between the attacks, the fires from Olivia, and the Amarok, Owen feared the worst but hoped for the best.

Not too much later, everyone left the club and gathered into multiple vehicles, and headed to the condo. The closer they got to the condo, the more he could feel the chimera rustling inside of him. Owen couldn't tell if it was the chimera, himself, or both that were eager to unleash vengeance upon Olivia. With Olivia out of the picture, not only would everyone be safe and their friends and loved ones avenged, but also the gem could finally be hidden for good. Owen presumed Isaac was still going to toss it through the magical gateway to the caverns. There, no one would be able to find it unless they were meant to.

The ride was silent but at least it seemed to go by quickly for Owen. When they were a few minutes away from the condo, Owen suggested a parking area that was near the condo but obstructed by trees and far away, but close enough to reach on foot. The group pulled into the parking lot and gathered outside of the vehicles and then made their way toward the condo. It was around midnight so the large gathering did not draw any attention since most people were asleep or in their homes at this late hour during a weekday. They quietly walked through parking lots and eventually made it to just in sight of the condo, where they took cover behind bushes that lined one of the nearby sidewalks.

"It looks quiet…too quiet," Cedric mentioned to everyone.

"There isn't a lot of cover from this angle once we pass the bushes. She will be able to see us from the balcony. Her light is off but that doesn't mean anything. However, if we circle around and enter from the other side of the building then she won't," Abigail suggested.

"That is a good idea. Let's get moving," Bailey said as she started to make her way down the line of bushes.

"Wait!" Owen loudly whispered. All eyes diverted to Owen as Bailey raised her arms out to either side in confusion. "She is smarter than that. She wouldn't leave herself that open to an ambush, no matter how invincible she thinks she is." Owen stared at the building, to the point of squinting and that is when he caught something.

"Wait a second. I think I see something," Owen said as he continued to stare at the building.

"How? It's so dark out there and most of the lights in the building are off," one of Cedric's men asked.

"I just have good vision," Owen said as he turned to the man and winked at him with his chimera eyes.

"He's right. I can see something too," Caine added.

"And how can you see that well?" Bailey asked.

"A vampire's eyes can see a lot and there are heat signatures moving all around in the building," Caine responded as he looked at Bailey with his blood-red vampiric eyes. Owen chuckled to himself because of how Caine was able to tell the truth but still mask his true identity.

"Do any of your men have binoculars?" Owen asked Cedric, who waved over one of his group members and took the binoculars to give to Owen. He surveyed the building with the binoculars and it confirmed what Caine and himself saw. "She has guards…none with any guns but they are everywhere."

"How do you know they are guards and not people who live there?" Selena inquired.

Owen swiveled his crouched body to look at Selena. "Because I made it a point to become familiar with the faces of the occupants within that building, especially the ones that lived near me, and now those faces are different."

"She made the entire building her new hideout. The occupants are either relocated or dead, and I am sure she has destroyed or re-routed the cameras. I despise her but you must admit, it's a smart play," Caine remarked. As much as Owen hated to admit it, Caine was right.

"How do we even get close to the condo without her knowing?" Avery asked.

"A distraction," Owen muttered.

"What's the distraction?" Selena inquired.

"Me…well Bailey and I. After Avery's death, it would make sense that we would be emotional enough to charge headfirst into battle. Even more with the rage that both of our creatures contain. As they are focused on us, then the rest of you can circle around and breach the other entrance. Cedric and his group will secure the perimeter before they come to our aid. Even then, I feel some of his group should stay out here and keep watch for anything. They can be our eyes and ears on the outside while we are fighting on the inside. The rest of us will meet in my old room and kill Olivia once and for all," Owen directed as he looked at Bailey, which she nodded with confidence.

"Let me go too. It will sell it more if they see me there too. Olivia knows I would not just let you run into a dangerous situation without providing any form of assistance," Abigail added.

Owen thought about it for a moment and then let out a small sigh. "Yes, you're right. You can come with us," Owen reluctantly responded. He knew she would be beneficial in their assault but he was trying to keep as few people as he could from the direct line of fire.

"Alright then. We will start to circle around and get into position to make our move as soon as you make your way to the condo. Good luck," Cedric said as he patted Owen on the shoulder. Each group took the opportunity to wish each other good luck.

"I truly hope to see each and every one of you when this is over…even you Caine," Owen announced to the group and then smirked at Caine, who nodded in acknowledgment. Bailey, Abigail, and Owen lined up and were about to go around the bushes and out into the open until Avery grabbed Owen's hand.

Owen turned and he noticed Avery was putting on a brave smile for him, regardless of how concerned she appeared to be between her glassy eyes and her increased breathing, as they continued to hold hands. Owen smiled gently back at Avery and for that moment in time, it was just the two of them. No words were needed to express how much they cared for each other and how worried they were for their safety. Within their moment, the two of them became more at ease.

"Owen, it's time…Owen…Owen," Abigail repeated herself, getting louder each time. Owen began to slowly back away while he continued to gaze upon Avery. He wanted to remember her smile and all that she meant to him as his fingertips gently slid away from her own.

"Owen!" Abigail loudly whispered. His smile continued until he took a deep breath and quickly turned around and hopped over the bushes and bolted toward the condo. Both Abigail and Bailey were not too far behind him. His speed increased, along with his rage and intensity, as he began to transition in anticipation of the fight that was soon to come.

CHAPTER 18

Owen made it almost three-fourths of the way there when he began to hear commotion from the building as the remaining lights began to turn on throughout all the rooms. Then, a handful of Olivia's men came out of the building and charged at them, all with varying creature eyes. Owen did not slow down and neither did Bailey or Abigail who were slightly behind him, with one on each side of Owen. He couldn't see them but he could hear their growls as they grew closer to the first wave of attackers.

As the oncoming group began to yell as they were about to engage, Owen leaped over them while spraying them with fire. He landed and quickly turned his head to see Bailey and Abigail slashing away at the attackers who were still standing and trying to extinguish the flames as they patted themselves. Knowing they were in a good position and could handle themselves, Owen continued toward the building.

He leaped onto the first balcony and then proceeded to stand on the rail and jump straight up to the next balcony, using his claws and the agile climbing nature of the goat to keep himself from falling. He pulled himself up and continued to move from balcony to balcony in an effortless fashion as he quickly scaled the building. Then, about halfway up, he finally reached a balcony that was occupied.

Unaware, Owen pulled himself up to be able to stand on the outside of the rail. As he did, Owen was blindsided by a right hook to the side of his face. The hit caused him to fall backward but he was able to grab onto the railing; however, even though the railing was bolted into the cement, it began to pull away from the balcony floor. As the rail squealed while it tore from its base, Owen had no choice but to let go and drop to the balcony below. He missed the railing and had to grab onto the small amount of cement protruding from under the railing. He grinded his teeth while his muscles flexed as he strained to keep himself from falling any further.

As the man was kicking the broken railing the rest of the way off the balcony so he can continue his pursuit, Owen sent a burst of flames, from his mouth, toward the guy which caused him to rear back and holler. That bought him the time he needed to escape his current dilemma. Owen pulled himself up and then over the rail and onto the balcony. Scaling the building was too risky now so he decided to use the stairs, which he was sure were guarded but at least he would have a solid ground to fight from.

Owen made his way through the room and out the door, being careful as he turned the corners of the hallway. He maneuvered his way up the stairwell since he did not know exactly how many of Olivia's people were in the building. He debated if he should stop and check all the rooms but Owen felt Olivia would not hide in just some random room. She thought too much of herself to hide in such a manner. Owen hurried up the stairs, skipping a few steps with each stride. He could hear the fighting further down the stairwell. This meant everyone must have reached the building and were in various sections of the condo at this point. Even with the siege, Owen knew Olivia would not retreat.

He reached the door that led to his floor but as he went to open it, the door barely moved. The door only opened slightly before it stopped which indicated to Owen that it was braced with something. It would make a lot of noise but he had to break the door down and

313

deal with the consequences afterward. Owen took a few long and steady breaths to calm his labored breathing from his journey up the many flights of stairs. Once he fully got his breath, he squared himself with the metal door and then sent a powerful front kick, while he roared, to the center of the door. The sound of the impact did not only loudly echo down the stairs and hallway, but the power behind the kick also sent the door flying off its hinges. The door laid in pieces around a splintered wooden post that was used to brace the door.

Owen slowly entered the hallway and wanted to see what would come from the disturbance he just made, and sure enough, he could hear someone walking down the hallway, so he waited. Owen hoped that being in his human form would cause the attacker to misjudge what they were up against, so he transitioned back to normal. He stood there with his arms crossed and with no expression on his face. He wanted to appear calm even though he was edgy with anticipation of what he was going to be confronted with. Finally, a female, maybe ten to fifteen years older than Owen, came around the corner. She stopped short and moved her auburn hair from her eyes to get a better look at Owen. She was dressed just as casually as Owen, who was in shorts and a t-shirt.

"Owen, I presume. Olivia said you would be the one to reach this floor first," she said. The woman appeared anxious as she looked around and rubbed the side of her head.

"You presume correctly. I am guessing she told you to kill me," Owen responded without emotion.

"She said to ask you if you had the gem. If you did, then I'm supposed to bring you to her. If not, then to kindly ask you to retrieve it and come back to this spot. If you refused, then I am to kill you and everyone else who entered this building in search of her. She said that I should do it in a very memorable way," the woman responded.

Owen grinned as he shook his head. "Yeah, that does sound like her. Well, I don't have the gem nor am I going to fetch it for her like

314

a good little boy so I guess that leaves the final option. By any chance, do you care to tell me what memorable way you are going to kill me?" Owen asked in a smug fashion.

Tears began to roll down her cheek which made Owen knit his brow in confusion. "I'm sorry. My family and I were in a rough spot and she promised me a wish from the djinn if I helped her, but what is about to happen is too far," she replied as she wiped the tears from her face.

"It's okay. We can work this out and I can help you. You don't have to be in this all by yourself. Just come with me and we can figure out how we can help your family. Just leave with me right now," Owen pleaded as he walked slowly toward her with his hands raised in front of him to help keep her calm. He could see the fear and desperation in her eyes…something that could not be faked. He felt sorry for her, as she was obviously just another pawn in Olivia's game and for that, he wanted to help her.

"I wish I could and I wish I would have met you first but it's too late," the woman replied as her voice cracked. She then began to rub her head even harder, while occasionally shaking it.

"Don't start making wishes yet. The djinn is not even here," Olivia commented as she turned the corner with a devious look on her face.

"Get behind me. I'll handle her," Owen called out as he stopped and glared at Olivia.

"Yes, by all means, please go to Owen," Olivia smiled as she nudged the woman who just kept shaking her head no.

"What have you done?" Owen asked Olivia.

"Nothing. Just bringing out an old, yet fun party trick. It takes a lot out of me to do it but man, it's worth it," Olivia raised her hand and pressed her fingers together like she was going to snap.

Owen's eyes grew wide as they moved from Olivia to the woman, and then back to Olivia. "Are you insane! Even if you succeed, the creature will be too close to a lot of people. This isn't a vast farmland. Many people will be killed and you will expose everyone, including yourself," Owen exclaimed.

"First off, if I can kill everyone in this building just so I can have the place to myself, I think I am fine with the carnage that will result in some peace and quiet. Second, I'm not stupid. If for some reason it makes it out of this building then I'll burn it to a crisp," Olivia responded in a carefree manner but her words were like daggers to the woman who kept flinching with the thoughts of what Olivia was telling Owen.

"Please, what if it escapes this building and you can't stop it in time and it ends up killing innocent people, or even children…I don't want that to happen," the woman cried as she talked.

"It's not my concern! You wanted a spot in line for the djinn, well here is your chance to earn it," Olivia coldly responded while she patted the female on her back.

Owen felt horrible for the poor woman involved which increased his hatred toward Olivia. However, he was able to pick up at least a few details from their conversation. Whatever the creature was, it had to be small enough to fit in the hallways but vicious enough to attack people. It still left a long list of possible creatures but at least he knew it may be able to be contained to the condo if needed.

"You're a monster," Owen muttered.

"I never claimed not to be," Olivia responded as she performed a slight head bow. "Which reminds me, how are the memories of you tearing Avery to shreds working out for you?" Olivia asked while she winked. Owen's eyes transitioned to the chimera for just a moment. Even though the chimera didn't kill Avery the idea, and her provoking attitude, did not sit well with Owen. It worked in Owen's favor to help keep the illusion that Avery was dead.

"Now, I am going to walk away and let you two have some alone time. Just to show that I am not a monster, I will give you a hint about what she is. When you are rifling through your long list of creatures that I'm sure Isaac had you memorize, start with the creatures within Egyptian mythology," Olivia smiled as she waved goodbye and walked back down the other hallway.

"What are you? Tell me, please." Owen begged the woman.

"I'm sorry. I am a…" the woman stopped talking at the same time Owen could hear a snap come from down the hallway. Before he could even react, the woman fully transitioned.

Owen shuffled a few steps back and transitioned deep into level two and he figured he may have to transition even further with what was in front of him. From its appearance, Olivia's hint was all that Owen needed to know what creature stood in front of him. It was a serpopard.

The beast had a leopard's body with a neck as long as its body. Its leopard's head was shaped sleek like a snake, and it had fangs and a forked tongue that flicked out multiple times. Its skin was brown from the combination of scales and short-length fur, with a slight hint of the leopard's spots. It dug its claws into the floor as it crouched down into a pounce position while its head waivered side-to-side as its neck curved. Even its growl had a hint of a hiss within it. From what Owen could remember, it was a worthy predator, for it was powerful, intelligent, fast, and most of all…it was very agile.

Owen went deeper into his transition, for if he wanted any chance of winning this battle, he needed more of the chimera to be present. That, and he needed the fearless nature of the beast as well, for his opponent was intimidating. Fur covered most of Owen's body as he crouched down with his razor-sharp claws extended. His breathing became heavier as his muscles tensed, both fueled by adrenaline. The serpopard began to slowly stalk Owen as a low growling hiss came from it while it raised its upper lip. Its neck was now coiled in a striking position. Owen held his ground…growling back at the creature as he showed his fangs. He felt no fear and had no intentions of backing down. He thought about just blanketing it with his flames but then he was nervous about burning the entire building to the ground so he had to be mindful of his use of fire.

317

When the serpopard was close enough, it struck quickly with its head. So quickly, that Owen just barely dodged the attack by shifting his upper body to the right as the bite narrowly missed his head. Owen went to swipe at the exposed head and neck but it retracted back as quickly as it sprung out at him, which caused him to swipe at nothing but air. It then pounced at Owen while he was out of position and sunk its claws into Owen's shoulder and chest as it tackled him to the ground.

As Owen was falling to the ground, he put his hands up in defense of another attack from the head of the beast, but he was tricked. The serpopard slid its head around Owen's arms and wrapped its neck around his body. It then began to constrict. Owen could feel the oxygen being squeezed from his lungs and his body began to ache from the increased pressure. He attempted to wedge his arms between himself and its neck to give him any leverage but there was not enough space.

Owen grabbed the neck with both of his hands and pierced the skin with his claws. The beast grunted in pain but it didn't break its hold. While still gripping its neck, he unleashed fire from his hands. The serpopard squealed as it unraveled its neck and jumped onto the wall, and in one continuous motion, took a few steps along the wall before it jumped and gripped the ceiling with its two front claws. It then turned itself around as it dropped back to the ground. The nimble predator was already facing Owen before he fully turned around.

It went in for another attack but Owen sent a small burst of fire from his hand to keep it away from him. The plan worked as it reared back and snarled at Owen. His body ached from the previous attacks and his wounds were bleeding, but not gushing. From his pain, he wondered if the serpopard cracked a few ribs.

As the serpopard coiled its neck again, Owen sent another small burst of flames at it to cause it to move and as it did, Owen darted forward. The beast snapped at Owen but its attack did not have the same speed as it did before due to it being out of position from Owen's small fire burst distraction. With this, Owen was able to swat its head away and then he attempted to jump onto the beast so he could bite it and hopefully immobilize it.

Even in his current situation, a small part of him wanted to save the creature, which was his reasoning behind immobilizing it. If the creature lived, then that poor woman would too. Unfortunately, it wasn't going to happen as the serpopard dodged his attack and scurried around him. Owen quickly swung around and slashed at the creature, but he missed. It was too quick for him. He needed another plan. Luckily, one did come to mind...one that he did not like. He had to let it constrict him again.

Owen stood up straighter and his claws were out, but he raised his hands higher than usual, leaving his midsection exposed. The beast coiled its neck again as it saw an opportunity. Owen roared at the serpopard to provoke it and as he did, it struck and quickly wrapped its neck around Owen.

This time, Owen was expecting it and was able to grab its head on the second pass around him with both of his hands. He quickly dragged his fingers over the eyes of the beast and then squeezed with all his might. As such, his claws punctured its eyeballs and dug into the skull of the beast. The creature wailed in pain as blood squirted from its eyes. He held his grip as the blood poured from both its eyes and head from where he had his claws embedded. It tried to unravel itself and retreat but Owen was not only able to hold his grip, but he also was able to lean his weight onto its neck so it was pinned on the floor. The serpopard clawed at him but was only able to get a few strikes in. The attacks hurt Owen, but not enough for him to release the beast.

Then, Owen sent fire through his hands and incinerated the serpopard skull while unleashing a deep roar as he held his grip tight. It didn't take long for the serpopard to stop trying to wiggle free and become still. Owen finally released his grip and slowly stood up, for he was in pain from the battle. The serpopard lied on the ground with its head bleeding and charred. The beast was finally dead.

Owen let out a sigh of relief but then held his ribs. If he didn't know any better, even more of them may have been fractured or broken. Luckily, the chimera was tough and he was able to endure the pain. He tried to stay deep in transition for as long as he could to try to heal himself to the point that he could transition back to human or at least close enough to it.

"Owen?" He turned around to the familiar face of Avery, who stood there with her axe that was stained with the blood of her enemies. He was still deep in transition so he knew his appearance, along with the dead creature, probably explained her shocked expression. He nodded back at her.

"Is that a…serpopard?" Avery asked.

"Was…yes," Owen responded with a deep, raspy voice. He was still breathing hard which did not alleviate the pain he was still feeling in his ribs.

"Are you okay?" Avery asked Owen.

"I'll live. Just trying to heal myself some more before continuing," Owen replied.

"Understandable but you can't continue in that state because you will be thinking more like the chimera than yourself. Look at you, even after the victory you still seem on edge," Avery commented as she started to approach him.

Owen raised his hand to stop her from coming closer. "Wait. I'm still revved up from the fight and I don't want to accidentally hurt you."

"If you didn't hurt me when you were the chimera then I doubt you will now. Just take some deep breaths," Avery calmly replied while she continued to approach him. She stood in front of him with her eyes staring into Owen's chimera eyes while she gently smiled at him. She then slowly raised her hand toward his face. He flinched but she only paused for a moment and then continued.

"Shhh," Avery slowly and lightly said as she gently touched the side of his face. Her warm, comforting smile never left her. With that, Owen felt a spark of calmness from within him beginning to grow and as such, he could feel his agitated state decrease. He transitioned down to his typical level two phase so he could continue to heal but also be able to be more rational.

"Thank you. I guess you could say..." Owen began to talk, more in his own voice now, but Avery interrupted him.

"Save the beauty tamed the beast comment for later. We still have a dragon to slay," Avery confidently said with a hopeful grin before she headed down the hallway. Owen softly chuckled to himself as he followed her. The two walked side-by-side down the hallway as they stayed alert for Olivia or any other signs of danger.

"She could be in any of these rooms. Do we just break each door down until we find her? We will be here forever doing that," Avery commented.

"And who knows what other fun people and creatures we may find behind these mystery doors. I say we check out my room first. It just seems like something her over-confident self would do," Owen said as the two picked up their pace down the hallway.

"Where are the others?" Owen inquired.

"We scattered once we entered the building. There were just so many different types of hybrids, and even a couple of common creatures, that it was hard to stay together as one big group in all that commotion. I feel like some of our group can't be too far behind," Avery responded.

"As much as I want to wait for everyone, I don't know how much longer Olivia will stick around. Confident, yes...stupid, not so much," Owen added.

"Then we can keep her busy until the rest arrive," Avery said as she firmly grasped her hammer axe with both of her hands.

"Keep her busy it is then. I just hope our friends arrive sooner rather than later," Owen commented. Part of him feared the same result that occurred with Michael but Avery was right. They had to do something since Olivia was not going to wait around for the odds to not be in her favor, especially confined to the small rooms and hallways of the building. Owen hoped with them being on the offensive, instead of being surprised on the hotel rooftop like before, would yield a different fate. Owen could now see his door as they jogged down the hallway.

"Stay behind me. I am going to kick the door down and we can rush in afterward," Owen directed as he stopped in front of his door but as he was about to kick it open, Avery stopped him by putting her hand on his shoulder.

"Curious," Avery whispered as she stood in front of him and put her hand on the doorknob. She slowly twisted it and opened the door. "Confidence means you don't lock the door," Avery whispered again as she slowly began to walk into the room with Owen right behind her. She had her axe lifted and ready to strike.

"So our friends can enter easier," Owen whispered as he held onto the door and put the door jam in to keep it propped open. The two quietly and cautiously walked into the room and checked the closets and the individual rooms. There was an eerie silence but it allowed Owen to listen and sure enough, he could only hear Avery's heartbeat which grew faster with each step.

"She's not here," Owen said as he eased up and tapped his fingers to his ears.

"The balcony door is open," Avery commented. She lowered her guard and walked onto the balcony and did a quick scan. "No one is out here. I guess she retreated," Avery said as she shrugged and turned around to walk back into the main room. Before she even passed the threshold Owen saw Olivia, who was apparently hovering above the balcony, descend quickly behind her.

"Avery, behind you!" Owen called out. Avery's eyes quickly transitioned as she turned and swung her axe at the same time. Olivia caught the hammer axe handle with her hand and then pushed the axe back toward Avery, causing the hammer side of the axe to smash into her face.

Avery fell backward to the ground and was barely conscious. Owen rushed toward Avery but Olivia placed the blade side of the axe near Avery's head. "Stop!" Olivia demanded. Owen came to a sudden halt as his eyes widened with fear.

Olivia grabbed Avery with her other hand and hoisted her off the ground and spun her around so Avery was facing Owen. Olivia then tossed the hammer axe off the balcony and put one hand around Avery's throat and the other around her waist to help hold her wobbly body up. Owen could see Avery's dazed eyes, which had reverted to human. He also noticed a nasty bruise on her forehead and her nose was bleeding and bruised too.

"Owen, Owen, Owen…I must admit you are quite fascinating! I think I am going to hold off on killing you just to see what else you can surprise me with. Your control over the chimera is astounding. To the point that you were able to hold off on killing sweet little Avery here. That must have taken real restraint and willpower over the beast to pull that off. I could understand Abigail because of the whole chimera thing but Avery…you must really have strong feelings for her," Olivia said as she deviously smiled.

"Please, let her go. I'll do anything. Just please, let her go," Owen pleaded as he transitioned to human so he wouldn't provoke Olivia. The pain caused by the serpopard rushed over Owen but it was outweighed by the fear of Olivia killing Avery.

"I'm sure you would, now that I have your precious Avery. Everybody just loves her. I've been wondering if maybe I haven't made myself clear. I thought I did with Michael but I guess I was wrong so maybe people will now listen once I snap Avery's little neck," Olivia coldly responded as her face became emotionless. Olivia's hand then moved from Avery's neck to her chin while her other hand moved from around Avery's waist to grab behind Avery's head.

"No! I'll get the gem for you right now in exchange for Avery's life. I'll even add myself to the exchange. I'll work for you or you can even just kill me. Come on…me and the gem for Avery's life. Please!" Owen's plea was laced with panic and desperation as his body and voice trembled with fear.

"Very tempting, but it's too late. My patience has run dry," Olivia countered with a hint of frustration in her voice as her eyes narrowed.

"Owen…it's okay," Avery faintly said. His eyes drifted to Avery. She let out a faint smile but all Owen could do is stare at her with his glassy, worried eyes.

"No, Owen…it's not okay and her death will be on your hands. I want my gem," Olivia demanded.

"Olivia…please don't do this. I'll get it for you. I swear," Owen begged.

Olivia snapped Avery's neck while she stared at Owen with a sinister smile. She continued her smile while Avery's body crumbled down Olivia and onto the ground.

Owen gasped before yelling, "No!" He then transitioned and lunged toward Olivia but she flew off into the night sky, cackling as she did. His instinct kicked in as he sent a stream of fire at her but she was too far away for the flames to come anywhere close to her.

Owen watched her quickly disappear into the night sky, but then reverted to human after he turned and saw Avery lying on the ground with her lifeless eyes staring back at him. He dropped to his knees and picked her body up to cradle it while he continued to kneel on the ground. He used one of his hands to keep Avery's head from dangling as he began to bawl.

"Somebody help me!" Owen called out in desperation but he didn't hear anything but silence. "No, no, no, no…Avery…please no, stay with me. You can't be dead. It will be okay…I'm here," Owen spoke in disbelief through his tears. "Please…someone help!" His cry for help was once again lost in the stillness of the night.

"Please don't leave me. I can't imagine my life without you." Owen's words were almost unrecognizable through his grief and hysterical crying as his tears poured down his face.

Owen tightly closed his eyes and yelled from the heartache he was now experiencing. A pain that easily surpassed any injury he had ever received before. Owen then raised his head and let out a loud roar into the night sky, as the pain and heartache he felt exploded inside of him. His core…down to the deepest regions of his soul was shattered, for Avery, the person he cared for most in this world…was dead.

CHAPTER 19

Owen gently closed Avery's eyelids and held her head close to his heart, while he still cradled the rest of her body. He slowly rocked back and forth, while still on the ground, as he held her while he wept. He had no idea what else was going on in the building or even how much time had passed while he mourned Avery, nor did he care.

"I'm so sorry Avery. I should have tried harder to stop you from coming here and I should have done more to protect you. I wish it was me that she killed and not you. I never got a chance to tell you how much you truly mean to me. I don't even know how to begin to go on without you. Without seeing your smile or hearing your voice. Not ever experiencing how wonderful you made me feel, regardless of what was going on. Not being able to talk to you about everything and anything." Tears ran down his face as Owen softly spoke to her through all his hurt and pain.

His mind was flooded with the memories he had of her, especially all the good times they had together. Then, those fond memories were tainted as he dwelled on the fact that he will not have any of those moments with her again. In addition to that, her lifeless eyes continued to haunt his memories even after he closed her eyes. Before he lost control, he emptied his mind and just sat and continued to hold her. Owen didn't know what else to do. All he knew was that he didn't want to let her go.

Owen heard a gasp from the main room. He turned his head and saw Bailey and Abigail standing at the balcony door, in utter shock as both their jaws dropped and their foreheads crinkled from the hurt expressions on their faces. Owen, who still had tears running down his cheeks, didn't say anything. He just turned his attention back to Avery.

"Is she...dead?" Bailey nervously asked as her lips quivered. Owen didn't respond or look at Bailey. He simply nodded. A single tear ran down Bailey's face as she shook her head in disbelief. She then walked toward Owen and dropped to her knees next to him. Her hand trembled while she gently moved the hair from the side of Avery's face. Bailey then wrapped her arms around Avery and Owen and began to sob.

"What happened?" Abigail cautiously asked as she walked onto the balcony.

"Olivia happened," Owen responded without looking at Abigail.

"I'm so sorry," Abigail sincerely said as she kneeled next to Bailey and Owen and put her hands on each of their shoulders. Tears formed in her eyes too for not only did she like Avery, but she also knew what she meant to Owen. "Where did Olivia go?"

"She flew away," Owen replied. Around that time, Cedric walked into the room and stopped short as he got to the balcony doorway. His eyes grew wide, "Oh, no...I'm sorry."

"Everyone keeps saying that but it doesn't change the fact that Avery is dead and Olivia is alive," Owen coldly countered.

"We are on your side, Owen. Without knowing where she is, we can't do anything until that changes. Selena and Caine are securing the remainder of the building and will be up here shortly," Abigail mentioned.

"I know things are horrible now but we have to stick together as a team and think this through rationally," Cedric added. A low growl came from Owen. Enough to make Bailey remove herself from Avery and Owen and for Cedric and Abigail to take a step back.

Owen slid one arm under Avery's knees and the other arm he had around her back as he stood up and proceeded to carry her inside. Her head and the arm not against Owen dangled as he walked over to the couch and gently laid her down, being careful to rest her head on the pillow. He then leaned over and kissed Avery on her forehead and whispered, "Goodbye Avery. Thank you for always being there. Love you." Owen stood up and wiped the tears from his face before muttering the words, "No more tears."

"It's okay to grieve, Owen. Especially after losing someone like Avery," Abigail commented. Abigail was privy to how Owen really felt for Avery and the knowledge of what Avery confessed to the chimera. She knew this was hurting Owen a lot more than people realized.

"I'm done grieving…I'm done being nice…I'm done playing by the rules. What I want is for Olivia to suffer before I kill her and I have so many ideas of how I can make that happen," Owen said, without emotion, as his eyes transitioned to the chimera.

"Come on. I understand how you feel and I know you want revenge but you must think about this logically. You can't go up against her. She is a psychic, a vampire, and a dragon who is crazy and has tons of followers. All you will do is end up getting yourself killed," Abigail sternly said to Owen as she stepped in front of him.

"I understand the need for revenge and no one is saying you can't have it. All we are saying is that you need to have a plan first," Cedric added as he stood next to Abigail.

"I want blood!" Bailey yelled as she punched a hole in the wall and quickly transitioned to level two. Her fangs showed as she snarled and breathed heavier than before as her skin grew more hair. She then tore the couch to shreds with her claws in a fit of fury.

Owen grabbed her arm to get her attention, but he should have waited for her to calm down. As soon as Owen touched her arm,

Bailey swung her other arm around to slash at Owen. He was able to catch her hand before her claws came anywhere close to him. She glared at him with her pale-yellow eyes, which were wild with rage. "You will have it but you can't do it if you fully transition. Channel your rage and save it for Olivia," Owen commanded. He silently hoped his tactic would work to keep Bailey from fully transitioning.

Bailey pulled away from Owen and stormed out onto the balcony and screamed. Afterward, she leaned onto the railing and Owen could tell she was starting to slowly come out of transition. Her breathing began to slow down and her fur started to disappear. He wasn't mad at her for attacking him, for Owen understood the rage. Everyone became silent after the exchange until Owen spoke again a few moments later.

"I'm tired of stalling and planning. The longer we wait the more time she has to find more creative ways of hurting and killing all of us." The chimera's amber eyes were fierce as they filled with hatred.

"Stop letting the chimera think for you!" Abigail exclaimed.

"Maybe I should be letting it think more for me," Owen snapped back. "Besides, I plan on going alone."

"You promised me blood," Bailey commented as she came in from the balcony. She had fully transitioned back to human, but Owen could see the strain on her face from controlling all the rage inside of her.

"Yes, you can rip through her precious followers and if I fail, you can be next in line to kill Olivia, but I need to go alone on this one. I can kill her, especially if I can catch her off guard. I just can't do it if I am worried about anyone else getting killed." Owen explained. Bailey gritted her teeth before reluctantly nodding her head in agreement.

"Thank you. Besides, if I'm wrong, then at least I die trying to avenge not only Michael and our friends who perished at the mountain but now Avery as well. I need to do something and it must be now before anyone else is added to that list." Owen then turned around to Abigail and Cedric. "Step aside," Owen demanded but the two didn't budge. "Are we going to have a problem?" Owen sternly asked through his teeth.

"I don't know…are we?" Cedric asked as he straightened up and fearlessly stared Owen in the eyes.

"Listen to yourself, Owen. Are you really going to hurt us to get to Olivia? Has Olivia gotten that much inside your head?" Abigail calmly asked. "Besides, you don't even know where to look. She could be anywhere."

Owen sent a quick burst of flames at their feet which caused them to dance out of the way. He purposely sent just enough fire to get them to move without having a direct altercation. As they were distracted, Owen walked past them and toward the balcony. The entire time, Bailey simply was observing what was transpiring.

"Fine! If you are so eager to run off on a suicide mission then go ahead," Cedric blurted out. "She's at the old abandoned warehouse a couple of miles east from here, in the manufacturing district. I had one of my men whose creature can fly keep watch in case Olivia tried to flee. When she did, he tailed her to that warehouse," Cedric explained.

"Why did you tell him that?" Abigail asked. Her brow furrowed and her hands raised off to her sides to show how frustrated she was.

"I'm all about helping people, especially friends and family, but if he is willing to hurt us to do what we have been pleading with him not to do then fine, it's his life. We tried our best to warn him," Cedric aggressively responded.

"I'll ignore the fact that you were withholding that information from me," Owen said as he glanced over his shoulder as he continued to walk to the balcony.

"If you are going after Olivia no matter what we say then at least let me come with you. Let anybody who is willing to fight to come with you to join in," Abigail begged.

"No! I will go alone. I'm all out of saying goodbyes to people I care about today," Owen countered as he reached the balcony. His face was absent of emotion.

"Owen!" Abigail shouted. Her face was originally tense from frustration but it then softened. Owen looked at her but then turned around and walked toward the railing and grabbed a hold of it.

"Owen!" Bailey called out as she walked onto the balcony. He looked over his shoulder at her. "Make her suffer," Bailey added in a low tone and a stern face. She was doing her best to control her anger. Owen slightly smiled and nodded his head.

Owen transitioned before he jumped over the railing and onto the balcony below. He then repeated what he did, effortlessly, from balcony to balcony until he reached the ground. As he was about to head toward the warehouse, his eyes caught a glimpse of something in the grass and when he investigated, it was Avery's hammer axe.

He squatted down next to it and ran his fingers across the blade. An idea passed through his mind…an idea that made him smile. Typically, Owen didn't use weapons but this time, he was going to, and what a fitting end to Olivia if it was by the stroke of Avery's axe itself. It was as if Avery was right there alongside him, helping him defeat Olivia. Owen grabbed the handle of the axe and picked it up. He stood there for a moment while staring at the axe. "Let's finish this," Owen whispered to the axe before he slipped his head under the strap on the axe that allowed it to rest on his back. He then sprinted off across the small open field and in the direction of the warehouse.

As he approached the set of buildings at the end of the field, which was mainly made up of small business shops, Owen leaped onto the side of the first building he came to and scaled it with ease. He then leaped from rooftop to rooftop, except for the ones that were either too far apart or significantly taller than the building he was on. With those exceptions, Owen would jump onto the side of the building and use his claws and whatever footing he had from ledges and imperfections to scale the building to the roof. His momentum never faltered and the closer he got to the warehouse, the deeper into transition he fell as his determination flourished.

Owen could see the warehouse off in the distance as he continued his way from building to building. The chimera's essence was fueling him to the point that he didn't feel exhausted from his journey. He finally stopped at the last building before the warehouse. The warehouse itself looked old, rusted, and worn down with patches of holes scattered throughout the roof. The perimeter had a chain-link fence, at least ten feet tall, with barbwire at the top. He scanned the area and even with his chimera eyes he could not see Olivia; however, he noticed a hint of an orange glow emanating from the holes in the roof. Then, Owen caught a glimpse of something moving in a tree off to the left of the warehouse, outside the fence line. He quickly turned his head and sure enough, there was a person within the tree.

Before Owen could react, the person floated away from the back of the tree to remain hidden. He then waved at Owen, raised one finger, and pointed hard at the warehouse, indicating Olivia was inside and alone. Owen nodded his head and gave a partial wave back to apparently, Cedric's lookout person. With that, the man flew off in the direction of the condo. Now that Owen knew she was indeed inside the warehouse, he could feel his predatory instincts beginning to grow as he began to stalk his prey.

He jumped down to the ground and stayed low and crept around to the same area where the man had perched not too long ago. The area was off to the side, just enough to be out of sight from the front entrance and any windows. Owen carefully made his way around to the tree with the veil of darkness and the shadows keeping him hidden. As he reached the tree, he glanced around and did not see Olivia or any patrols that Cedric's man may have missed. After a moment of surveillance, Owen decided to breach the fence.

His initial thought was to climb the fence but that would have been too much noise. He then debated about trying to make a hole in

332

the fence by either cutting it with the axe, melting it with his flames, or pulling it apart with his own bare hands. Cutting it would also be too noisy and melting it would send a bright light over to Olivia that he was there. He contemplated pulling the fence apart but then decided not to since it would take too long. Instead, he decided to go over the fence.

Owen climbed the sturdy tree until he found a strong branch that he could leap from, that was also near an open enough spot for him to not hit any of the other branches when he jumped. With the red leaves from the red maple tree providing him cover, he had time to make sure that he was ready. He grabbed onto the larger branches on each side of him and made sure his footing was firm against the union of the branch and trunk. Owen gritted his teeth and then pushed as hard as he could and catapulted himself over the fence. He lightly chuckled to himself because ironically, he landed on his hands and feet.

Owen then scurried over to an old rotten pile of wooden pallets to keep him hidden. From there, he couldn't see many other spots to take cover. He had to take a chance and make his way over to the building without being seen. He took a deep breath and sprinted toward the side of the warehouse while he kept his eyes on the front of the building in case she heard something and came outside.

Once he reached the building, Owen crept along the side of it. His heart was racing with anticipation the closer he got to the corner of the building. As he neared the corner, he closed his eyes and listened but he could not hear anything. He then slowly peeked around the corner and his vision confirmed his hearing…nothing. Owen briskly walked around the corner and to the front door, which was closed. He didn't want to open it, for he feared that the large metal door would squeal. Luckily there was a large enough window next to it for him to climb through and as such, Owen was inside the warehouse.

The appearance of the inside confirmed his suspicions from

when he first saw the warehouse…it was abandoned. From the old dusty desks and chairs to the cobwebs found near the rusty filing cabinets, he appeared to be in the front office. Owen made his way to the back of the office area to what seemed to be the door that led out to the warehouse. He grabbed the handle and very slowly turned it until it wouldn't turn anymore. Then, he carefully pulled the door open, holding his breath as he did in fear of the older door making a creaking sound, but luckily it opened quietly.

As the door opened, he could see light coming from within the warehouse. He quickly, yet quietly, closed the door and softly walked to a nearby beam that went from the floor to the ceiling. The rusted metal beam was wide enough to conceal Owen. He could hear Olivia talking off in the distance but he could not make out what she was saying. She wasn't speaking softer and even though she sounded like she was further down the warehouse, that wasn't the reason. It was the fact that Olivia was speaking in a language that he didn't recognize. The tone of the conversation seemed to be frustration, which spawned arguing. From what he could gather, but it also could have been the dialect of the language. While she was engaged, Owen took the opportunity to peek around the beam to get a better idea of the layout of the warehouse.

It was a large area about half the size of a football field with ceilings just as tall and wide. Toward the back of the warehouse were old metal racks that he figured were used to store the inventory. The front of the warehouse, where he was located, seemed to be more for staging and packing the inventory to ship out due to the faint yellow lines on the ground that led to a large bay door where the truck would back in to load. The floor was concrete but some areas were already cracked and crumbled.

The light source was coming from random burning piles of wooden pallets and furniture that he presumed Olivia set on fire. The room was illuminated enough to see the inside of the warehouse but not bright enough for the light to fully escape the large holes in the ceiling. Of course, he saw Olivia in the middle of the warehouse pacing back and forth as she spoke on her phone. Owen had to restrain himself to keep from charging at Olivia and tearing her to shreds as the images of Avery's dead body began to fill his mind again. He wanted Olivia dead but if he attacked now then she would see him coming and he would lose any advantage he had over her, or she would just fly away through the holes in the ceiling. He thought about closing the gap between them by sneaking over to another beam but they were spread out far enough throughout the warehouse where he might be seen.

Olivia finished her conversation and Owen could now hear her walking back in his direction. He steadied his breathing and closed his eyes so he could hear her footsteps as they grew closer. He attempted to gauge where exactly she was in comparison to him. There was a large enough space between the beam he was hiding behind and the beam to the right of him that if she walked in the middle or closer to the other beam, he would not be able to attack her without being seen. From what he could tell, she was closer to him and probably because the office door was more on his side.

Owen slowly grabbed the hammer axe and pulled it back over his shoulder and gripped the handle tight as he raised the blade near his face. He caught a glimpse of his reflection on the blade. It was hard to make out between the lighting and the blood on the axe, but he could at least see his eyes. For a moment, he didn't recognize the set of cold eyes staring back at him; however, it didn't bother him. Owen was there for a reason and he was about to fulfill what he sent out to do. He slowly positioned himself to be able to strike at any moment.

Owen tried to imagine how tall Olivia was compared to him, as well as what she wore when he last saw her at the condo. She was not wearing heels so he figured she would come to almost the base of his neck. He needed to swing the axe as hard as he could and that swing had to be level at his chest or slightly lower. That way, he would have a greater chance of striking her. He wanted to take her head with the axe but he was fearful she may either duck out of the way or that he would accidentally swing the axe over her head. His best chance was to drive the axe into her heart.

As her footsteps grew closer and closer, Owen phased deeper and deeper into transition. He wanted to wait until the last moment to go as deep into transition as he could to keep from losing his patience and just attacking. Owen could hear Olivia about to walk past the beam. He took a deep, quiet breath to steady himself. He slowly opened his eyes before he went deep into transition and then swung his axe with all his power.

Olivia screamed and turned away as she caught the staff portion of the axe that was close to the blade but she didn't catch it quick enough. The axe lodged into the lower part of her left side rib cage. Even though she was able to divert the axe from striking her in the chest, the axe still did enough damage just being a couple of inches into her flesh and bone.

She grimaced and moaned from the pain as she turned her head to see Owen with a sadistic smile on his animalistic face. "You know this won't kill me, right?" Olivia commented as she strained to get the words out of her.

"I know but I'm just getting started," Owen replied with his deep, raspy voice as he grabbed her by the neck and while the axe was still inside of her, he picked her up by the throat. Owen's hand quickly moved from her throat to the axe handle, and he then slammed her onto the ground. The force of the impact caused her to grunt as the axe went slightly deeper into her body. She was also dazed from her head smacking against the concrete floor. Owen put his foot on her chest, just above the axe's blade, and yanked it out of her. He could hear the satisfying crackling sound of the axe dislodging from her ribs and flesh. She yelled in agony as blood poured out of her gash. Her pain was his joy because not only was it the first time he had seen her truly injured, but his revenge was finally being carried out.

Owen raised the axe above his head and at that time, his smile and joy were replaced with a hardened face that was filled with pure hatred as the memories of his loved ones entered his mind. As Owen was about to send another brutal attack down to sever her head, Olivia gained enough awareness to raise her hand toward Owen and transition enough to send a stream of fire up at him.

It was difficult for him to dodge the attack entirely since she caught him as he was stretched out with the axe above his head. Luckily, Owen was able to at least twist his body and lean away enough to only get hit with just a small portion of the intense flame. He dropped the axe and stumbled back as he patted himself to extinguish the flames from his shirt. He could feel parts of his chest and arms burned and could even see some redness and blisters, but the chimera's intensity allowed him to keep the pressure on. Even though the element of surprise was gone, she still took on a lot of damage from his attacks. She was weak enough that he felt he still had a fighting chance.

Olivia smirked as she stared back at him with her green dragon eyes and her body now covered in green scales. She winced as she stood up. "Let's expedite some of this healing, shall we?" Owen thought she would go deeper into transition with the dragon but instead, the scales disappeared and her eyes converted from the green dragon to the blood-red eyes of the vampire. Owen knew the healing powers of the vampire were quicker than the dragon and she could go deeper into transition much easier as a vampire. He could see the blood from her wound slowly change from pouring to just a trickle. He had to think of something or else she would be fully healed and any advantage he had would be gone but then he realized, she was now a vampire and not a dragon.

Owen flung his hand forward and sent a wave of flames in her direction. Her eyes grew wide and her jaw dropped from the surprise move by Owen. The fire hit her and for a moment, he could see the burn marks as she screamed but then the screaming suddenly stopped. Olivia grinned as she finished extinguishing the flames on her clothes with her hands. He could see she transitioned back to the dragon to withstand the fire, which was unfortunate. However, he was pleased to see that he could see some scorch marks on her body, as well as her wound from the axe still causing her pain as she held it with her hand. Olivia had a slight hobble as she walked toward him and stopped just a handful of feet away from Owen.

"Feisty…I like it," Olivia commented with a playful smile, but then her body twitched from the pain.

"Then you will love this," Owen said as he ran toward her and began a melee of slash attacks, with the first attack knocking away the arm she used to defend herself. Owen then sent a follow-up attack by slashing Olivia across her face. He then immediately sent another slash across the other side of her face which caused her head to snap sharply to the other side. Owen proceeded with another attack but his claws slashed her shin, not her head, as she flew into the air. He saw her glance over her shoulder at one of the holes in the ceiling, contemplating her escape.

Owen had to act swiftly and with him still being deep into a level three transition he did not hesitate to turn and leap onto the column. With his hands around the flat edges of the beam, he got his footing and pushed off into the air, and intercepted Olivia as she was trying to escape. The two landed on the floor, toward the middle of the warehouse, as Owen drove her body into the concrete. Olivia pushed Owen up and then slashed at him. She caught him across his chest since he used his arms to protect his face and neck. Owen grabbed his chest and his face squinched from the pain. Then, he could see the orange glow forming in her mouth and was able to roll off her and away while just barely avoiding the flames that came toward him.

"I'm going to make you suffer," Owen coldly said as he stood up while Olivia staggered to her feet. He could see only scratches on her face from his attacks but he didn't care because she was wounded which proved she was not invincible. Owen continued, "For all the pain you have caused everybody in the name of that gem, I am going to use it against you." Olivia's brow crinkled from being puzzled by Owen's comment.

"If you manage to leave here alive, I am going to figure out the same method that you did to harness the djinn's power to get wishes of my own. Do you want to know what my first wish will be?" Owen asked with a devious grin.

"To have friends that don't die so easily?" Olivia sarcastically responded while she smiled.

Owen scoffed. "No. I am going to wish that you lose all your powers and abilities and become just a normal, everyday human." Olivia's carefree expression melted away and was replaced with a worried one as her eyes grew wide and her mouth slightly opened.

"Your priceless expression on your face indicates the fear of knowing what comes next. As a normal human, you will not only feel powerless, but you will also be vulnerable to any form of attack or torture that I see fit. When it is all done, and you are begging for me to end your suffering, I will be merciful and grant you your wish...no pun intended. I will kill you...slowly," Owen added. His eyes were just as cold as his words.

"That is some dark stuff there, Owen. If I didn't know any better, I think you have been hanging out with Caine too much. Still...I like this darker version of yourself," Olivia commented as the smile returned to her face while she held her side. Owen grinned as he began to approach Olivia.

"Besides, do you think you can actually pull that off? Do you think your goodie-goodie soul will allow you to keep up this dark pace? Heck, do you know how long it took me to find the correct ingredients, the spell, and how to perform the spell to get it to work? Quite a long time and even with the gem in hand, I wonder if you will even live long enough to figure it all out," Olivia countered.

Olivia then sent a burst of flames, from her hand, at Owen which he dodged to the right of it. He then flung his hand forward and unleashed his own wave of fire back at Olivia as he charged. His move caused her to raise her arm to shield her face. Owen knew the flames would not cause much harm to her at this point but that wasn't the intention. While her vision was temporarily obscured by his fire, Owen leaped into the air.

As Olivia was blindly shooting fire from her other hand, Owen tackled her to the ground. The two rolled along the ground and when they came to a stop, Owen immediately grabbed her by the shoulders and in one motion, stood up and threw her against a nearby metal beam. Olivia slammed against the beam and slid down to the ground. She held her head and slowly stretched her back, while partially dazed.

Owen began to charge toward her but quickly stopped when he saw her regain focus. Olivia unnervingly smiled at him as the flames danced around inside of her mouth, while the dragon's emerald eyes stared at him. She then stood up and glanced over her clothes which had scattered burnt holes throughout them. She looked at Owen and he could see the flames were gone. Apparently, the flame attack that Owen thought she was going to use was more of a warning.

"I'm not going to lie…I hope you can keep this evil Owen streak alive. I like this rough and tough bad boy vibe you got going on," Olivia said as she playfully smiled.

Owen growled as he charged at Olivia with an overhand slash but she swatted his hand away and backhanded him across the chin. As he stumbled back, she sent her claws across his chest again, and while Owen grabbed his chest and recoiled from the pain, Olivia sent a slash toward his face. He was able to get his arm up in time to protect his face but his forearm suffered a large gash from her attack. She grabbed him by his shirt and yanked him forward so her face was inches from his own.

"I like to play rough too," she loudly whispered. She appeared to go in for a kiss so Owen went to headbutt her but it was a ruse. His head went forward as her head went around his and she sank her fangs into the base of his neck. Owen yelled and tried to break free but her grip around him was too powerful and she was too close to maneuver away. Then, he could feel his neck begin to burn as fire was beginning to brew within her mouth.

Out of desperation, Owen could think of only one idea that could set him free. He reached down to the side she was still favoring and dug his claws into her wound from the axe attack earlier. Olivia shrieked in pain as she released her bite and grabbed his hand and tried to pull it out, but Owen's claws were in too tight and her skin began to tear from her efforts. Olivia dug her claws into his forearm to force him to let go but Owen held tight and growled and showed his fangs as he did. She was finally able to step far enough back to punch Owen across his face. He was dizzy from the hit but he held on. Olivia let out a deep, low growl and then sent two more punches back-to-back, causing Owen to finally let go.

As he began to stagger back, dazed, Olivia grabbed him by his shirt and began to repeatedly punch him in the face. His arms were too injured to block due to both of his forearms being clawed earlier, and he was too dizzy to counter. Half a dozen strikes later, Owen fell to his knees. His face was bruised, swollen, bloody, and battered. Also, his forearms and chest were bleeding and he had random burn marks on his body.

Owen roared, which was laced with pain, as he tried to stand up, but he could not. His will to fight and live was still strong, but his strength has left him. Olivia strolled over to Avery's axe and picked it up. She returned to Owen and stood to his side with the blade of the axe under his chin. At this point, Owen was aware of his bleak situation but was unable to do anything to stop it.

CHAPTER 20

Her brow arched. "I like your spirit. I'll give you one last chance. Join me and I will make your allegiance worth your while with a wish from the djinn. Two if you can retrieve the gem for me," Olivia offered.

Owen was still breathing heavily from his injuries but then he gathered himself enough to respond. "You have taken so much from me. To the point that I don't even care if I live or die. If I can't kill you…if I can't spoil your plans, then at least I tried and didn't submit to be one of your henchmen. Besides, if I don't stop you, there are still plenty of people out there that will."

"Such a shame. You had such potential. Even Klayden, as stubborn as he was, finally gave in to wanting a wish from the djinn," Olivia said as she lifted Owen's chin higher with the blade. Even with his death just an axe stroke away, Owen still wondered if Klayden was good all along, but turned evil only in desperation to bring back his family. If so, Owen didn't want to share the same path that Klayden took.

Olivia slowly moved the blade from under his chin to the back of his neck. "I hope when they find your decapitated body, they will appreciate the irony of you being executed by Avery's axe. It's a shame you couldn't keep her alive, but please…send my regards to her when you meet her shortly." She raised the axe high in the air with her right hand as she held her side with her other hand. Olivia swung the axe down with enough power to lodge the blade within the concrete. The problem was that Owen was not there anymore.

Her brow knitted as she stared at the spot where Owen's body should have been. She glanced around and her eyes widened when she saw Owen about thirty feet further down, toward the back of the warehouse. Before she could truly see anything else, she felt something smack the side of her face as she fell to the ground. Olivia looked up and saw Caine standing above her with a look of disgust.

"Owen, let me heal you. You look terrible," Selena said as she kneeled beside Owen with her hands on his shoulders. Owen was still partially out of it as he looked back and forth from Caine to Selena. It took him a moment to realize what just occurred.

"I feel like that is becoming your job here lately," Owen weakly responded while he tried to focus.

"Healing good people never felt like a job to me," Selena responded with a small smile as she rested her forehead on top of Owen's head. He began to feel the powers of her healing consume him.

"Thanks, but just enough to get me back out there. I can't let her get too much of the upper hand," Owen added as his head became clearer and he began to feel his pain melt away.

"Nobody uses me and gets away with it!" Caine exclaimed, and with his fury fueled by his hatred for Olivia, he kicked her in the face, sending her flat on her back. He then walked over to the axe and ripped it from the concrete.

"Let me guess, you're going to do a reenactment of Owen's dialogue and describe all the horrible things you are going to do to me," Olivia responded in an annoyed tone as she slowly stood up. She was still transitioned as a dragon, but also still in pain from her injuries.

"Why talk about it when I can do it," Caine countered as he held the axe with both hands and lifted it over his head, and with an overhand swing, threw it at Olivia. She dodged to the side as it soared past her and lodged itself in the wall near the door that led to the office area.

"You missed," Olivia said while she grinned. Caine's only reply was a devious smile back at her. He then dropped his smile and went to attack but Olivia put up a wall of flames in front of her with both hands. Even with his vampire speed, he ended up in the flames and had to back off while violently slapping his body to extinguish the fires on himself. He then sped back over to Owen and from what. Owen could see, Caine had burn marks on his body, and his clothes had some burnt holes scattered about. Caine frantically checked himself over again to make sure he was still not on fire.

"I think I am good enough. Thanks," Owen hastily commented as he put his hand on top of Selena's hand while the two stood up. Owen, who was still deep in transition, still felt pain but at least the bleeding had stopped and he was able to use his arms more now. He was also able to focus better now that his blurry vision and dizziness had left him. Olivia's eyes narrowed as she glared at the three standing before her. She began to slowly walk toward them, with flames around her hands.

"You saved my life. I guess now your debt is paid. Thank you," Owen said as he extended his hand out to Caine, but Caine didn't shake his hand in return.

"What…that…no. I did that just to annoy Olivia. My debt to you has been paid for a different reason," Caine said with a peculiar smirk. Owen looked at Caine and squinted his eyes while tilting his head, for he was confused at his comment. Caine responded back to Owen's confused expression by nodding toward the office door. Owen turned and looked around Olivia to see Cedric, Abigail, Bailey, and one that he did not expect to see…Avery!

Owen dropped immediately out of transition at the sight of her as his jaw dropped and his eyes widened. A few tears rolled down his

344

face as he felt all the air leave his body. Avery looked at Owen and gently smiled at him after she pulled the axe out of the wall. Owen lightly chuckled and gasped at the same time before he smiled back at her. He was astonished at Avery's appearance.

"How? That's impossible. She was dead before you could have done anything to save her," Owen commented as he turned to Caine.

"Then it's a good thing that I too believed your concern about Avery coming along on this mission. I believed it enough that I slipped my blood into that vile mixed drink that I served her earlier," Caine responded in a smug manner.

Owen put his hand on Caine's shoulder, "Thank you. You have no idea how much this means to me and words cannot express how grateful I am. Still, I thought you were against blood sharing?"

"I knew how you felt toward Avery, for I share a similar connection with Selena. That night, you not only saved Selena, but you saved me too. It was the least I could do to slip a few ounces of my blood into her drink," Caine responded. Owen could see Selena smile out of the corner of his eye but as Owen's eyes drifted back to Avery, he noticed something was different. The cyclops's blue eyes were not present anymore. Instead, her eyes were now purple.

"Wait. If Avery died with vampire blood in her system does that mean she is a vampire or some weird mix of a cyclops and a vampire?" Owen asked.

Caine put his hand on Owen's shoulder, "Details best discussed for another time. Now my friend, let's bag ourselves a dragon," Caine added with a crooked grin.

Owen nodded and patted Caine on his shoulder before he turned to face Olivia. By that time, Olivia had already turned around and watched the others form a half-circle around her. Owen, Caine, and Selena completed the other half of the circle. For the first time ever, Owen saw Selena with weapons...twin daggers. Olivia was now surrounded by the entire group that was also now in transition. Olivia's flames vanished as she rolled her eyes.

"I don't know how you do it but someday you will die…permanently," Olivia exclaimed to Avery and then her eyes moved away from her. Avery confidently smiled for a moment before her face became stern again. Olivia scoffed. "Back to business. First, the obvious. I am a dragon, a vampire, and a psychic. You will not win this, so…I'll make you this offer. Whoever tells me which one of you has my gem, or hands me the gem itself, not only will get to live but will also get two wishes from the djinn. I will have plenty so don't worry about me," Olivia added with a quick raise of her brow and a smirk.

"Bargaining now…is that fear I sense in you?" Caine rhetorically asked.

"Not fear…frustration. I grow weary of this game and I want my gem," Olivia retorted without expression as she glanced around at everyone.

"How about this counteroffer…we stop you one way or another, here and now," Owen called out.

Olivia smiled as she raised her hands out to either side. "If that is what you choose then fine…attack at your leisure."

The group engaged Olivia, which her counter to that was to fly straight up toward the ceiling. However, Owen leaped into the air and grabbed onto her ankles which caused her to slow down but she was still gaining altitude. Abigail joined the effort and grabbed onto Owen's legs to add more weight. This caused her to stop flying higher but she was still holding steady. Olivia lowered her hand toward the two and was about to set them ablaze when Owen used the same trick as before. In one movement, he yanked himself up with Abigail still holding on. His arm extended and he sunk his claws into her wound. She yelled as the three went crashing to the ground.

Owen and Abigail rolled away as Cedric and Bailey attacked. Cedric's claw smashed against the back of her head, which sent Olivia down to one knee. Then, Bailey slashed a couple of times at Olivia, which scraped across her arms as Olivia defended. Cedric sent another heavy claw attack toward her head, but she swiftly stood up and spun around him. As he turned around to face her, she performed a front kick that hit him in the chest so hard that it made him fall back and slam into Bailey.

As soon as the two hit the ground, Selena and Avery joined the attack. Avery swung the axe but Olivia moved her head back as the blade just missed her nose, but Avery immediately swung again. The hammer side of the axe rammed into Olivia's chest, which caused Olivia to be jolted backward and straight into Selena's blades. The force of the impact caused the blades to enter a few inches into Olivia's back. Olivia hollered as Selena used the leverage from the blades and flung her toward Abigail and Owen, who sent their fists from either side of Olivia, into her stomach. While she was bent over and holding her stomach, Owen and Abigail grabbed her by the back of her shirt and threw her head first into the metal beam.

The group surrounded her again as she grabbed the beam to help herself up. Owen could see she was hurt and winded and even saw blood trickling out of her wounds and bruises on her face and arms. Unfortunately, the attacks themselves didn't cause nearly as much damage as they would have on any other typical hybrid. He knew they had to keep the pressure on her because eventually, as strong as she was, even she had to fall. With that thought, Owen led the next series of relentless attacks against Olivia.

Each one of them kept the pressure on her by attacking her with one or two hits before either Olivia knocked them down or they were able to escape to allow another attack by someone else. With the number of attacks that Olivia was constantly facing from all directions, she could not fly away or defend herself properly. She did attempt to use her fire from time to time but when she did, Owen and Abigail took the lead due to their agility while the others hung back. Caine was just as agile but it appeared at this point, he only stepped in to help Selena if she was in too much danger. The group continued the onslaught and Olivia was weakening more and more each time, but unfortunately the rest of them were becoming battered and worn out more quickly than she was.

Olivia started to become more ingenious with her attacks with each round, to the point that Owen began to wonder if she was analyzing their strengths and weaknesses while they fought. She first hit Cedric with a wave of fire at close range after he missed with one of his claw attacks, knowing he was slower than the rest and could not avoid her fire as efficiently.

As he rolled away to put out the flames, Avery came across and swung her axe but Olivia caught the axe and in the same motion, hip-tossed her into the beam. She then turned around and swung Avery's axe at Abigail's legs, but she jumped to the side; however, Olivia had already planned for that. She surprised Abigail with another attack as she immediately twirled around for another swing. This time, the blade sliced Abigail's thigh, which caused her to grab her leg in pain as she fell to the ground. Olivia sent the axe down upon Abigail but Owen stepped in front and caught the axe handle. He strained as Olivia pushed harder. His arms began to shake as he roared and went deeper into transition to hold Olivia off as Abigail dragged herself away along the ground.

Olivia's mouth began to light up so Owen had to think of something quickly because he was too close to dodge the fire attack. As Olivia unleashed her flames, so did Owen. The two had fire pouring out of their mouths at close range and for a moment, their flames met in the middle of them. This didn't last long as Owen could see her flames becoming closer to his face as he began to feel the intensity of the heat from her.

Selena then came from behind Olivia and jammed one of her daggers into the main wound near Olivia's ribs. The stab caused Olivia to let out a deep roar and kick Owen in his side before she let go of the axe. Then, Olivia threw her elbow behind her and hit Selena between the eyes. While Selena stumbled back while she held her head, Owen grabbed the axe and swung it at Olivia as he stood up. She countered by catching the axe with one hand and yanked the axe toward her. As Owen stumbled forward, she rammed her knee into his stomach. The impact caused Owen to let go of the axe and bend over as he held his stomach. He was both in pain and nauseous from the hit. She shoved him to the ground and repositioned her grip on the axe.

Olivia didn't waste any time with her new weapon as she flung the axe toward Avery just as she got up. She saw the axe coming and dropped to the ground again to avoid the blade as it clanged against the beam. Olivia then quickly spun around and backhanded Selena, which caused her to lift into the air and fall hard onto the ground.

She stood over Selena with an evil grin. Olivia then pressed her lips firmly together as she pulled the dagger out of her wound and then she sent the blade toward Selena's heart. Once again, her attack hit nothing but concrete as Caine whisked her away. The group slowly stood up and surrounded Olivia again but now everyone was injured in multiple different ways. Owen started to worry that they were not going to win this fight, even with the numbers in their favor.

Olivia chuckled as a large smile appeared on her face. "Not only am I embarrassing each and every one of you, I think I figured out who has the gem," Olivia held out the dagger and began to point it at each one of them as she slowly turned around in a circle. The dagger stopped at Avery. "If I'm wrong, then we will see if a third time is a charm," Olivia commented as she drew the knife back behind her head. In response to Olivia, Avery raised her axe in front of her to help shield her while the group rushed toward Olivia and Avery. At the last moment, Olivia turned around and sent the dagger flying toward Caine.

The dagger pierced his chest with enough force that he stumbled back a few feet before he collapsed to the ground. Caine raised his head as blood poured from his mouth and his chest where the dagger entered his heart. His head then dropped back to the ground and his

349

arms flopped to either side of him as he stopped moving.

"No!" Selena yelled as she rushed over to him and pulled the dagger out of his chest while she cried.

"Selena, look out!" Owen yelled. Her eyes drifted up in time to tumble out of the way of Olivia's fire attack.

"Don't be dramatic. He'll live," Olivia said to Selena as she approached Caine. The group, including Selena, approached Olivia.

"Not any further unless you want me to make his death permanent," Olivia said with stern eyes as she hovered her flaming hand over Caine's body. The group stopped their progress and Owen could see the confusion on Bailey's face, for she did not know Caine's true nature. A topic he was sure he would have to discuss with her if they made it out of this battle alive. Olivia then looked at Selena and motioned her to go join the rest of the group, which she stared at Olivia with discontent before she followed her directions.

"It took me a while but when one of your prized fighters is more of an observer, it tends to draw more attention to them, not less," Olivia remarked as she extinguished the fire around her hand in order to check Caine's body for the gem. At this point, Owen's heart was in his throat. She was moments away from finding the gem and Caine's life was at risk. There was nothing they could do.

"I think we have a winner," Olivia commented as she pulled the pouch out of Caine's pants pocket. Owen could feel the dread embrace him as his eyes widened with fear, along with the rest of the group. Olivia opened the pouch to peek inside and a large smile appeared on her face. "Looks good."

Olivia let out a large sigh of relief while she closed the pouch and walked toward the group. "All of this pain and suffering you endured was for nothing because, at the end of the day, I still won. Now, not only did you suffer for nothing, you lost any chance at a wish. Even better, now you will go from living a long, oh-so-happy life, to dying in agony," Olivia added as she raised her hand toward the group and ignited it as a cold expression appeared on her face.

The injured group braced themselves but then Owen felt something weird and it wasn't just him. He noticed the others in the group was looking around at each other, and themselves. Even Olivia's flame vanished as she had the same puzzled look. The hair on Owen's arm began to rise.

Out of nowhere, Hailey dropped from the sky, and before she landed hard on the ground in a crouched position, her talons sliced Olivia across the face. Thunder could be heard across the sky. Hailey slowly stood up and Owen could see the electrical currents bouncing all over Hailey's body as she glared at Olivia.

"She's cut!" Cedric exclaimed and sure enough, Owen could see three large cuts across Olivia's face as the blood dripped down.

Before Olivia could react, Hailey screamed and stuck out both of her hands in front of her. Her scream sounded like a combination of Hailey's voice and the screech from the thunderbird. She projected a large electrical bolt at Olivia. The impact hit Olivia in the upper part of her chest and flung her back several feet as she landed hard on the ground and rolled to a stop. As Olivia slowly stood up, she grimaced and held the spot that Hailey just hit with lightning. From what he could see, it looked burnt.

Owen felt a wave of hope come over him for the thunderbird was able to have enough power to injure the dragon. The shock and fear in Olivia's eyes were a testament to that. It must have been the other reason why Olivia wanted Hailey out of the city. She must have feared that Hailey's thunderbird had enough power to kill her dragon. Owen then gasped as he saw the pouch laying on the ground between Hailey and Olivia.

The two of them looked at the pouch at the same time before they looked at each other again. "I believe that belongs to me," Hailey commented with a controlled, angry voice.

"No longer. It's mine now," Olivia sternly replied.

"I'm not afraid of you. If anything, you should be afraid of me," Hailey countered as she walked toward the gem. Olivia smiled and

351

dashed toward the gem and in return, Hailey bolted toward the gem as well.

Hailey arrived at the gem first and as she reached for it; she took her eyes off Olivia. When that happened, Olivia sent fire from both her hands and her mouth toward Hailey and the gem. The fire from her hands was used as a wall to prevent Hailey from grabbing the gem while the fire from her mouth hit Hailey. She yelled as she flailed her arms around and then glided a couple of feet in the air backward. She then fell out of control to the ground, where she rolled around until the fire was out. The group gathered around Hailey to make sure she was okay. Owen could see the burns and the blisters throughout her upper body, as well as the obvious pain she was in from her groans and crinkled face as she gritted her teeth. Luckily enough, she would live.

Olivia nonchalantly strolled over to the gem and picked it up. "Oh, what's the matter? Did we just learn a lesson that I am the only fire-resistant creature here?" Olivia mocked the group. "Keep that in mind if any of you decide to come for the gem again. I will burn you and everyone you love to ash," Olivia harshly added while still in transition. Owen, and the others, looked at each other as they all painfully transitioned back to human. Even though they were all scared for themselves and the thought of what would happen if Olivia escaped with the gem, she had the advantage now. The group transitioned back to human to not just keep Olivia calm, but they also felt defeated and worn out.

"Well, I'll be on my way now," Olivia added while she waved the pouch in front of them but as she was about to take off, the room became bright.

Everyone looked up and saw Isaac land firmly on the ground with flames covering his body. With the intensity of the heat and light coming from Isaac, the group had to partially shield their eyes while taking a few steps back. Isaac then grabbed Olivia's wrist. She seemed shocked as her jaw dropped and her eyes widened while she squeezed the pouch tightly. To Owen's surprise, even though she seemed caught off guard, she transitioned down to level one. That left only her dragon eyes and a few scales on her arms. Owen could see her face squinting in pain from his fiery grip but Isaac didn't advance in his attack.

"The phoenix's fire can burn through anything. She is fire resistant, not fireproof. You can literally incinerate her by your touch alone," Abigail called out.

"Do it, Isaac! She is the one who killed Michael and almost killed Avery. She has hurt all of us," Bailey added loudly.

"Isaac, she has the gem! What are you waiting for? Do it!" Owen pleaded. He hoped Isaac's good nature would not prevent him from doing what needed to be done.

"You wouldn't hurt me...would you?" Olivia pitifully asked Isaac. She frowned and her shoulders slumped as her puppy-dog eyes stared at Isaac. After a few moments, Isaac's flames disappeared and both Olivia and Isaac transitioned to human. Isaac then released his grip and took a step back as Olivia rubbed the red area on her arm from his fiery grip.

"What are you doing?" Owen yelled while everyone else looked back and forth at each other with knitted brows from Isaac's confusing move.

Olivia smiled and perked up, "I didn't think so. Good seeing you again." She then flew through one of the holes in the roof, with the gem, and vanished into the night sky.

"No!" The group collectively exclaimed as they watched Olivia escape. Isaac solemnly turned around to face them.

Owen charged Isaac and grabbed him by the shoulders and slammed him against a metal beam. His chimera eyes glared at Isaac as he raised his hand and extended his claws.

"Owen, don't!" Avery begged as she ran closer to Owen, with the rest of the group right behind her.

Owen didn't pay Avery, or anyone else, any attention. "Why did you let her go? She has the gem with her and has found a way to control the djinn. To the point that she can be granted as many wishes as she chooses. Who knows what wishes she will ask the djinn for and what havoc she will cause? Do you have any idea how dangerous she is? She's a threat to the entire world!" Owen scornfully interrogated Isaac but he didn't respond. He just stared back at Owen with no expression on his face.

"Are you working for her? Did you take her up on an offer to get a wish for yourself? That's why you let Olivia go, isn't it? Answer me!" Owen demanded while he still held Isaac against the beam. His face was only a foot away from Isaac's face as he yelled.

"Astrid," Isaac softly said as his eyes lowered.

"What?" Owen asked in a lower tone due to his confusion.

"Her name is Astrid," Isaac calmly said while he continued to look down.

"And how do you know that?" Owen asked in a stern tone.

Isaac's eyes slowly drifted up. He looked Owen in the eyes and in a soft tone responded, "Because…she's my daughter."

~ To Be Continued ~

Thank you for reading my book! I appreciate your support and I hope you enjoyed it!

You can find me on social media at:
Facebook: Author Brian Marotto
Instagram, Twitter, and TikTok:
@MeBrianNotBrain

If you enjoyed the book and would like to rate it, and even leave a review, I would really appreciate it if you did! Also, recommending my book to others is also very appreciated!

My books can be found at:
https://linktr.ee/AuthorBrianMarotto

DON'T MISS

THE AWAKENING

AND

THE IMPRISONED

BOOKS ONE AND THREE IN
THE CREATURE WITHIN
TRILOGY